More praise for Kay Hooper

FINDING LAURA

"You always know you are in for an outstanding
read when you pick up a Kay Hooper novel, but in
FINDING LAURA, she has created something really
special! Simply superb!"
—*Romantic Times* (gold medal review)

"Hooper keeps the intrigue pleasurably complicated,
with gothic touches of suspense and a satisfying
resolution." —*Publishers Weekly*

"A first-class reading experience." —*Affaire de Coeur*

"Ms. Hooper throws in one surprise after another. . . .
Spellbinding." —*Rendezvous*

AFTER CAROLINE

"Harrowing good fun. Readers will shiver
and shudder." —*Publishers Weekly*

"Kay Hooper comes through with thrills, chills,
and plenty of romance, this time with an energetic
murder mystery with a clever twist. The suspense is
sustained admirably right up to the very end."
—*Kirkus Reviews*

Bantam Books by Kay Hooper

FINDING LAURA
AFTER CAROLINE
AMANDA
ON WINGS OF MAGIC
THE WIZARD OF SEATTLE
MY GUARDIAN ANGEL

Finding Laura

Kay Hooper

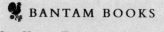
BANTAM BOOKS

NEW YORK TORONTO LONDON

SYDNEY AUCKLAND

This edition contains the complete text of the
original hardcover edition.
NOT ONE WORD HAS BEEN OMITTED.

FINDING LAURA

A BANTAM BOOK

PUBLISHING HISTORY
Bantam hardcover edition published November 1997
Bantam paperback edition / July 1998

ISBN 0-553-57185-0

Published simultaneously in the United States and Canada

Bantam Books are published by Bantam Books, a division of Bantam
Doubleday Dell Publishing Group, Inc. Its trademark, consisting of the
words "Bantam Books" and the portrayal of a rooster, is Registered in
U.S. Patent and Trademark Office and in other countries. Marca
Registrada. Bantam Books, 1540 Broadway, New York, New York
10036.

PRINTED IN THE UNITED STATES OF AMERICA
OPM   10 9 8 7 6 5 4 3 2 1

*F*OR MY NEPHEW, CLINT—
A VERY BELATED BIRTHDAY PRESENT

Family Tree

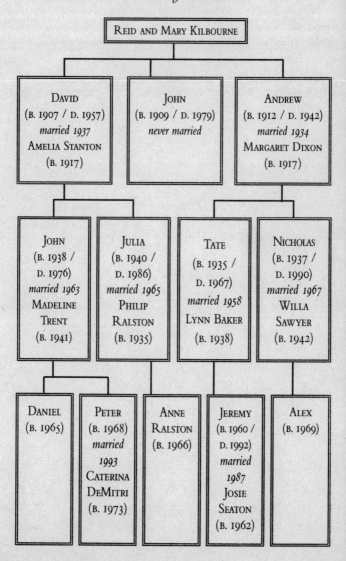

REID AND MARY KILBOURNE

DAVID
(B. 1907 / D. 1957)
married 1937
AMELIA STANTON
(B. 1917)

JOHN
(B. 1909 / D. 1979)
never married

ANDREW
(B. 1912 / D. 1942)
married 1934
MARGARET DIXON
(B. 1917)

JOHN
(B. 1938 /
D. 1976)
married 1963
MADELINE
TRENT
(B. 1941)

JULIA
(B. 1940 /
D. 1986)
married 1965
PHILIP
RALSTON
(B. 1935)

TATE
(B. 1935 /
D. 1967)
married 1958
LYNN BAKER
(B. 1938)

NICHOLAS
(B. 1937 /
D. 1990)
married 1967
WILLA
SAWYER
(B. 1942)

DANIEL
(B. 1965)

PETER
(B. 1968)
*married
1993*
CATERINA
DEMITRI
(B. 1973)

**ANNE
RALSTON**
(B. 1966)

JEREMY
(B. 1960 /
D. 1992)
*married
1987*
JOSIE
SEATON
(B. 1962)

ALEX
(B. 1969)

Finding

Laura

*S*he set the mirror carefully on the table, her fingers lingering unconsciously to trace the intricate swirls of polished brass. The eyes she raised to meet his were wide and disturbed.

"Why are you telling me this?" Her voice was unsteady.

"Because you have to know." He stepped nearer to her, his face tightening a little at her obvious distress. "Don't you see what it means, darling? Don't you understand?"

"I don't believe it."

"Catherine—"

She shook her head once, violently. "No. I don't believe it. How could I believe it? You're asking me to set aside all the teachings of my lifetime."

It had been a mistake to tell her, he realized that now. She was too deeply religious, her faith too absolute, to allow for acceptance of such a thing—even when it came from him. Something coldly uneasy stirred inside him as he gazed at her agitated face.

"It's all right, darling," he said soothingly. "Just a far-fetched idea of mine, that's all. Because I love you so much, it just seems to me—"

"No." She was looking at him as if at a stranger, a stranger with shocking ideas. "No, you believe it. You really believe it."

He wanted to deny that, to say anything to wipe away the frightened look on her face, the panicked bewilderment in her eyes. But he did believe what he had told her, and he knew himself too well to think he would be able to lie about it—especially to her.

Attempting the next best thing, he said, "Does that really matter, Catherine? There are other things we don't agree on, other ways we think differently. Why should this matter?"

The last vestige of color drained from her face. "You mean . . . all this time you've been going with me to church, and you didn't *believe*? You have no faith? You—you've been lying to me?"

"No, not lying. I just believe in a different interpretation of God's word, that's all. A different explanation of—"

But she was backing away from him, her wide eyes agonized. "I—I don't know you at all," she murmured. "How can I marry a man I don't even know?"

"Catherine—" He reached out for her, but she turned, stumbling a little, and rushed from the room.

For just a moment he stood there, cold with anxiety, with the hollow awareness of having made the biggest mistake of his life. Then he heard the cracked muffler of her beat-up jalopy roar with life, and his heart leaped into his throat as he raced for the door. It was pouring rain out, the roads slick as glass, and she wasn't a very good driver. . . .

Her car fishtailed out of the driveway as he climbed into his and started the engine with jerky urgency. He knew where she would go. To her church, where she had taken all the problems and questions of her life. But it was on the other side of town, with too many hairpin turns and steep hills to traverse at high speed in the pouring rain.

He wasn't far behind her, he thought, but he couldn't see much beyond the hood of his car and had to slow down, cursing under his breath. He could feel the tires slipping, losing traction even at the slower speed, and the coldness inside him spread outward like icy ripples in a pool.

She'll be safe. She has to. Her God will take care of her.

But then his car reached the top of one of the many vicious hills, and his headlights caught the ragged break in the old wooden fence that had been erected as a pitiful barrier. Frantic, he stopped his car and wrenched the door open, already calling her name. He was soaked in the seconds it took him to reach the gap in the fence, water streaming in his eyes and blinding him so that he almost catapulted over the edge of the embankment before he could stop himself.

He swiped a hand across his eyes and peered through the driving rain. Lightning flashed, offering a quick, stark glimpse of what lay below. It was her car, canted at an impossible angle, a red glow underneath it hellish evidence of terrible danger. He started forward, slipping in the mud, thinking of nothing except getting to her.

He was still twenty feet from the car when there was a hollow *whomp,* and the explosion lifted the vehicle briefly into the air. The blast of heat knocked him backward off his feet, and by the time he struggled to sit up, flames had engulfed the car.

Paralyzed with horror, with the first razor slashes of agony, he saw, in the cruel light the fire provided, Catherine's hand. It lay across the ledge of the driver's-side window, limp and unmarked by the shattered glass all around it. And on the third finger, the diamond he had given her glittered with bright and mocking promise.

Chapter 1

*J*ust a couple of hours tomorrow morning, I promise. Come on, Laura—it'll be fun."

Laura Sutherland pulled her sunglasses down her nose to peer at her companion, wincing at the brightness of the afternoon light bouncing off the blue water of the apartment complex's pool. "Fun for who? Cass, I hate antiques. You know I hate antiques."

Basking in the hot sunlight a few feet away from her umbrella-shaded friend, Cassidy Burke rubbed more suntan lotion onto a brown thigh and made a sound of frustration. "It won't be just antiques, Laura. According to what I've heard, there'll be all kinds of things—and furniture in all kinds of styles. Besides, haven't you always wanted to get inside the Kilbourne estate?"

"Not particularly." Laura looked at Cassidy's effortless tan with envy and shifted a bit to make sure her shoulder remained in the shade of the umbrella. Life really wasn't fair. With Cass's pale blond hair and blue eyes, she should have burned to a crisp on a day like this. But did she? Oh, no. She just tanned a golden brown. Laura, on the other hand, not only didn't tan effortlessly, she didn't tan at all; cursed with extremely fair skin, sunlight either burned her badly or else peppered her with freckles. She was ghost pale—and it was the end of yet another long, hot Atlanta summer.

"How can you not be curious?" Cassidy demanded. "The Kilbournes were here long before Sherman marched through, and the intrigues in that family have been grist for the newspapers for generations. You know they say that old Amelia Kilbourne killed her husband? And Amelia's son died mysteriously, everybody knows that, when his two sons were just kids—"

"Cassidy." Laura pushed her sunglasses back up her nose and shook her head. "Even supposing any of that 'they say' and 'everybody knows' stuff is true, do you really expect to see or hear anything of interest at an estate sale? If any of the family is even there, they'll be behind satin ropes in rooms off-limits to the public. Bet on it."

It was Cassidy's turn to pull her sunglasses down her nose, and her bright blue eyes peered at Laura with undiminished interest. "Oh, the whole house is off-limits. The sale's taking place in the side courtyard of the house. The way I heard it, when the prodigal son came home, he took charge with a vengeance. And no way was he going to permit strangers to tromp through the ancestral halls— even if he did want to sell them a few trinkets."

"The prodigal son?" Laura asked despite herself.

"Mmm. Daniel Kilbourne. Amelia's oldest grandson. He's been up north enlarging the family fortune. Some kind of financial wizard, I take it. So, anyway, Amelia gets it into her head that the bursting attics and basement of the house badly need emptying, and announces an estate sale. And before you can say 'scat,' here comes Daniel to arrange everything."

"Is there anything those newspapers of yours *don't* know?"

Cassidy laughed and relaxed in her lounge, pushing the sunglasses back up her nose. "Not much. For instance, while the boys' mother, Madeline, is said to be meek, mild, and completely willing to live in Amelia's house and do as she wishes, both of her sons get away with murder— Daniel because he does what he wants despite the old lady, and Peter because he charms her into giving him his way."

"Sounds like a lovely family," Laura noted dryly.

"You haven't heard the half of it. Honest, Laura, it's like a soap opera! The old lady still technically controls most of the family fortune, but Daniel's been running things for years, and word has it he has to fight Amelia every step of the way. *He*'s supposed to be hard as nails, and because of some kind of legal arrangement Amelia's husband made just before he drowned in his own swimming pool, Daniel's set to inherit everything when Amelia goes. *Everything*. The rest of the family will have to either be real nice to Daniel or else go out and get jobs once the old lady's gone.

"And there are several relatives living in the house, you know. There's Josie Kilbourne, some sort of cousin by marriage, I think; she doesn't get along with Amelia's granddaughter, Anne—who's the daughter of Amelia's daughter, who supposedly died mysteriously, and—"

Laura held up a hand in protest. "Enough! Cass, you've lost me."

"I haven't even mentioned Peter's wife, Kerry," Cassidy said in an innocent tone. "Don't you want to know about her and the chauffeur?"

"Jeez, is there just a normally dull and boring Kilbourne?"

"Not so you'd notice. I'm telling you, it's Peyton Place revisited."

Laura shook her head. "Well, anyway, I'm really not interested in an estate sale, Cass. Or the Kilbournes, for that matter. I have better things to do with my Saturday morning, thanks."

Cassidy smiled slightly and, without looking at her friend, murmured, "You know, I bet they'll have mirrors. Bound to, with a house that big. Just think—mirrors. Old ones, God knows how old. Mirrors you could never find anywhere else. . . ."

After a long moment, Laura said, "You're evil."

Cassidy turned her head and grinned at her friend. "I'll drive. Oh—and can I borrow your blue blouse?"

LAURA'S OBSESSION WITH mirrors had been a part of her life for as long as she could remember. As a child, her family had teased her for her vanity, not understanding that it wasn't her own reflection she gazed so intently into mirrors to see but something else. Something she couldn't explain even to herself.

As she grew older, Laura learned to downplay her obsession, just as she had learned to downplay the other inexplicable things she felt, the things that made her different from those around her. She turned her obsession into something acceptable. She became a collector. She collected mirrors, hand mirrors. That might raise a few brows from time to time, but no one thought she was crazy to collect mirrors. Lots of people collected odd things.

She was still teased from time to time, but those who knew her best looked high and low for interesting mirrors when a gift was needed, because Laura was unfailingly delighted with them.

But no one, not her family, not even Cassidy, who was her closest friend, knew just how deeply her obsession ran. They didn't know that she still looked into every mirror she encountered, not to check her hair or makeup, but still searching for that mysterious something she couldn't even put a name to. They didn't know that her collection of mirrors went far, far beyond the thirty or so examples she displayed in her apartment.

Packed away in numerous boxes in the small second bedroom she used for storage were literally hundreds of hand mirrors. She didn't buy every hand mirror she saw, of course. Some were too large or too small, too ornate or too plain, or whatever material they were fashioned in didn't suit her. She had no mental list of characteristics, yet always knew instantly if a mirror just somehow wasn't "right." And eventually, all those she bought left her vaguely dissatisfied, no matter how excited she had been initially.

It occurred to her that she was searching for a specific mirror, but she had no idea why she would be. Or what that mirror represented to her. She didn't even have a clear picture in her mind to go by, only flashes of intuition and the evidence of what she had collected through the years. Looking at those, she could guess that it was a fairly small hand mirror, fashioned out of some kind of metal and with an intricate design on the handle and back.

But why she searched so intently for such a thing, or what it could possibly mean to her, Laura had no idea. She knew only that it wasn't possible for her to pass up a chance to perhaps find a wonderful new mirror, any more than it was possible for her to willfully stop the beating of her heart.

THE KILBOURNE ESTATE was set in one of the old and gracious suburbs of Atlanta, well back from the road and surrounded by fencing made up of red brick and wrought iron. The house stood amid stately oak trees on property that was thirty acres of immaculately groomed, meticulously planned and landscaped perfection. Various magazines and historical societies had named it the Most Beautiful Estate in Atlanta for so many years that it had been tacitly retired from consideration in recent years so that other estates might carry the banner.

The huge house itself was very Southern, a plantation style more common to the Louisiana river country. Double galleries with six Doric columns on each level extended across the entire front of the main section, while two large wings stretched out to either side. The architectural details of the mansion mixed several periods, from the Doric columns that were classical, through proportions and symmetry that were Greek Revival, and right on into French and baroque touches.

Laura fell in love with the house immediately, which surprised her. She had never been drawn to places, and though her artist's eye could appreciate beauty, no other house had ever made her fingers itch to paint it or called out to her soul to come in and explore its many nooks and crannies.

Not that either was possible, of course. The house hadn't had its portrait painted since 1840, and during today's estate sale, the interior of the house was quite firmly off-limits to all but family. There were uniformed guards standing about to make sure no one wandered inside or ventured out into the vast and celebrated gardens of the estate.

"They're awfully fussy about having strangers about, considering how much of their business is public," Laura murmured to Cassidy.

Bright-eyed with interest, Cassidy nodded. "No kidding. I guess we meekly follow the signs, huh?"

"I guess."

There was a clearly and plainly marked path from where they had been told to park along the wide driveway at the front of the house around the north wing to a rear courtyard near the huge garage that was empty of cars—and filled with the furniture and items that were to be sold. The garage doors were all open, and there were also several long tables set up near the garage, so that all items could be viewed prior to the auction.

Like everyone else attending, Laura and Cassidy had to stop at a registration table first and present a valid I.D. in order to acquire bidding numbers. With that accomplished, they moved toward the garage, where there were already a couple dozen people moving about even though the auction was still nearly two hours away.

"It looks like most of the big furniture is at this end," Cassidy noted as she scanned the area. "The smaller stuff seems to be in that far corner. Listen, since I'm hunting a table for my bedroom and you're looking for mirrors, why don't we split up? We can meet back out here where they'll hold the auction."

Laura, who had caught the distant gleam of something shiny, nodded a distracted agreement and angled off to enter the middle garage door in a shortcut that would take her to the far corner. The interior was well lit and, since it was a reasonably cool morning, comfortable. Temporary shelving had been set up in rows at the far end of the garage to hold small items, and it was to that area that Laura was drawn.

She was virtually alone back there, since most browsers had started at the other end and hadn't reached this area yet. It was very quiet, auction attendees being serious about their bargain-hunting and tending toward low voices and narrowly focused attention.

Laura's attention focused very narrowly. She saw several wall mirrors first, hanging near the garage door in a grouping, and was, as always, drawn to them. She inspected each one, noting only in passing carved and gilded frames that were lovely. Her gaze was drawn to the bright, reflective surfaces of the mirrors. She stood before each one for at least a full minute, looking intently at the reversed image of the room behind her. That was what she scanned searchingly; she never noticed her own reflection, only what lay behind her.

But whatever it was she hoped to see remained elusive and inexplicable. Sighing, disappointed as always, Laura turned away and began moving along the nearest row of shelves. She saw pretty much what she expected to see, given that an attic and basement had been cleared out after generations of a family had stored away what was broken or disliked. Old vases and figurines, decorative bowls, candlesticks, a pair of nice bronze bookends, several small lamps, ornate picture frames, mechanical clocks, stacks of old books, and so on.

She walked along slowly, absently noting that some items had been tagged with a price, meaning that the auctioneer would have a floor for the bidding and could not accept less than the tagged price. Other items bore only numbers, for sale to the highest bidder even if that high bid was only a few dollars.

Laura saw a couple of items she was mildly tempted by, but nothing grabbed her until she reached the last row of shelves. Halfway down the row and on the middle shelf, in a cleared space with nothing near it, was a mirror.

It was about fifteen inches long and seemed to be made of brass, though the metal was so badly tarnished it was difficult to be sure. The handle bore an intricate, swirling design that was stamped or cut deeply into the brass on both sides, while the nearly heart-shaped mirror was held lovingly between an edging of an even more elaborate pattern. Laura didn't have to look to know that the back of the mirror would also be stamped with the swirling design; she didn't recognize it, yet she felt an odd sense of familiarity.

More than that, she was conscious of a certainty that was immediate and absolute.

This was the mirror she had looked for all her life. She knew it.

She felt it.

Her heart was thudding against her ribs, and Laura saw that her hand was shaking when she reached out slowly to touch the mirror. She merely touched it at first, tracing the complex design stamped into the metal with her index finger. Then, as if the precision of every movement were desperately important, she wrapped her fingers around the handle and lifted the heavy mirror.

She didn't realize until she held the mirror before her face that she had closed her eyes. She was afraid to open them. Afraid of what she would see—or not see—when she looked. Afraid, suddenly, to find an answer to the puzzle of her obsession.

But finally, Laura drew a breath and opened her eyes.

She saw herself. Red hair and green eyes. A face even more pale than usual. A face that was never quite what she expected to see, somehow. And beyond her face, behind her, were the rows of shelving filled with items, and the square of brightness that was the open garage door.

Nothing more.

So. Only half the mystery solved. This was the right mirror, Laura was sure of it. But she still had no idea what it was she expected to see beyond her own reflection. Or if she would ever see it.

After a long moment, Laura gently returned the mirror to the shelf. She didn't move away, but stood there gazing down on it, reaching out to touch it lightly again and again, while she waited for the announcement that the auction was about to begin.

"IT'S UGLY," CASSIDY said, taking her eyes off the road long enough to glance aside at the mirror held gently in Laura's lap. "And you got it for five dollars. How good can it be if it costs five dollars?"

"It won't be ugly when I polish it," Laura said. "And

you know as well as I do that auctions are great places to find bargains. This mirror is old, Cass. Real old."

"Old doesn't make it beautiful."

"You're just being grumpy because that guy outbid you for the table you wanted."

"It was *my* table," Cassidy said rather fiercely, her competitive and possessive nature outraged by the loss.

Laura couldn't help smiling, however distractedly; she didn't take her gaze off the mirror in her lap. She still felt as shaken and exhilarated as she had when she'd first seen the mirror, and could hardly wait to get home and polish away years of tarnish. She wanted to see it, to explore the intricate design of the metal, to learn everything she could about it. She could feel something stamped into the brass on the back, numbers or letters set unobtrusively within the intricate design, but due to tarnish and age couldn't make out what it was.

There was a nick on the side of the handle, as if the mirror had struck a sharp edge at some point. And a worn spot where many thumbs must have rested over the years. And Laura was certain the original glass part of the mirror had been somehow broken and replaced.

It could no doubt tell some tales, this mirror, Laura thought.

". . . then again, I could always just go on talking to myself."

Laura blinked, and turned her head to look at her friend. "Oh, sorry."

"Never mind." Cassidy shook her head, her expression wry. "We're home now." She was just turning her two-year-old Mazda into the parking lot of the apartment complex where they lived.

"I'm sorry you lost that table, Cass, really."

"Oh, never mind the damned table. I suppose you'll be drooling over your mirror all afternoon and not be fit for company."

"I never drool," Laura protested mildly. "But as a matter of fact, I thought I'd spend the rest of the day at home." She didn't try to defend her desire to close herself away with the mirror, because she knew Cassidy wouldn't understand. *Hell, I don't understand it myself!*

The two women went into the lobby of their building, waved at the security guard, and went up in the elevator. Cassidy got off on the third floor to go to her apartment, still not in the best of moods and declaring that she was going to order a pizza for lunch and then spend the rest of the afternoon at the pool. Laura continued on to the fourth floor, where her apartment was.

They had both lived in the building for five years, meeting in the laundry room and hitting it off instantly. Both came from large families they weren't particularly close to, and with time and space to themselves for the first time in their lives, neither was in any hurry to exchange the single life for couplehood or kids. Cassidy worked in a bank and considered Laura's job as a commercial artist far more glamorous than her own, while Laura envied Cass her ease with people and her ability to flirt.

Laura didn't flirt, and she was by nature a loner. She had always been intense in her emotions, perhaps because she was creative, and that intensity made her wary of any casual relationship. She had friends, of course, but most were acquaintances she saw infrequently, with the exception of Cassidy.

As for men, in the years since college she had gotten involved with two men seriously enough to contemplate taking them home at Christmas to meet her family. Neither man had made it to the small coastal Georgia town where she had grown up, the relationships faltering and then failing even before the tinsel and lights of downtown Atlanta began to pall on everyone. Laura accepted the blame for the breakups, knowing herself to be moody and emotional around the holidays, but comforted herself with the certainty that someday, someone would sense and understand her peculiar whims and moods.

Today, however, she just wanted to be alone with her mirror.

She went into her corner apartment, which was bright and airy due to numerous windows and the southeastern exposure she had requested. The small kitchen was divided from the much larger space of the living room by a breakfast bar with two high stools that took the place of a dining table. There was space for a dining table just beyond the kitchen, but that was occupied by Laura's drafting table and, sometimes, an easel and stool.

There was an easel there now, holding a half-finished painting that was Laura's latest attempt to discover whether or not she could *really* paint and make her living that way instead of working on ad layouts and the like. The verdict on this attempt was no, a conclusion Laura had dismally reached a couple of days ago. Whatever spark it took to inflame the creative soul of an artist was lacking in Laura. For now, at least. But she refused to give up. Someday . . .

To the right of the living room, beside the doorway that led to the short hall and two bedrooms of the apartment, Laura's collection of hand mirrors was displayed, some on a set of freestanding shelves and some artfully arranged on the wall above it. It was a varied collection, with mirrors fashioned from brass, silver and silver plate, copper, pewter, and two from gleaming wood. They ranged in size from hardly more than palm sized to nearly twenty inches long, and the mirrors themselves were formed in nearly every possible shape. There was even one small triangular mirror set in wrought iron.

Laura didn't even glance toward them.

She went into the living room, dropping her shoulder bag onto the comfortable overstuffed chair and pausing only long enough to set the mirror carefully on the polished wood of her coffee table before going in search of what she would need to clean her prize.

IT WAS AFTER five o'clock that evening when the security guard downstairs called up to tell Laura that she had a visitor.

"Who is it, Larry?"

"It's Mr. Peter Kilbourne, Miss Sutherland," the guard replied, unaware of the shock he was delivering. "He says it's in reference to the mirror you bought today."

For just an instant, Laura was conscious of nothing except an overwhelming urge to grab her mirror and run. It was nothing she could explain, but the panic was so real that Laura went ice-cold with it. Thankfully, the reaction was short-lived, since her rational mind demanded to know why on earth she felt so threatened. After all, she had bought the mirror legally, and no one had the right to take it away from her. Not even Peter Kilbourne.

Trying to shake off uneasiness, she said, "Thank you, Larry. Send him up, please."

She found her shoes and stepped into them, and absently smoothed a few strands of hair that had escaped from the long braid hanging down her back, but Laura didn't think or worry too much about how she looked. Instead, as she waited for her unexpected visitor, she stood near the couch and kept glancing at the mirror lying on several layers of newspaper on the coffee table.

It looked now, after hours of hard work, like an entirely different mirror. The rich, warm, reddish gold color of old brass gleamed now, and the elaborate pattern stamped into the metal, a shade darker, showed up vividly. It was a curious pattern, not floral as with most of the mirrors she had found, but rather a swirling series of loops and curves that were, Laura had discovered, actually made up of one continuous line—rather like a maze.

It was around the center of this maze that Laura had discovered the numbers or letters stamped into the brass, but since she hadn't yet finished polishing the back, she still didn't know what, if anything, the writing signified.

A quiet knock at her door recalled her thoughts, and Laura mentally braced herself as she went to greet her visitor. She had no particular image in her mind of Peter Kilbourne, but she certainly didn't expect to open her door to the most handsome man she'd ever seen.

It was an actual, physical shock to see him, she realized dimly, a stab of the same astonishment one would feel if a statue of masculine perfection suddenly breathed and smiled. He was the epitome of tall, dark, and handsome—and more. Much more. Black hair, pale blue eyes, a flashing smile. Perfect features. And his charm was an almost visible thing, somehow, obvious even before he spoke in a deep, warm voice.

"Miss Sutherland? I'm Peter Kilbourne."

A voice to break hearts.

Laura gathered her wits and stepped back, opening the door wider to admit him. "Come in." She thought he was about her own age, maybe a year or two older.

He came into the apartment and into the living room, taking in his surroundings quickly but thoroughly, and clearly taking note of the mirror on the coffee table. His gaze might have widened a bit when it fell on her collection of mirrors, but Laura couldn't be sure, and when he turned to face her, he was smiling with every ounce of his charm.

It was unsettling how instantly and powerfully she was affected by that magnetism. Laura had never considered herself vulnerable to charming men, but she knew without doubt that this one would be difficult to resist—whatever it was he wanted of her. Too uneasy to sit down or invite him to, Laura merely stood with one hand on the back of a chair and eyed him with what she hoped was a faint, polite smile.

If Peter Kilbourne thought she was being ungracious by not inviting him to sit down, he didn't show it. He gestured slightly toward the coffee table and said, "I see you've been hard at work, Miss Sutherland."

She managed a shrug. "It was badly tarnished. I wanted to get a better look at the pattern."

He nodded, his gaze tracking past her briefly to once again note the collection of mirrors near the hallway. "You have quite a collection. Have you . . . always collected mirrors?"

It struck her as an odd question somehow, perhaps because there was something hesitant in his tone, something a bit surprised in his eyes. But Laura replied truthfully despite another stab of uneasiness. "Since I was a child, actually. So you can see why I bought that one today at the auction."

"Yes." He slid his hands into the pockets of his dark slacks, sweeping open his suit jacket as he did so in a pose that might have been studied or merely relaxed. "Miss Sutherland—look, do you mind if I call you Laura?"

"No, of course not."

"Thank you." He nodded gravely, a faint glint of amusement in his eyes recognizing her reluctance. "I'm Peter."

She nodded in turn, but didn't speak.

"Laura, would you be interested in selling the mirror back to me? At a profit, naturally."

"I'm sorry." She was shaking her head even before he finished speaking. "I don't want to sell the mirror."

"I'll give you a hundred for it."

Laura blinked in surprise, but again shook her head. "I'm not interested in making money, Mr. Kilbourne—"

"Peter."

A little impatiently, she said, "All right—Peter. I don't want to sell the mirror. And I did buy it legitimately."

"No one's saying you didn't, Laura," he soothed. "And you aren't to blame for my mistake, certainly. Look, the truth is that the mirror shouldn't have been put up for auction. It's been in my family a long time, and we'd like to have it back. Five hundred."

Not a bad profit on a five-dollar purchase. She drew a breath and spoke slowly. "No. I'm sorry, I really am, but . . . I've been looking for this—for a mirror like this—for a long time. To add to my collection. I'm not interested in making money, so please don't bother to raise your offer. Even five thousand wouldn't make a difference."

His eyes were narrowed slightly, very intent on her face, and when he smiled suddenly it was with rueful certainty. "Yes, I can see that. You don't have to look so uneasy, Laura—I'm not going to wrest the thing away from you by force."

"I never thought you would," she murmured, lying.

He chuckled, a rich sound that stroked along her nerve endings like a caress. "No? I'm afraid I've made you nervous, and that was never my intention. Why don't I buy you dinner some night as an apology?"

This man is dangerous. "That isn't necessary," she said.

"I insist."

Laura looked at his incredibly handsome face, that charming smile, and drew yet another deep breath. "Will your wife be coming along?" she asked mildly.

"If she's in town, certainly." His eyes were guileless.

Very dangerous. Laura shook her head. "Thanks, but no apology is necessary. You offered a generous price for the mirror; I refused. That's all there is to it." She half turned and made a little gesture toward the door with one hand, unmistakably inviting him to leave.

Peter's beautiful mouth twisted a bit, but he obeyed

the gesture and followed her to the door. When she opened it and stood back, he paused to reach into the inner pocket of his jacket and produced a business card. "Call me if you change your mind," he said. "About the mirror, I mean."

Or anything else, his smile said.

"I'll do that," she returned politely, accepting the card.

"It was nice meeting you, Laura."

"Thank you. Nice meeting you," she murmured.

He gave her a last flashing smile, lifted a hand slightly in a small salute, and left her apartment.

Laura closed the door and leaned back against it for a moment, relieved and yet still uneasy. She didn't know why Peter Kilbourne wanted the mirror back badly enough to pay hundreds of dollars for it, but every instinct told her the matter was far from settled.

She hadn't heard the last of him.

IT WASN'T UNTIL late Sunday morning that Laura was finally able to make out what was stamped in the mazelike pattern on the back of the mirror. It was almost unnoticeable, designed so cleverly that it seemed a part of the pattern, but in the center of the maze had been stamped a tiny heart. There was a curving line through the heart, dividing it in half, and in each half was a letter. *S* in one half and *B* in the other.

Below the tiny heart was a date. 1778.

At first, Laura thought that might indicate the date the mirror had been made, which would make it well over two hundred years old. But then she found an additional date on the back of the handle, near the bottom. 1800.

The second date, if it indicated the date the mirror was made, would mean that it was just shy of two hundred years old.

Two hundred years.

Then again, Laura told herself, the numbers might not be a date at all, either set of them. They could be some kind of brassmaker's marks, or even something stamped into the metal by someone trying to make the mirror appear older than it actually was.

That was her common sense talking. But when Laura touched the mirror, when she traced the swirling pattern in the brass, she *felt* age. She sat there on the couch for a while longer, gently polishing the mirror, letting her mind muse over those two initials in the heart. Because that had to be it, of course—the initials of lovers. The mirror must have been a gift from a man to his lady, and the date stamped just below the heart might commemorate a wedding or birth, or perhaps the date they had met.

Laura still had no idea why she should feel so strongly about a mirror that was very likely almost two hundred years old, and she couldn't help wondering if there was any way she could find out its history. Surely that would give her something to go on, something to explain why she was so drawn to the thing.

When she heard someone knock on her door, Laura assumed it was Cassidy. She left the mirror on the coffee table and went to open the door, startled to find two neatly dressed middle-aged men standing there. Before she could do more than ask herself why Larry hadn't announced visitors, one of the men opened up a folded wallet and showed her a badge.

"Miss Sutherland? I'm Detective Bridges, this is Detective Shaw. Atlanta Police. May we come in and talk to you, please?"

God, surely he didn't tell the police I stole the mirror! "Talk to me about what?" she asked, aware that she sounded rattled.

Neither detective seemed surprised that she kept them standing at the door. Detective Bridges said pleasantly,

"Where were you last night, Miss Sutherland? Say, between eight P.M. and midnight?"

Must not be the mirror, then. The relief was overwhelming. "I was here," she said.

"Alone?" Detective Shaw asked.

She didn't like the way he was staring at her, so suspiciously. "Yes, alone. Why?"

Detective Bridges spoke again, still polite, his gaze seemingly pleasant. "Can anyone verify that, Miss Sutherland?"

She frowned at him. "This is a secured building; the front lobby entrance is always manned by security, and you can only enter or leave the rear door with a keycard. The guard downstairs last night would have me in his log if I'd left the building— Hey, why didn't he announce you two?"

"We asked him not to, Miss Sutherland." Bridges was still polite.

More belligerent, Shaw demanded, "How do we know you didn't leave by the rear door?"

Laura's earlier uneasiness returned full force. What was this all about? Slowly she said, "Every time a card is used, a computer records whose it is. Check with Larry—the guard downstairs. My card wasn't used last night."

"You could have used somebody else's," Shaw pointed out nastily.

"Maybe I could have, but I didn't," Laura snapped. "Look, what's this all about?"

Bridges smiled again. "I believe you know Peter Kilbourne, Miss Sutherland?"

"No. That is, I've met him. Yesterday, as a matter of fact. But I don't know him. Why?"

"He came here late yesterday afternoon?"

"Yes."

"Why?"

Laura gritted her teeth and promised herself this was

the last question she'd answer until her own was answered. "I bought a mirror yesterday from his family's estate sale. He showed up hours later and said it had been put up for auction mistakenly. He wanted to buy it back. Now, what the hell is going on?"

Bridges must have realized she was about to stop being cooperative. Or maybe he just knew how to time an announcement to create the maximum amount of shock. In any case, he chose to answer her.

"Peter Kilbourne was murdered last night. And as far as we can determine, you were one of the last people to see him in the hours before his death."

"And," Shaw added in a voice of frightening satisfaction, "he checked into a motel last night not three blocks from here—with a redhead."

Chapter 2

They didn't believe me." Laura was curled up in her big chair, drained and more than a little frightened.

"They can't have any real evidence, because you didn't do it," Cassidy reminded her.

"I can't prove I didn't leave the building last night, that's what they kept coming back to. Even though the door guard didn't see me leave and my keycard wasn't used, they said I could have used somebody else's. Nearly thirty people left the building last night between eight and midnight, according to the computer log, and that one cop is convinced I used one of their cards." Laura shivered and tried to think of something else. "By the way, how was your date?"

"Never mind my date." Cassidy, sitting on Laura's couch, was a little pale and definitely worried. "It was cruddy and I came home early—and this is no time for small talk. Look, once everybody who used their card last night verifies that, you'll be in the clear. Right?"

"I don't think so. When they got the printout from

Larry, he said something about at least a couple of people in the building losing or misplacing their cards. If those lost cards were used last night . . ."

"You don't have a motive, you'd just met the man."

"Yeah, well. The nicer cop said they'd check with the family and see if anyone could verify that he came here to see a stranger about a mirror she'd bought at the estate sale. All the driver knew was that he brought Peter to this address, and that Peter mentioned my name."

"Somebody in the family is bound to verify it, Laura."

"Maybe. But I don't know that it would matter if they did. The police could always say that Peter did know me and used the mirror as an excuse to see me. Those newspapers of yours weren't kidding about his charm, and I'll bet the woman last night wasn't the first one he'd taken to a motel. He made a move on me, for God's sake, and we'd just met."

"I hope you didn't mention that to the police," Cassidy said ruefully.

"No, of course not." Laura put a hand up and rubbed her eyes tiredly. "I just wish that so-helpful chauffeur had driven Peter when he went back out last night after he left here and went home. But Peter drove himself—and his car was found parked two blocks from here. Dammit, I think it looks bad, and I *know* I'm innocent."

"Look, if he was with another woman, maybe his wife—"

"His wife is—or was, since she's probably on her way home now—visiting relatives in California. Haven't you read the special edition of the newspaper they put out this afternoon?" She nodded to the untidy stack of newspapers on the floor beside her chair. "I looked at it while I was waiting for you to get back from your tennis date. Peter Kilbourne's murder is a front-page story. They didn't have a lot of details, but they had a few. Seems the wife is the only one of the family with a strong alibi. The rest of them were scattered about last night, several at home with no proof they stayed there, and one or two out on the town, possibly with witnesses."

"Then the police will find the woman he was with," Cassidy offered.

"Oh, yeah." Laura sighed. "Seen late at night by a sleepy hotel manager who remembers only that she was a redhead. Hotel rooms being what they are, I'll bet the police found enough fingerprints to paper a billboard. And whoever killed him had the presence of mind to wipe the handle of the knife, so that probably won't help identify anyone." Laura shivered again. "I hope the newspaper exaggerated. It said he had been stabbed a dozen times. God, Cass, how badly would you have to hate a man to stab him a dozen times?"

"Don't think about it," Cassidy said, looking a bit sick herself.

"I can't help it." She managed a wavering smile. "I don't have your ability to compartmentalize, remember? You're the mathematical one; I'm the one with the vivid imagination. Even though I didn't do it, I . . . I can see it, Cass. In my mind. How it must have happened. The violence of it. The blood . . . God help me, I could probably paint it."

It was Cassidy's turn to shiver. "That's creepy."

"Tell me about it. There's a downside to everything, including imagination."

"Then let's use logic," Cassidy suggested. "We know who *didn't* kill him—you. So who could have done it, and why?"

"I don't know. How could I?" Laura stared at the mirror on her coffee table and frowned. "All I know is that Peter Kilbourne came here to buy back that mirror—and he wanted it badly enough to offer me five hundred dollars for it."

"Is it worth that much?" Cassidy wasn't nearly so

scornful of the "ugly" mirror today, but whether because Laura had polished it up or because it appeared to be far more important than it had yesterday was something she didn't explain.

"I don't know enough about antiques—even antique mirrors—to know what it's worth, but I'm willing to bet he didn't want it back because of its intrinsic value. No, there was something odd about the whole thing."

"What do you mean?"

Laura's frown deepened. "Well, for instance, he said it had been in the family a long time, implying that it was an heirloom. But you saw the condition it was in when I bought it. That mirror's been stuck in a trunk or box, or lying on a dusty shelf somewhere, for years. Maybe even decades. That's not the way a devoted family takes care of an heirloom. And then there's the way he reacted to my collection of mirrors. He asked me if I had *always* collected mirrors, not as if the idea of collecting them surprised him, but as if my collecting mirrors meant something else to him."

"Like what?" Cassidy asked, puzzled.

"I don't know. It was all inflection, and something in his eyes, too brief for me to really get hold of it. But . . ." Laura hesitated, then went on slowly, "you know, I have the weird feeling that he left here without the mirror only because he saw my collection over there. When he got here, he had every intention of offering me whatever it took to get the mirror, but something changed his mind."

"Maybe he knew how obsessive collectors could be, and realized you wouldn't sell."

"I don't think that was it. He seemed to . . . recognize something. It was almost as if, when he saw my collection, he suddenly understood something that had been a puzzle to him until then."

"Why you bought a mirror, maybe?" Cassidy shook

her head before Laura could respond, and said wryly, "No, people buy all kinds of things at estate sales, so that shouldn't have puzzled him."

"I don't think it did. But something did. Until he saw my collection."

Cassidy watched her brooding friend for a moment, then said, "So, what happens next? I assume the police will be asking all of us about our keycards, but what about you?"

Laura's mouth twisted. "The nice one asked me if I would—voluntarily—consent to having my fingerprints taken. The implication being that if I didn't agree, they'd charge me, or arrest me, or officially take me in for questioning. Or do whatever it took to get my prints whether I like it or not."

"I guess you consented?"

"I'm supposed to go first thing tomorrow morning, before work."

"Well, okay—we both know they won't find your prints in that motel room, and without that, they have nothing. I mean, Laura, all they really have is the fact that Peter Kilbourne spent fifteen minutes here hours before he was killed. So you're a redhead—big deal. How many redheads are there in Atlanta? And that's assuming the hotel manager saw what he thought he saw—late at night when he was sleepy, as you said."

"All that's perfectly true," Laura admitted. "And it's undoubtedly why I wasn't arrested this morning, because they don't have any evidence against me. But, Cass, it's virtually certain I was one of the last people to see him alive, and if they can't find another redhead lurking somewhere in his immediate past, then they're going to concentrate on me. They'll be looking for connections between me and Peter Kilbourne."

"But there aren't any," Cassidy protested.

"You know that, and I know it, but the police are

going to want to find out for themselves. They'll examine me and my recent past, if not my entire life, with a microscope. Talk to people who know me. Maybe have me followed. God knows what else. And when the press gets hold of my name . . . damn. At best, my life is not going to be fun for a while."

"And at worst?"

"At worst, the police won't be able to find another suspect." Laura managed a smile, but she wouldn't have wanted to see what it looked like. "And even if their case is too weak for a courtroom, I'll bet the press will be able to come up with all sorts of scenarios in which I murder Peter Kilbourne."

"But if you're not even arrested—"

Laura heard herself utter a sound that might have approached amusement. "Come on, Cass. If you don't think they'll rush to judgment, you haven't been paying attention to the news in the last few years."

"Then what'll you do?" Cassidy asked soberly.

Returning her gaze to the mirror on the coffee table, Laura said slowly, "The police weren't at all interested in the mirror, except for it being the *alleged* reason why Peter came here yesterday. So they won't be investigating that. But I think somebody should. I can't help feeling that it's important for me to find out why he wanted to buy the mirror back. I think I need to find out as much as I can about its history, about how it came to be in the possession of the Kilbourne family."

"How will you do that?"

"I've been thinking about it," Laura said, not admitting that she had decided earlier to do this on her own account, to attempt to explain why she felt so strongly about the mirror. "You remember that college student I used last summer to do research for me?"

"Yeah. You said she was good."

"Very good. I think maybe I'll give her a call and see if she wants to earn a little extra money."

"Researching a mirror?"

Laura shrugged. "There are a couple of dates on the back to give her a place to start, so why not? Maybe she won't be able to find anything. But maybe she will. Maybe she'll be able to tell me where the mirror came from and how it ended up in the possession of the Kilbournes."

"And what do you expect that to tell you?"

"Why it was so important to Peter Kilbourne, I guess."

"Do you really think this mirror had something to do with why he was killed?"

"No. I don't know. It's the only thing I've got to go on, Cass. The only thing I know of Peter Kilbourne is that he wanted this mirror back the day he died. I have to find out why."

After a moment, Cassidy shook her head. "Sounds like a long shot to me, Laura. But I guess you have to do *something* about this situation."

"I can't just sit around and wait for the police to decide I didn't do it," Laura agreed, then frowned. "Problem is, it'll take a while to get the research done, even if Dena gets lucky. And she'll have to start with the origins of the mirror—I think nearly two hundred years ago. That's an awful lot of ground to cover before getting to the Kilbourne family."

"Unless they had it all along," Cassidy pointed out. "That could be it, you know. Maybe the mirror was passed along from generation to generation and finally ended up in the attic because some Kilbourne lady decided she liked silver better than brass for her dressing table. It could have lain forgotten up there for a long time. And maybe, after the auction, somebody in the family was looking over the list of things sold and saw the mirror listed. Recognized it—and went ballistic."

"Maybe." But Laura didn't really believe that. She had nothing more to go on than her feelings, but those told her the mirror had a different history, that it had come into the possession of the Kilbourne family fairly recently. "But if not, if Dena has to comb through records from Revolutionary days to the present, then it's going to take a while before I have any tie to the Kilbournes."

Cassidy looked at her steadily. "Logically, of course, there is another way to look for the information. Go right to the source. Having the mirror in your possession should at least get your foot in the door."

That possibility had been lurking in Laura's mind for hours, but she instantly said, "I don't think I'd have the nerve to go to their door, Cass. Especially now. According to the papers, they'll bury Peter Tuesday afternoon. I just . . . I don't think I could go to them and ask about the mirror."

"I don't think you're going to have a choice," Cassidy said. "If you want to figure this thing out for yourself, I mean. The police might possibly tell you if somebody in the family confirms that Peter came here to discuss the mirror, but I bet they won't bend over backward to tell you much more than that. And only somebody in the family can tell you what reason Peter might have had to try and buy the mirror back."

"They'll be in mourning. And I've been all but accused of murdering Peter; what if they know that?"

"They probably will know it, if the police concentrate on you," Cassidy pointed out. "Especially once the press gets hold of it. But being suspected doesn't mean you're guilty, Laura, and even if the press rushes to judgment, surely the family will want to know the truth."

"If someone I loved was murdered," Laura said, "I wouldn't want his accused killer in my house. Period."

"You haven't been accused. The police have questioned you, like they've no doubt questioned other peo-

ple. Because he was here hours before he was killed. But
he left here alive, remember that, with his chauffeur to
verify that fact. You're an innocent woman trying to find
out if this mirror you bought at their estate sale might have
something to do with his death. Period."

Laura managed a smile. "That sounds so nice and logical. But it might just take more nerve than I can muster."

Cassidy unwound from her curled position on the
couch and got up, stretching absently. "You have plenty of
nerve, friend. You've just never needed it before. As a
matter of fact, I've always thought that quiet manner of
yours hid pure steel underneath."

"I don't know how you could have gotten that idea,"
Laura murmured.

"No?" Cassidy smiled wryly. "Because, like me, you
come from a big family. Because your being the third
oldest out of eight kids, and the oldest girl, means you
spent your childhood with plenty of responsibility heaped
on your shoulders. Because you had five younger siblings
clinging to you and two older ones teasing you—and if
that doesn't toughen up someone's hide, nothing will.
And lastly, because you walked away from all that at eighteen and have seldom looked back since. You're strong
enough to do whatever you have to do, Laura. Believe *me*
if you don't know it yourself."

This time, Laura's smile was easier. "Thanks. I'll have
to think about it, though—going to the Kilbournes."

"Well, let me know what you decide. I need to go
home and get ready for work tomorrow. Want to split a
take-out order for supper?"

"I don't think so, thanks. I'll talk to you tomorrow,
Cass."

"You bet."

When she was alone in the quiet apartment, Laura
leaned forward in her chair and picked up the mirror. She
held it in her lap for several moments, tracing the pattern

on the back, then lifted it and turned it until she could see her reflection. But as always, she looked past herself, as if she expected to see something just beyond her shoulder.

"What is it?" she murmured. "What do I always expect to see?"

As always, there was no answer. But Laura had to wonder if perhaps one of the Kilbournes could answer that question for her. Or answer another one, why Peter had wanted the mirror back. Either way, this mirror now connected her with the Kilbourne family, for good or ill.

The only thing she knew for sure was that Cassidy had been right. The mirror was likely to do one thing, at least. It was likely to get her in the door of the Kilbourne house.

If she had the nerve to make the attempt.

JOSIE KILBOURNE HUNG up the phone and rubbed her eyes with a sigh. Between the calls of sympathy, and the funeral arrangements it had fallen to her to make, Monday morning had been a busy one for her. She'd barely had time to think, and suspected that the shock of finding out about Peter's murder in the early hours of Sunday morning was still a long way from wearing off.

It seemed unreal to her still, that he was gone. That someone had violently ended his life. She could even think with detachment how ironic it was that he had died in a run-down motel—Peter, who had always demanded and usually got the best of everything.

She looked at the stack of notes before her that were ready to be folded into envelopes and mailed. They were handwritten, the notes, in a spidery but steady and beautiful hand on elegant notepaper, and Josie couldn't help wondering if Amelia had stayed up all last night to respond personally to the calls and messages of condolence that had come in yesterday. If so, it was nothing the old lady didn't normally do; Josie had known her to walk the quiet halls of the house at all hours.

Still, after the murder of a favorite grandson, anyone would think that Amelia, who had celebrated her eightieth birthday earlier in the year, would have spent less time at her desk being polite and more time grieving with Peter's mother and his widow.

That thought had barely crossed her mind when Josie grimaced. How could she even mentally criticize Amelia for staying away from Madeline when Josie herself hadn't been able to bear the overwhelming grief of Peter's mother? And Kerry obviously didn't want comforting or company in her mourning; Peter's wife—widow—had arrived back home today white and calm, saying little to anyone.

But Madeline had gone instantly to pieces when the news of Peter's death had come, and she was no better now. Still, Daniel was the only one Madeline seemed to need, and he at least was patient enough to spend hours letting her cling to him while she alternately sobbed and talked brokenly about her "baby."

Josie couldn't help wondering if Daniel knew his mother would never grieve so violently for him, if he should predecease her. Peter had been her favorite, and though she had always looked to her older son for help and support, she had never been affectionate toward Daniel and seemed, in fact, a bit nervous around him. But if Daniel knew—or cared—that he was the least favored of his mother's sons, he never let on. And he would remain with his mother, infinitely patient and uncomplaining, as long as she needed him.

But Amelia was another matter. To her, open and un- abashed grief was . . . unseemly. Amelia was of a differ- ent generation, raised in a different and much more formal time by undemonstrative parents; maybe that was why she appeared—at least outwardly—unmoved by tragedy. Why she pushed aside grief to respond politely to the condolences of people who knew the family, and why she had no patience with the unbridled emotions of her daughter-in-law. And of course she didn't look any different today than she had last week or last month, since it wasn't possible to wear a darker shade of black to separate the degree of fresh grief from that forty years old.

Josie glanced down at her own darkly sober skirt and blouse and felt a twinge of uneasiness. Had she donned the funereal outfit in deference to Peter's death or because it had become automatic? She honestly couldn't remember. *My God, am I becoming Amelia?*

It was a distinctly unnerving thought. Five years had passed since Jeremy Kilbourne's death in one of the odd accidents that seemed to befall so many of the Kilbournes, leaving Josie a widow at thirty. As a fairly distant relation of Amelia's husband, and not on the wealthy branch of the family, Jeremy had also left his wife virtually penniless. So Josie, grieving and broke, had come to work for Amelia as her personal assistant.

It wasn't a bad job by any means. The money was good, she got her room and board here, and the work was usually light. But as she looked down at herself, Josie couldn't help wondering if she shouldn't have gotten out of this house years ago.

"You should never wear a frown. It spoils the perfection of that alabaster brow."

The mocking voice brought her head up, and Josie smiled slightly as Alex Kilbourne came into the room to perch on the corner of her desk. At twenty-eight, he was years younger than she was, yet he seemed older, extremely self-confident and sometimes uncomfortably perceptive. He was a very handsome man, tall and well built, a rare blond Kilbourne with greenish eyes, and he drew the attention of women almost as effortlessly as Peter had.

For the first time, Josie wondered who else he was sleeping with.

"It's a day for frowning, I'd say," she told him in a tone of mild reproof.

Alex lifted an eyebrow, his smile turning a bit wry. "Because one of his women finally took Peter out of circulation? You forget—I didn't like him."

"No, I hadn't forgotten that. But you should at least be wearing an armband, Alex. It's only decent."

"You're wearing enough black for both of us, sweet," he told her.

She resisted an urge to glance down at herself again. "I look the same as always," she said a little defensively.

"I know."

He had never before commented on her habit of wearing dark clothes, but something in his voice now told her that he had certainly noticed it—and quite likely understood it. Unwilling to think too much about that, Josie changed the subject.

"Do you happen to know if Daniel is still with Madeline?"

"No, I haven't been upstairs. Did I see the doctor go up a while ago? Not for Amelia?"

"No, Daniel said to call him to see Madeline. I imagine he could hold out during another night of her weeping, but if she doesn't get some sleep before the funeral tomorrow, she won't make it through." Josie sighed. "And even though she *looked* awfully calm, the doctor gave Kerry something too; he said he wanted her to sleep until tomorrow morning."

Alex gazed down at her intently. "How are you holding up?"

Josie shrugged. "I've been too busy to think much about it. But I looked at the newspapers this morning, and—"

"Ignore them," he advised firmly. "Groundless speculation, mostly."

"They said Peter checked into that motel with a redheaded woman."

Alex looked at her gleaming auburn hair for a moment, then said, "So?"

"So I'm the only redhead in the family, Alex. The
only one in the house, as a matter of fact. What if the
police decide I'm a suspect?"

"You were with me Saturday night."

"Until just before ten. They said Peter was killed
around midnight."

"You had no motive, and he wasn't your lover. I
would have said Peter wasn't stupid enough to be carrying
on with a relation by marriage living in the same house
with his wife." His eyes narrowed suddenly. "Or is there
something you haven't told me?"

Josie shook her head, but under his steady gaze finally
sighed a bit impatiently. "He made a small pass—once—
when I first came to live here."

"You mean right after you'd buried Jeremy?"

She nodded.

"Christ," Alex muttered.

"Well, he wasn't exactly Mr. Sensitivity, despite his
charm, we both know that. Anyway, I told him to leave
me alone, and he did. It was probably just a knee-jerk
reaction to a new woman nearby and meant nothing. You
know how he was. Besides, unlike you, he didn't seem too
interested in older women."

"Insensitive *and* stupid," Alex decided. He leaned
down and caught both her hands in his, pulling her gently
up out of her chair. "You've been shut up in here all day,
and your imagination's beginning to work overtime; why
don't we go for a walk? There are still a few flowers
blooming in the gardens, and it's cool out."

"No, I have to mail all these notes for Amelia today. And there are some messages she should see, and—"

Alex drew her closer and kissed her, cutting off her words and her refusal quite deliberately. His mouth moved on hers with the seductive skill that never failed to astonish her and make her weak with longing, and she heard herself make a sensual little sound when his arms went around her and she felt the strength of them. Unexpected strength in one who moved almost lazily and never seemed to exert himself.

"Don't," she murmured against his lips. "Somebody might come in."

He tipped his head back and looked at her, smiling just a little. "Josie, we've been sleeping together for two months. Do you really think there's anybody in this house who doesn't know?"

Startled, she said, "Not Amelia, surely."

He laughed. "She knew before anybody, sweet. You couldn't sneak a secret past that old lady in pitch darkness a mile away from her."

"She hasn't said anything," Josie protested.

"What would she say? We're both over twenty-one and unattached, and despite the way she dresses and some-times acts, Amelia is well aware of what decade we're in. As long as we're reasonably discreet, what's she got to complain about?"

"She'll think I'm cheating on Jeremy," Josie said almost to herself.

Alex didn't let go of her, but his arms loosened slightly and his expression was abruptly unreadable. In a level voice he said, "Jeremy is dead, Josie. He's been dead for five years. You are not cheating on him."

"I know that, but—but Amelia might not see it that way. She's been a widow for *forty years* and still wears black, still keeps a place for David at the dinner table, and his picture by her bed, and—"

Alex framed her face in his hands. "Amelia wears black because she knows she looks good in it. As for the rest, if you think it's emotionally healthy to keep an empty chair ready for a man who stopped needing it forty years ago, all I can say is that you ought to talk to somebody about this, sweet."

Josie eyed him, conscious of brief amusement. "I take it you think the picture by the bed *isn't* excessive?"

"Well, it's not as bad as an empty chair. Do you keep a picture of Jeremy on your nightstand, by the way? Since you've never let me into the inner sanctum, I have no way of knowing."

Back on balance now, Josie merely said, "I have his picture on my dressing table, not the nightstand."

"When you move it into a drawer, or tuck it away in a photo album, let me know."

"Why?"

He kissed her lightly and then released her. He was smiling, but his face was still unreadable. "Because then I'll ask for an invitation into the inner sanctum."

That surprised her somewhat; it implied that he didn't want Jeremy looking over his shoulder while he made love to his cousin's widow. But Alex had never shown a sign of being uncomfortable about their relationship. In fact, he had always talked to her easily and casually about Jeremy, before and since they had become lovers. But Josie chose not to question him, preferring not to look too deeply into Alex's feelings about her dead husband.

"Walk with me in the garden," Alex suggested again.

"I have all this work—"

"The work isn't going anywhere, Josie, and nobody but you expects you to work all day without a break." Alex got off the desk and took her hand, leading her firmly toward the door. "For the sake of your health, we're going for a twenty-minute walk. You can finish up the work for Amelia later. No arguments."

Josie offered a final protest. "But don't you have work to do?" Alex, with a law degree earned several years before, was "in training," as he termed it, to take over as the Kilbourne family lawyer when the current one retired.

"Our office handles only one client, remember?" Alex said, pausing at the door to smile at her. "The Kilbourne family. And since Preston Montgomery doted on Peter, and since he's amazingly emotional for a lawyer—even an old one—the firm of Kennard, Montgomery, and Kilbourne is closed for the week. The only thing I have to do officially is read Peter's will to the family after the funeral."

"You don't have to sound so cheerful about it," Josie felt honor-bound to say.

Alex shook his head slightly, still smiling. "After all this time you still don't expect me to be conventional, surely? Josie, I refuse to grieve for a man I didn't like, or respect his memory as if death made him a saint. I know he was blood, but he was bad blood. He was in a seedy motel room with another woman while his wife was away—and it wasn't the first time. If you want to see me offer sympathy, you should have been there this morning when I picked Kerry up at the airport. She's the one I feel sorry for."

Since Josie felt the same way, it was difficult to criticize Alex for his attitude, but Josie had been raised by conventional parents and it was hard for her to discard their teachings. "I do too, but—"

"But?" He waited politely.

She smiled suddenly. "Never mind. You're right—I should never expect conventionality from a man who wears Looney Tunes neckties within the hallowed halls of a venerable law office."

He winked at her. "Now you're catching on."

Josie felt peculiar chuckling as she let him lead her toward the back of the house, but she couldn't help it. She doubted there was anything Alex took seriously, but his casual attitude had frequently brightened her mood, so she seldom complained. Besides, she did need to get out of the house for a few minutes, to walk in a cool garden with a man who made her laugh, and forget the violent death of another man . . . even if only for a little while.

BY TUESDAY MORNING, Laura had received both good news and bad news from the police. The good news was that her fingerprints had not been found anywhere in the motel room where Peter Kilbourne had died or in his car. The bad news was that one of the keycards used in her building on Saturday night belonged to a tenant who had gone off into the wilds hunting—and nobody seemed to know when he'd be back. Until he returned, and assuming he verified that he himself had used his card to exit the building at eight thirty-five on Saturday night, Laura could not be eliminated as a suspect.

She didn't think she would be even then, unless the police found another suspect. A suspect they didn't seem to be looking for. They had already spent time at the company where she worked, asking questions about her of her boss and other employees, and everybody in the apartment building had also been questioned.

A friend who worked at her bank had told her that the police had obtained her banking records, looking for God knows what, and she was willing to bet they also had her phone records to find out if she had called Peter Kilbourne—or he had called her. Neither of which, Laura was certain, would provide the police with the connection they were seeking.

Laura tried to work all day Tuesday, but her concentration was spotty and she kept thinking about the fact that today was the day they were burying Peter Kilbourne. And it was early that afternoon when she received her first call from a reporter, which rattled her so much that she didn't have a hope of getting any more work done.

She finally went to her boss and asked for a leave of absence, explaining truthfully that since the press now had her name and would undoubtedly be pestering her until the police solved the murder, it would be better for both her and the company if she took some time off.

"Take as much time as you need, Laura," Tom Sayers said, more sympathetic than many employers would have been. "I'll shift your projects to some of the others in the meantime."

"I'm really sorry there's been so much trouble, Tom."

He smiled at her, a middle-aged man with a weathered face and sharp brown eyes. "I don't see how you could have prevented it," he told her. "All you did was buy a mirror."

Laura was grateful that he believed in her, but not particularly surprised; he had hired her at eighteen on her innate artistic ability alone, training her himself and encouraging her to take night courses to get a college degree in the field of commercial art. Now, ten years later, Laura had her degree and was one of the top artists in his small but profitable graphic design business.

"Just take care of yourself," he told her as she left his office. "And don't let a bunch of nosy reporters turn your life upside down."

Good advice, Laura thought as she drove home. But the situation had already turned her life upside down. Here she was, hiding out from the press—and taking an unpaid leave of absence from her job to do it, which meant money would be very tight if she couldn't go back to work soon. And when she got home, it was to find on her answering machine several requests for interviews and a number of rude questions, which was definitely upsetting. She finally had to turn the phone off just to escape the constant ringing.

This is what I get for having a published number—even with just my initial in the book!

That afternoon she managed to get in touch with Dena Wilkes, the college student and researcher who had worked for her before, and Dena enthusiastically agreed to come over in the morning and get all the details as well as take photographs in order to start researching Laura's mirror.

Laura spent Wednesday afternoon trying to paint. Her best efforts had always come purely from her imagination, so she tried to just let her mind wander and her fingers paint what they would. Not surprisingly, she found herself painting the mirror—but the perspective was interesting, she decided. The image taking shape on canvas was the mirror being held by a hand—a feminine hand.

Maybe when it's finished, I'll know what I'm supposed to see in the damned thing!

Cassidy arrived that evening, offering her company and Chinese take-out, and Laura was happy to accept both. In a determined effort to forget the murder, they watched an old movie on television and discussed the careers and sex appeal of all their favorite movie stars. Still, as soon as her friend went home, Laura was left with too many anxious thoughts.

Patience was hardly her strong suit, especially when she was all too aware that others—namely the police—were possibly in charge of her destiny; she wanted to do something herself, to put her fate back in her own hands. She told herself there was nothing she could do except find out about the mirror, but that undoubted fact did nothing to soothe her restlessness.

Then, on Thursday morning, she found among her usual mail two letters. One was positive, a motherly type of letter assuring her that of course she hadn't killed Peter Kilbourne and that everything would be all right if she would just put her faith and trust in God. The other was a vehement and crudely worded invitation to her to burn in hell for her sins and crimes.

Both were from total strangers.

Laura's rational mind told her they were the types of letters anyone experiencing a sudden—and negative—notoriety might easily receive, and that she shouldn't let them get to her. But the mere fact that two strangers had somehow discovered she was the "female acquaintance of Peter Kilbourne being questioned by the police" was more than unnerving.

She dropped the letters as if they burned, staring down at them for a long moment. Then she went to turn on her phone, and hunted up the business card Peter had given her. She had a hunch he used the "business" cards more for social contacts than anything else, and when her call to the number on the card reached an answering service, she was sure of it. Without leaving a message, she hung up, wondering uneasily if the police were keeping track of calls made to Peter's number now that he was dead.

Pushing that unnerving possibility out of her mind, she placed a second call, this one to a number she knew well. "Cass? Listen, didn't you say that the Kilbournes banked there? I know you shouldn't, but . . . can you get me the phone number at the house?"

ALLOWED THROUGH THE gate by an expressionless security guard, Laura drove her Cougar up the long driveway to the Kilbourne house at four o'clock that afternoon. She was still surprised to be here at all—surprised both because she'd found the nerve to call and request an appointment, and because that request had been granted so quickly.

She didn't know quite what she would say to whichever member of the family had granted her request, but she had several Polaroids of the mirror in her purse as well as the receipt she'd been given at the auction for her cash purchase. Just in case.

She parked her car in the small turnoff near the walkway leading to the house and walked slowly up the brick pathway toward the front door. The house looked even bigger and more imposing than it had when she had first seen it days ago, and even though Laura felt the same affinity with it that she had felt then, she was also all too aware now that it was a house in mourning.

The funeral wreath still hung beside the front door.

Reaching it, she took a deep breath in an attempt to steady her nerves, and firmly rang the doorbell. The response came so quickly that she actually stepped back, startled, as the door was pulled open.

A lovely woman with beautifully pale skin and auburn hair stood there, looking at Laura intently out of wide gray eyes. Dressed very plainly in black slacks and a dark blue, silky blouse, she was inches shorter than Laura and slightly built; a delicate, almost doll-like woman who might have been any age between twenty-five and thirty-five.

"Miss Sutherland? I'm Josie Kilbourne. Please come in."

As she stepped into the entrance hall, Laura realized that it was Josie Kilbourne she had spoken to on the phone, even though the other woman had not identified herself then. Though her manner was brisk, her voice was curiously childlike and sweet, and instantly recognizable. But it was not she who had granted Laura's request; after listening to it, she had gone away for a few minutes and then returned to set today's appointment.

Barely giving Laura a chance to look around at the vast, marbled entrance hall, Josie said, "If you'll come into the library, I'll tell Mr. Kilbourne you're here."

Which answered the question of who had agreed to see her. Except, wasn't there more than one Mr. Kilbourne in residence? Hadn't the newspapers mentioned a lawyer in the family? He was probably the one.

The library, just off the entrance hall, was book-lined and very pleasant. There were two big windows, curtained in a dark gold fabric that went well with so much wood, and the hardwood floor was covered with a rug in muted tones of gold and burgundy. There was a huge desk in one corner, a smaller one closer to the door, and two long leather sofas faced each other at right angles to the magnificent fireplace.

"Make yourself at home," Josie invited, using the common and informal phrasing that sat oddly in this decidedly grand house. She went out of the room, leaving the double doors open.

Too nervous to sit down, Laura moved slowly to the fireplace and gazed up at the big painting hanging above it. The little brass plate on the bottom of the gilded frame said *Amelia Kilbourne, 1938.* Nearly sixty years ago. She had been beautiful then, strikingly so, a slender, elegant woman with jet black hair arranged—unfashionably but definitely flattering—in a pompadour that lent her a turn-of-the-century air. And that impression was intensified by the high-necked, lacy dress she wore—again, not at all fashionable for the 1930s.

Laura studied the lovely face of a young Amelia Kilbourne, noting the high, sharp cheekbones that reminded her of Katharine Hepburn, and the dark eyes that contained a glimmer of mischief. And that smile, like Mona Lisa's, hinted at mystery.

Her imagination touched, Laura wondered how that lovely face had aged in nearly sixty years. The woman who wore it had buried her husband and both her children as well as a grandson, and had lived through what were arguably the most turbulent years in her country's history. And so much had changed. Travel by air had been exotic when she was a child; she had lived to see space travel. Television, personal computers, cable and satellite dishes, cellular phones, electronic security—had any of it changed Amelia? Or was she still the woman who had worn a pompadour in defiance of fashion because it suited her?

Laura didn't know what made her turn suddenly, except the certainty that she was no longer alone. And her reaction, when she saw him standing in the doorway, was so powerful it was as if an actual electric shock had stopped her heart beating. In a moment of infinite silence, she stared at him, taking in his unusual height and wide, powerful shoulders, his gleaming black hair, and the palest blue eyes she had ever seen. He wasn't handsome, but his harsh face was unforgettably compelling, and intensity radiated from him almost visibly, like the shimmer of heat rising from a fire.

Then, the utter silence was broken by his voice, deep and low, the tone measured. "I'm Daniel Kilbourne," he said.

She swallowed hard and managed to say "Laura Sutherland" in an unsteady voice.

"Tell me, Laura Sutherland. Did you kill my brother?"

Chapter 3

She wasn't what Daniel had expected. Beautiful, yes; Peter had said she was beautiful, and Peter had been a connoisseur of female beauty. She was tall, voluptuous without an ounce of excess flesh, and her face was strikingly lovely. Her hair, pulled back from her face and arranged simply in a long braid hanging down her back, was a bright and burnished red-gold, and she had the unmistakable fair skin of a true redhead as well as clear green eyes.

She wore her pale slacks and silky green blouse with a certain unconscious elegance, and though her voice had wobbled a bit when she had introduced herself, her shoulders were squared with determination and her chin was raised. She had guts, he thought, to come here even knowing what they all must think of her.

But she was still . . . more than he had expected.

"Did you kill my brother?" he repeated when she remained silent.

"No." She shook her head a little, her wide eyes never leaving his. "No, I didn't kill him. I didn't know him."

Daniel came into the room slowly, relying on the control built over a lifetime to keep his expression unreadable. He went past her to the compact wet bar between the windows. "Drink?" She shook her head, and Daniel fixed a small Scotch for himself. He wasn't a drinking man, but he needed one now.

Turning once again to face her, he moved toward her until he could rest a hand on the back of the couch between them. He sipped his drink, watching her, then said, "Peter went to see you Saturday. So you did know him."

"I met him then," she said, steady now. "But I didn't know him. He spent less than fifteen minutes in my apartment, and then he left. That's the only time in my life I've ever seen your brother."

"Do you expect me to believe that?"

"It's the truth."

"Of course, you would say that, wouldn't you?"

She drew a little breath, her fingers playing nervously with the strap of her shoulder bag. "You know I bought a mirror at your estate sale Saturday?"

He nodded. "Yes. The police asked me to verify that Peter had gone to see you because of the mirror."

"You verified it?"

"Yes."

"Then you know I was a stranger to him."

He smiled slightly without amusement. "I know that's the way it appeared."

"It's the way it *was*. He came to see me because he wanted to buy the mirror back. Do you—do you know why?"

Daniel looked down at his drink, moving his hand to swirl the ice cubes around in the glass. "No."

He's lying. Laura knew it. She didn't know why he was lying, but she knew he was. She watched him lift the glass to his lips, her gaze fastening onto his right hand. He wore a big gold ring with a carved green stone that might have

been jade or emerald, and there was something eerily familiar about how he held the glass with only his thumb
and two fingers.

It was difficult for her to think clearly; she was still
shaken and bewildered by the instant physical attraction
she had felt to him. She had never been a woman who
reacted to men quickly, cautious in that as she was in no
other area of her life, and she wasn't quite sure how to
cope with what she felt. He was a stranger, and a man
moreover who thought her at least capable of being a
killer, yet she couldn't take her eyes off him, and all her
senses had opened up so intensely that she felt nakedly
unprotected.

Daniel lacked Peter's beauty, but his harsh features
were compelling in a sensual way that made the younger
brother seem almost absurdly boyish in retrospect. Daniel's
big, powerful body moved with uncanny grace, with the
ease of muscles under absolute and unthinking control,
and his very size and strength spoke of command, of natural forces just barely contained. She thought of a big cat
moving silently through a dark and dangerous jungle, and
the image was so strong she could have sworn there was a
scent of primitive wildness in the room.

To Laura's bewilderment, her body seemed to open up
just as her senses had, to soften and grow receptive as if in
invitation. Her skin heated, her muscles relaxed, her
breathing quickened. Her knees felt weak, shaky. She felt
an actual physical ache of desire.

My God, what's happening to me?

Struggling inwardly to control what she felt, to concentrate on what she had come here to find out, Laura
managed to speak evenly. "You don't know why Peter
wanted to buy the mirror back, but you know that's why
he came to see me on Saturday?"

"As I told the police." His pale eyes were fixed on her
face, intent, almost hypnotically intense. He was absently

swirling the ice around and around in his glass, the movement causing his ring to flash shards of green.

His hand was long-fingered and strong; she wondered if his touch would be sensitive or if it would overpower with its strength. A flare of heat burned inside her as speculation created a rawly sexual image in her mind. "You don't know why the mirror was important to Peter?" she asked with an effort.

"That's what I said." His voice was even, his gaze unreadable.

Whatever she felt, he seemed unaffected, and seemed not to notice that she hardly shared his composure. Laura tried to draw a steadying breath without making the need for one obvious. "He said the mirror was an heirloom. Is it?"

"As far as I know, Miss Sutherland, it was one of many unused, unwanted items packed away in the attic by God knows who, God knows how many years ago." He had only a trace of a Southern accent, something common to people who had lived and traveled much outside the South.

"Would anyone else in the family know more about it?"

"I doubt it." He was abrupt now, a slight frown narrowing his eyes. *And it's not really the best time to ask them,* he might as well have added.

It struck Laura for the first time that Daniel seemed completely unmoved for a man who had buried his brother two days before. Had the two men disliked each other? Or was Daniel merely a controlled man who gave away little of his emotions? He certainly *looked* hard, with those harsh features and chilly blue eyes, and though his attitude toward her said plainly that he was not inclined to believe her relationship with his brother had been either recent or innocent, he didn't appear angered or in any way disturbed by the possibility that his brother's murderer might be standing before him.

Still, he was obviously at least conscious that his was a house of mourning, and she wondered if that was why he had agreed to meet and talk to her—so that other members of the family, closer to Peter, would not be disturbed.

Slowly she said, "But you don't believe the mirror has any value to anyone in the family?"

"I don't believe anyone else will wish to buy it back from you, no," he replied indifferently. His wide shoulders moved in a slight shrug, drawing her eyes and causing her concentration to waver yet again. There was so much of strength and power about him, so much of force or the possibility of force. And yet she wasn't afraid of him, she thought.

Aware, suddenly, of a silence that had gone on just those few seconds too long, she said hastily, "Then you won't mind if I try to find out why Peter wanted to buy it back."

He lifted an eyebrow. "Mind? No. But just how do you propose to do that?"

"It's an old mirror; it's bound to have a history. I have a researcher looking into that."

"Why?"

Laura hesitated an instant before answering him. "I . . . collect mirrors, so I probably would have done it anyway just out of curiosity. But since your brother tried to buy the mirror back, and then was killed hours later, I need to know if there was some connection to his murder. For my own peace of mind."

"I see."

Hearing something in his voice, she said tightly, "The *only* connection between your brother and me is that mirror, Mr. Kilbourne. I was not having an affair with him, if that's what you think."

His eyes were narrowed again, fixed on her face, and

his voice was very deliberate when he said, "I haven't quite made up my mind what I think about you, Miss Sutherland. Let's just say I knew my brother very well. He never met a beautiful woman he didn't try to get into his bed. And that was not something at which he often failed."

Laura ignored the backhanded compliment. "Be that as it may, I'm not in the habit of sleeping with men on fifteen minutes' acquaintance. Or married men at all, for that matter. Whatever you think of your brother's morals, you have no right to make assumptions about mine." *He'll incline his head slightly to the side in that mocking way.*

He did just as she expected, the gesture familiar to her for no reason she could explain to herself.

"I was brought up never to call a lady a liar," he said dryly. "So we appear to have a standoff. I don't *quite* believe your relationship with my brother was innocent, and you have no way of proving it was."

The fact that he was all too right about the latter point was something Laura found distinctly unsettling. She didn't want anyone to believe she had been sexually involved with Peter Kilbourne, not the public, not the press, not the police, not the family—and most certainly not this man.

"At least believe I didn't kill him," she said, hearing the plea in her voice.

She thought that harsh face might have softened imperceptibly, thought there was a glint of warmth in the chilly eyes, but whatever Daniel would have replied to her plea was lost forever when a new force entered the study.

"Why didn't you tell me we had a visitor, Daniel?"

I would love to paint her, was Laura's first thought.

Amelia Kilbourne, without question. She was a tiny old woman, hardly over five feet tall and seemingly frail, walking with a silver-headed cane even though her posture was upright. Her face hadn't changed all that much in sixty years, retaining the high, sharp cheekbones and jaw so obvious in the painting, as well as the high-bridged nose and clear dark eyes. Her snowy white hair was arranged in a smooth and immensely flattering pompadour, her turn-of-the-century–style black dress was floor-length, high-necked, and made of lace over some shimmery material that seemed more suitable for a dinner party than an afternoon of a day of mourning. But, like the hairstyle, the old-fashioned style of clothing suited her to perfection.

Daniel looked at the old lady before he spoke, and for an instant it seemed to Laura that there was a silent battle of wills going on, his pale eyes hard and her dark ones holding an expression that was somewhat defiant and—afraid?

Then Daniel said expressionlessly, "This is Laura Sutherland. My grandmother, Amelia Kilbourne."

"Mrs. Kilbourne," Laura murmured, not knowing what to expect from this member of the family.

Amelia moved across the room with apparent ease and without leaning on her cane, and sat down at Laura's end of one of the leather sofas. She gestured to the other one with an elegant hand and said pleasantly, "Hasn't my grandson asked you to sit down? Do, please."

Laura did, overwhelmingly aware of Daniel standing silently behind her. "I didn't mean to intrude, Mrs. Kilbourne. I—I know this is a terrible time. You have my sincere condolences on the death of your grandson." It occurred to her only then that she had not offered sympathy to Daniel for his brother's death, and she wondered if that oversight had been because his effect on her had pushed politeness aside or because she had sensed immediately that he would not want condolences from her.

"Thank you, Miss Sutherland. Or may I call you Laura?" Her voice was soft, her accent more Alabama than Georgia.

"Of course."

"And everyone calls me Amelia. I hope you will."

"Thank you." Laura could almost feel Daniel's sardonic gaze on the back of her head, and wished to heaven he'd move around the sofa where she could keep an eye on him. It was like having the big cat of her imagination crouching in darkness behind her, ready at any moment to spring forward and devour—or at least seize—his prey.

And she felt more than a little uncomfortable facing his grandmother, wondering how swiftly Amelia's gracious manner would desert her when she found out just who their visitor really was. But then Amelia spoke again, her tone still pleasant, and it became clear that she knew exactly who she was entertaining.

"I understand the police are looking for evidence connecting you to my grandson, Laura."

It was hardly a question, and the suddenness of it caught Laura off guard, but she tried to keep her voice steady when she said, "I met Peter for the first time on Saturday, Mrs. Kilbourne."

"Amelia, my dear. Please."

"Amelia, then. Thank you. He just came to my apartment to talk about a mirror I bought here that day."

"Yes, my dear, so the police said." Amelia brushed the mirror aside, uninterested. "But it appears that Peter was seen several times in the company of a beautiful redhead, and it seems the police want to cast you in that part." Her tone was brisk and matter-of-fact, and if she found it distressing that her grandson should have been seen in the company of a woman not his wife, she didn't let her feelings show.

His voice level, Daniel said, "Have you been talking to the police, Amelia? I thought we agreed that I would handle them."

"You forget, Daniel, the commissioner is an old friend of mine." She glanced up at him, a hint of pleased triumph in her eyes. "He called to tell me how the case was progressing."

"And obviously," Daniel said grimly, "let his tongue run away with his judgment."

"Nonsense. Why shouldn't I be told the facts? I'm Peter's grandmother, after all."

"The facts, Amelia? You'll learn the facts if this ever gets to a courtroom. In the meantime all you'll hear are theories and speculation. Because that's all the police have, until they find evidence. Peter is dead; that's a fact. Somebody killed him; that's another fact. And that's all we know."

The hard force of his words didn't seem to affect Amelia unduly; she merely moved her thin shoulders in a delicate shrug. "If you're hoping to protect Kerry from public speculation about Peter's women, I would say it's too late for that, Daniel. Far too late."

Laura sat very still, watching Amelia and listening to her and Daniel talk as if no third person were in the room. She was trying to define the undercurrents she felt between these two, trying to understand what it was she heard in their voices and saw in their manner toward each other. Was it dislike? A natural struggle between two powerful, willful people, or something more? Daniel seemed to choose his words carefully, yet it was clear he was at odds with his grandmother; Amelia appeared somewhat wary of her grandson, and yet there was also defiance in her attitude.

And neither of them, so far as Laura could tell, was grieving much for the man they had buried two days ago.

"It may be too late to spare Kerry's feelings," Daniel said to Amelia, still grim, "but I don't think Laura should be dragged through the mud with nothing more than circumstantial evidence against her—and precious little of that. Was it you who gave the press her name, Amelia?"

Laura turned her head to stare at him, conscious of a

little shock to hear him use her name so casually. "How did you know they had my name? It hasn't been printed in the newspapers."

Daniel looked down at her briefly. "I know because several reporters called here asking insolent questions."

"Did you tell them not to print my name?" she wondered.

"I reminded them that freedom of the press did not include the right to libel, and since you had not been arrested, it wouldn't be wise of them to print your name in connection with my brother's murder."

She wanted to ask him why he was bent on defending her from the press when he was himself suspicious of her, but he returned his attention to his grandmother then and repeated his question.

"Did you give them Laura's name, Amelia?"

"No, of course not. Why on earth would I have done that?" she demanded, frowning.

Laura turned her head back to stare at the old lady. *But you did, Amelia.* Just as she had known with Daniel, she was sure that Amelia had just lied. She had given Laura's name to the press. The question was, why? It made no sense to Laura, no sense at all.

"I don't know why you would have," Daniel said. "But I think it would be . . . wise of you to leave the investigation in the hands of the authorities. And let me deal with the police. All right, Amelia?"

As polite as the words seemed, Laura could have sworn she heard a subtle threat in them and in Daniel's suddenly gentle tone, and judging by Amelia's reaction, she heard it too. The old lady's dark eyes flickered, and her lips tightened slightly as her gaze fell.

"Very well, Daniel."

What's going on between these two? Then Laura remembered that according to Cassidy's tabloid newspapers, all the family's financial power was held between these two, with Amelia technically in control but Daniel running things—and fighting his grandmother at every step. If that was true, maybe it explained the undercurrent of hostility she felt, as well as Daniel's clear attempt to bend his grandmother to his wishes.

What surprised Laura somewhat was how quickly Amelia gave in. But then she caught a glint in the dark eyes that turned suddenly back to her, and Laura had the odd notion that a plan was forming behind that elegant face—and that she was meant to play some part in it.

"Well, child, it's obvious to me that a lovely girl like you would never be mixed up in Peter's sordid goings-on, so we won't speak of that again." With a wave of her elegant hand, she swept away her grandson's death and any possibility that Laura might have had a hand in it. Swept it away regally. "I understand you're an artist?"

"Yes. A commercial artist." The police commissioner again? Or did Amelia have yet another source of information?

Amelia's gaze flicked toward the portrait hanging over the mantel, then returned to Laura's face. "It's time to replace that old thing with something more accurate, I'd say. Do you accept commissions?"

Startled, Laura shook her head. "I don't think you understand, Mrs.—Amelia. I don't paint portraits. I do graphic design, advertising layouts in magazines, things like that. Commercial art."

It was Amelia's turn to shake her head, smiling a little. "I can't believe that's the extent of your ambition, Laura."

She hesitated, very conscious of Daniel's silence behind her, then said with painful honesty, "I'm not good enough to be a painter, especially a portraitist. I make an attempt from time to time, but—"

"You haven't given up?" Amelia's voice was gentle, encouraging.

"I . . . can't quite bring myself to." Laura was more

than a little surprised to hear herself confide that, since even Cassidy had no idea that she still cherished hopes of being a "real" artist someday.

"Then that's fine. You can attempt to paint me." Humor suffused Amelia's face, transforming it amazingly from cool hauteur to warm charm. "Between us, I think we can decide if the attempt is successful. If it is, I'll have a wonderful portrait by an up-and-coming artist. And if it isn't, neither of us will have lost anything of value. In any case, you'll be paid for your time and for the effort."

"But—"

Briskly, Amelia quoted an amount that widened Laura's eyes. "A generous commission, I think, for an unknown artist," the old lady added.

"More than generous," Laura said. And incredibly tempting, given her current tight budget. "But you must see how impossible it would be for me to accept your offer. Even if I felt able to complete the commission, the police suspect me of being involved in your grandson's murder. They would certainly find it odd if I spent so much time here, and I doubt other members of your family would be happy about it either."

"You didn't kill Peter," Amelia stated with absolute confidence.

Do you know who did, Amelia? Is that why you're so sure of my innocence?

"No," Laura said, "I didn't. But until the police find out who did kill him, most people are going to suspect I was somehow involved. How would it look if I spent so much time here? And what would the police think?"

"The police needn't concern you," Daniel said. "I'll . . . explain the situation."

Laura turned her head quickly and stared at him. "Don't tell me *you* think this is a good idea?"

His smile was somewhat sardonic. "I think my grandmother wants you to paint her portrait. Amelia usually gets what she wants."

It wasn't the reason he was giving his approval to this scheme, Laura thought, but whatever his real reason was remained hidden behind his enigmatic eyes. And between the two of them, Amelia inexplicably requesting—demanding, really—that she spend a great deal of time in the coming weeks among the Kilbournes, and Daniel allowing it despite his stated feelings about her, Laura felt uneasily that she was being drawn into something she would be better off avoiding.

Her vivid imagination might be working overtime, of course, but Laura had a sudden image of herself as a pawn being maneuvered by these two in some kind of subtle gamesmanship only they understood. And all she knew about pawns was that they were sacrificed during the game.

"You could work on the portrait in the evenings," Amelia was saying, still brisk, "so it wouldn't interfere with your job."

"I've taken a leave of absence from my job," Laura said automatically, still rattled by the suddenness of all this.

"The press?" Daniel asked.

She glanced back over her shoulder at him again. "It just seemed like a good idea, that's all."

He said nothing to that, just looked down at her expressionlessly.

Amelia, however, was delighted. "Wonderful, you can concentrate on the portrait without distractions. We'll even have a room prepared for you here in the house, so you won't have to drive back and forth every day."

The sensation of being drawn in was even stronger, and Laura felt a jolt of panic. Quickly she got to her feet. "I . . . I'll have to think about it, Amelia. It's a very generous offer, and I thank you for it, but I'll have to think about it."

For an instant it seemed Amelia would protest and insist on an answer now, but then she smiled and rose gracefully. "Of course, Laura."

The relief Laura felt was so strong that she told herself it was absurd; what did she think they would do, keep her here by force? "It was a pleasure meeting you," she told Amelia.

"And you. I hope we'll see each other again soon."

"I'll show you out," Daniel said, setting his glass aside.

Laura was tempted to say she could find her own way, but instead walked beside him through the double doors and out into the entrance hall. She was a tall woman, but her head barely topped his shoulder, and she was overwhelmingly conscious of his size, his nearness, the physical heat of his body. And that sense of his strength and power was even more compelling now when she was so close to him. *God, what's wrong with me?* She could smell his aftershave or cologne, and the musky scent appealed to her so potently that she wanted to just close her eyes and breathe him in.

At the front door he paused with his hand on the handle and looked down at her. "I'll speak to the police to explain why you came here today," he said. "And I'll tell them that my grandmother has offered you a commission to paint her portrait."

She got a grip on her senses and managed to ask, "You think that will . . . allay their suspicions?"

In a considered tone he said, "I think that the acceptance by the family of your presence in this house will carry some weight with them, yes."

"Will you tell them *why* I'm accepted in this house?" Laura asked.

"Certainly." He opened the door and stood back to allow her to leave. "I'll tell them we feel you had nothing to do with Peter's murder."

Baffled, Laura could only shake her head. He was willing to defend her to the press, to explain her visit here to the police and to proclaim her innocence to them, and yet she was certain Daniel was doing it all to further some agenda of his own. And Laura couldn't figure out what that might be.

"Good-bye, Laura," he said.

She looked up into that hard, expressionless face and could only shake her head again helplessly. "Good-bye, Daniel," she said, using his first name as deliberately as he had used hers. Then she walked out of the house.

DANIEL STOOD LOOKING after her until he saw her car pull out of the turnoff near the house and head toward the front gate. Only then did he slowly close the front door. He crossed the entrance hall and returned to the study, finding his grandmother standing by the fireplace as she contemplated the portrait painted some sixty years before.

"You pushed, Amelia," he said pleasantly. "You frightened her. Not very subtle of you, was it?"

Her lips tightening slightly, Amelia said, "And what about you? Standing there like a rock, chiding me as though I were no more than a lackey here to obey your commands. That might have put her off just a bit, don't you think?"

"Oh, she wasn't liking me very much even before you came in here," Daniel told her dryly.

Amelia sent him a sharp, knowing look. "You got more charm from your father than you let on, even if Peter did get the lion's share; why didn't you make yourself agreeable to her? She's beautiful."

"Maybe because I don't want my brother's leavings."

With an abrupt sound of amusement that was not quite a laugh, Amelia said, "If he was sleeping with her, I doubt he would have been in a motel room with another woman."

"If he was with another woman."

"You think she killed him? No, there's not enough rage in her."

"There might have been—Saturday night."

Amelia shrugged. "I suppose anyone could snap if they were pushed too far. But that girl never killed anyone." Then, eyeing him shrewdly, she said, "So you'll speak to the police, eh? Smooth the way so Laura Sutherland can come here and paint me? Trying to keep me occupied and out of your way, Daniel?"

It was his turn to shrug. "Just trying to please you, Amelia, as always."

"You may have charm," she told him, "but humility passed you by. So don't think I believe a word of it. No, pleasing me is no more than incidental to your plans. But that's all right."

His eyes narrowed as he watched her walk to the door. When she reached it, she half turned to look back at him. She was smiling.

"I know about the mirror, Daniel," she said softly. "I know what it means." She left the room, moving, as always, with elegant grace.

Daniel didn't move for a long minute. He might not even have breathed. Finally he broke the silence of the room with a low, vicious curse and went to fix himself another drink.

"IT'S A LITTLE weird," Cassidy decided later that evening as the two women were sitting in Laura's living room.

"A *little* weird? It's totally bizarre." Laura lifted her hands in a gesture of bewilderment. "It started out okay, mind you. I didn't lose my nerve. The guard at the gate let me in. I was shown into the study by this Josie Kilbourne, who was very polite, and Daniel came in a few minutes later, and—"

"And what? Your face just changed. What happened when Daniel came in?"

"I just remembered. Jeez, that shows how rattled they've got me. When Daniel came in, after he told me who he was, he asked me very calmly if I had killed his brother."

"Like that? Straight out?"

Laura nodded. "Oh, yeah. I'd venture to say he isn't the kind of man who beats around the bush very often."

"He made quite an impression on you, I see."

"You could say that." Laura looked away from her friend's intent gaze and went on quickly. "Anyway, like I said, barring Daniel's question, things started out okay. Normal. Expectable. I asked about the mirror. He said he didn't know why Peter would have wanted to buy it back, that it was junk as far as he knew. He made it clear he thinks I was sleeping with his brother at the very least, but he was more . . . controlled than angry. Then Amelia came in."

"And things got crazy?"

Laura made another baffled gesture. "I just don't get it. There's no way she can have any idea of my skill, yet she offers me a commission to paint her portrait—a generous commission. Me, a woman she knows damn well is under suspicion for her grandson's murder. And she's so . . . insistent. That old lady is absolutely determined that I paint her. She even said they'd get a room ready for me at the house in case I didn't want to drive back and forth, for all the world as if I lived on the other side of the state."

"She invited you to stay in the house?"

"It wasn't an invitation so much as a matter-of-fact assumption."

"And what did Daniel say?"

"Very little. He wasn't happy that Amelia had been talking to the police, and he all but accused her of being the one to give my name to the press, but he didn't object once to the idea of me hanging around to paint Amelia. In fact, he said he'd explain the situation to the police."

"And you think it's all some kind of power struggle between them?"

"There was *something* going on, that much I know. I felt it. And whatever it is, both of them mean to get me involved."

Cassidy hesitated, then said, "Aren't you reading an awful lot into an admittedly odd request to paint an old lady's portrait?"

"You weren't there, Cass. It's hard to explain because it was all under the surface, a matter of how they sounded as well as what they said. How they looked at each other. All I can tell you is that I felt as if each of them wanted something of me, wanted to . . . to use me in some private plan."

"Like a pawn."

Laura nodded. "Like a pawn."

"Well, then, it's simple—refuse the commission. Don't go back there."

That was the simple answer, Laura thought. Certainly the most logical answer, and undoubtedly the smart one. Her rational mind told her that if she went back to that house, if she got involved with that family, she would be asking for trouble; the instinct for self-preservation buried deep inside her warned that the trouble would be bad.

But other instincts, other desires, were tugging at Laura, and what they urged was not nearly so cautious, or so clear-cut. She needed to find out about the mirror, and despite Daniel's dismissal, she felt certain that someone in that family could tell her what she needed to know. And she thought Daniel was right in saying the police might not consider her so strong a suspect if the family was seen to accept her; there was that. And then there was the portrait, an opportunity for Laura to find out if she was good enough to paint; capturing Amelia's aged beauty, her haughty elegance, would certainly be test enough. And the money undeniably would come in handy.

But most of all, what she had felt when she had first seen Daniel, the eerie sense of familiarity and the instant, almost overwhelming attraction, was something she had never before felt in her life—and something impossible to push aside or ignore.

He didn't "quite" believe her relationship with Peter had been innocent, and he hadn't "quite" made up his mind about her—but he had defended her to the press. And he would profess her innocence to the police. And he had not objected to her presence in his family's home.

But Laura had no idea what lay behind his expressionless face and enigmatic eyes. She had no idea what part he meant her to play in his quiet, intense gamesmanship with Amelia. She didn't know how he had felt about his brother, or his brother's death.

She didn't know what he thought of her.

"Laura?"

Meeting her friend's concerned gaze, she said slowly, "I don't think I can refuse the commission, Cass. I have too many questions that can only be answered if I go back there."

"Questions about the mirror?"

Laura nodded. "That. And other things. Daniel didn't show a flicker of emotion about his brother's death, and Amelia was almost offhand about it. Why? Even if he was a womanizer, Peter Kilbourne was a handsome, charming, immensely likeable man. How could he have passed from their lives, and so violently, with such little effect on them? I knew him for fifteen minutes, and I feel more shock about his death than they showed."

"Surely you don't think one of them killed him?"

"I don't know. But a sleepy motel manager isn't a very good witness; anybody could have been with Peter that night. A jealous husband could have burst in. Or someone in the family, outraged because he was cheating on his wife. The point is, an outsider can never know what's going on *inside* a family—unless they spend some time there. I've been invited to come inside."

"Said the spider to the fly," Cassidy murmured.

Laura had to smile, albeit wryly. "Yeah. That's just the feeling I got."

"Then have you considered the fact that it might not be safe for you to spend time in that house? Laura, it's at least possible that someone in that family killed Peter, isn't it?"

Slowly, Laura said, "Possible, I guess. And—Josie's a redhead."

"So there could be a killer in that house. Laura, you say you feel drawn in to a situation you don't understand; maybe you'd better listen to your instincts."

"I don't have to decide tonight. I'll think about it."

Cassidy nodded, but her expression said she knew what Laura's decision would be. Still, she didn't say anything else about the Kilbournes until she got up to go to her own apartment a little later.

"Those newspapers of mine say Daniel isn't nearly as pretty as Peter was. True?"

"True enough," Laura replied.

"But?"

Laura frowned at her. "But nothing. Peter was better-looking."

"All right then, *don't* tell me."

Giving in, Laura said, "Daniel isn't handsome, but he's sexy as hell—is that what you want to hear?"

"If it's the truth."

"Oh, it's the truth. The instant I saw him, I . . . Well, let's just say that for the first time in my life I understood how someone could fall into bed with a stranger without hesitating."

Cassidy's eyes widened, and she grinned. "Well, well. Maybe this mess will have a happy ending, after all."

"I don't think so."

"Why? No sparks in return?"

"Worse than that." Laura smiled faintly. "At the very least, he thinks I was his brother's latest mistress. And I can't prove I wasn't."

Cassidy shook her head. "If you do go back there and spend any time around him at all, he'll know you weren't, Laura. Any man would."

"I don't know about that. Do you know what the name Daniel means?"

"What?"

"Judge."

"Then he'll judge you innocent." Cassidy smiled. "See you tomorrow, okay?"

"Good night, Cass."

Laura thought about her friend's confident words later that night as she got ready for bed, and she couldn't summon up much belief in them. In fact, her emotions were in such turmoil that she couldn't even sort through them—or her thoughts. All she had were questions and painful feelings.

Why was Amelia Kilbourne so hell-bent on having her portrait painted by an unknown artist? Why did she seem so uncaring about the death of a charming grandson? Were she and Daniel struggling for control of the family? How long had it been going on? Who was going to triumph? And why did Laura feel that she had somehow become a part of that battle?

Then there was Daniel. Seemingly unmoved and unmoving as granite, he nevertheless was filled with an intensity Laura had sensed strongly. What did he really feel about his brother's death? What did he feel about the grandmother he addressed by her given name, about the struggle between them?

What did he feel about Laura?

She lay there in her comfortable bed in her silent apartment and felt the dull ache deep inside her. Emptiness, that's what she felt. Longing. Desire for a man she had never laid eyes on before this day, a man who had not so much as touched her hand, a man who thought the absolute worst of her.

I can't go back there.

I have to.

It went around and around in her head, and when Laura finally fell into a weary sleep, she still had no idea what she would do.

Chapter 4

Y our mirror," Dena Wilkes told Laura on Saturday morning, "was made in 1800. It was commissioned by a Brandon Cash, to celebrate the twenty-second anniversary of his marriage to his wife, Sarah. It was actually made by a silversmith in Philadelphia. And the mazelike pattern is created out of a single, unbroken line without a beginning or an end, meant to represent eternity. In fact, that's how the silversmith listed the pattern, as Eternity, and he noted that the design was created by commission for Brandon Cash and would never be duplicated."

"I'm impressed," Laura told her.

Pleased, the vibrant college student patted her dark hair in a preening gesture. "Am I good, or what?"

"You're brilliant. How did you find it so quickly?"

"I got lucky," Dena confessed with a laugh. "The silversmith kept very good records, and since he ended up rather famous, his work is well known. He didn't do much in brass, and what he did is well documented. Your mirror's worth a fair price, by the way."

Laura shook her head. "I'm not interested in its value, just its history. And the history of the people who owned it."

"So you said, but I thought I should mention it."

They were sitting at Laura's breakfast bar with coffee, and Dena sipped hers before consulting the notebook lying in front of her. "Okay. We got lucky again with the Cash couple. His family was well known in the Philly area, and there are a number of contemporary accounts in various newspapers, letters, and journals. Luckily, most of this stuff is on the library net, so going up there won't be necessary."

"Good," Laura said dryly. "I can barely afford you, let alone plane tickets."

"So I assumed." Dena grinned at her. "Let's see, now . . . I didn't know how much you wanted, so I got as much as I could. Brandon Cash was born in 1760 and lived a good long time. Died at seventy in 1830; no cause of death is listed, but there was a flulike epidemic at the time, so that probably got him.

"Sarah Langdon was born in 1762, and she also lived to be seventy, dying of what a doctor noted as a broken heart in 1832."

Laura was startled. "A broken heart? He actually wrote that?"

"Yep. Said she just slowly wasted away after her husband died, and that he was convinced she died of a broken heart. Listen, apparently these two had quite a romance, and everybody was touched by it." Dena consulted her notes again. "Brandon and Sarah met in 1777, when she was fifteen and he was seventeen. Both families considered them too young, but they were passionately determined to get married—and did, a year later.

"Seems they had a good life. No money worries, and their health was certainly good. Sarah bore three children without complications, and the kids grew up strong and healthy. And all through their marriage, people commented on how devoted they were to each other. Not just affectionate, but as if each were incomplete without the other. Neither left a journal, but in a letter to his sister just after he died, Sarah said that they hadn't spent a single night apart in all the years they were married, and that she couldn't bear that empty bed."

"So maybe she did die of a broken heart," Laura murmured.

"It's sad, isn't it?" Dena shook her head, but then her naturally positive nature asserted itself. "On the other hand, they had more than fifty years together."

Laura nodded. "More time than most people get." But her imagination conjured the image of an old woman lying still and silent in her half of a lonely bed, and it made her heart ache. With an effort, she shook off the feeling. "What about the mirror?"

Dena, obviously untroubled by lives lived more than a hundred years before she was born, nodded briskly. "Sarah didn't have a will, but the mirror is listed along with a bunch of other household items that went to her daughter, Mary. This was just after Sarah died, of course, in 1832. Not much known about Mary, but in any case she didn't keep the mirror long. I guess she needed some quick cash; she sold the mirror back to the silversmith who originally created it."

"Do you know what he did with it?"

"Yep. He kept it for more than twenty years, because his own wife loved it. Then she died, and he sold the mirror in 1858. Actually his son sold it. To a young lady by the name of Faith Broderick. A few months later the silversmith's son, Stuart Kenley, and Faith Broderick were married."

Dena looked up from her notes briefly. "I didn't get much further before I had to quit yesterday. So far all I've found out about them is that Stuart was born in 1833, and

Faith in 1836. I'll be able to keep following the trail on Monday."

Laura shook her head admiringly. "You've already found out more than I expected, especially this soon. Do you think you'll be able to trace the mirror all the way to the present?"

"No way to be sure, really. I've been surprised we've been this lucky; people don't usually keep track of a brass mirror when it passes from hand to hand. But this one seems to have meant something to everyone who owned it, so they made note of what happened to it. Cross your fingers our luck holds out, and the next owners cared enough to record what happened to the mirror."

Dena had typed up her notes so that Laura would have a copy of this first chunk of research, and after the college student had gone, Laura spent some minutes studying the material. Dates, brief comments, not much information, really. Dry facts. That a boy and girl had met and fallen in love in Revolutionary times. That they had married and had a family. That they had been especially close, especially in love, so much so that others noticed and commented. That he had commissioned a mirror to be made to honor his wife and their love.

That they had died less than two years apart, after more than fifty years together.

Then the next steps on the mirror's journey to the present. Back to the silversmith who had fashioned it, and to his wife, who had loved it. Then, years later, put back in a shop window, where it attracted the attention of a young lady, who came in to buy it—and apparently fell in love with the man who sold her the mirror, the silversmith's son.

Laura didn't know what she had expected. Maybe a giant red flag indicating why Peter Kilbourne had wanted to buy the mirror back, or at least some hint of his reasons.

But there was nothing that she could see. Not so far, anyway.

She left the notes on the bar and went to her work area, staring at the beginning of the painting of a feminine hand holding the mirror. She had barely worked on it the day before, though she had spent a great deal of time staring at it. A great deal of time moving restlessly around her apartment while her thoughts chased around and around in her head and common sense and logic clashed with yearnings she didn't even understand.

I can't go back there.

I have to.

Laura rubbed the ache between her eyebrows fretfully and was just about to go in search of aspirin when the phone rang. Calls from the press had tapered off, so she had turned the phone back on the previous afternoon, but Laura still approached the instrument warily.

"Hello?"

"Laura? This is Amelia Kilbourne."

She didn't relax. If anything, she grew tenser. "Hello, Amelia."

"Forgive my impatience, child, but at my age time is a matter of some concern. Have you decided to accept the commission?"

"I—I still don't know, Amelia. I'm sorry."

"If you're troubled about the family, don't be. They've been informed, and no one objects."

Laura wondered if it was a case of no one daring to object, but she didn't voice her reservations on that point. Instead she said, "If the police didn't suspect me, it might be different, but—"

"Daniel spoke to the police—and I spoke to the commissioner." Amelia uttered a little laugh, slyly pleased at having disregarded her grandson's wishes again. "They admitted they have no evidence against you, Laura. They can't connect you to Peter in the past—or that night. They showed that photo you gave them to the motel manager, and he's sure it wasn't you he saw in the car. As far as the police are concerned, you're no longer a—what do they call it?—a prime suspect."

It was a relief to hear that, even though Laura had told herself often that no evidence of a relationship existed because there had been no relationship. Still, mistakes were sometimes made, and innocent people were sometimes convicted of crimes they had not committed. Laura would not feel entirely safe until Peter Kilbourne's killer was in jail.

"I'm glad to hear it, Amelia," she said. "Thank you for telling me."

"Does it make it easier for you to accept the commission, child?"

Sidestepping that question, Laura said, "Amelia, wouldn't you rather get a real artist with recognized ability to paint your portrait?"

"You are a real artist, Laura. And what's wrong with my choosing to advance the career of an unknown? I can guarantee you that if you produce work we're both happy with, you'll have more commissions than you can accept within a month." There was no conceit in her voice, but simple certainty; she might not be the leader of society she had once been, but Amelia Kilbourne knew that there were still many people in Atlanta who would follow her lead.

"I don't think you'd be happy with the result, Amelia."

"Let me be the judge of that. In any case, how will you know if you don't try?"

Laura closed her eyes, wavering. She felt the pull of Amelia, the sensation of being drawn in, and every instinct urged her to be wary. This was wrong somehow. There was danger in this offer, in that house. But there was also Daniel.

I can't go back there.
I have to.

Opening her eyes, Laura said steadily, "All right, Amelia. I accept the commission, thank you. We can get started on Monday, if that's all right with you?"

MADELINE'S FORK CLATTERED to her plate, and she turned wide blue eyes, still pink-rimmed from crying, to her mother-in-law. "Oh, Amelia, no," she whispered.

"It's all right, Mother," Daniel said quietly from his place farther down the table. "The police believe Laura Sutherland had nothing to do with Peter's murder."

"She's coming here, Madeline," Amelia said in a matter-of-fact tone. "She'll be here Monday, and she'll continue to come here until the portrait is finished. I've asked her to do all the work on it here at the house."

"She isn't moving in?" Alex asked politely. "I thought I heard you give orders that a room's to be prepared for her."

"In case of need," Amelia replied, and her lips tightened slightly. "She prefers to return to her apartment each evening, but I've told her the room will be ready should she decide otherwise."

Alex looked across the table at Josie and let his eyes widen slightly, asking silently—and sardonically—why anyone would prefer not to spend the night in this house. Knowing all too well that he considered the place gloomy and the current atmosphere unnecessarily depressing, Josie looked away hastily and encountered Madeline's anguished gaze.

As Daniel had, Josie spoke gently. "It really is all right, Madeline. I met her, and she seemed very nice. I'm sure she'll be . . . sensitive to your feelings."

"I wonder if she'll be sensitive to Kerry's," Alex mused.

Josie glanced at the empty chair beside her, where Peter's wife—his widow—normally sat; Kerry was spending the weekend with a sister who lived here in Atlanta. Josie said, "Surely she will. I mean, we don't even know that she was—was involved with Peter."

"I'd bet hard cash on the probability," Alex said.

"That's enough," Amelia snapped, sitting up even straighter than usual in her chair at the head of the table. "Laura will be here as my guest, and I expect you all to behave accordingly."

Amelia's granddaughter, Anne, sitting between Madeline and Daniel at the long table, said, "Whether we like it or not." Her voice was flat.

Amelia looked at her, frowning. "This is still my house, and I'll thank you to remember that fact."

Anne, a dark-haired, brown-eyed woman with her grandmother's elegant features spoiled by a discontented expression, shrugged pettishly. "Oh, I remember. How could I forget, when you remind me almost daily?"

"I shouldn't have to remind you."

"No, I suppose not. After all, everything done in this house has to have your stamp of approval or it just doesn't get done. I couldn't choose wallpaper for my room without your okay, and we're all forced to eat this bland, unimaginative food because it suits you, not because any of us like it." She shoved her plate away with an angry gesture.

"You don't have to live here," Amelia reminded her coldly.

Josie intervened before Anne could voice a retort, saying quietly, "I think we're all still coping with shock, and—"

"Don't help me!" Anne told her in fierce resentment. She pushed her chair back and stalked from the room.

There was a little silence, and then Josie sighed. "No

matter what I say or do, I always seem to rub Anne the wrong way."

"She's jealous of you," Amelia said with a shrug.

"She shouldn't be." Josie felt distinctly uncomfortable. "I . . . think I've eaten all I can. Excuse me, please?" Receiving a gracious nod from Amelia, she left the table and the room, hearing Madeline's plaintive voice behind her.

"But, Amelia, this girl—!"

Josie frowned a little as she went to the library and the small desk she used. She didn't really have any work to do, beyond sorting and filing copies of some of Amelia's notes from the last day or so. Amelia was an inveterate letter writer at all times, maintaining a steady correspondence with friends all over the country, and she insisted on keeping copies of letters received *and* written for the family archives. Recent letters and notes concerned Peter's death, of course, and Josie had been too busy to get them all filed.

Not that Amelia either asked or expected her to be working on a Saturday evening, but Josie was restless and needed to be occupied. She was worried. In many ways, Peter hadn't exactly been an asset to the family, but his death had upset a careful balance, and the result was a great deal of tension—and suspicion.

Josie didn't want to think that, but during the past days she had come to the reluctant conclusion that someone inside the family might have had something to do with Peter's death. For one thing, the police seemed far more interested now than they had been initially in the whereabouts of family members the night Peter had been killed; they had returned twice during the week, polite but full of questions. And for another thing, the faces around her seemed guarded and wary when they hadn't been before.

Even Alex . . .

"You surely aren't planning to work tonight?"

Josie looked up as Alex came into the room, and after a slight hesitation placed a crystal paperweight atop a stack of Amelia's notes. "No, I guess not. I was just restless."

"After that little scene at the supper table, I'm not surprised. Madeline is still upset, and Amelia lost patience with her. So it's left to Daniel to try and calm his mother down."

"I can't say that I blame Madeline, really," Josie said. "To bring any stranger into the house right now would be upsetting, but Laura Sutherland? What's gotten into Amelia? This sudden obsession with getting her portrait painted, and by an unknown artist, seems so . . ."

"Crazy?" Alex supplied wryly.

Josie got up and absently pushed her chair neatly back under the desk. "Eccentric, let's say."

Alex laughed shortly at her careful choice of words. "She's up to something, that much is certain. So's Daniel."

Josie looked into his speculative greenish eyes and felt a little chill of unease. "What do you mean?"

"I mean . . . things are going to come to a head in this family, and soon, if I'm not much mistaken. The only question is, how many of us are going to be left standing when it's all over."

"You make it sound like a war."

He shrugged, suddenly careless. "Nothing for you to worry about, sweet. Both Amelia and Daniel like you." He reached out and took her hand, smiling. "Anyway, let's not think anymore about that. You're restless, and I've had about all of this house I can take for the moment, so why don't we get out of here?"

"You're on." Josie didn't know what he had in mind, but she didn't really care. She didn't want to think or worry anymore, at least for a while, and Alex was the best cure she had ever found for too much introspection.

• • •

THE CLOCK ON his nightstand proclaimed the hour of midnight when Josie stirred beside Alex. She was reluctant to move, very reluctant, but she had never yet spent an entire night in his bed and wasn't about to start now. Whatever he said, Josie doubted that Amelia would like her secretary and the soon-to-be family lawyer openly sharing a bed right here in the family house.

"Where are you going?" he murmured when she pushed the covers back.

"To my room, of course."

Alex hooked an arm around her waist, hauled her easily back to his side, and shifted his weight so that he held her trapped. "I don't think so."

"Alex—"

He leaned down and kissed her, his half-open eyes gleaming at her in the lamplight as his mouth played on hers. His tongue glided sensuously, his teeth nibbled gently, in a caress that was blatantly sexual.

Josie felt his hard shoulders under her hands and wasn't surprised that she had reached for him. He knew just how to touch her, just how to arouse her until she was beyond protest. Beyond herself. No matter how closely she tried to guard herself, he always found at least this way in.

Her body arched into his, pressing closer, and she made a little sound when his hand slid up her rib cage and cupped her breast. Her flesh responded instantly to the gentle kneading, to the rhythmic brushing of his thumb back and forth across her tightening nipple. She made another sound, harsher and more urgent, hearing it throb in her throat, which ached just as the rest of her body ached for him.

His eyes still slitted, still gleaming enigmatically at her, he murmured against her lips, "You don't really want to leave me, do you, sweet?"

She looked at him dazedly, then caught her breath when he lowered his head so that he could brush his lips across the straining tip of her breast. He held her gaze while his tongue darted out and flicked lightly, while his mouth captured and sucked her sensitive flesh.

"Do you?" he demanded insistently, his low voice as seductive as his caresses.

Josie wanted to say yes. She wanted to be able to be strong, to prove at least to herself that Alex had changed nothing in her. But her body had changed, had learned to respond to his touch, and as much as she would have liked to deny that, he knew it as well as she did. He was feeding at her breast, not like a child but like a man hungry for the taste of her, and the hot sensations were driving her mad. With every pull of his mouth, the empty ache deep inside her intensified until she couldn't be still—or silent.

"No," she said huskily, her fingers threading through his silky blond hair. "No, I don't want to leave you. Oh, God, Alex—please . . ."

"You'll stay all night?" His mouth toyed with her nipple while his hand slid down over her belly and probed gently between her thighs.

Josie shuddered, her body going as taut as a bowstring when his long fingers penetrated, his thumb stroked and teased. She tried to find the breath to answer him, realizing dimly and with an oddly relieved sense of surrender that if he had asked her to walk through fire or over broken glass, her reply would have been the same.

"Yes. Yes, Alex. Oh—!" She couldn't help crying out, writhing against him when she felt his teeth rake her nipple gently and his fingers plunge deep. "Alex, for God's sake!"

"Not for yours?" he murmured, raising his head at last and smiling at her.

A little wildly, she said, "What are you trying to do to me?"

Whether he heard in her voice that she was pushed to her limits or simply lost patience himself, Alex answered her with his body. He slipped between her thighs, drawing them high around his waist, and slowly entered her.

Josie was so close to the edge, and he kept her there, moving with exquisite care, the strain showing on his face and in quivering muscles. He seemed bent on drawing out the lovemaking until neither of them could stand another moment more, and though Josie wanted to protest, she couldn't find the breath or a single coherent word with which to do so.

It seemed to go on forever, pleasure that rippled through her in tiny, rhythmic waves that grew more and more powerful, until finally she was swept up in a hot, dizzying whirlpool of sensation so intense that she was blind and deaf to everything except the overwhelming satisfaction of her climax.

Josie became aware of her surroundings once again just as Alex rolled onto his back, carrying her with him. He was still breathing harshly, and she lay with her cheek against his chest and her eyes closed while her pillow gradually steadied into a slow rise and fall.

"That wasn't fair," she murmured at last.

His arms tightened around her, and Alex didn't pretend to misunderstand. "No, I guess not. But you've been slipping out of my bed like a nervous schoolgirl for two months, and I couldn't take it anymore."

She raised her head and looked down at him gravely. "You never said anything."

"Would it have done any good?" And when she remained silent, he nodded. "Yeah, I thought so."

"Amelia—" she began, but Alex was shaking his head.

"Don't kid yourself, Josie. You don't creep back to your own room in the middle of the night because you're worried about what Amelia might say. You do it because in your mind you've put this affair of ours into a nice, neat, safe little category. It's sex. Just sex."

She frowned. "Isn't that what you want?"

He gazed up at her for a moment, a little smile playing around his mouth. Then he said, "Sure. But having sex makes us lovers, sweet, and lovers sometimes sleep together—all night—in the same bed. I want that too. But you don't have to worry. It won't make us married. It won't even make us in love. So you don't have to give up Jeremy."

Josie moved off him jerkily and yanked the covers up to hide her nakedness. "I don't know what you're talking about."

"Yes, you do." He raised up on an elbow, his handsome face a little mocking. "If it's just sex between us, then it's no threat to your memories of Jeremy. If you slip back into your own bed in the night, the bed you've turned into your marriage bed and keep sacrosanct even though he never slept in it with you, then you haven't really been unfaithful to him."

"He's dead," Josie said shakily.

"Yeah, but you haven't buried him. You haven't let go of him." Alex smiled slightly, seemingly a little amused. "Oh, don't look so horrified, Josie. It doesn't bother me. If you want to wear your widow's weeds for the next forty years like Amelia and keep Jeremy's ageless picture on your dresser to smile at every night, that's your business. Hell, it might even be just the way he'd want you to live out the rest of your life. But since he'd have a bit of trouble performing his husbandly duties as things stand now, I doubt he'd begrudge us an hour spent together here and there. Or even a night. Who else would he expect to see to his widow's needs, after all? I am his cousin."

With a choked sound, Josie flung back the covers and scrambled from the bed. She didn't look back at Alex, but was highly aware of his silent attention as she found her clothes scattered on the floor and dressed hastily.

"You said you'd stay all night," he reminded her coolly.

She threw him a single incredulous look and fled from his bedroom as if something with teeth and claws pursued her. She was automatically quiet as she hurried down the dimly lit hallway, carrying her shoes, and didn't realize she was actually holding her breath until she was inside her own bedroom and leaning back against the door. Then her breath escaped raggedly, catching at the end in a dry little sob.

She felt a little sick, and more than a little shaken. Alex had never before been cruel to her, never. He had never taunted her about Jeremy, and he'd certainly never uttered anything like his mocking words of tonight. So why had he tonight? Why had he said things he must have known would upset her terribly? It was so unlike him. . . .

Growing gradually more thoughtful and less shaken, Josie undressed again and went into her bathroom to take a shower. Her movements were automatic, her thoughts wholly occupied with Alex. Finally, as she was drying her hair, she toyed with the idea that he had said what he had because he had *not* wanted her to spend the night in his bed—whatever he said. Was that possible? He had asked her numerous times to spend the night in his bed, but he'd never protested when she had refused—until tonight. Yet when she had given in and agreed, he had almost immediately begun taunting her.

Why?

Josie put on a nightgown and robe, chosen without thought from her dresser drawer, and when she looked down at herself she had to wonder yet again if she was, in fact, becoming Amelia. The gown was black, high-necked, long-sleeved, and not in the least sexy, the robe a dark and dull gray. Did she feel the need to mourn Jeremy even in her sleep? Or was this some kind of symbolic apology to her dead husband after she came from the bed of another man?

She looked at the silver-framed picture on her dresser

that showed a darkly handsome, smiling man, and for the first time, she wanted to turn it facedown.

"Damn you," she said softly.

There was, of course, no response, and Josie paced around her bedroom for some time trying to sort through her tangled emotions. In the end all she knew was that she wouldn't sleep at all if she didn't go back to Alex and at least try to find out why he had behaved that way.

She opened her bedroom door very quietly and began to slip out into the hallway, then froze. She and Alex shared the second floor of this wing of the house—or had—with Peter and Kerry, who had separate bedrooms, and with Daniel. As Josie looked down the hallway, she saw Alex come out of the bedroom that had been Peter's. He was fully dressed, appeared to be carrying something clenched in his right hand, and looked a bit grim.

Instead of going to his own bedroom, Alex continued on to the end of the long hallway and knocked lightly on Daniel's door. It was opened almost immediately, with Daniel also fully dressed and wide awake despite the lateness of the hour.

They were too far away for Josie to hear what was said, but the low conversation went on for some time, with Alex opening his hand at one point to show Daniel whatever it was he held. Finally, Daniel nodded and drew back into his own room, and when Alex started to turn, Josie jerked back into her own bedroom.

She heard Daniel's door close quietly, then another door a few moments later, and when she looked, the hallway was empty.

With all thoughts of going to Alex pushed aside now, Josie softly closed her own door and went to sit on her bed. Her earlier uneasiness had returned, and now it was stronger. Much stronger.

What was going on?

. . .

"HOW MANY PRELIMINARY sketches will you do?"
Amelia asked.

Laura looked up from the first tentative strokes of her
charcoal pencil and smiled. "As many as it takes. I did
warn you."

Amelia smiled. "So you did. Don't worry, child; I'm
perfectly willing to sit for you as long and as often as you
require. If I may talk, that is. If not, we may have a problem."

"Talking is fine," Laura told her. "In fact, it may help
me. Doing a portrait is capturing a personality, and that
isn't accomplished by the eyes alone."

"You *do* know how to go about it," Amelia said in
satisfaction. "I knew you would."

"Let's reserve judgment on that until we see the re-
sults," Laura suggested ruefully, not at all sure of herself.

It was late Monday morning, and she and Amelia were
in the conservatory at the rear of the house, which was
flooded with light and vibrant with lush green plants and
potted flowers. Amelia had begun to show her the house,
but they had barely covered the ground floor when they'd
reached the conservatory, and Laura had suggested they
stop here for a while so she could sketch.

She had made the suggestion for more than one reason. Though Amelia didn't act frail, the old lady quite
likely was, and Laura thought a short rest could do no
harm. And the house was so huge that Laura felt quite
overwhelmed; she needed a bit of time herself before going on. And lastly, the background this room provided, so
luxuriant and vivid, was a wonderful contrast to Amelia's
black and silver coolness.

She sat as Laura had requested in a fan-backed wicker
chair, while Laura sat at a slight angle in another wicker
chair. Requesting no particular pose—"just try to relax"—Laura had ended with a subject who sat almost rig-
idly upright with hands folded in her lap.

Laura took what she was given and began sketching with a bit more confidence, listening with half her attention as Amelia talked on.

"This room would probably be a good one in which to work when you finally begin the actual portrait, Laura. Plenty of light. Though I don't think this background—"

"We'll decide on a final background before the portrait's begun, Amelia. But I want to sketch you in several different places."

"Probably wise," Amelia decided. "By the way, you'll meet a few more of the family today at lunch. Alex, who is a cousin of mine, is at the law office, of course; he'll be taking over as our family lawyer, and so he works in the city most days. And Anne—my granddaughter—took it into her head to go shopping today. But you'll meet my daughter-in-law, Madeline. And, of course, Peter's wife, Kerry."

Laura glanced over the top of the sketchpad to see her subject smiling pleasantly, and wished she could capture in charcoal or oil that bland tone of voice that seemed so odd under the circumstances. If it was a part of Amelia's personality, then it was certainly a fascinating part—if a little eerie.

"I want you to make yourself at home here, Laura," Amelia went on. "When we aren't working on the portrait, I hope you'll feel free to wander around and really get a feeling for the house and gardens. I've lived here for sixty years, so this house *is* me. I've put my mark on it, from the attic to the cellar. This house will tell you much about who I am."

"I don't doubt it," Laura murmured, using a thumb to gently smudge the line defining Amelia's cheekbone.

Amelia kept talking, musing about the time she had spent in this house, the parties held here in years past, the detailed planning of the gardens. She talked quietly, almost gently, seldom requiring a response from Laura, and Laura became so absorbed in her work that she looked up with a start when Amelia chuckled and asked her if she realized they had been here for two hours.

"I'm sorry—" Laura began.

"It's quite all right, child, I'm fine. But I believe I'll go and make sure lunch is almost ready, if you'll excuse me."

"Of course. I think I'll stay here and tinker with this a bit."

Amelia rose gracefully as if she had not spent two hours sitting in the same position. There was no cane in evidence today. "May I see the sketch?" she asked.

Laura hesitated. "If you don't mind, Amelia, I'd rather wait until I've made another sketch or two. Give me time to get the feel of this, if you will."

With a smile, Amelia said, "Certainly, child. I'll be back in just a few minutes." She almost glided from the room.

Left alone, Laura studied her sketch with a frown. It was okay, she thought. Not great, but not bad. She tinkered a bit, adding shading here and there and trying to get those dark eyes right, then finally closed the sketchpad with a sigh. Sketches weren't perfect. They weren't supposed to be. They were preliminary work designed to familiarize an artist with the subject.

She gazed toward the rear of the conservatory and the atrium doors that opened out onto a veranda above the gardens, not really seeing anything. She had tried not to think too much about anything since arriving here, concentrating on Amelia and the commission. But she hadn't been able to ignore the odd stillness of this huge house, the sense of tension she felt here.

It felt almost empty, this house, an impression reinforced by the fact that she had seen only Amelia since arriving here. Amelia had even opened the front door to her, and though she had said that the cook/housekeeper was working in the kitchen, and that a couple of maids who came daily were upstairs cleaning, there was no sound to betray any of them.

Amelia hadn't mentioned Daniel. Was he here? Did a man who held the financial reins of a vast family business have to "go into the city" to work on weekdays, or was the big desk in the study meant for him? He lived here most of the time, Laura believed, though he made frequent trips out of Atlanta on business and sometimes stayed away for weeks or months.

Was he here?

Of course, Laura's information was culled almost entirely from Cassidy and her tabloid sources, and there was some doubt as to its accuracy. He was single, that much seemed certain, and there had been no mention of a particular lady friend. He was thirty-two, though he looked older. A financial genius, it was said. A hard man, it was said.

Was he here?

"Already hard at work?"

His deep voice came so suddenly upon the heels of her wistful musings that Laura jerked and looked up at him with wide eyes. He was standing no more than a few feet away, moving on panther feet she hadn't heard, and he was dressed less formally than she'd last seen him, in dark slacks and a white shirt with the collar open and the sleeves rolled carelessly back over his forearms.

He was . . . *more* than she remembered, though that hardly seemed possible. He was bigger, more powerful-looking, a more intense jolt to her senses. She felt oddly light-headed, looking at him, as if she had lurched too suddenly to her feet. It was a sensation that was both familiar and strange, like the echo of something she had felt at some other, long-ago point of her life.

Realizing he was waiting for a response, she got a grip on herself. "Why not? Amelia wants her portrait."

He slid his hands into his pockets and nodded slightly.

"So she does. And you want to find out if you're a real artist. What's the verdict so far?"

"It's too early to tell. I've only done one sketch." Try as she might, she couldn't read what lay behind the pale sheen of his eyes, and that hard face gave away nothing of his thoughts. Did he still believe she had been his brother's mistress?

"Have you been bothered any more by the press?" he asked.

Laura shrugged. "Not very much, no. Or the police. Try as they will, they can't connect me to your brother before the day he was killed."

Daniel smiled slightly. "Still protesting your innocence to me, Laura?"

She hugged the sketchpad to her breasts, wishing it were a shield. "I don't like knowing that you don't believe me. Especially now. I'll be spending so much time here, under your roof—"

"It's Amelia's roof," he interrupted. "As long as she lives, this house is Amelia's. So why does my opinion matter?"

She stared at him, baffled by what she felt, by the longing to go to him now with the pure and simple attraction of iron filings to a magnet. Yet she was wary of him, not afraid but apprehensive and uneasy, sensing once more an intensity she couldn't define lurking just below his calm surface. When he showed so little, how could she possibly know what it was he felt?

"Laura? Why does my opinion matter?" he asked very softly.

"Because it matters," she whispered.

"Why? Why do you care what I think?"

She felt her heart beating. It was beating very hard, because she could feel it throughout her body, in every limb and under every square inch of her flesh. And she could have sworn she could hear it as well, thumping through the wall of her chest, through her breasts, against the sketchpad she held so tightly.

His eyes had changed. There was warmth there, heat, shimmering like molten silver. It was desire. No, more than that, far more. It was the same longing she felt, the same aching need, something so powerful it was essential to his very being. It was alive in him as it was in her, struggling to escape, to find satisfaction. It called to her like a siren song.

Laura had no idea what she might have said or done if Amelia had not come back into the conservatory just then. But she did come back, her brisk voice cutting through a silence that had become profound.

"You have a phone call, Daniel. Laura, lunch is ready."

Laura looked at her, blinking as though she had just awakened from a deep sleep. Then she looked back at Daniel, and his eyes were enigmatic once more. *Or have they always been? Am I imagining what I want to see?*

"Thank you, Amelia," he said politely. "May I join you and Laura for lunch?"

"Of course." She was equally polite.

"Then I'll see you both shortly." He turned and went into the house, moving easily for a big man, gracefully.

Laura couldn't stop watching him until he was lost to sight.

"Ready for lunch?" Amelia asked brightly.

Still holding her sketchpad to her breasts, Laura slowly got to her feet. Her whole body was aching, and not because of sitting for so long. She moved to meet Amelia, not really conscious of the other woman until thin fingers gripped her arm tightly.

"Child—I have to warn you."

Laura stopped and looked down into worried brown eyes. "Warn me? About what?"

Amelia glanced around nervously, then lowered her voice until it was hardly more than a whisper. "Be careful of Daniel. He's a dangerous man, Laura. He's a very dangerous man." She released Laura's arm and quickly moved toward the house, almost scurrying as though she were panicked.

Laura stared after her, chilled.

Chapter 5

*S*he caught up with Amelia just as the old lady went into a parlor down a hallway from the conservatory, but as desperately as she wanted to, Laura was unable to press Amelia on the subject of Daniel for the moment. The parlor was occupied.

"Laura," Amelia said, bright and seemingly untroubled once again, "I'd like you to meet Kerry, Peter's wife. This is Laura Sutherland, Kerry."

Kerry Kilbourne came as a total shock to Laura, and quite effectively distracted her from confused thoughts about Daniel. Kerry was young, for one thing, probably no more than twenty-three or twenty-four. But her age wasn't the real shock. Her appearance was. In most any eyes she would have been seen as plain at best, with a thin, pale face and indeterminate features. Her hair was by far her best feature, thick, shining, and the lovely shade of creamy gold that could never come out of a bottle; she wore it simply, pulled back and tied at the nape of her neck with a dark ribbon. She was about Laura's height, but carried too little weight, and her angular body appeared positively bony in an ill-fitting dark blouse and too long skirt.

Unwarned but innately sensitive, Laura managed not to wince when Kerry turned her head toward the guest, revealing the left side of her face. It was badly scarred. From just under her eye all the way down to at least the collar of her blouse, her pale flesh was puckered and furrowed in what must have been the result of some kind of terrible burn.

Both her eye and her mouth were undamaged, and when she offered Laura a tentative smile, the scarred half of her face seemed to writhe and darken, as if mocking the gesture. "How do you do," she said softly, her polite tone that of a child with manners drummed into her.

To the courteous greeting, Laura could only reply, "Fine, thank you, Mrs. Kilbourne. I—I'm so sorry about your husband."

Kerry's smile was unutterably gentle, and there was nothing in her hazel eyes to hint at her thoughts or emotions about Laura's presence here, or even the general strain she had to be feeling. "Thank you."

"There are too many Mrs. Kilbournes in this house, Laura," Amelia said in a decided tone. "We'll be less confused if you use everyone's Christian name."

Laura saw an almost imperceptible nod from Kerry, and said, "All right, Amelia, I'll do that."

"Fine. Kerry, where's Madeline?"

"I haven't seen her, Amelia."

"Anne?"

"No. I suppose she's still out shopping."

Amelia was obviously displeased, but all she said was, "Well, we'll start without them then. This way, Laura."

Kerry moved with striking grace, her angular body seeming to flow and take on an almost sensual presence, and as Laura followed the younger woman and Amelia from the parlor, she had to wonder if fate had a sense of justice or merely cruelty to attempt to balance ugliness with traces of beauty.

She also had to wonder at the decidedly odd couple Kerry and Peter had been. They couldn't have been married more than a few years, and since it seemed certain that Peter had been in a motel room with another woman the night he died, he had clearly not been faithful to his young wife. Why had he married her? Had he, in his own way, loved her? Pitied her?

And what about Kerry? Married to an incredibly handsome and charming philanderer, what had her life been like?

Laura couldn't help remembering Cassidy's merry recitation of tabloid gossip. *"I haven't even mentioned Peter's wife, Kerry. Don't you want to hear about her and the chauffeur?"*

Somehow, Laura doubted that this sweetly smiling, damaged young woman was playing footsie with the family chauffeur, but one never knew, after all. Perhaps she *had* found a lover when her husband's attention had wandered. Perhaps theirs had been a marriage based on the understanding that each was free to find pleasure elsewhere, or perhaps they had married for purely businesslike reasons and emotion hadn't entered into it.

Laura told herself that no outsider could possibly know what brought two people together, and that she was being unfair in trying to understand Kerry and Peter's marriage when she knew so very little about them both. But it was yet another odd note in this situation, and there was no way she could keep herself from speculating.

That speculation was cast aside, however, when they reached the formal dining room to find Daniel there. Either his telephone call hadn't required more than a minute or two of his time, or else he had considered being here more important; Laura didn't know which it was, but would have bet the latter, if only because she had the idea nothing went on in this house without his awareness and attention.

"You can leave your sketchpad on the sideboard, Laura," he told her, and it was only then that she realized she was still holding the thing like a shield. She put it where he suggested, then saw Amelia make a slight gesture indicating where she was to sit, on the old lady's right hand. Daniel immediately pulled out the chair for her, and Laura was so rattled by then that she took her place with awkward stiffness.

"That's normally Alex's place, Laura," Amelia said, waiting regally for her grandson to hold her own chair, "but I believe I'll move him across the table to Peter's chair."

Kerry was quietly taking a chair on the other side of the table and one place down from Amelia's left hand, not waiting for Daniel to seat her and apparently unmoved by Amelia's words. It was Daniel who spoke, as he seated his grandmother, his tone indifferent despite the hint of sarcasm in his words.

"This house is full of rituals, Laura, most of them Amelia's."

"There's nothing wrong with a routine," Amelia retorted. "I like for things to be in their proper places."

"And people as well," Daniel noted, but not as if he cared one way or the other.

It seemed everyone had his or her assigned place at the dining table, at any rate, Laura thought. There was a place set beside Kerry on Amelia's left hand, empty at present; the other three chairs on that side of the table bore no place settings. On Laura's side, there was a place setting at the chair next to her, then a chair without a place setting, and then one last place setting.

Daniel went to his place, leaving two empty chairs between him and Laura. She turned her head slightly to glance at him as he sat down, and she was afraid her disappointment showed because she could have sworn she caught a hint of amused understanding in his pale eyes.

"He's a very dangerous man."

The truth? Or merely another chess piece moved in the subtle game between Amelia and Daniel? Was the old lady genuinely concerned about Laura's safety and well-being, or was she bent on making certain that Laura was *her* pawn rather than Daniel's?

Laura had no way of knowing. But after Amelia's seemingly panicked "warning," she felt more than ever that she had let herself get involved in something far beyond her understanding. Something dangerous.

"Where's Josie?" Amelia asked.

"Coming," Daniel replied. "The phone caught her as I left the library."

"And Madeline?"

"Sleeping. The doctor left some pills with me, and I thought she needed sleep worse than lunch."

Daniel's voice was matter-of-fact and certainly without provocation, yet Amelia stiffened and stared down the table at him as if he had quite deliberately offended her. "I wanted her to meet Laura."

Daniel smiled pleasantly as he unfolded his napkin. "You didn't want a scene, did you, Amelia? Mother isn't far from a breakdown, I think we both know that. Sleeping today will help. She can meet Laura tomorrow."

Before Amelia could respond to that, Josie hurried into the room, apologetic and somewhat harassed. "I'm sorry, Amelia—it was that dratted plumber again, making excuses for not being here today when he promised he would be. Tomorrow, and this time he *swears*. Hello, Laura."

"Hello, Josie." Even more than before, Laura felt that insidious sense of being drawn into this household, this family. It was unsettling. The matter-of-fact acceptance of both Kerry and Josie made her more wary than at ease, and she couldn't help being thankful that at least one person in this house—the missing Madeline—seemed to be behaving normally regarding Peter's death. The poor lady was also no doubt upset by Laura's presence here in the house, something Laura completely understood.

In fact, Laura would have felt better if one or two of the people seated at this table looked at her in open suspicion or even haughty dislike. That at least would have seemed more normal. More expected. And Laura would know, then, how to attempt to defend herself; she would know why she felt so uneasy and threatened. As it was, all she knew was that she felt very much out of place despite the calm acceptance of those around her.

Only Daniel had expressed any suspicion of her, any reservations about her explanation of her relationship with Peter, and even he now seemed casually accepting of her presence. *Seemed* being the operative word; Laura was well aware that he remained unconvinced of her complete innocence.

As soon as Josie slid into her chair and unfolded her napkin, the swinging door to the butler's pantry opened and a sedately uniformed maid began serving lunch. The food was good, if a bit unimaginative, and conversation around the table was generally sporadic and fairly innocuous, but Laura found it difficult to relax.

On the one hand, she was overwhelmingly conscious of Daniel, which resulted in an upsetting but hardly unpleasant jumble of emotions and a heightened sensitivity to every sound and movement around her; on the other hand, she was ill at ease in this house and wary of undercurrents she didn't understand. Which meant that her emotional state could best be described as confused and apprehensive.

Not exactly at her best.

"How's the sketching going?" Josie asked Laura half-way through the soup course.

"As well as can be expected, I suppose." Laura smiled a little.

"Feeling tentative?" Josie guessed, her own smile understanding.

"Very much so."

"I imagine it must be tough to push yourself artistically. Still, I envy anybody who's creative. I can't draw a straight line that *looks* like a straight line, and even the pictures I take with a camera never resemble whatever it was I pointed at."

"I always wanted to write music," Kerry said in her soft voice. "But I've enjoyed playing other people's compositions so much that I just never tried writing my own. Afraid I couldn't measure up, I guess."

"What instrument do you play?" Laura asked.

"Piano."

"She's very good," Amelia said.

"When you spend enough time doing it, you can be good at almost anything," Kerry said.

"Only if you have talent in the first place," Josie told her with a smile.

Laura agreed silently with Josie, but Kerry's statement made her wonder if Peter's widow had turned herself into a recluse because of her scars. Was this house and its secluded and protected grounds her prison? She had gone to Peter's funeral, Laura recalled from the news coverage on TV—but heavily veiled. And Laura couldn't remember any mention of Kerry being scarred in all the newsprint following the murder, or in Cassidy's reports of tabloid stories. Was it not publicly known, or were even the tabloids being uncharacteristically kind in simply not mentioning it?

"Kerry plays for us sometimes in the evenings," Amelia told Laura. "Perhaps you'll decide to stay overnight once or twice while you're working on the portrait, and she can give us a recital."

"I'd be delighted," Kerry said in that tone of one with manners drummed into her, giving away nothing of her true feelings on the subject.

Laura smiled quickly at her, but said only, "Perhaps I will, Amelia. But my plan, as we discussed, is to leave each day by late afternoon. I don't want to intrude on the family any more than necessary."

"And I told you it wouldn't be an intrusion," Amelia reminded her gently. "You're more than welcome in this house, Laura. And I meant what I said about you spending time here even when you aren't working on the painting."

Daniel spoke then, his tone dispassionate. "Surely you don't mean Laura to spend all her time here, Amelia. This commission, like any job, demands a certain number of hours, but I imagine she also has a personal life outside her work. Family of her own. Friends. You can't ask her to give up all the rest only to paint your portrait."

Instead of bridling at her grandson's implied criticism, Amelia turned it into a handy opening, smiling at Laura and asking, "Do you have family in Atlanta, child?"

Laura shook her head. "Not in the city, no."

Amelia wasn't deterred by the brief answer. "Oh? But in Georgia?"

"My parents live in a small town on the coast, fairly close to Savannah. A younger sister still lives there as well." Laura shrugged. "We aren't very close."

"That's a shame," Amelia said seriously. "Family is very important, Laura. Blood ties matter."

Yet you seem unmoved by the death of your grandson. Why didn't that tie matter, Amelia? "I have a different philosophy," Laura offered with a faint smile. "Some families shouldn't try to be close. Because the members are too alike—or too different. Or because they never should have been a family in the first place." She regretted the words the instant they left her mouth, and could only hope she hadn't sounded as biting as she thought she had.

"We pick our enemies and our friends," Daniel said. "Our families, sometimes unfortunately, are chosen for us."

Laura glanced at him, wondering if he was offering sympathy or referring obliquely to his own family. It was impossible to tell. But before she could comment or he could add anything, Amelia spoke again.

"Surely you aren't completely alone in the city, Laura?"

"I have friends. Co-workers. I'm not alone, Amelia. I'm just . . . without family. Which suits me just fine."

"Is there a man in your life?" It was Josie who asked, and almost immediately looked as though she wished she hadn't.

But Laura answered steadily, completely ignoring the notion of the police and the press that she had been involved with Peter. "No one special. I date occasionally, but I'm more likely to go out with friends or groups. To be honest, my social life is incredibly boring."

Josie grinned at her, obviously relieved that her unthinking question had been handled gracefully. "Have you ever hit rock bottom and caught yourself actually looking forward to your high school reunion? That happened to me a couple of years ago."

"No, but when a childhood acquaintance from my hometown came into Atlanta a few months ago, I seriously considered going out with him. And he was completely unbearable as a little boy."

"Maybe he improved with age?" Josie suggested.

"No such luck. He's a minor politician and had just given a speech at some garden club a friend of mine attended. She said if he ever made it into the larger political scene, it'd set the South back a good twenty years."

"Set us back in what way? Economy? Industry or business? Race relations? The respect of the rest of the country?"

"All of the above."

Josie chuckled. "Ouch. A definite loser."

"Yes. But I did pass on my ten-year high school reunion, so maybe there's hope for me yet."

"Well, I've always thought that things happen in their own time, for their own reasons," Josie offered. "So I keep telling myself fate has a plan for me."

"The only problem with that," Laura said, "is that you might not recognize the beginning of the plan. I mean, with all the decisions we make in our lives, how do we know we haven't turned left when fate meant us to turn right?"

"That is a point," Josie conceded ruefully.

Daniel spoke then, his gaze on Laura and his voice thoughtful. "You believe you're the captain of your fate? That your decisions alone determine the course of your life?"

She looked at him, unsettled by how sharply his voice affected her and by the tug of attraction she felt in merely gazing at him. As for his question, it wasn't something Laura had thought about much, so she was a little surprised to find that she had very definite ideas on the subject. "No, not my decisions alone. If someone else makes a decision that affects me, then clearly it would influence the course of my life in one way or another. None of us can truly be the captain of our own fate."

"Do you believe in destiny?"

Again, Laura surprised herself. "Yes . . . I guess I do. Like Josie, I believe that some things are meant to happen, in their own time and way." She made an effort to lighten her tone, to sound offhand about it. "Especially in the short term. Any catalyst sets a series of events in motion, and sometimes those events seem inevitable. That's a kind of destiny, isn't it?"

"I'd call it that," Josie offered. "I must admit, I have a hard time swallowing the idea that my life was planned for me before I was born."

Laura nodded. "Me too. But I think some things are planned, in a sense, because they're stamped into our genes. Take my being an artist. I always wanted to be one, from the time I was very small. Yet I was never exposed to art as a child. There was no rhyme or reason to it, and as far as I know, there isn't an artist on the entire family tree. So I can only assume that in me the mix of genes and chromosomes combined unexpectedly; I was genetically predisposed to be artistic. Being an artist, in effect, became my destiny."

"I never looked at it that way," Josie said musingly. "But you know, it makes sense."

Amelia, who had listened silently to the discussion, now said, "But suppose you had been unable to get any training at all in art, that you were forced to do something entirely different in order to simply survive and had no time at all to devote to exploring your artistic nature."

Laura nodded. "Then that circumstance would have changed my destiny. Or delayed it."

Amelia nodded in turn, her dark eyes thoughtful. "Interesting. So you have a . . . qualified belief in destiny. Some things are meant to be, but our environment and our decisions may alter those things."

Laura couldn't help but laugh a little. "That's me—on the fence as usual."

Amelia smiled at her. "If I've learned anything in my life, child, it's that there are very few things about which we may be absolute—or absolutely certain."

After that, the conversation around the table became inconsequential once again, which rather relieved Laura. She had enjoyed the discussion of destiny, but couldn't get rid of the disturbing notion that either Amelia or Daniel had during the course of it moved another chess piece.

Josie, she thought, wasn't involved in the power play, and it seemed doubtful that Kerry was either. No, that concerned only Amelia and Daniel, and it was so subtle, so much under the surface of politeness and family ease, that Laura doubted the other two women were even aware of it. She wondered if anyone else in the family was.

She wondered if her own imagination was working overtime.

When everyone had finished eating, Amelia signaled the end of the meal by rising, and Laura found herself rising automatically as well, just as the others did. Then a little scene unfolded that Laura was absolutely sure had been planned beforehand.

"Laura," Amelia said, "I always rest a couple of hours after lunch. When I come back downstairs, we can continue working on the portrait. In the meantime, why don't you explore the house and grounds?"

"I'd be happy to show Laura around, Amelia," Josie said promptly. "My desk is cleared for the day, so I'm free."

Laura glanced at Daniel just in time to see his lips tighten slightly, and couldn't help wondering if he had meant to take advantage of Amelia's usual naptime, when Laura would be alone to . . . to what? To further his own agenda?

Smiling at Laura, Amelia said, "You'll be in good hands with Josie, child. She knows this place and this family quite well. I'll see you in a couple of hours, all right?"

"Of course, Amelia." What else could she say? That she would much rather have been alone—just in case Daniel wanted to further his agenda? *If he really is dangerous,* she thought, *I'm in big trouble.*

Daniel didn't stick around. Instead, with a pleasant "Ladies," he nodded to Josie, Kerry, and Laura and strolled from the dining room.

Kerry didn't linger either, smiling at the other two and leaving only seconds after Daniel and Amelia.

"I could use a walk in the garden," Josie told Laura. "How about you? It's a good place to start."

Laura thought fresh air might just possibly clear her head a bit, so she was entirely willing. Getting her sketchpad from the sideboard, she followed Josie from the dining room.

They went back through the east wing of the house and through the main section to get to the conservatory. Laura was beginning to get a sense of the place, helped by the fact that there were numerous large rooms and logical hallways rather than the rabbit warren of small rooms and odd halls that seemed so common to huge houses.

It was an impressive house. The money and attention poured into it over the years was easily visible in the woodwork, the rugs and draperies, the furnishings. Yet it was oddly melancholy even in its beauty, or so Laura thought. The dark colors chosen made the large rooms seem smaller and certainly less airy and bright than they would otherwise have been, and the heavy textures of all the draperies as well as the dense patterns of the wallpaper lent the place a somber, closed-in feeling.

That was it, Laura thought. This house made her feel oddly cut off from the world outside it, isolated in a place different from any other place she'd ever known. No wonder she felt uneasy, trapped.

"It's a bit gloomy," Josie said over her shoulder with a faint smile as they moved through the main house toward the conservatory. Then she laughed. "No, I didn't read your mind; it's just that everyone feels that way at first. Amelia likes dark colors, and of course that has an effect—not a positive one, I'm afraid."

"It's a lovely house," Laura said, then added honestly, "but oppressive too."

"I've heard that word used more than once. I suppose

I've grown used to it—although I walk in the garden every day, so maybe my subconscious feels it more than my conscious mind does."

Laura drew a slightly relieved breath when they passed through the bright colors and verdant atmosphere of the conservatory, then a deeper, happier breath when they reached the veranda. Today was cool for the end of September, and the air had that crisp, clear bite that signaled the arrival of fall. Some of the trees scattered over the vast gardens were beginning to turn, lending hints of red and gold to the lush green of their lingering summer foliage, and here and there was a splash of blue and purple and bright yellow as the last of the summer flowers bloomed in a desperate race with the approach of autumn's first frost.

"Now, this," Laura said as they paused on the veranda to gaze out over the gardens stretching into the distance, "I like."

"My favorite place in the whole world," Josie confessed. "It's taken fifty years to get these gardens absolutely perfect, and I think it was worth every day's work. The head gardener's been here for thirty years, and he's a real artist."

Scanning what she could see of the acres and acres of landscaped grounds, Laura thought she saw something surprising off toward the southwest. "Is that a maze I see?"

Josie nodded happily. "Yeah, and it's great. Amelia's husband, David, had it designed back in the fifties; he was a great one for puzzles, I'm told. And this one's absolutely diabolical. It took me nearly a year of trying before I discovered the key to the thing. Now I can go straight to the center—where there's a lovely little gazebo, by the way—and straight back out without taking any wrong turns. But I can't tell you how many times I got lost and finally had to yell for help."

Laura, who was also a great one for puzzles, said hastily, "Don't tell me the key. Maybe I'll have time to explore."

"Of course you will," Josie told her. "Amelia rests after lunch every day, as she said, so you'll have that time for sure."

"You mean you won't be baby-sitting me every day?" Laura asked, a smile taking the sting out of her words.

Josie laughed. "It's not as bad as that, I promise you. Amelia asked me to look after you today because she wants you to feel comfortable here. Plus, I can answer a lot of the questions you no doubt have about the family. Come on, we'll take the path to the maze."

Laura was more than willing, but as they crossed over yards of manicured lawn to reach the path, she said, "Isn't there a swimming pool? I don't see one."

"You're walking over it—literally," Josie said. "Amelia had it filled in forty years ago after David drowned in it."

Remembering now that she had heard something about that, Laura said, "Was he a bad swimmer?"

"No, a very good one. But he apparently slipped on the tiles around the pool and fell in, hitting his head on the edge. At least, that's what the investigators determined; there weren't any witnesses." She shook her head slightly. "There's been a great deal of misfortune in the Kilbourne family."

Laura knew that Josie herself was a widow, but it didn't seem quite the time to probe into that. So she merely said, "That often seems the case with very powerful families."

Josie nodded. "As if fate takes away as much as it gives. Here—this is the path to the maze."

The path was gravel, scrupulously neat, and wound lazily among azalea bushes that had long since lost their spring blooms, and groups of rosebushes still providing valiant color, and flower beds and lush green plants of every kind. There was even a babbling brook crossed by an arched wooden bridge.

Laura took in the beauty of her surroundings, absently contrasting this sprawling, flourishing, vividly *alive* place with the dark stillness of the house, but what she said was, "So Amelia expects me to ask questions about the family?"

"Well, she didn't say in so many words," Josie replied frankly. "But I certainly expect you to. Look, I don't see any reason to be coy about any of this, Laura, and I hope you agree."

"I do." Laura glanced at the woman walking beside her, wondering which was most important here, Josie's apparent willingness to be open or her auburn hair.

"Good. So we both know that the police considered you a suspect in Peter's murder, at least for a while, and that the newspapers are hinting without much subtlety that you were his mistress."

"I wasn't," Laura said firmly. "I met him for the first and only time the day he died, when he came to my apartment to try and buy back the mirror I'd bought here that day."

Josie looked up at her curiously. "That's what Amelia said. It's funny about that mirror, though."

Laura felt her pulse quicken. "You know something about it?"

"The mirror itself? No. In fact, I can't remember ever seeing it. Which is why I find it odd that Peter wanted to buy it back from you. I mean, if it had been important to the family, I think I would have known about it."

"That is why he came to my apartment," Laura heard herself say a touch defensively.

Josie smiled quickly. "I believe you. Or at least, I believe that's what he told you."

Laura frowned. "What he told me?"

With a faint smile, Josie said, "Peter was a womanizer. Or, more accurately, I think, he was a sort of serial lover. One woman after another, one conquest after another. It fed his ego, and maybe something more, I don't know. If he saw you at the estate sale—and it's quite possible he did—then I'd expect him to pursue you any way he could. The mirror could have been a handy excuse to meet you."

That was a possibility Laura had not considered, but after she thought about it for a moment, she shook her head. "No, I don't think that was it. He really wanted to buy the mirror back."

"He didn't make a pass?"

Laura hesitated, then said, "A small verbal one. But it was the mirror he came after, I'm sure of it."

"Well, if you're right about that, I'm really puzzled." It was Josie's turn to frown. "I saw the inventory before the sale, sort of checking up on Peter, if you want the truth, and I didn't even notice the mirror."

"Peter was in charge of the inventory?"

Josie nodded. "Amelia put him in charge when she decided to have the sale—and before Daniel came back home. Peter was supposed to take a look at every item and make sure it wasn't something we didn't want sold. It shouldn't have been a very difficult job, since most of that stuff in the attic and basement had been there for years and years. All he had to do, really, was get an appraiser to check out everything. Which he did. Anything deemed especially valuable was tagged with a floor price, and the rest tagged to be auctioned to the highest bidder."

"Daniel wasn't involved in the sale?" Laura asked, remembering Cassidy's remarks on the subject.

"Well . . . yes and no. By the time he heard about it and came home, most of the details had been covered. But he did make sure Peter had gotten a really good appraiser, and I know he went over the list of items the appraiser considered too valuable to sell without a floor." She paused, then added, "As a matter of fact, he didn't see the entire inventory until after the sale, late that afternoon. I remember him asking Peter about it."

"You didn't hear them discuss the list, did you?"

Josie shook her head. "No, I left the library and went upstairs for a few minutes. When I came back down, neither of them was in the library."

Laura thought about it, wondering inevitably if it had been Daniel who had noticed the mirror on the complete inventory, and if it had been he who had sent Peter to buy it back. But why, then, would Daniel show so much disbelief of Laura's story if he knew it was the truth? What possible reason could he have for pretending he knew nothing about the mirror?

It didn't make sense.

Josie was also silent while they followed their path around a weeping willow tree, through a section of lush fernlike plants, and finally to a long wooden bench placed on a hill overlooking the huge maze. Then she said, "If you stand here long enough and concentrate, you can work out the key to the maze. Why don't we sit down for a few minutes?"

"Sounds good to me." Laura was happy to sit here in the cool, sunlit garden and look down on the neatly clipped hedges that made up the maze. She didn't concentrate on trying to figure out the secret, just admired the fully four acres of a living puzzle. She could see, in the center, the pagodalike roof of the gazebo protruding above the greenery, a visible but elusive goal.

Laura half turned and looked at her companion, then impulsively unclipped from the sketchpad the small pouch containing her charcoal pencils and opened the sketchpad, turning to a fresh page. "Do you mind?" she asked. "I could use the practice."

Josie looked startled, then shrugged. "Sure, go ahead. Should I sit a different way, or—"

"No, just relax. And keep talking. Tell me about Amelia."

"Amelia . . . What can I say about her? She took me in and gave me a job when I didn't have anywhere else to go. She's always been kind to me. Never made me feel like a . . . poor relation living on charity. She has a mind like a steel trap, and her memory is incredible."

Sketching rapidly, glancing from the pad to Josie's lovely face, Laura said, "She's had quite a bit of tragedy in her life."

Josie nodded, looking out over the maze but not really seeing it. "Yes, she has. She and David had twenty years together, but his death was so sudden and unexpected. . . . She still mourns him, you know. That's his place at the foot of the table. And she still wears black." Josie frowned slightly.

Wondering what had caused that brief disturbance, Laura said neutrally, "Forty years is a long time to mourn."

"Yes." Josie shook her head as though throwing off an unpleasant or unnerving thought. "But she had other losses during those years. Her son, John—Daniel and Peter's father—died in 1976, in a hunting accident; he was out with a party of friends, and tragically—inexplicably— two of them accidently shot him."

"That was tragic," Laura noted.

"Par for the Kilbourne family history," Josie told her. "Take Amelia's daughter, Julia, for instance. She was Anne's mother—you'll meet Anne later. Anyway, Julia was killed in 1986, in another gun-related accident. She and her husband, Philip, thought they heard a prowler one night, so he got up and got his gun. Instead of staying in bed where he'd left her, Julia followed him. If she had called out to him . . . but apparently she didn't. He mistook her for the prowler and shot her."

Laura stopped sketching and stared at Josie. "My God."

"Yeah. There was some talk at the time—naturally—but the investigation found it an accidental shooting. Philip had some kind of breakdown, I was told, and ended up moving to Europe. He hasn't seen any of the family, even Anne, since."

"I'd say guns and Kilbournes don't mix," Laura said.

"No kidding." Josie's smile was a little strained suddenly. "My husband, Jeremy, was killed five years ago. He was at a convenience store one night when it was robbed. There was an off-duty cop there who shot the robber. But in a bizarre twist nobody could ever really explain, one of the cop's bullets ricocheted off an iron support post and went through Jeremy's heart."

Laura couldn't think of a thing to say except to repeat, "My God."

"Another odd chapter written in the Kilbourne family history." Josie smiled again, this time with more ease. "You know, a couple of years ago, I went back over the family tree just out of curiosity, and the most interesting thing I found was that there hasn't been a Kilbourne to die of disease in nearly a hundred and fifty years. All the deaths were in some way violent and/or accidental. Jeremy's father was killed in a boating accident, for instance, and his uncle died as the result of a fall."

"And now Peter," Laura murmured.

Josie nodded. "Now Peter. I asked Daniel once if he wasn't wary of the Kilbourne family curse. He said there was nothing he could do about curses, and that playing it safe sounded incredibly boring."

After a moment, Laura returned her gaze to the sketch and absently added some shading beneath the angle of Josie's jaw. The sketch was turning out unexpectedly well, which made Laura wonder if she should stop thinking so much about what she was doing and just do it. Her fingers seemed better at their job when her mind was preoccupied by something else.

And her mind was certainly preoccupied. "Do you believe there's a curse?" she asked Josie.

The older woman pursed her lips thoughtfully. "My logical mind says there's no such thing as curses. But there's no denying a streak of the bizarre in this family's history. I don't know, Laura. Maybe destiny just laid down an odd pattern for the Kilbournes. Maybe they're paying off a lot of bad karma. Or maybe they've just been unlucky."

"How did Peter feel about it?"

"I doubt he even thought about it, to be honest. He wasn't an especially thoughtful man, if you know what I mean." When Laura lifted an inquiring brow, Josie went on slowly, "Peter was always concerned more with the physical than the philosophical. I don't just mean his women, although that was certainly part of it. He had strong appetites in other ways. He enjoyed good food and wine, and although he was basically lazy in some ways, being physically active appealed to him. He played a mean game of tennis and squash, ran in a few marathons. But he wasn't interested in discussions, in conversation."

"What about Kerry?"

Josie didn't ask Laura to be more specific. She sighed. "I just don't know. I never saw a single gesture of affection between them, even though they've lived together here at the house since they were married about four years ago. Kerry's so sweet and gentle you'd think any man would be at least kind to her, but Peter always seemed indifferent. More punctilious than anything else, as if he owed her courtesy—and nothing more. I don't even know how they met or why they got married. I was living here when Peter brought her home—they'd married at the office of a justice of the peace—but I was still grieving over Jeremy's death and wasn't really interested in what went on here in the house."

"They married before he brought her here?"

"Yes, and I don't think Amelia was too pleased. She likes Kerry, mind you, but I have a vague memory of her really ripping into Peter about it. I can't recall what was said, just that Amelia thought Peter had made a mistake by not telling her what was going on."

"What was going on?"

Josie frowned. "Well, that he'd met Kerry and decided to marry her, I suppose."

Laura wondered if that was all, but it was clear Josie wouldn't know the answer even if there had been something else "going on" with Peter. "Did Kerry ever go out with him?" she asked curiously.

"No, not that I know of. It's like they were married in name only, if you can believe that in this day and age. They even had separate bedrooms—without a connecting door. And since my bedroom is in the same wing, I can tell you there was never any traffic back and forth that I saw—although, when they were first married, I did see Peter come out of Kerry's bedroom a few mornings. But no sign he set foot in there in years."

Laura thought of Kerry's gentle voice and smile, of the unreadable hazel eyes and the thin body and scarred face, and she couldn't help wondering. There had to be anger there somewhere, bitterness—didn't there? The anger of a fragile, vulnerable woman married to an indifferent man who found his pleasures elsewhere. The bitterness of a man who loved beautiful women married to a woman reluctant to show her scarred face in public. Between that very odd couple and within that very odd marriage, might there not have been rage enough for murder?

"She was out of town when Peter was killed," Laura heard herself say.

Josie looked at her, understanding. "Yes, she was. But

. . . Kerry is always pretty well veiled when she travels. Swathed in scarves and hidden behind big sunglasses, with that special makeup that hides her scars. So I suppose . . ."

"The police would have checked her alibi," Laura said.

Josie laughed suddenly, a rueful sound. "Yes, of course. And it's ridiculous anyway. Kerry couldn't hurt a fly."

Chapter 6

*L*aura shook off the idea as well, at least for the moment, and held her sketch at arm's length to study it. Not bad, she decided.

"May I see it?" Josie asked.

After an instant's hesitation, Laura turned the sketchpad around so that Josie could see her likeness.

"Hey . . . you're pretty good," Josie said slowly, wide eyes staring at the sketch.

"Not good enough." Laura smiled. "I caught the shape of your face, the curves and angles, the shadows. But not the life. Not the spark that makes your face different from every other face. Until I can do that, I won't be good enough."

Josie nodded after a moment, but said, "You don't have far to go, I'd say. Not far at all."

"Thanks." Laura closed the sketchpad and clipped the pouch of pencils back in place.

Josie got up, saying, "Why don't we take the other path back toward the house; that'll take us along the other side of the gardens."

"Suits me. Listen, if I decide to try my hand at the maze—"

"Tell somebody you'll be in there," Josie said firmly. "Always. There's an oddly muffling quality about the shrubs in the maze, so yelling for help won't do any good unless somebody's close by." She grinned. "However, if you turn up missing, I'll check the maze first thing."

"Thanks."

"Don't mention it." Josie indicated the second path that had ended here overlooking the maze, and they began strolling back. "Along this path we have a Japanese-type section with a coy pond, three trellises covered with prize-winning roses, a fantastic rock garden—"

"And a partridge in a pear tree?"

Josie chuckled. "We just might. Suggest to Avery— he's the head gardener—that the twelve days of Christmas might be a dandy theme, and he'll design something incredible."

Laura shook her head. "It's already incredible. I didn't think gardens like this existed, not in a private home."

"Not many do. The cost of upkeep is pretty well prohibitive unless you have money to burn. The Kilbournes, for all their strange paths to destiny, have it. Especially now. Kilbourne Data is one of this country's biggest designers and producers of computer equipment, as well as electronic components for military aircraft and satellites. And thanks to Daniel's foresight, there's now a division of the company engaged solely in research and development; real cutting-edge technology. Daniel's a financial genius, to say nothing of having a genuine feel for what might be needed in the future."

"I've heard that." Laura glanced at her. "I've also heard that he and Amelia don't always agree on financial decisions."

Josie hesitated, then shrugged. "I couldn't really say, since I'm Amelia's personal assistant and rarely have anything to do with family business. But I do know that while Amelia can veto some financial decisions, she has no say in others—or at least, so it seems to me. Apparently, David left the family money tied up in some odd, complicated way it'd take a team of lawyers to understand." She hesitated again. "There's been some tension from time to time. But I'd guess that kind of thing was normal in a family like this one. Nobody's going to agree all the time."

Laura knew only too well that Josie was right; nobody agreed all the time, and within families—especially powerful families—dissension was probably closer to being the rule than the exception. But she wondered if the curious division of power within the Kilbourne family had grated on two strong, dominating personalities, turning them into adversaries.

"How was Peter involved in the family business?" she asked, curious.

"Well, he wasn't, really. Some family stock, of course, but no voting power, and he didn't have much of a say in what went on. He did things for Amelia, checked out investments and the like; she has some money of her own, you see, and that's separate from family holdings."

Laura was a little surprised that Josie was being so forthcoming, but had a hunch it was less a matter of her discretion and more a matter of Amelia's instructions. What she didn't understand was why Amelia would want her questions about the family answered. To enable her to paint a better portrait? It didn't seem likely. Why, then?

"I wish they'd find out who killed Peter," Josie said suddenly, her tone anxious. "It's so awful not knowing."

Nodding, Laura said, "I read a book once where there was a murder and all the innocent people tied themselves into knots, agonizing over it. In their imaginations any of them could have done it, so they were suspicious of each other. The point of the story was that the innocent suffer more than the guilty do when they don't know the truth."

Josie glanced at her quickly. "I don't believe any of the family did it. How could I believe that?" When Laura said nothing, she added, "It must have been the redhead with him. The police think so."

Laura nodded, hearing the aching uncertainty in the other woman's voice; Josie had plenty of doubts and suspicions. "Probably."

As they passed through the lovely rock garden, Josie looked distractedly around, her expression showing no pleasure in beauty at the moment. Almost to herself, she said, "I hate not knowing. I hate it."

"So do I. And I hate being suspected of something terrible I didn't do," Laura said steadily. "That's why I've been asking nosy questions about the family. If you were wondering."

"Well, I was wondering," Josie said after a moment. "But I can see how you might think it was a good idea to learn all you could about the family."

"It's the only thing I can do. I was pulled into this because I bought a mirror here and later talked to Peter about it. And even though the police can't connect me to his murder, the press is having fun trying. If the truth doesn't come out, I'll always have that black mark of suspicion and doubt against me."

Josie stopped on the path and looked at her. "I hadn't thought about it that way. But you're right, of course. If the truth doesn't come out . . . we can never be sure about a lot of things. Including the people around us." She drew a breath. "But do you really think that something you learn about the family can help you find that truth?"

Laura hesitated, then said, "I think Peter was murdered because of the kind of man he was. Somewhere along the way, he made a bad enemy, and that enemy killed him. Maybe that redhead he checked into the motel with killed him. It certainly looked like a crime of passion, it seems. But maybe his death was just *supposed* to look that way. Maybe we're all making wrong assumptions. I don't know, Josie. I'm not a detective."

"Yet you can't leave it to the detectives, the police?"

"No, I can't. I have to find out for myself why Peter died. And why I was one of the last people to see him alive."

Josie nodded soberly. "I can't say that I blame you for that. But be careful, Laura. In all the books the amateur almost always ends up hip-deep in trouble."

It was a friendly warning, Laura thought.

At least, she hoped it was.

The two women continued along the path through the gardens to the house, neither of them with much to say now. Laura was debating with herself as to whether she should ask Josie where she was the night Peter was killed. She needed to know that, if only to eliminate the delicate redhead as a candidate for Peter's mysterious lover, but at the same time she didn't want to upset the feeling of casual harmony between them.

And chances were good Josie wouldn't like the question.

They were still silent as they went up the steps onto the veranda, and both stopped almost automatically as a man strolled out of the conservatory to meet them. He was tall and blond, a strikingly handsome man with greenish eyes and a lazy smile. He looked to be about Laura's own age, she thought, and the sober elegance of his business suit was offset somewhat by the loosened, brightly colored tie peopled with cartoon characters.

"Hi, Josie," he said amiably with a faint smile for the redhead, and then, looking at Laura, he added, "You must be Laura. I'm Alex Kilbourne."

The lawyer, Laura realized as she nodded a greeting. "You're . . . Amelia's cousin?" she ventured.

"Yes, but only in the vague Southern sense, meaning that we're related. Actually, my grandfather was the youngest brother of Amelia's late husband. There were three brothers; everyone in this house is descended from or related by marriage to those three brothers."

Laura sighed. "I think I need to see a family tree," she murmured almost to herself.

Josie spoke finally, directly to Laura. "Amelia began a genealogy years ago, so there's a fairly complete chart going back several generations; I'll show it to you later, if you'll remind me."

"Thanks, I will." Laura became aware then that here was yet another undercurrent among the Kilbournes—this one between Josie and Alex. He seemed relaxed, yet his glances at Josie held an odd entreaty; and though Josie remained expressionless, Laura could feel her tension.

"How did you like the gardens?" Alex asked Laura, his tone still pleasant.

"Very much. This is a beautiful place."

"It has its charms." He smiled. "Amelia's just come down, I believe, and is waiting for you in her parlor."

"I'll show you the way, Laura," Josie said instantly.

Laura was tempted to tell Josie she could find her own way, since she was certain Alex wanted a moment alone with the redhead, but she decided not to interfere, having no idea what kind of relationship they had. It was interesting, though. Very interesting.

"Nice meeting you, Alex," she said instead.

"My pleasure. See you around, Laura. Josie."

They left him standing there on the veranda, and when Laura glanced at Josie's face as they moved through the conservatory, she found the older woman wearing an unhappy frown. Tentatively, Laura said, "He seems very nice. He lives here in the house?"

Josie nodded. "Since he joined the family firm of lawyers a couple of years ago. Amelia likes to have family around her, and the house is certainly big enough." Her voice was distracted and the frown remained.

"Did Alex and Peter get along?" Laura wondered.

Josie didn't answer immediately, and when she did her voice was no longer distracted. "No. No, they didn't." Before Laura could respond to that, Josie added quickly, "But he was here the night Peter was killed. Besides, they didn't hate each other, they just didn't get along especially well."

"I see."

"And a woman killed Peter. That's what they said, isn't it?"

"Yes. That's what they said." *But only because a woman was seen with him at the motel. We don't really know for sure that she killed him. A man could have come along later and done it.*

As if she had read Laura's thoughts, Josie's expression of unhappiness intensified. But all she said was, "Here, this is Amelia's parlor. I'll see you later, Laura." She didn't exactly run as she continued down the hall toward the front of the house, but her need to get away was pretty obvious.

Laura hesitated an instant, then went into the small parlor where she had met Kerry earlier. It was, now that she had heard it termed "Amelia's parlor," very characteristic of the old lady and her style. Almost Victorian, it was furnished with antiques and held so many small tables and pictures and bric-a-brac that an unkind person would have called it cluttered. The draperies were heavy velvet, the wallpaper dark, and spread over the hardwood floor was a tapestry rug fashioned in unusually dark colors.

She had barely noticed the room during her first visit this morning, but now it had a strong impact on Laura. She couldn't help wondering what in Amelia's background or personality had produced this near obsession with dark colors and heavy textures. So many losses? So

many bouts with grief? Had her life given Amelia a dark
and gloomy vision of the world around her?

Amelia was sitting in a delicate Queen Anne chair and
smiled as Laura came in. "I hope Josie took good care of
you, child."

"Very good care of me, Amelia. We walked through
the gardens."

"Ah, good. Then shall we continue working? I
thought you might like to sketch me in here. I spend a
great deal of time in here."

Looking at Amelia in gleaming widow's black surrounded by the stifling colors and clutter of her room,
Laura thought the background was ideal. She picked an
angle, found a chair, and began sketching.

ALEX CAME INTO the library and closed the doors firmly
behind him.

Josie looked up, stiffened, and said immediately, "Daniel will be back in here—"

"Not for half an hour or so, he won't," Alex told her.
"I asked him to give us a little while."

She pushed her chair back and stood up, glaring at
him. "You had no right to do that. Dammit, Alex—"

He came to the desk, but didn't attempt to go around
that barrier to touch her. "Josie, you've been avoiding me
since Saturday night. You scuttle away when I get close,
leave a room if I come into it, and lock yourself in your
bedroom right after supper."

"Get it?" she snapped.

Alex grinned faintly. "I'd have to be an idiot not to.
You're avoiding me. Okay, so let's talk about it."

"There's nothing to talk about."

"I think there is. Listen, I know I upset you—"

"Upset me? First you convince me to spend the night,

and then you needle me until I change my mind. Why would that upset me?"

"Josie—"

She gestured angrily, cutting him off. "If you want to end it, Alex, just say so. Maybe men your age like playing games, but I'm a little beyond that, so let's cut to the chase, all right?"

He sighed and folded his arms across his chest. "Age has nothing to do with it, Josie—not yours and not mine. I won't let you use that as an excuse."

"You won't let *me*? Since when is this my fault? Dammit, Alex, *you're* the one who ran me off Saturday night—and don't you dare try to deny it."

"All right, I won't."

His mild agreement took the wind out of her sails, leaving Josie feeling unexpectedly flat. "Well, why?" she demanded.

He shrugged. "Because . . . you didn't want to stay. Oh, you agreed to, but only because I more or less forced you to. And when that happened, I realized it wasn't the way I wanted it to be. I didn't want to wake up in the morning and see you regretting we'd spent the night together."

Josie frowned at him. "Then why didn't you say something about it instead of—of being cruel and driving me away?"

"Was I cruel? No, Josie—unless the truth is cruel." He smiled slightly, his greenish eyes very intent on her face. "I know I probably sounded harsh, and I suppose that was intentional. It just seems to me that it's time you said good-bye to Jeremy. Unless, that is, you really do want to end up like Amelia, still wearing black and living in a mausoleum forty years from now. Is that what you want?"

No! But she couldn't quite voice that answer, as badly as she wanted to. Something held her back. Slowly she said, "My feelings about Jeremy are none of your business."

"They are when he sleeps between us in my bed," Alex said bluntly. "A ménage à trois isn't quite what I bargained for."

She felt hot tears sting her eyes, and wasn't even sure why. "You didn't complain in the beginning," she said shakily. "Why start now?"

He hesitated, then said, "Maybe because it offends my sense of justice to see a beautiful young woman bury herself with her dead husband. Maybe because I can't believe Jeremy would have wanted you to stop feeling when he died. Or . . . maybe I just resent knowing there's a ghost in my bed. Take your pick, Josie. It really doesn't matter."

"It does to me."

"Does it?" Alex shrugged again. "All right, then. I don't like it, sweet. I just don't like it. Every time I take you in my arms, I know damned well you think you're cheating on Jeremy. And I really don't enjoy feeling like the other man. I took it as long as I could, and now I just can't take it anymore."

Josie drew a breath. "I can't help how I feel."

"Neither can I." He leaned forward, bracing his hands on the edge of her desk, and held her gaze steadily. "Make no mistake, Josie—I want you back in my bed. But not until it's just the two of us. Leave Jeremy in your inner sanctum if you have to, his picture on your dresser. Apologize to him there, if you have to, for being with another man, and do penance if he demands it of you—or you demand it of yourself. But the next time you come to me, you come alone."

Josie didn't say a word, watching silently as he straightened, turned, and walked to the door. She didn't call him back, as badly as she wanted to, when he opened the door and went out, leaving her alone in the room.

When he was gone, she sank down into her chair and

looked rather blindly at the schedule of Atlanta's upcoming charity events she had been studying when he had come in. She couldn't think of anything beyond Alex's ultimatum and the confusion of her own feelings.

And when she could think, long minutes later, she realized that her uneasy questions about what he'd been doing in Peter's room later on Saturday night, and what he and Daniel were up to, had completely slipped her mind when he was standing in front of her and might have answered them. But now those questions tormented her as surely as his ultimatum did.

Alex had gotten up and dressed after she'd left him, and she had to wonder if it had been the first time. Or had he, the previous Saturday night, also dressed and left his room—and possibly this house—after she had returned to hers?

". . . a woman killed Peter. That's what they said, isn't it?"

Laura had agreed, Josie remembered. But her expressive face had said clearly what had occurred to Josie—that it was believed a woman had killed Peter only because a woman had been seen with him that night.

There was no reassurance in that thought. Only doubts.

Too many doubts.

"SO THIS IS Amelia Kilbourne." Cassidy studied the second sketch Laura had made at the house, shaking her head almost unconsciously. "She looks like something out of the last century."

Curled up in the chair in her living room, Laura sipped the hot chocolate she'd just made—as a sort of defiant good-bye to summer, whether it had really gone or not—and nodded. "She's just that way, in looks. Sort of the way she talks sometimes as well. But I get the idea it's because she favors a more elegant time—and knows she looks good in the setting.''

Cassidy put the sketchpad aside and eyed her friend thoughtfully. "That sounds awfully . . . calculated.''

Laura was momentarily surprised, but then nodded. "I guess so. I think Amelia is very aware of how things look. Not just appearances, but the meanings behind them. She's . . . an interesting woman.''

"Umm. What about the others? That sketch you did of Josie is especially good, by the way; I'd certainly know her if I saw her. Your best work.''

Laura smiled, but shrugged off the compliment. "I like Josie. And, at a guess, she wasn't involved with Peter because she is involved with Alex Kilbourne. I just think so, mind you—I don't know for sure. But there seemed to be a lot of tension between them. A man/woman kind of tension. The thing is, I think it occurred to Josie just today that just because a woman was seen with Peter the night he was murdered doesn't necessarily mean a man couldn't have killed him. She's worried. I don't know if something in particular is bothering her or if it's a general uneasiness because we don't know who killed him, but she's pretty anxious.''

"Think maybe she suspects Alex?''

"Maybe. She said he was at the house Saturday night, but she was awfully quick to defend him. I mean, to say that even though he and Peter didn't get along, it wasn't hatred. Ergo, he wouldn't have murdered him.'' Laura shook her head. "I don't know, she might suspect he had something to do with it.''

"What do you think?''

"I talked to the man for barely a minute, hardly enough time to make that kind of guess.''

"Guess anyway,'' Cassidy suggested.

Laura frowned. "He seemed perfectly nice, charming. Not exactly the buttoned-down lawyer type, judging by his necktie—Looney Tunes characters. But he *is* a lawyer, and I can't see this particular lawyer stabbing a man to death in a motel room."

"Okay. What about Daniel?"

Laura's first reaction to that question was an instant and definite negative. *No.* No, not Daniel. He hadn't killed Peter. It wasn't possible. That kind of hatred wasn't in him. He hadn't stood over his brother's body in that shabby motel room driving the knife in again and again. . . .

"Laura? Hey, what's wrong?"

"It's cold in here," she heard herself murmur. "That's all."

"That's not all. You went white. What is it?"

After a moment, Laura said, "I keep forgetting the reality of it. That a man was brutally murdered. And then, suddenly, something makes it real to me."

Cassidy nodded in understanding, but asked, "What made it real to you this time? That I asked about Daniel?"

"Not so much that as . . . I just got an image in my head. How it must have happened. I told you imagination was a curse."

"I guess so." Cassidy studied her thoughtfully and added, "I hate to repeat the question, but . . . ?"

"Daniel?" Laura tried to think objectively, and when she couldn't, tried to at least convince Cassidy that she was able to. "I don't know, Cass. He seems awfully calm and . . . controlled. And way too smart to do something so hasty and reckless—to say nothing of illegal and immoral. I just can't believe he went to a seedy motel and stabbed his own brother to death."

"No matter what the provocation?"

Laura lifted her shoulders in a helpless shrug. "I don't know that there *was* provocation—I mean, beyond the usual type of sibling rivalry. Apparently, Peter didn't have much to do with the family business, so I doubt he was involved in this power play I think is going on between Daniel and Amelia. And so far nobody's said a word about Daniel and Peter not getting along."

Cassidy nodded, obviously not convinced but willing to move on. "Okay. How about the Widow Kilbourne? You met her, right?"

Realizing only then, Laura said slowly, "You know, every woman in that house with the Kilbourne name is a widow. Amelia and Josie, Madeline—and Kerry. All of them are widows."

"Doesn't say much for the longevity of the Kilbourne males, does it?"

Laura started to mention Josie's comments about the history of the family being filled with untimely deaths by accident or violence, but decided not to get into all that. Instead she said, "It's Kerry you're wondering about, isn't it? Peter's widow?"

"Right."

"She was in California, remember? At least, I haven't heard anything to indicate otherwise. Josie says she usually travels swathed in scarves and wearing heavy makeup, but there doesn't seem to be any doubt that it was her—"

"Wait a minute. Scarves and heavy makeup?"

"I would have thought your tabloid sources would have mentioned it," Laura said a bit dryly. "Kerry is badly scarred, Cass. Most of one side of her face. It looks like a burn or something like that."

Cassidy looked shocked. "Scarred? *Peter's* wife? How?"

"Well, I don't know. To be honest, I didn't even think to ask Josie—and Amelia isn't exactly someone I *could* ask about it. The scars don't look recent, though, and something about the way Kerry speaks and acts tells me she's been that way for quite a while."

It was Cassidy's turn to shrug helplessly. "Does this mean anything about Peter's death?"

"God knows." Laura sighed, feeling abruptly tired. "I spent an entire day at the house, and I'm more confused than ever. Nobody seems to be grieving over Peter's death—except his mother, naturally, and I haven't met her yet—but nobody's admitted to hating him, either. I feel definitely odd asking them where they were the night he was murdered, and besides, the police *must* have. So all I can do is go on sketching Amelia and pick up what I can."

"Any luck finding out about the mirror?"

"Still more questions than answers. Josie said she didn't see how it could be valuable to the family, or she would have known about it, and she's probably right about that. But she also said that Peter was in charge of doing the inventory before the sale, and that Daniel didn't see the entire inventory until it was over with—that afternoon. Shortly before Peter came to see me."

"So . . . now you think Daniel might have been the one to want the mirror back? But I thought he said he didn't know anything about it?"

"He did. But I thought—felt very strongly—at the time that he was lying. That he does know something about the mirror. I don't know *why* he would have lied, though. And the fact is, I still don't know why Peter tried to buy the mirror back. Whether it was his idea or someone else's."

Cassidy pursed her lips thoughtfully. "It's sounding more like a long shot every day that the mirror had anything to do with the murder."

"I know."

"But you still think there's a connection?"

"I think I have to find out if there is."

"Mmm. So you go back to that—what did you call it?—that oddly dark and repressive house?"

Laura nodded. "Tomorrow morning at nine."

Unusually grave, Cassidy said, "Look, be careful, okay? I don't know if any of these people murdered Peter Kilbourne, but it sounds to me like most of them have things to hide. And people protect their secrets."

"Yes," Laura said. "I know."

"SO, YOU'RE LAURA." She came into the west wing den where Laura was waiting on this overcast Tuesday morning for Amelia to return from a phone call, a young woman a little older than Laura who very much resembled a younger Amelia. "I'm Anne Ralston. Amelia's grand-daughter."

Laura nodded a greeting. "You look like her," she offered.

Anne didn't seem entirely pleased. "Yeah, so I'm told." She eyed Laura, frowning, and said abruptly, "You look like someone Peter would have hit on."

Laura was taken aback, but only momentarily. She glanced down at the current sketch of Amelia, then returned her gaze to meet Anne's almost defiant stare. "Do I?" Her voice was mild.

Anne found a chair and slouched down into it. "Oh, I'd say so. He liked redheads. But you already know that, don't you?"

"I've been told." Laura was determined not to let this angry woman put her on the defensive. "Actually, though, I hear he just liked women. All kinds of women." Unobtrusively she turned to a fresh page and began sketching Anne with rapid, spare lines.

Anne's lips tightened. "You sound just like the press, painting him as a horny son of a bitch who couldn't keep his fly zipped." She didn't seem aware of being sketched.

"Is that what he was?" Her hair was easy, Laura decided absently, as severely short as Amelia's was elegantly long, almost spiky, and suited to her narrow face and sharp features.

"He was okay," Anne declared, her chin rising.

"Maybe the press thinks he was nothing but a womanizer, and maybe certain members of this family can write him off without a second thought, but Peter was okay. He was a lot smarter than some people think, I can tell you that."

"Smarter how?"

"He had plans. He was going to make people sit up and take notice." Her voice was truculent. "Maybe Daniel thinks he's the only one who can make money for the family, but—"

"Anne, I thought you were due at the Moretons' this morning," Amelia said as she came into the den.

"They canceled." Anne shrugged, her face taking on a sulky expression that made her look rather like a thwarted teenager.

"Then why don't you take advantage of the time to begin going through your clothes? We'll be into cold weather sooner than you think."

"Do we *have* to go through this twice a year?" Anne demanded, rolling her eyes. "In the spring we pack away winter clothes, and in the fall we pack away summer things. My closet's big enough for both, so I don't see—"

"You don't have to see, Anne. You only have to accept that things are done a certain way in this house."

"This house is full of rituals, Laura, most of them Amelia's," Daniel had said. It appeared that this seasonal sorting of clothing was one of those rituals. Laura listened as she sketched quickly, trying to capture Anne's discontented face before she left the room. As she was obviously about to do.

On her feet now, Anne said, "Things have always been done a *certain way* in this house and this family, and I'm sick and tired of it. It's stifling! And it's dangerous, Amelia. You think I don't know that Peter died because of the *certain way* this family conducts business?"

"Anne." Amelia's voice was icy. "Peter died because he was a married man having a sordid affair. And that affair

had nothing to do with business." She held her grand-daughter's gaze for a long minute, then went to the chair where she had earlier posed for Laura and sat down. "And now, if you don't mind . . ."

Without even glancing toward Laura, a burning flush coloring her high cheekbones, Anne turned and stalked from the room.

Amelia sighed and smiled a bit tiredly at Laura. "I'm sorry you had to see that little scene. I try to make allow-ances for the child—Josie told you about what happened to her mother?"

Laura nodded. "Yes. A terrible thing."

"She was already an adult when it happened, but it was still a tremendous shock, of course. I try to remember that. But she's difficult. Very rebellious, even now—she just turned thirty-one, though she certainly doesn't act it. And everything is always my fault, without question."

"She does seem very angry," Laura ventured, aban-doning the hasty sketch of Anne and returning to the one of Amelia she'd been working on earlier.

"She didn't say anything terrible to you, did she, child?" Amelia was anxious.

"No, nothing like that." *He had plans.* What had Anne meant? And why was she so convinced that Peter had died because of the way the family conducted business?

"Good, that's good. She often speaks without think-ing, you see. Take that remark about Peter and the family business; she knows very well that Peter was never in-volved in the family business. But I suppose it's simply difficult for her to accept that his own immoral behavior got him killed." Amelia nodded sadly as though to herself. "They were close, you see."

But she didn't say "the family business," Amelia. She said "the way this family conducts business." And I think that's a different thing entirely.

But Laura merely nodded and focused her gaze on the

sketch, unwilling to question Amelia on a point that seemed elusive even to herself. But even as her fingers worked skillfully, her mind was fixed elsewhere. Anne was probably a woman damaged by the tragedy of her father accidentally killing her mother; who wouldn't be? But though that might well explain her sulky and discontented personality, it didn't really explain, Laura thought, her pointed remarks about the "certain way" the Kilbourne family conducted business.

The question was, did Anne know something about Peter's murder, or was she merely speculating? And, either way, how could a seeming crime of passion have anything to do with business?

Laura looked beyond the sketchpad at Amelia, finding the old lady sitting primly as usual, smiling faintly as usual, and couldn't help wondering if her dismissal of Anne's remarks had been as offhand as it had seemed. Was Amelia convinced Peter had died by the violent hand of a mistress? Or *was* there something odd in the way family business was conducted, something that might have resulted in his death?

Laura smiled. "Amelia, if you could lift your chin just a fraction—there. That's perfect." And she concentrated on getting those dark eyes just right.

AS SEEMED TO be her habit, Amelia left Laura shortly before twelve in order to "check on" lunch; Laura assumed it was another indication of the precision with which she ran this house, that she wanted to inspect preparations for lunch before the meal was placed before a guest. Then again, it seemed likely that she did the same thing even if a guest was not present, simply because she was a perfectionist.

That realization made Laura eye her sketch uneasily. Would this suit a perfectionist? Probably not. The only positive note was that Amelia had not asked again to see the sketches, and Laura hoped she wouldn't. It was going to be unnerving enough having her view the actual painting once she began working on that; these preliminary efforts, though improving, were not meant to be judged by a perfectionist.

Laura closed the sketchpad with a sigh, then looked up as she heard a few unhappy notes from a piano. The music room was just across the hall, she remembered, and she guessed that Kerry was getting in a bit of practice before lunch.

She left her sketchpad on the chair and went out into the hall, thinking only that the music sounded awfully despondent and that no one should be that alone. But she didn't realize until she was a couple of steps into the music room that it wasn't Kerry sitting on the padded bench of the baby grand and playing the sad notes.

It was—had to be—Madeline Kilbourne.

The wide, pale blue eyes she turned to Laura were red-rimmed and a bit puffy from crying, and also had that slightly vague look that came from some sedatives. But despite the drugs, she was perfectly dressed in an elegant black suit with pearls, and her attractively graying dark hair was flawless. So was her makeup.

"Oh, excuse me," Laura murmured, not venturing from her place just inside the doorway and not at all prepared for this meeting. "I expected Kerry."

"You're Laura." Madeline's long, elegant fingers left the keys and drifted to her lap, and she tilted her head to one side as she considered the stranger. "Amelia wants you here."

"Yes. I'm very sorry about your son," Laura said uncomfortably.

Those dazed blue eyes filled with tears, and her voice shook. "He was my baby. Such a beautiful boy, so sweet-tempered, so full of charm. He was like his father, you know. He was all I had left of John."

Laura hadn't meant to speak, but heard herself say, "You still have Daniel."

Madeline frowned a little and seemed briefly confused. Then she shook her head. "No, he's not at all like John. And he was never mine, not like Peter was. He never came in and sat on my bed in the evening to tell me about his day. But Peter did. He never told me all his secrets. But Peter did."

Again, Laura heard herself speaking when she hadn't intended to. "Did he tell you about the mirror, Mrs. Kilbourne?" Somehow, she couldn't bring herself to address this woman by her first name.

The question seemed to recall Madeline's attention from some distant point, and she frowned again. "Mirror? That's why you said he went to see you. Because of some mirror."

"Yes. A mirror I bought here at the estate sale. He wanted to buy it back. Do you know why?"

"Peter wasn't interested in mirrors. He wasn't vain," Madeline explained anxiously.

The last thing Laura wanted to do was to grill this dazed, grieving woman, but she couldn't seem to stop herself. "He said the mirror was a family heirloom, Mrs. Kilbourne. A brass hand mirror. Do you recall it?"

"I don't know anything about a mirror." Madeline's voice was dull now, but as she looked at Laura, her cloudy eyes cleared to become as sharp as a knife's edge. "Did you kill my son?" she asked in the tone of someone who desperately needs an answer.

"No." Laura cleared her throat. "No, Mrs. Kilbourne, I swear I didn't. I had nothing to do with his death."

Those urgent blue eyes remained fixed on Laura's face for a moment, then tracked past her suddenly and widened. "Oh," she said softly.

"Mother, you should be resting."

Laura didn't start at the sound of Daniel's quiet voice, because she had been unconsciously braced for it. She felt him behind her. But she heard her breath catch when he touched her for the first time, one of his powerful hands on her shoulder as he gently guided her to one side a step so that he could pass her there at the doorway.

He didn't look at Laura as he passed her, but went to his mother and took her arm, urging her to her feet. He didn't appear to use force, but she rose immediately, looking up at him with a kind of entreaty.

"You should be resting," he repeated as quietly as before.

"Yes. Yes, of course I should." She looked at Laura, eyes cloudy again, and said with vague politeness, "You will excuse me?"

Not trusting her voice, Laura nodded.

Daniel led Madeline from the room, his gaze meeting Laura's only once, fleetingly and unrevealingly.

Alone, Laura stood there for a moment before she realized how tense she was. She lifted her hands and stared at them, unaware until then that her fingers had been curled so tightly that her nails had dug crescent imprints deep into her palms. She rubbed her hands together slowly.

She felt ashamed of herself for having questioned Madeline, especially since the answers were useless to her. And she was afraid she had earned yet another black mark in Daniel's book because of it.

Before she could do more than consider that unhappily, Laura was distracted when a gleam of sunlight found its way through the narrow opening of the draperies and reflected brightly off a wall mirror above a side table. The light was brief as the sun ducked back behind the gray clouds that had been present all day, but Laura hardly noticed that. She had only looked into this room before

and hadn't seen the mirror; now, as always, she was drawn
to it.

She wasn't even aware of moving until she stood before the mirror. It was a big mirror, two feet by three feet,
in a gilded frame, all details Laura noted only in passing.
As always, she ignored her own reflection to study the
room behind her, past her right shoulder. And as always,
what she saw left her with a gnawing sense of disappointment, because whatever it was she looked for was not
there.

"Damn," she whispered.

MADELINE WAS NOT present at lunch.
Neither was Daniel.

his is getting really interesting," Dena said on Tuesday evening when she stopped by Laura's apartment with her second progress report. "Not to say tragic."

Laura couldn't help wincing. "Don't tell me. The mirror's cursed?"

Dena sat down on Laura's couch and made a slight gesture. "I wouldn't go that far. Yet." She opened her notebook. "Okay. As I told you before, in 1858, the mirror was purchased from the son of the silversmith who made it by a Faith Broderick, who later married the silversmith's son. Ready for their story?"

Laura sat down in her chair. "Go ahead."

"Right. Stuart Kenley, the silversmith's son, was born in 1833; Faith Broderick was born in 1836. They both lived in Philadelphia, but apparently had no contact with each other until she walked into his father's shop after spotting the mirror in the window."

"You know that for sure?"

"Yeah. Faith left a journal. It's in some archives in

Philly, but a helpful librarian copied a few relevant pages and faxed them to me. According to Faith, it was love at first sight for both her and Stuart. She waxed fairly poetic about it, talking about twists of fate—that kind of stuff. I copied the pages for you, so you can read them yourself later."

Laura nodded without comment.

"So we have a young couple in love," Dena went on. "The kicker is, she's already engaged, and in those days, engagements aren't so easily broken. She doesn't waste any time, however, in breaking it off. Not much comment in the journal about what must have been a terrible scandal— beyond Faith's unhappiness at hurting a good man. Anyway, she and Stuart plan to marry just a few weeks after they meet. The day before the wedding, Faith receives a note from her former fiancé asking her to come to his home. Still feeling guilty about having dumped him, she does. And finds his body. He's hanged himself, leaving another note placing the blame squarely on Faith's shoulders."

"What a prince," Laura said.

"Yeah, I thought the same thing. He couldn't have her, but he made damned sure she'd never forget him." Dena shrugged. "On the other hand, maybe he was truly heartbroken and just wanted her to know. Anyway, all Faith says about it in her journal is that she's sorry he could find nothing else to live for."

"She married Stuart?"

"Very quietly the next day, though their church wedding was canceled. They left Philly almost immediately for Washington, D.C., where they were living when the Civil War began. Stuart joined the Union army and was killed in battle, at the age of thirty, in 1863. Five months later, in 1864, Faith died in childbirth at the age of twenty-eight. The child died with her."

After a moment, Laura said, "I'd call that tragic. I mean, the whole thing."

Dena nodded. "No kidding. The only positive thing in the whole story was the love Faith felt for Stuart—and he, apparently, felt for her. She said—well, you'll read it for yourself. It's really sweet." She turned a page in her notebook, and added, "Okay, after Faith died, the mirror went to a sister, who apparently kept it until her own death more than thirty years later. The sister's estate ended up being sold at auction, in New York City, around 1897 or 1898. I'm working now on running down the records of the auction."

Laura accepted the folder Dena held out to her, but didn't open it and read this part of the report for herself. Instead she said, "I'll say it again—I'm impressed. No kidding, Dena, you're doing great."

"Thanks, but I still say we're lucky that everybody so far has made a note about what happened to the mirror. I mean, Faith left a will and left the mirror very specifically to her sister. And the sister was a prominent society widow, childless, so there was public note of what happened to her estate." Dena looked reflective. "But it's the earlier stuff that got me. Finding that mirror way back in 1800, and then being able to get information on it and the people who've owned it was more than lucky. Funny. It's almost as if . . ."

"As if?"

"Well, as if you were meant to find out about the mirror." Then she grinned. "Of course, I'll deny I said that if the trail ends at this New York auction house."

Laura smiled. "I have absolute faith in your ability to trace the mirror all the way to 1997 and the Kilbournes' attic."

Dena got to her feet with a chuckle. "I'll do my best. In the meantime, I've got to get home and get ready for a test tomorrow. I'll be back in touch by the end of the week, I hope."

"Thanks, Dena."

"Don't mention it."

When she was alone in her apartment, Laura opened the folder and read Dena's brief report. Again, it was a dry recitation of facts and dates, this time about a young couple with far fewer years together than the first, and with more than their share of bad luck. Then Laura continued through the file to find photocopies of a journal's pages, and instantly the spidery handwriting leaped out at her.

> I cannot explain it even to myself. It was the mirror that drew me, as mirrors have always drawn me, catching the light in the window even as it caught my attention. But when I went in to inquire about the price, when I saw him, it was as if fate itself had planned that we meet. Why else was I there, that day, in a part of the city I have never before seen? Why else was he working, that day, in the front of the store when he was always in back? Both of us felt it, felt that it was intended we be together.

Then on another page, on another day:

> I should feel wicked that I have hurt a good man, and I am sorry, but what else could I do? I love Stuart.

Then, finally:

> We are as two halves of the same soul, utterly content and at peace with each other. Our passion is like the embers of a fire, glowing long into the night, warming our hearts even as it warms our

bed. If we have only this night together, this week,
this winter, it will be enough.

That last entry was dated 1859, during their first winter together, and someone—apparently the helpful librarian—had noted that it was the final entry of the journal.
Either her life had become too busy for the daily discipline
of noting the day's events, or else Faith had simply said all
she needed to with that last happy entry. Five years later,
almost to the day, she would be dead.

Laura closed the folder and leaned forward to place it
on her coffee table. Another couple through whose hands
the mirror had passed. Another couple whose love for
each other seemed unusually powerful. And so . . .
what? What, if anything, did it mean?

She brooded over it for the rest of the evening while
she took care of the usual chores daily living demanded.
She stripped her bed and remade it, took a trip down to
the laundry room, halfheartedly dusted the living room.
She fixed supper for herself and watched a newsmagazine
on television, then took what was meant to be a relaxing
bath and got ready for bed.

She couldn't sleep. Her mind was too full of Anne's
bitter anger and Madeline's overwhelming grief. Too full
of questions. Every time she closed her eyes, it was to see
those two meetings replayed in her memory, every flicker
of expression and nuance of voice incredibly vivid, as if her
subconscious had recorded all the details for a reason.

But try as she might, considering those details left
Laura no closer to understanding. She had met, today, an
angry and bitter woman just past thirty whose sulky manner and discontented expression made her seem far less
mature than her years. And she had met a dazed and grieving mother who had clearly worshiped her dead younger
son and who seemed oddly apathetic about her older son.

Each woman had said something Laura couldn't stop

thinking about. Anne's comments about Peter's "plans" and her contention that he had died because of the way the family did business; and Madeline's statement that Peter had told her all his secrets. The question was, did either woman know something that might help explain Peter Kilbourne's murder?

Or was Laura merely looking for complications in what was in essence a very simple, straightforward crime of passion?

WEDNESDAY WAS A grim, overcast day, though the rain held off all morning. They were into October now, a month the forecasters were promising would be unusually stormy and unsettled. Laura didn't know if the weather added to her tension, but by the time she and Amelia had as usual spent the morning alone together and then had joined Josie for lunch, she was more than ready to get out of the house for a while.

Before Amelia could hand her off to Josie, as she had done on both previous days, Laura forestalled her by saying she wanted to spend Amelia's rest time just walking over the estate by herself. If Amelia didn't mind, of course.

After an almost imperceptible hesitation, Amelia said, "Why, no, child, of course I don't mind. But it's due to start raining any minute now, so don't get too far from shelter."

Laura agreed to that and, when Amelia had left the dining room, said to Josie, "I've been itching to try the maze."

Josie smiled quickly, the preoccupation she'd shown during the meal not so obvious now. "I thought you might be. Just remember, there's no shelter in there until you reach the gazebo. Why don't you grab an umbrella from the stand at the end of the hall, just in case?"

"Thanks, I will."

"Okay. See you later."

Laura elected not to take her sketchpad with her, leaving it on a chaise in the conservatory as she passed through on her way outside. The house was very quiet as she left it, and she wondered where everyone was. There hadn't been a sign of any of the family except Amelia and Josie, and no one else had been mentioned.

The rain was still holding off, so Laura carried her umbrella closed, but the air was damp and the temperature cool enough that she felt a bit chilled even in her lightweight jacket. It was going to rain, she was certain; her left arm was aching dully, something it always did when rain was present or on the way, though she had no idea why. Her mother had called her the family weather forecaster, always far more reliable than those paid to do the job, and had ascribed Laura's ability to a grandfather who had also been able to predict the weather from the aches in his bones. Laura didn't really care from whom she had inherited the ability; she just knew it was going to rain, and soon.

She walked quickly along the path to the maze, knowing she'd have only a couple of hours before Amelia would be back downstairs and ready to sit for another sketch; she could no doubt get good and lost in the maze in that length of time.

She encountered no one in the garden, and it was so quiet along the way that she caught herself glancing around a bit uneasily. Not that she was afraid, of course—but it was very quiet. Even the birds seemed subdued. She paused on the hill overlooking the maze and looked down on it for a few moments, not trying to find the key but simply getting the pattern in her mind. Then she continued along the path down the hill to the opening of the maze.

She hadn't expected it to . . . loom as it did. The hedges forming the maze were easily eight feet high and neatly squared off. The graveled path ended at the opening; the roughly three-foot space between the hedges where one walked was grass, so that anyone entering the maze was surrounded by green.

Laura didn't suffer from claustrophobia, and she thought that was a good thing. There was sufficient light despite the overcast day, but . . . The leafy walls rose on either side of her, still and a bit damp, the short grass was soft beneath her loafers, it was eerily quiet—and it would have been all too easy to feel a panicked sense of being trapped.

Shaking off the first tendrils of that, Laura concentrated on using her sense of direction to pick her way through the maze. She encountered a dead end within minutes, amused to see that a section of the wall of green blocking her way had been clipped artistically to provide a subtle but skillful likeness of an indolent poodle, so that it seemed to peer out at her from a bank of greenery. Backtracking, she chose another green alley and this time made progress.

For a while, Laura was completely intent on working her way through the maze, amused at dead ends to find other topiaries—all animals and most of them comically rendered. But as she moved deeper into the maze, her sense of isolation grew sharper, and the tendrils of that earlier panic slithered around her. She caught herself looking up often just to assure herself that the leaden gray sky still remained above her, that she was not, in fact, boxed completely in by the leafy walls.

It grew dimmer as the clouds darkened threateningly, and Laura checked her watch uneasily to find she had been in the maze for more than an hour. And she had no idea if she was even near the center. She paused when she was presented with a choice of paths, her sense of direction confused now, and jumped as if she'd been stung when there was a sudden, eerily silent burst of light almost in her face.

After the first moment of surprise, Laura had to laugh, albeit shakily. Not a *burst* of light, she realized—but light. Cannily hidden within the hedges, evenly spaced lights shone upward, providing illumination without in any way diminishing the mystery of the maze. Obviously, the lights must have been wired to an optical sensor; the darkening of an already overcast day had simply tricked them into their night mode.

The explanation was reasonable, and Laura was momentarily cheered by the lights. But she moved on tentatively, almost wishing she'd left a trail of bread crumbs so that she could find her way back out of this living puzzle; clearly, she was not going to find the center, at least not on this first attempt. And despite Josie's warning that it had taken her nearly a year of trying before she had found the key, Laura had hoped to be luckier. She was usually good with puzzles.

So now what do I do? Swallow my pride and yell, or just keep wandering around out here until Josie comes to find me?

She wandered a little farther and came upon an intersection—with three possible paths. "Damn," she muttered.

"Laura?"

His voice sounded so near that she nearly jumped out of her skin a second time, and for an instant she couldn't reply. Then, clearing her throat, she said, "Daniel?" even though she knew it was him.

"Stay where you are," he called to her. "I'll come to you."

He had been close, because it was only seconds before he appeared around a bend in the right-hand path and approached her. He was wearing dark slacks and a black leather jacket over his open-necked white shirt, his hard face unreadable, and for a moment Laura felt a sudden urge to run, to get away from him. How long had they both been in the maze, moving in silence as he trod familiar paths and she tried to learn her way? Had he known she was here? Had he followed her?

"He's a dangerous man, Laura. He's a very dangerous man."

Was that it? Did she believe Amelia? Or was it simply that this was too eerie and isolated a place in which to encounter a man who unnerved her? She heard a rumble of thunder as he neared, and it seemed to her that it was abruptly hard to breathe.

His pale eyes narrowed slightly as Daniel reached her, but his low voice was mild and matter-of-fact. "I saw your sketchpad in the conservatory and thought you might have come out here."

She nodded hesitantly. "I wanted to try my hand at the maze."

"You're close to the center. Did you know?"

"No. I was more or less lost," she confessed.

"It's a tough maze if you don't know the key." He glanced upward at the brooding clouds, and as another rumble of thunder rolled toward them, said, "The sky's about to open up, I think. The closest shelter is the gazebo. I'll take you to the center." He held out his hand to her.

Laura hesitated, but when she met his steady gaze, she realized that he was as conscious of reaching out to her as she was. And that he had done it very deliberately. There was something infinitely patient in the way he waited for her to take his hand, as if he would have stood there all day if that were necessary.

Still holding her umbrella in one hand, she finally lifted her free hand and placed it in his. She thought she was braced for it, but the shock of his flesh touching hers was so powerful it was as if she had touched a live wire. And her involuntary response was the same as if an actual electrical current had formed its unbreakable connection between them—she couldn't have pulled away from him even to save her own life.

His long fingers closed around hers in a strong but painless grip, and he smiled very slightly. But all he said was, "This way," and guided her to turn onto the left-hand path.

Laura didn't say a word as she walked beside him. The urge to escape him was still very much with her, yet at the same time she felt an odd sense of fatalism, a powerful inner certainty that some things were simply inevitable—and that this meeting was one of them.

I'm losing my mind, she thought with a touch of desperation. *It's all that stuff Faith wrote in her journal about her meeting with Stuart, that's what it is. I've let it all go to my head.*

But she hadn't read Faith's journal excerpts when she had first met Daniel, and yet she had felt this same aching awareness, this sense of familiarity and the unnerved sensation of being nakedly vulnerable to him. So how could she blame Faith and her journal?

Daniel didn't speak either, guiding her along the path and through three more turns without a word. It wasn't until they came abruptly to the heart of the maze that he spoke again. "The jewel at the center of the puzzle," he said.

It was, Laura thought, an apt description. The heart of the maze was an opening at least sixty feet square, landscaped with numerous low-growing shrubs, planters containing late-season flowers, and even a lovely fountain splashing quietly. Stepping stones formed a path that meandered around, stopping here and there at delicate white wrought-iron benches where the reward at the center of the puzzle could be enjoyed.

And the heart of it all was the gazebo, unexpected in its style and mysterious even as it enticed. It was large, at least twenty feet from front to back, a French country structure with a peaked, cedar shake roof, and painted white—which was the end of practicality. On seven sides a half wall rose, with delicate posts providing support from there to the roof, and to each post were loosely tied filmy white curtains like the draperies of an elegant four-poster bed. Through the eighth side, which was open, could be seen delicate, white-painted wrought-iron furniture to match the benches outside.

There were several surprising touches within the surprising structure, such as vases of cut flowers on the two wrought-iron tables, and comfortable white cushions on the two chairs and the chaise longue. There were even a few blue throw pillows to provide both colorful contrast and further comfort.

Soft lighting came from inside the gazebo, obviously wired to the other maze lights, and the result was so inviting that Laura was completely charmed. "You're right," she said. "It is a jewel."

Daniel's fingers tightened briefly around hers, and then he was leading her toward the gazebo. "We're about to get wet," he said.

He didn't release her hand until Laura had climbed the two steps up into the structure. She felt bereft the instant the warmth of his fingers left hers, but tried desperately not to let him see that as she leaned her umbrella against the half wall and began exploring. He remained in the doorway, one foot on the floor of the gazebo and the other on the first step as he leaned back against the support post and watched her. She could feel his gaze, but Laura didn't look at him until she had explored the lovely, comfortable interior. The first drops of rain thudded against the roof as she sat down on the foot of the chaise and met Daniel's intent gaze.

"Who takes care of it?" she asked.

"The gardeners take care of the plants and flowers,

of course. Kerry's responsible for keeping the interior so . . . inviting."

Laura thought of Kerry out here, making a place of comfort for herself that was surrounded by both beauty and isolation, and for a moment she felt like an intruder.

"She won't mind," Daniel said, reading her thoughts or her expression. "Kerry isn't quite as fragile as she seems."

There was nothing unkind in his tone, but as Laura frowned at him, she had the odd feeling he was trying to tell her something. The rain was coming down harder now, yet it was still a peaceful sound in the gazebo. Laura wished she could feel peaceful. "Isn't she?"

Daniel shook his head. "She survived an accident that would have killed most people. It left her scarred, but it also left her stronger."

"What happened?"

"It was a car accident. Kerry was about ten, riding in the backseat while her mother drove. Another car ran a stop sign and hit them broadside. They ended up jammed between the car that had hit them and a big tree. Before rescue people could get to the car, it had begun to burn. They got Kerry out, but not before she was badly burned. Her mother wasn't so lucky."

Laura wanted to ask how Kerry and Peter had come to marry when they'd apparently been so distant with each other, but she was afraid Daniel would take the question as a too personal interest in Peter. Instead she said, "You care about Kerry."

"Is that so surprising? She's my sister-in-law."

Laura hesitated again, then said, "But not the wife of a . . . loved brother."

Daniel didn't seem surprised. "No." He smiled slightly at her reaction. "I've shocked you."

"Not shocked. It was something I felt was true. I just —didn't expect you to admit it," she said honestly.

"Because we're supposed to love our relations unconditionally? Tell me, Laura, do you love everyone in your family?"

The question caught her off guard, and so she answered more honestly than she might otherwise have done. "No. Some of them I do, but—no."

"And you feel guilty about it."

"Sometimes."

"You shouldn't." Daniel's broad shoulders lifted and fell briefly in a shrug. "Remember our discussion at lunch the other day? We don't choose our families, and sometimes they're so different from us that even tolerating them is a difficult thing to do."

"Was it that way between you and Peter?"

Again, Daniel shrugged. "Something like that."

Before she could stop herself, Laura blurted out, "Where were you when he was killed?"

Daniel's face changed slightly, though Laura wasn't sure just how or why. All she knew was that he didn't like her question. But he answered it, his voice deliberate.

"I was out until after midnight. At a charity dinner. With a hundred or so witnesses."

"I'm sorry." Again, she spoke without thinking, aware of nothing but the need to make him forget her question.

"Sorry about what, Laura? That you had to ask where I was? That you thought there was a possibility I might have murdered my brother?"

Refusing to look away from his hard gaze, she said, "Why shouldn't doubt work both ways? You haven't said you believe I didn't kill him."

"Haven't I?"

"You know you haven't."

After a moment he nodded. "Fair enough. All right, then. I don't believe you killed Peter. I even doubt—in the face of my own knowledge of my brother—that you were his mistress."

Instead of the relief she expected to feel, Laura was wary. "Why the change of heart?"

"I don't believe you killed him because I've come to realize it isn't in you to kill. No one who could sketch Kerry and Anne with so much understanding and Amelia with so much bafflement is capable of murder."

"You looked at my sketches?"

He nodded without apology.

Laura felt her cheeks warm as she thought of the sketch of him she had secreted—she hoped—at the back of the sketchpad; he hadn't mentioned it, so she could only hope he hadn't seen it. "I did Kerry from memory," she said.

"And with compassion," he noted. "Which is what makes me doubt that you could have been sleeping with her husband."

She digested that for a few moments, absently listening to the rain beat against the roof of the gazebo and thunder rumble distantly. "*. . . and Amelia with so much bafflement . . .*" What had he meant by that? Had she so totally failed to capture Amelia in her sketches? But before she could nerve herself up to ask him, he distracted her completely from the subject of sketches.

"I, on the other hand, am probably quite capable of murder, given enough provocation," he said matter-of-factly.

Laura stared at him, uncertain.

Daniel smiled and added gently, "But I didn't kill Peter."

"Do you know who did?"

"The mysterious redhead, I assume."

He's lying again. Laura knew it as certainly as she had known it once before, when he had denied knowing why Peter had wanted to buy back the mirror. He could have given her that answer. And whatever he thought of his brother's death, he did not believe some "mysterious red-head" had killed him.

So once again, Laura was left with mixed emotions. She was glad he now seemed convinced she was innocent—both of murder and of being Peter's mistress—but he was not telling all he knew or suspected, and that was deeply disturbing to Laura. Why had he lied? What did Daniel know, and why was he so unwilling to tell her the truth?

"You're frowning," he said, his tone still gentle.

Saying the first thing that came into her mind, Laura responded, "I was just thinking that Amelia will be expecting me back at the house."

"I told Josie I was coming out here to look for you," Daniel said. "I'm sure she'll tell Amelia where we are."

And that's what you want, isn't it, Daniel? You want Amelia to know you're out here with me. That we're alone together. But why? Why? Am I nothing more than a pawn to you, a chess piece to be maneuvered in your game with Amelia?

Laura looked at his harsh face and enigmatic eyes and wondered how on earth it was possible to feel so much familiarity about a man and yet have so little knowledge of him. She *knew* him—how he stood and walked, how he held a glass, the way he would tilt his head slightly in faint mockery. She knew the rhythm of his voice, the feeling of his presence even if he came up behind her, and she thought she would have recognized the touch of his hand even in the dark. She knew when he lied to her.

Yet she didn't know him at all. She had no idea how the mind of Daniel Kilbourne worked. She didn't know if he was quick or slow to trust, if he was easily amused, if he knew or even cared that his brother had been the favorite son. She didn't know the books he read, the music he preferred, the kind of women he favored. She didn't know if he was a good man, or if he hid his negative characteristics beneath the surface as easily as Peter had hidden his beneath charm. She didn't even know if he liked the rain.

The strange thing was, there was a sense of frustration and bewilderment far back in Laura's awareness, a vague but nagging feeling that she *should* know all those things about him. She didn't understand it, couldn't explain it— but that didn't change the feelings.

"Laura?"

She blinked, realizing she'd been staring at him for several moments too long. "Oh . . . sorry," she murmured. "I was miles away."

"You were thinking about me," he said.

After an instant of shock, Laura managed to say—albeit a bit unsteadily—"Don't flatter yourself."

"I'm not. You were thinking about me." His voice was calm.

She knew another denial would ring hollow, but the uneasiness Laura felt about him and her response to him wouldn't allow her to admit the truth. So, with a panicked sense of burning at least one of her bridges, she said lightly, "Oh, right—I guess I was. Amelia warned me about you, and I was just trying to decide if I believed her."

Daniel's eyes narrowed. Softly he said, "She warned you about me. What did she say?"

"She said you were a dangerous man. Are you?" She tried to sound merely curious, as one seeking the answer to an idle and unimportant question.

"Only to my enemies." His answer was, just faintly, preoccupied, and his gaze seemed to be turned inward for a moment or two. But then he was looking at Laura again, seeing her, and there was a tiny frown between his brows. "Why did Amelia feel the need to warn you?" he wondered.

"I couldn't say." Laura paused, then added deliberately, "Aren't you going to return the favor and warn me about her? What's going on with you two, anyway?"

Daniel replied to the first question rather than the last. "Why would I want to warn you about Amelia?" But there was something thoughtful, even speculative, in his tone.

It made Laura feel distinctly uneasy, and she cast about in her mind for something outrageous to get them off the subject. "Oh, I don't know. According to gossip, she killed her husband—your grandfather. Is that true?"

"I've always believed it was," he replied mildly.

Laura sat up a bit straighter and stared at him. "You're kidding."

"No." He shrugged. "There were no witnesses to the . . . accident. And though something had obviously cracked his skull open, nothing was found around the pool with blood on it. According to my father—who told me about it, since it happened before I was born—the police always suspected Amelia. So did my father."

Clearing her throat, Laura said, "You're just saying that because I dared you to warn me about her . . . aren't you?"

"Am I?" Daniel's smile was hardly there, and his eyes were as enigmatic as they had ever been. "There was a curious thing about my father's death as well. He was supposedly shot by friends in a hunting accident. But those *friends* were actually friends of Amelia's."

"You're not suggesting—"

"I'm not suggesting anything. I'm merely mentioning an odd circumstance of my father's death."

Laura felt a sudden chill and absently drew her jacket more closely around her. He wasn't serious—was he? She got no sense of him lying, but surely he didn't believe his grandmother had killed her husband and then somehow arranged the death of her son?

"You're just trying to scare me," she murmured finally.

After a moment, in a much gentler tone, Daniel said, "If I did that, I'm sorry. You have nothing to fear from Amelia, Laura. You aren't at all likely to . . . get in her way."

"I can't imagine why, but that didn't reassure me," she told him, all too aware that it was easier for her to believe Daniel's "warning" than it had been for her to believe Amelia's. Then a sudden thought occurred, and she added, "Peter. You don't think she—"

Daniel was shaking his head. "She's eighty, and physically frail. There's no way she could have killed Peter."

"Does she have an alibi?"

"She was on the phone with a friend on the West Coast until almost midnight, according to her—and verified by the phone company *and* the friend."

"You sound almost disappointed," she noted.

"Well, it would have been simpler if she'd done it. One killer is all any family needs—" Daniel broke off and stared at Laura, obviously surprised. Somewhat grimly he said, "You've a beguiling way about you, Laura."

She wasn't listening. "You think someone in the family killed Peter?"

"I think," he replied, glancing at his watch, "that Amelia is probably waiting for you and that it isn't going to quit raining anytime soon. So if you'll grab that umbrella, we'll head back despite the rain."

Almost automatically she got up from the chaise and got the umbrella. "You do think it was someone in the family. Who? Why?"

"Whatever I may suspect," he said, "I haven't any proof." He took the umbrella from her and held it pointed outside the gazebo to open it, then took her hand rather than ask her to give it.

Laura looked down at their hands as she joined him

under the umbrella, unnerved by the way her fingers compulsively twined with his. That and the physical jolt that was becoming a familiar sensation distracted her for several minutes, and it wasn't until they had left the heart of the maze for the narrow leafy corridors of the puzzle that she spoke again.

"I don't suppose you've confided your suspicions to the police?"

"No."

She looked up at his face, shadowy under the umbrella, and wished she knew whether or not to believe him about any of this. They were walking so close together that she was overwhelmingly aware of him, and that kept clouding her thoughts. His hand was warm and hard, and she had to fight a ridiculous urge to lift it and rub her cheek against it.

His fingers tightened a little as though he had read her mind again, but all Daniel said was, "Leave it alone, Laura. Do what you came here to do. Paint Amelia's portrait. Let the police investigate the murder."

"That's easy for you to say. You haven't been a suspect."

"I've been a suspect in your eyes."

She hadn't meant to, but Laura heard herself say, "No. Not really."

His fingers tightened again. "Definitely a beguiling way about you."

"Then maybe I should take advantage of it. Tell me about the mirror, Daniel." This time she didn't look up at him.

"I have nothing to say about it." His response was so prompt that it seemed obvious he had expected the request sooner or later.

"Then tell me why you never asked to see it."

He was silent for several steps. "Lack of curiosity, I suppose."

"Well, you know, that's a funny thing. You really should have been curious. I mean, a stranger comes to you and tells you that hours before his death, your brother tried to buy back a mirror she'd bought from your family's estate sale earlier that day. That he offered her an incredible price for the mirror. And you never even ask to see it."

"So?"

"So it isn't . . . natural. You should have been curious. Why weren't you curious, Daniel?"

"I had just buried my brother. I didn't care about mirrors." There was a touch of impatience in his voice now. "Besides that, I'd learned all I needed to from the inventory of the sale. The mirror was not a Kilbourne family heirloom and was therefore of no interest to me."

You just lied again, Daniel. She wanted to pursue the matter, but it was clear that he had no intention of telling her what he knew about the mirror—for the moment, at least. Besides, there was so much in her head now that she could barely think straight.

She fell silent, walking beside him with her hand in his and taking only vague notice of the turns he made. Which is why she was surprised when they emerged from the maze in remarkably short order.

Sighing, she said, "I should probably ask for the key. But I'm not going to."

"Why do I get the feeling you're a very stubborn woman?"

"Why do I get the feeling that was a rhetorical question?" She glanced up, saw him smile, and wished it didn't make her feel so absurdly pleased.

The rain was light but steady, tapping against the umbrella rhythmically as they followed the graveled path back up to the house. When they neared the veranda and passed over the flat patch of ground that had once housed the pool, she couldn't help saying, "You don't really think she killed your grandfather, do you?"

After a moment he replied, "No, of course not."

And he was lying.

Wishing she hadn't asked the question, Laura walked beside him up onto the veranda and then into the conservatory. He released her hand only then and occupied himself in shaking out the umbrella and leaving it by the door.

"Amelia's probably in her parlor," he said.

"Yes, I imagine so." She got her sketchpad off the chaise where she had left it, holding it against her like a shield. "Thanks for the rescue," she added lightly.

"My pleasure." He looked at her as though he wanted to say something else, but finally shook his head a little and headed toward the doorway to the house.

Alone, Laura hesitated a moment before going in search of Amelia. She opened her sketchpad and flipped through the pages rapidly, finding everything as it should be. Except for one thing.

The secret sketch of Daniel was gone, torn neatly from the pad.

And Laura didn't know which possibility unnerved her more. That Daniel had taken it—or that someone else had.

Chapter 8

*A*melia didn't mention Laura's having been with Daniel until later in the afternoon, when Laura was just finishing up a sketch of Amelia against the background of the elegant marble fireplace in the front parlor.

"Did you enjoy the maze, child?"

Laura, who had been trying very hard without much success to not think of her subject as a possible murderess, answered more or less at random. "Very much. And the center's absolutely beautiful."

"You found your way there so quickly?"

"Well, no. Actually, I was lost."

"Then Daniel took you to the center?" Though her voice was pleasant, something in the way she asked the question made her displeasure evident.

"It was about to start raining," Laura said. "The gazebo was the closest shelter." Aware that she sounded a bit defensive, she added hastily, "I'm going to have to figure out the key to the maze; even though I enjoyed wandering through it, going directly to the center certainly has its own rewards. It's a wonderful maze, Amelia."

"Yes, David loved it," Amelia said. "I haven't been out there in years, I'm afraid."

The implication was clear—that the old lady couldn't bear to spend time in a place her dead husband had loved so much. Laura looked at Amelia over the top of the sketchpad, studying that aged but still elegant face, those enigmatic dark eyes and the faint, sad smile, and she tried to imagine what Amelia must have been like forty years before. Could she have had something of Anne's wired anger and discontent? Could there have been rage enough in her then to drive her to hit her husband with something heavy enough to kill him?

And could she, afterward, mourn him so devotedly for decades?

Laura closed her sketchpad and, abruptly, before she lost her nerve, asked, "Amelia, why did you warn me about Daniel?"

"Because I'm concerned about you, child." The reply was prompt, and Amelia did look suddenly anxious. "You're a beautiful young woman, and Daniel isn't immune to that. But he's a hard man, Laura. He . . . uses people. I don't want him to use you."

It sounded reasonable enough on the face of it—an elderly lady's concern for the vulnerable heart of a young friend. But Laura didn't quite believe it. Amelia's first warning had been too intense, her demeanor too nervous, almost frightened, and that had suggested more a fear for Laura's physical well-being than concern over her love life. Yet now the old lady claimed merely to be worried that her grandson might seduce, and presumably abandon, Laura. It didn't ring true. It was almost as if Amelia had thought about it in the days since and had decided—for whatever reason—that a less agitated and more specific warning might carry more weight.

After a moment, Laura said mildly, "Thank you for your concern, Amelia, but I'm twenty-eight, not eighteen. And I'm no innocent."

If anything, Amelia looked even more anxious. "I'm sure you think so, child, but I doubt very much if you've encountered a man like Daniel before. He is dangerous, in his way. He'll stop at nothing to get what he wants, and he doesn't care who he hurts. Just . . . be careful, that's all I'm saying. Don't believe everything he tells you." Her face changed slightly, and she added softly, "Peter charmed his way through life. Daniel is far more ruthless. He doesn't let anyone get in his way."

"You aren't at all likely to . . . get in her way," Daniel had said.

It didn't surprise Laura that the words were so similar, because she was certain both Amelia and Daniel wanted something, that they were quietly and subtly battling each other for what they wanted, and that each of them was already, in some way, using Laura against the other.

What she couldn't figure out *because* it was all so subtle was exactly what was going on and how she, a virtual stranger, could be involved. How could she be used—as a weapon or a pawn—when she had no stake in their battle?

Or did she?

Finally, Laura said, "I'll be careful, Amelia." Then she smiled. "But I think you're exaggerating both my appeal and Daniel's interest—to say nothing of my own. I'm here to paint your portrait, that's all."

Amelia nodded, though she was patently unconvinced.

Laura was just about to say that she should probably be on her way home when the storm that had been lurking about all afternoon chose that moment to attack. And it definitely sounded like an attack. Thunder boomed so strongly that the walls and windows of the big house vibrated audibly, wind-driven rain pelted the windows, and a brilliant flash of lightning lit up the room.

Frowning, Amelia said, "Laura, you can't drive home in this mess. It wouldn't be at all safe to be on the roads now. Why don't you just stay the night? We have a room all ready for you."

"Thank you, Amelia, but surely it'll slack off in a little while—"

Another rolling boom of thunder kept Amelia from answering for a moment, but then she said, "According to the forecast, we'll have a series of storms all evening. Stay, Laura, please. For my peace of mind if nothing else."

Laura really didn't like to drive in the rain, let alone a storm. Besides which, refusing Amelia's courteous—and practical—invitation would have been rude in the extreme, and although Laura found the house too dark and stifling to be very comfortable, she didn't want to make that fact obvious to Amelia.

Nodding, she said, "Thank you, Amelia, it's very kind of you."

"Oh, nonsense, child. I've wanted you to stay here from the beginning, as well you know." Amelia got to her feet, a bit more briskly than usual and seemingly not in the least stiff from sitting so long. "Now, why don't I show you to your room? You can rest awhile if you like. We have dinner at six."

As Laura rose, she glanced down at her slacks, knit shirt, and casual linen blazer, and thought that while she looked okay for supper, she was undoubtedly underdressed for dinner at the Kilbourne house. But before she could comment, Amelia was going on matter-of-factly.

"You and Kerry should wear the same size, I think, so we should be able to find you something to sleep in. As for dinner, I ask that everyone dress for that meal as they would a meal out at a nice restaurant; I'm sure Kerry can find you a pretty dress or skirt."

Laura felt more than a little disturbed by the idea of sharing clothing with Peter's widow, but told herself firmly not to be absurd. As long as Kerry didn't mind, of course.

"She won't mind?" she asked Amelia.

"Not at all, she's a very sweet girl. I'll see her after I take you to your room."

Laura found herself following meekly after Amelia. Ten minutes later she was standing alone in the largest of four guest suites on the second floor of the main section of the house, looking around her with an odd feeling of unreality. The suite consisted of a bedroom, sitting room, and bathroom, all sized generously. There was a private phone line for the convenience of guests, Amelia had said, and the television in the sitting room was, of course, hooked up to cable.

The suite was the prettiest set of rooms Laura had seen in the house, and not nearly as dark as most of the other rooms seemed to be. The wallpaper was a bit ornate, and the four-poster bed had a canopy with elaborate flowing draperies, but the filmy curtains at the big windows let in plenty of light, the furniture was delicate rather than heavy, and there was a working fireplace in the sitting room.

"I shouldn't have luggage," Laura muttered to herself. "I should have *trunks*." She had never in her life been in a private home with this kind of elegant, ostentatious accommodations for guests. In fact, she hadn't realized that such places still existed.

Then again, how many private homes had grounds with extensive gardens and a four-acre maze?

Shaking her head a little, Laura found herself drawn across the sitting room to a mirror hanging above a side table. As always. And as always, when she reached it she stood looking at the reflection of the room behind her as it appeared over her right shoulder. But whatever she was looking for wasn't there, and the room seemed oddly empty.

She turned away finally and glanced at her watch, see-ing that it was four-thirty. After a moment's thought, she used the private phone line to call Cassidy and leave a message on her answering machine.

"Hi, Cass, it's me. Guess where I'm sleeping tonight?"

IT WAS FIVE when there was a soft knock at the sitting room door, and Laura answered it to find Kerry. The younger woman, who was wearing a dark terrycloth robe and smelled of soap, had an armful of clothing and smiled tentatively in greeting.

"Hello, Laura."

"Hi, Kerry." Laura stepped back in invitation, and as Kerry came into the sitting room, added, "Look, I hope you don't mind, but Amelia—"

"Of course I don't mind." Kerry placed the clothing over the back of a chair and turned to smile less hesitantly. "I imagine Amelia didn't give you much choice, any-way—about wearing some of my clothes, I mean. She can be a bit . . . overpowering."

"You can say that again."

"She likes things done a certain way here, as I'm sure you've noticed. Life is more . . . peaceful . . . when the rest of us go along."

Laura looked at Kerry's plain, scarred face with its clear, gentle hazel eyes, and wished suddenly that she could spend more time with this woman. She had a feeling that of all the women in this house, Kerry would turn out to be the most complex. And the most interesting.

"We meet downstairs in the front parlor at six," she told Laura helpfully. "Dinner is actually at six-thirty. Amelia likes to hear what everyone's done during the day before we sit down to eat. And she likes us to dress well—whether elegant clothes suit us or not."

"I see. Thank you," Laura said, wondering absently what kind of clothing Kerry would prefer, given a choice.

"I picked out a few things for you to choose from," Kerry went on with a glance at the clothing she'd put down. "Long skirts, I thought, to better match your shoes. Mine would be two sizes too large."

Laura couldn't help looking down to compare, and thought that the other woman would wear a size or two larger than her own size six. "That was very thoughtful," she said gratefully. "It had just occurred to me that loafers aren't too dressy."

Kerry smiled. "These days, when women are wearing clunky boots with thin skirts, I don't think it would matter very much. But these should do fine. And don't be self-conscious; Amelia's been trying to dress me properly for years now, and I can't seem to satisfy her. I'm her project."

There was nothing of self-consciousness in Kerry's soft voice; if anything, she seemed amused by her failure to live up to Amelia's standards. Once again, Laura thought that she'd really like to get to know this woman. *But, of course, I had to be suspected of her husband's murder. And of being his latest mistress.*

"I imagine most people fall short of Amelia's expectations," Laura said a bit wryly.

"Sooner or later," Kerry agreed, again with that hint of amusement. "Now I'd better go finish getting ready, and leave you to. If you need anything else, please don't hesitate to ask, Laura. My room is in the west wing—the first room on the right."

"Thanks, Kerry."

"Don't mention it."

When she was alone again in the sitting room, Laura went through the things Kerry had left for her. A very pretty long nightgown and matching robe; a simple black ankle-length dress; a dark green skirt and blouse; and a royal blue dress. Everything was in excellent taste—for

Laura. She saw immediately that the outfits had been chosen with care and with her coloring in mind, and she knew the styles would suit her beautifully.

Which was interesting, Laura thought. Because Kerry had picked from her own closet clothing that would look wonderful on Laura and yet was clearly wrong for Kerry's angular body and washed-out coloring. In other words, she had displayed excellent taste in dressing another woman in her own clothes.

Laura had a hunch that Kerry's seeming inability to dress "properly" enough to suit Amelia was less a matter of ineptness and more a matter of gentle rebellion. No woman, Laura thought, who moved with Kerry's sensuous grace could fail to *know* how to wear clothing well, even if she chose not to. It was another sign of an interesting and complex personality.

Thinking about that, Laura went to take a quick shower, ruefully amused to find in the bathroom a basket of toiletries that included everything from a new toothbrush wrapped in plastic and a selection of shampoos and skin care lotions to a set of very nice combs and brushes. Either the Kilbournes—meaning Amelia—believed in being prepared for the unprepared guest, or else Amelia had fully expected Laura to spend a night here sooner or later.

Laura decided not to think about that too much. She showered and then got dressed, choosing the black dress because her loafers were black and also because she knew black was one of her best colors; the extra measure of confidence, she figured, couldn't hurt.

She freed her long hair from its braid and brushed it out. There was so much of it—enough for three people, her hairdresser claimed—that she seldom left it loose, but she did now because it seemed to suit the simple, almost Oriental style of the dress. She had only the makeup in her purse, which meant foundation and lipstick, but since that was all she normally wore, it was enough.

It was ten minutes to six when Laura gathered her nerve and left her suite to go downstairs. The quiet struck her immediately, especially since she'd had the TV in her sitting room on just for the company. Was it another of Amelia's ideas of how things should be done that it was always so quiet in the house?

She went down the broad staircase and crossed the foyer to the front parlor, which was across from the library. She expected at least several family members to be already in the room, but there was only one.

Daniel.

He was standing at the marble fireplace, where a cheerful gas-log fire crackled in the hearth and sought to both warm the slightly chilly room and provide a comforting contrast to the storm rumbling outside. He didn't realize she was there immediately, and in the moment or so before he did, Laura took advantage of the rare opportunity to study him without his awareness.

The dark suit he wore was sober, the tie tasteful and conservative, yet neither could diminish or disguise the latent power of his body; Daniel Kilbourne could never be unobtrusive. He would always be noticed. Particularly, she thought, by women. At least, that was the reason she offered to herself for this growing hunger inside her every time she saw him.

That had to be the reason.

He gazed down into the fire, the flickering light throwing an occasional shadow to make his face appear masklike. Yet he was not, now, as enigmatic as he had always seemed to Laura. For the first time, she saw a hint of strain around his mouth, and the frown drawing his brows together looked very much like worry. She thought, looking at him, that he was beginning to feel the burdens he carried.

He looked up then, seeing her, and just as in the maze, Laura felt that it was suddenly difficult to breathe. She couldn't look away from him, and her heart was thudding against her ribs, and she was so powerfully drawn to him that she felt an almost physical tugging at some deep part of her. She could have sworn there was a flashing response in his pale eyes, a heat as vivid and real as the fire crackling beside him. She could have sworn he—almost—reached out to her.

But then he moved his head slightly, and it was gone. It was all gone.

"Good evening, Laura." He was polite, his voice pleasant and detached.

I've got to stop imagining this! I've got to . . . "Good evening." Her voice was calm, she thought, so at least she wasn't making a total fool of herself.

"The others should be down shortly. Would you like a drink?" He nodded toward the wet bar in the corner by the door.

"No, thank you." She moved farther into the room, circling around the grouping of sofas, chair, and coffee table before the fireplace to take up a position behind one of the sofas and near the windows. She had half-consciously put most of the room in front of her, with her back to the wall, and it was only as she did so that she realized just how wary and unsettled she felt.

Daniel didn't appear to notice or, if he did, chose not to comment.

"You were wise to decide to stay the night," he said, as thunder crashed and rolled and the sounds of the wind outside became audible.

Laura wondered if Amelia had told him, or if he had simply assumed when she appeared dressed for dinner, but didn't ask. "I hate being out in a storm," she said. "Driving in one, I mean."

"Most people do." He continued to look at her with detachment.

Laura felt a flicker of irritation, wondering if he had

any intention of moving beyond banal small talk; somehow she didn't think so. Looking at him now, she could hardly believe he had, only hours earlier, told her that he believed his grandmother had murdered his grandfather.

Oh, hell, maybe I imagined that too . . .

"Hey, thought I'd be the last one down. Where is everybody?" Alex strolled into the room, his dark suit sober and formal, and his necktie spotted with bright green frogs in various stages of leaping. He nodded at Laura, seemingly unsurprised to find her still here.

Rather than answering the question, Daniel said, "Care to be bartender?"

"Sure. What'll you have?"

"Scotch."

Alex nodded. "Laura?"

"Nothing, thank you."

Alex went to the wet bar and fixed drinks for himself and Daniel. He had just taken his glass to Daniel and returned to the bar when Josie and Kerry came in. "Ladies?" he asked, indicating his role with a sweeping gesture.

Josie shook her head and Kerry asked for a small whiskey. When she came in a moment later, Anne requested Scotch.

"Is your mother coming down?" Alex asked Daniel.

"I believe so. She seems . . . better today."

Josie came to sit on the sofa nearest Laura, joined a moment later by Kerry, while Anne slouched down on the sofa across from them. Anne was dressed more casually than the other women, in a skimpy silk T-shirt and long print skirt—and a pair of the clunky ankle boots Kerry had earlier commented on. Josie was in very dark green, a beautiful long dress with a deep V neckline, and wore her auburn hair piled on her head with casual elegance.

Kerry wore a long black satin skirt and dark blue silk blouse, an outfit that would have looked fine except for the peculiar sweater vest she had chosen to wear over the blouse.

"I thought that dress would suit you," she remarked softly as she sat down and looked back over her shoulder at Laura.

Unable to return the compliment, Laura merely said, "Thanks again, Kerry."

"So, what did you think of the maze?" Josie asked, half turning to look up at Laura with a smile.

"I think it's diabolical." Laura very carefully didn't look toward Daniel, but she knew he was listening. "But fascinating. And the center is just lovely." She looked at Kerry. "The gazebo especially."

Obviously pleased, Kerry said, "I change the interior in the spring and late fall, so it's almost time. Darker, warmer colors for winter."

With a sigh, Josie said, "I'd spend hours every day out there if I could. Even after you learn the key, it's a nice, brisk walk to the center, and then you just want to stay there."

"It's my favorite place in the world," Kerry said.

"It's a bunch of bushes," Anne said petulantly, swirling the ice around and around in her glass. "We ought to use the space for a tennis court."

Looking across at the dark woman, Laura couldn't help wondering if Anne was always so fractious, or if Peter's murder and its aftermath had affected her more than the others. She certainly seemed wired, her entire thin body tense and her movements jerky, and her voice was so sharp that it cut off even an attempt by the others to keep the conversation going.

Madeline walked into the silence. Wearing a simple black dress of a medium length, her hair and makeup once more flawless, she smiled vaguely at the assembled group. "How nice. Amelia isn't down yet?" Her eyes were clearer than they had been the day before, so her manner ap-

peared to be more normal and less influenced by sedatives—but Laura had to wonder if the positioning of the
comment and question implied what it seemed to.

It was Alex who chose to answer her, his tone light and
somewhat careless. "I'm sure she will be now that the
audience is here. Can I get you something, Madeline?"

"No, dear, the doctor says not," she told him as she
went to sit on the opposite end of Anne's sofa. "But thank
you." Then, in the same sweet tone, she added, "You
really shouldn't say such things about Amelia, Alex. She
wouldn't like it."

"It's all right, Madeline. Amelia and I understand each
other."

Amelia came into the room, elegant and regal in her
usual black, leaning only slightly on her silver-headed
cane. "Do we, Alex? Have you been insulting me?"

With a wounded expression, he said, "Never. I'm always admiring, Amelia. Always. Sherry?"

"Yes, thank you." She went to the chair in the grouping around the fireplace and sat down, smiling pleasantly at
the others. "You all look very nice," she said in satisfaction, and although it was obvious she more or less ignored
Anne's outfit, she did add, "Kerry, dear, not the vest."

"Sorry, Amelia," Kerry said meekly.

Alex brought Amelia her drink, and was just turning
back to the bar when the doorbell rang. "Who'd be out
on a night like this?" he muttered. "Should I get it,
Amelia, or ignore it?"

Laura found the question a bit odd, but no one else
seemed to. Amelia was frowning just a bit, and she seemed
more resigned than gracious when she said, "They got past
the gatehouse, so I don't see that we have a choice. See
who it is, Alex."

He went promptly, and the others waited in silence.
They heard the low sounds of voices, both male, and a few
moments later Alex came back into the parlor with an

expression that was both wry and somewhat guarded. As another man came into the room behind him, Alex said to the room at large, "Not a social call, I'm afraid."

The newcomer was tall, broad-shouldered though not heavily built, and his black hair glistened wetly from the rain. He was a strikingly handsome man, with hawklike features and penetrating gray eyes. He had obviously discarded a raincoat, since his very nice suit jacket was dry, and he didn't seem at all disturbed to walk into a room filled with numerous Kilbournes.

"Hello, Brent," Daniel said.

"Daniel. Ladies." His gaze fell on Laura, and he added, "Hello again, Miss Sutherland. I don't know if you remember me, but—"

"I remember you very well, Lieutenant." How could she forget? Laura wondered. She had spoken briefly to this man while still trying to scrub ink off her fingers from the fingerprinting the Monday after Peter's murder. Brent Landry, a homicide lieutenant, had asked her only a few questions, and those politely, but he hadn't expressed much belief in Laura's innocence.

Amelia, who had her back to the door and, so, to the guest, and who made no effort to turn, said sharply, "I detest this modern habit of calling on people at the dinner hour to be certain of finding them at home."

No one seemed surprised by the old lady's temper. Laura, watching curiously, saw Brent Landry lift his eyebrows at Daniel questioningly. With a slight gesture indicating his own position, Daniel gave way for the other man, joining Laura behind the sofa nearest the windows, and Landry went to stand at the fireplace, where he could see everyone in the room—and where Amelia did not have to turn to see him.

"Well?" she demanded, frowning at him.

"I'm sorry for the hour, Miss Amelia," he said gravely. "But policemen do sometimes have to be rude."

"Your grandmother would turn in her grave. She taught you better. How's your mother?"

"She's fine, Miss Amelia. And, as Alex said, this isn't a social call."

From that brief exchange, Laura gathered several things. That Brent Landry was evidently what Amelia would consider her social equal rather than a mere policeman, that he knew the family rather well, and that he had, gently but firmly, resisted Amelia's obvious attempt to reduce him to the status of boyhood. He was not going to hand over command of this situation to the old lady no matter how well she had known his grandmother.

His steel seemed to impress Amelia, or at least win her grudging respect, because her voice was milder when she said, "Very well, then. If this is official, let's have it. What is it you want of us?"

"I have a few questions, Miss Amelia, that's all. I thought it would be better if I came out here and asked them. Quieter."

"About Peter's death, I assume?"

Madeline made a little sound, an intake of breath that was audible only because the room was so quiet in that moment, and her large blue eyes fixed on Landry with painful intensity. "Do you know who—?"

Landry hesitated almost imperceptibly, then said gently, "No, not yet. I just have a few questions."

"Then ask them," Amelia ordered impatiently. "Though God knows you people have asked us enough questions already. But I'd like an answer to a question or two of my own, if you don't mind."

Without committing himself, he merely raised his eyebrows interrogatively.

"Why, suddenly, are you involved in this, Brent? We've had policemen here since Peter was killed, but this is the first we've seen of you."

"I was given the investigation a few days ago," Landry explained readily. "You'd have to ask my superiors why."

Laura glanced at Amelia in that moment, and when she saw those thin lips move ever so slightly in a Mona Lisa smile, she wondered suddenly if Amelia's friendship with the commissioner had anything to do with Landry's involvement. Had Amelia decided that a friend of the family would be better in the investigation? Did she expect to be able to control, or at least influence, Landry, in the event he focused his suspicions on any of the family?

And if she had arranged Landry's involvement, was it because she fully expected that someone in the family would fall under suspicion?

Nodding a response to his explanation, Amelia said, "All right, then. If you're in charge, why aren't you out searching for Peter's killer?"

"I am, Miss Amelia, I promise you. And in that search, certain . . . evidence has come to light. You do want me to be thorough, of course?"

"Yes." But her eyes were narrowed now, and her lips tight.

"Very well." His gaze tracked around the room, touching each person fleetingly, and he spoke with measured calm. "In the motel room where Peter was killed, we found several strands of red hair, one of them caught in his fingers. This seemed to be further evidence that the redheaded woman the motel manager saw Peter arrive with might have been his killer."

"So far," Daniel said, "this is not news."

Landry shook his head slightly, his sharp eyes still scanning the people in the room. He was good at holding his audience. Very good. And even the storm seemed to wait for him, to quieten, so that his voice was the only sound in the room. "No, it isn't. But the lab analysis was. It seems the hairs came from a wig."

Laura's first reaction was sheer relief, and the fleeting glance from Landry seemed to confirm her own thought: Why would a redhead wear a red wig? No good reason, unless her own hair was in some way damaged—and Laura's, very obviously, was not. She couldn't even remotely be a suspect now—could she?

But hard on the heels of that relief other questions tumbled. If the woman the motel manager had seen with Peter had been wearing a red wig, then the field had widened rather than narrowed. And why had the woman worn a wig? As a disguise, to hide her natural hair? Because Peter had wanted to have sex with a redhead?

Alex, who had moved to lounge negligently against the back of the sofa between Madeline and Anne, said quietly, "All right, you've got our attention. But we haven't heard any questions yet."

"You will." But Landry wasn't about to allow himself to be rushed. He continued to speak in a calm, methodical way. "The hairs came from a very expensive wig. Not many of them made in that particular shade of red, and even fewer sold here in Atlanta. It took some time, but we managed to trace those wigs to the buyers. There were three. Two have been eliminated as possible suspects in Peter's murder."

"And the third?" Daniel asked.

Landry allowed the tension to build for a beat or two, then said, "The third wig was sold, just a month ago, to Anne Ralston."

But she's his cousin, was Laura's first thought. But as she stared at Anne's white face and the dark, darting eyes, she realized that the older woman definitely knew something—and that she was terrified.

"What—what would I want with a wig?" she demanded tensely, staring down at her glass now rather than at the policeman.

"You bought it, Anne. The store owner identified you from a photo."

Anne tried a laugh that didn't come off. "Okay, so I bought a wig. So what?"

Alex, frowning, said slowly, "As one of this family's attorneys, I'd have to advise Anne that she has no obligation to answer your questions. In fact, I'd have to urge her not to say anything else. I haven't heard the Miranda warning."

"Anne isn't under arrest," Landry said. "I'm merely asking her a few questions to help me in my investigation."

"Be that as it may, you know better, Brent."

Landry looked at the lawyer, then turned his gaze to Amelia. Calmly he said, "The sooner we clear this up, the sooner I can . . . move on to the next piece of evidence."

Amelia was staring at Anne. "Do you know anything about this, Anne? Do you?"

"Amelia," Alex warned.

"We'll hear this now," she snapped, her dark eyes fierce. "Right now. Anne, did you kill Peter?"

"No!" Anne gasped. "Oh God, Amelia, I *swear* I didn't!"

"Where were you the night Peter was killed, Anne?" Landry asked her, his voice subtly harder now, more commanding.

She sat hunched and tense, both her hands wrapped around her glass and her eyes darting around the room, and she made Laura think of a wild animal in a cage, desperate to escape.

"I was out," she whispered. "I already told the police—I was out. I went to a party. I *told* them—"

"The party started at nine," Landry said. "Nobody remembers seeing you until around midnight."

Peter was killed around midnight, Laura remembered.

Anne gulped air, tears beginning to trickle down her ashen cheeks, and she wailed, "I didn't kill him! I didn't!"

"But you were with him that night, weren't you?" Landry insisted. "It was you in his car, you the motel manager spotted. I showed him your photo, Anne. What do you suppose he said?"

She looked up at him finally, stricken, guilt written so clearly on her face that it might as well have been in indelible ink. Her voice shaking, hardly more than a whisper, she said, "I was with him. All right, I was—was with him. But *I didn't kill him!*"

Laura drew a breath, her gaze going immediately to Kerry. But Peter's widow was utterly calm, showing no reaction as she looked across the coffee table at Anne. And it was in that moment that Laura suddenly felt like an intruder. She shouldn't be here, shouldn't be listening to this—

There was some thought in her mind of just slipping out of the room, of leaving this family to their pain, but before she could move, she felt Daniel's hand lock around her wrist. She started in surprise and looked at him quickly, only to find him gazing at Anne with as little expression as Kerry showed. No one else would have noticed him holding her wrist, since the back of the sofa hid it, and Laura didn't want to draw attention by struggling with him.

At least, that's what she told herself. What she knew was that his grip, though painless, was as unbreakable as if it had been made of iron.

Amelia's voice fell like chunks of ice into the sudden silence. "Do you mean to tell me that you were having sex with your cousin? Your married cousin?"

A hectic flush of sheer humiliation brightly colored Anne's pale cheeks, and she sent Amelia a look that was part resentment and part shame. "I didn't rape him, for

God's sake! I didn't even seduce him. Why can't you blame *him* for it, Amelia? He made the first move, saying forbidden fruit tasted sweeter. Why can't you—"

"Peter is dead, Anne," Amelia reminded her, still icy. "Whatever sins he may have committed appear to have caught up with him."

Landry spoke then, his tone as dispassionate as hers was disgusted. "How long had the affair been going on, Anne?"

"It wasn't an *affair*." She was eager now as she looked up at him, anxious to deny the importance of her being with Peter that night. "It was only the second time, I swear it was. And he was alive when I left the motel at eleven-thirty. He'd just taken a shower and—and the cab driver must have seen him, because he went to the door when I left and he was only wearing a towel—"

Breaking into the breathless account, Landry asked, "Did you call for the cab?"

She nodded. "I don't remember which company, but it was the first one listed in the Yellow Pages. But the driver must have seen Peter, must have seen him standing there alive when I left—"

"All right, Anne. I'll check out your story." From his voice, it was impossible to tell whether or not Landry believed her. He glanced at the silent tableau around him, then added politely, "In the meantime, I think I've delayed your dinner long enough. I'll see myself out."

As he walked past Alex, the lawyer said dryly, "Come again sometime when you have another little bomb to drop on us."

Landry's only response to that was to say "Good evening" to the room at large and then walk out of it. Nobody moved or spoke until they all heard the front door open and close a moment or so later. And the first to speak was, oddly enough, Madeline.

"Well," she said, "that was certainly . . . unpleasant." She was not looking at Anne.

"I call it nauseating," Amelia said roundly, her gaze practically skewering Anne to the sofa. "How you could do such a thing—"

Anne squirmed visibly, obviously without an answer that would have satisfied her grandmother.

"I've got to know," Alex drawled. "Why the wig?"

"Why not?" Anne demanded belligerently. "It was a good disguise and—and it was exciting. And Peter likes—liked—redheads."

"Dear God," Josie murmured not quite under her breath.

Scrambling to her feet, Anne said, "You're all staring at me as if I were a—a—"

"I wouldn't finish that sentence if I were you," Alex murmured.

She glared at him, then the others. "You don't understand. None of you understand how it was. Peter made me feel—"

"Spare us the details, if you please," Amelia requested frigidly. "If you can't find an ounce of proper shame, at least have the consideration not to offend the rest of us—particularly Peter's mother and his widow."

Laura watched Anne realize just how indefensible her position was, watched it sink in to her that there was not a person in the room sympathetic to her. That it came as a shock to her was some indication of just how self-centered she actually was.

With a choked little cry, Anne dropped her heavy glass to shatter on the marble hearth and ran from the room, the sounds of her clunky boots thudding on the stairs gradually fading to silence.

"I'll get a broom," Josie said, rising.

"No, leave it." Amelia got up as well, leaning on her

cane a bit more than she had earlier. "We'll go in to dinner
now."

Laura doubted that anyone had an appetite, but she
wasn't at all surprised to see the other members of the
family move obediently to follow Amelia's lead. Except
Daniel. He didn't move, and he didn't release Laura's
wrist. They both stood there behind the sofa nearest the
windows and watched the others leave the room behind
Amelia, and only Alex sent them a curious glance before
following the rest out.

"Why didn't you let me leave?" Laura asked Daniel.
"Before, when I wanted to, why didn't you let me leave?"

He looked at her, and his face tightened slightly. "You
want to know who killed Peter, don't you, Laura? Then
you can't leave. You can't run away from any of this."

He still hadn't released her wrist, and Laura didn't try
to pull away. She just stood there and looked up at him.
"Did you think it was Anne? Is she the one you suspected?"

Daniel hesitated, then said, "I knew she was involved
with him."

"And knew she was capable of murder?"

"It was possible. As I said, suspicion isn't proof."

Laura felt his hand slide down over hers, his fingers
twine with hers, and she tried to concentrate on what she
thought she saw in his face. "But you aren't very relieved
to know she's probably in the clear—or will be if that cab
driver remembers her. Why not?"

"Because it isn't over." He squeezed her hand gently,
then released it. "Go on with the others, Laura. When
Amelia asks, tell her I stayed behind to clear up the broken
glass."

"Daniel—"

"Go on."

After a moment she obeyed, hesitating at the doorway
long enough to look back and find him watching her with

the same expression he'd worn in the maze when he had waited for her to give him her hand. Patience. Infinite patience.

Not at all sure why that unnerved her so much, Laura hurried out of the room and after the others, hoping to catch up before Amelia even realized that two had lagged behind.

YET ANOTHER STORM rolled through just after midnight, waking Laura from a restless sleep, and she got out of bed to go to the window and watch. The window was at the back of the house and overlooked the gardens, and Laura had noticed earlier that there were numerous lights out there illuminating the paths as well as some of the shrubs and trees. They lent the gardens an eerie appearance as rain sheeted down and the wind yanked the trees back and forth viciously. Shadows leaped and crawled like living things, seeming to jerk and tremble in terror when the thunder boomed and lightning flashed.

Laura had always enjoyed watching storms even if she hated driving in them, so she leaned against the window casing and watched, absently rubbing her left arm to soothe the ache. She didn't expect the storm to last long, and within minutes the rain had slacked off to a hesitant drizzle and the wind died to a fitful breeze. Thunder still rumbled distantly, and there was an occasional streak of lightning across the dark sky, but it was apparent that the storm had spent most of its fury.

She was just about to go crawl back into the very comfortable four-poster bed when a hint of movement below just outside the conservatory caught her attention. Someone was leaving the house, she realized, hurrying across the veranda and down into the gardens. It was diffi-cult to be sure, but Laura thought it was a woman.

The figure was cloaked in some long and shapeless

garment, and there wasn't enough light to enable Laura to see any identifying characteristics, so she could only speculate as she watched whoever it was hurry along one of the garden paths and disappear among the trees.

Someone, it seemed, had a late appointment. But who was it? And where was she going?

Chapter 9

ou mean everything just . . . went on as usual?" Cassidy demanded incredulously.

"As if nothing had happened." Laura handed her friend a cup of hot chocolate and then curled up in a chair across from her with her own cup. "Nobody said another word about it. Very polite small talk at the dinner table, and afterward Kerry played the piano for us. Beautifully, by the way. But it was as if that cop had never been there, as if none of us knew who was with Peter in that motel room before he was killed. Anne didn't come downstairs again last night, and I didn't see her at all today."

"What about Daniel?"

Laura looked down at her drink. "Him either. Josie said at breakfast that he'd had to go into the city for the day with Alex."

"So you didn't get a chance to talk to him again after he said in the parlor that it wasn't over yet?"

"No. He came along to dinner just a few minutes after I did, but he didn't say much at all, and he slipped out at some point while Kerry was playing for us later." Laura shrugged. "The only good thing to happen, from my point of view, was that Madeline apparently decided to accept me being there. She was very polite, sweet even. Treated me pretty much the way she does Josie, as if we were a couple of nice young nieces."

"Well," Cassidy said dryly, "after Anne's little confession, Madeline probably felt pretty sure you weren't the one involved with Peter."

Nodding agreement, Laura said, "Which leaves us with a very big question. Who killed him? If that cop can verify that Anne left the motel at eleven-thirty, with Peter very much alive, and went on to her party, then she's in the clear. His body was found around one A.M. and the medical examiner puts the time of death at just about midnight. Anne couldn't have gotten back in time to kill him, and besides, witnesses put her at the party around midnight. So . . . who went into that motel room, just minutes after Anne left, and stabbed Peter to death?"

"You think it was one of the family?"

"I . . . don't know. Amelia and Daniel both seem to have airtight alibis. Madeline didn't do it; I flat-out don't believe in mothers killing their grown sons, especially not this mother. Anne may be in the clear. Kerry was in California. That leaves Alex and Josie—and she said Alex was at the house that night."

"But you said she was worried?"

"Yeah. And she's still tense, preoccupied. Either she knows something or she suspects something. Alex . . . I don't know. I still can't see him stabbing a man to death, but I've hardly spoken to him."

Cassidy frowned. "You said that Anne said something about Peter dying because of the way the family conducted business—what about that?"

"That's been bothering me," Laura admitted. "She could have just been shooting off her mouth—I'd say she's the type to do that—but she seemed awfully certain. And she also said Peter had had plans, and that Daniel wasn't the only one who could make money for the family."

"Which means?"

"I don't know. But Anne was in that motel room with Peter the night he died, and she said it was their second time together. So since she was the woman he was sleeping with, he might have told her something. I mean . . . he might have been involved in some kind of business deal that maybe went wrong somehow. Maybe he stayed at the motel after she left because he was planning to meet someone else there. And that someone killed him."

"Doesn't that argue pretty shady business?" Cassidy wondered. "Would a Kilbourne have been involved in something like that? It's not like he needed the money."

Laura thought about it briefly. "If I'm reading the family right, Peter was virtually shut out of any meaningful family business, except whatever crumbs Amelia threw his way. And my understanding confirms what you picked up from the tabloids: when Amelia goes, Daniel's left in sole charge. Time was running out for Peter. Maybe he did need to show the family he could—I don't know—put a big deal together, or something. And to do that, maybe he had to walk the shady side of the street."

"So how can you find out if that's true?"

Laura's shoulders rose and fell in a shrug. "The same way I've found out what little I already know, I guess. Poke around and ask questions, and listen when they talk to me."

Cassidy looked at her curiously. "You're . . . different about this now. Do you realize that?"

"I don't know what you mean."

Still studying her friend, Cassidy spoke slowly. "When you first went to the Kilbourne house, you were . . . uncomfortable with the whole idea. You didn't like being there because they were mourning Peter—or should have been—and because you were a suspect in his murder. But you *felt* like a suspect in the murder and you wanted to find out if that mirror had anything to do with it. So you went. And then you were uneasy because some kind of power struggle was going on between Amelia and Daniel, and whatever it was made you feel like a pawn."

"Yes. So?"

"So now you're different. You've been drawn in to the family, into their personalities and lives. But your priorities seem to have shifted. You don't feel like a suspect anymore. You seem to be almost avoiding the issue of the mirror. I mean, even though you asked Daniel about it, you didn't push him, didn't tell him you knew he was lying about it. You just let him deny everything. And, Laura, you do realize, don't you, that you've already chosen sides in this power struggle you don't even understand?"

Laura didn't respond for a moment, but finally she looked at Cassidy with a faint smile. "You know, I keep telling myself that Amelia is probably right. Daniel is a dangerous man. I know nothing about him, and I feel too much, and I can't escape the belief that his—his secrets have something to do with me. Half the time I want to run from him, and the other half . . ."

"You want to run to him?"

With a faint sound that might have been an unsteady laugh, Laura said, "Exactly. I don't know what's wrong with me. Cass, you *know* me. I'm so cautious about men, you've laughed at me for years over it. But this man, a man I've known barely a week, has somehow managed to get under my skin. And he's done it almost despite himself. When he hasn't been expressionless, he's been enigmatic, showing barely more emotion than a sphinx. He's lied to me consistently. He believed, at least for a while, that I was his brother's mistress and possibly his murderess. And he's touched my *hand*. Only my hand. Now, does that sound like a man a woman should find herself obsessed with?"

"Should? Maybe not, Laura. But you obviously are, so what does should have to do with anything?"

Accepting the truth of that with another sound of spurious amusement, Laura leaned her head back against the cushion and closed her eyes briefly. Then she opened them and looked at her friend. "Amelia's asked me to stay at the house this weekend. I'm considering it."

Uneasy, Cassidy said, "I know you stayed last night and nothing terrible happened, but, Laura, do you think it's a good idea to go on staying at the house? You said it was oppressive, for one thing, that the house itself made you apprehensive. That doesn't sound too good to me. And you still don't know that someone in that family didn't kill Peter. For that matter, you don't know that Amelia didn't kill someone years ago. Daniel himself told you he suspected her of murdering his grandfather, and you said he didn't lie about that."

"He didn't lie—but suspicion isn't proof," Laura said, conscious of echoing Daniel's words.

"Okay, granted. Maybe the old lady's perfectly innocent of killing her own husband; after forty years and her spotless reputation, we should probably give her the benefit of the doubt. And maybe, just maybe, none of the family killed Peter. But there's still that thing going on between Daniel and Amelia—and pawns *are* sacrificed, Laura. That's why they're in the game."

"I know, I know," Laura murmured.

"Do you? You don't seem to have too many defenses where Daniel is concerned, and you're not real good at hiding your feelings. So what if he's recognized the beginning of an obsession? Do you really think it's a good idea to sleep in a bedroom just down a short hallway from his?"

Laura started to correct Cassidy, to say that Daniel's room was down a *long* hallway from the guest suite—in a different wing of the house, in fact. Josie had conducted her through the entire second floor of the big house Laura's second day there, so she knew where everyone slept. But she realized she was focusing on trivialities in order to avoid the real issue, and so said instead, "Probably not."

Patiently, Cassidy said, "Then why are you considering doing just that?"

"You'll think I'm crazy."

"Don't let that stop you. I already think so."

Laura sighed. "All right. I'm considering staying at the house this weekend because I have this weird feeling that I have to be there."

Cassidy stared at her. "A weird feeling. Laura, is this one of those peculiar things about you that *you* can't even explain—like why Christmas depresses you horribly, or why you can't cut your hair?"

The latter "peculiar" thing had started when Laura was about five or so. In her family of eight children, money had been tight, and so her mother had saved a few dollars by cutting her children's hair herself. Once a month or so, she would line her children up to take their turn sitting in a kitchen chair with a towel pinned around their necks while she—quite skillfully—cut their hair.

However, around the age of five or six, Laura had begun to fight her mother. She could, vaguely, remember it even now, remember sobbing and feeling a terrible grief and pain she couldn't have put into words even if there had been words within a desperate little girl to explain the inexplicable. The battles had grown worse and worse, with Laura becoming nearly hysterical whenever her turn came, until finally her exasperated and baffled mother had elected to let Laura wear her hair long.

Hardly aware that she was speaking aloud, Laura murmured, "I cut it short once when I was sixteen and rebelling. It nearly broke my heart. I felt as if I'd somehow betrayed someone. And I didn't know who—or why."

"I remember you telling me about it," Cassidy said, recalling Laura's attention to the present. "So, is this feeling that you need to spend the weekend at the Kilbourne house the same kind of thing?"

"Yes—no. I don't know, Cass. Every time I set foot in that house, I feel so much that it's hard to sort one thing from another. I just . . . I just think I need to be there this weekend."

"So you'll go over there tomorrow with a bag packed for the weekend?"

Laura hesitated, then nodded. "I think so, yes."

Cassidy leaned forward to set her cup on the coffee table, and then picked up the mirror Laura had been staring at when she'd come in. "Going to take this with you?" she asked.

"Yes." Laura hadn't even realized it was in her mind until she said it.

"Why? I get the feeling you're fairly sure now that it had nothing to do with how or why Peter was killed. That's true, isn't it, Laura? This mirror . . . it's between you and Daniel now, isn't it?"

"He lied about it. He knows something about it."

Cassidy set the mirror down gently and then leaned back, frowning at her friend. "I think I was wrong before. You haven't been ignoring the mirror at all, have you? It's more important to you now than it was at first. Why? Because Daniel lied?"

Laura managed a smile. "Stop asking me questions I can't answer, Cass."

"You're very frustrating as a friend, you know that?"

"I'm amazed you've put up with me so long," Laura said gravely.

"Yeah, well, so am I." But Cassidy was smiling ruefully. "Look, call me every night from the house, will you?

Tell me what's been going on, reassure me that you haven't developed the habit of walking in your sleep—down that hallway to Daniel's room. Okay?"

"Sounds like a good idea to me," Laura said.

"IT'S A BIT late to be out here, isn't it?" Alex asked as he stepped into the gazebo.

Josie looked up with a start, and stared at him for a moment before glancing around the gazebo as if she expected to see a clock. "Is it?"

"Nearly eleven." He had changed, as she had, from the more formal clothing he'd worn for dinner, and was dressed now in jeans and a sweatshirt, and Josie couldn't help wondering if he'd come out here in search of her or if this was another of his nighttime rambles.

"If Amelia wants me—" she began.

"I'm not Amelia's messenger boy," he said a bit sharply.

His edginess didn't do much to ease her own, and Josie frowned at him. "Sorry."

Alex drew a breath and shoved his hands into the front pockets of his jeans. "No, I'm sorry. I didn't mean to snap. Look, I saw you from my window as you crossed the veranda, and I thought . . ." He shrugged. "I thought that since I was getting awfully damned tired of this polite dance we've been doing all week, I'd come out here and—try to change the music."

"Change it how?" She felt at a slight disadvantage, since she was leaning back in the chaise and he was on his feet, looming over her, but she didn't move to get up.

"Would it help if I apologized?"

Josie swung her feet to the floor, but still didn't get up. With an effort, she kept her face expressionless. "I'd say that all depends. Would you mean it?"

He opened his mouth as if for a quick affirmative, but

then hesitated. Finally he shook his head. "No, dammit, I probably wouldn't. I still don't want three of us in my bed."

"And I still can't help how I feel," she said steadily. "I—I don't know why I can't let him go, Alex."

"Maybe because you loved him," he said just as steadily.

Josie nodded slightly, even though she had more or less faced a different truth days ago. It wasn't because she had loved him that she couldn't let go of her dead husband. It was because his memory, painless now, was safe and shielded her heart, and if she let it go, there would be nothing protecting her from being hurt again.

"Josie?"

She looked up at him, at that handsome face and those shrewd, perceptive greenish eyes, and the jolt of pain she felt told her that she might not, in the end, have a choice to make. With or without her assent, it seemed that her shield was weakening. Because something else was, suddenly, stronger.

"Josie . . ." He stepped to the chaise and went down on one knee, both his hands covering hers as they lay in her lap. "I was an idiot, all right? I pushed you, and I shouldn't have. I won't make that mistake again."

She freed one of her hands and touched his face almost curiously, frowning a little as she wondered when it had happened. "You said you had a right," she murmured.

"I was wrong. Josie, we can go back to the way things were before. It'll be enough."

"Will it?"

His face tightened beneath her fingers, but Alex's expression remained calm. "Yes."

She traced the shape of his bottom lip slowly with a fingertip. "But you said the next time I came to you, I'd have to come alone."

"As you may have noticed, you didn't come to me. I

came to you." Alex uttered a soft laugh and then caught her hand against his cheek and pressed his lips against her palm. "Pride sunk and ultimatum in pieces. And after only a few days, yet. You should be proud of yourself, sweet. It takes a lot to bring a Kilbourne to his knees."

"That's not where I want him," she said.

The chaise was narrow and the night was chilly, but neither condition had much of an effect on their passion. And if either of them realized that someone else might have been wandering the maze and would come upon a very private scene at the center, that didn't inhibit them either.

Their clothing was discarded hastily, dropped on the floor of the gazebo. Shoes were kicked aside and pillows scattered. They were so frantic for one another that there was no time or patience for foreplay, and no need. Within minutes, Josie was lying back on the chaise, her thighs cradling Alex and her fingers gripping his shoulders as he pushed inside her almost roughly.

It was as if they had been apart for months instead of days, as if desire had built inside them both like pressure inside a boiler. All that mattered was the release of that pressure, and they found release in each other.

Lying limply beneath him, Josie finally found the energy to murmur, "We didn't even untie the curtains."

Alex pushed himself up on his elbows to look down at her. Smiling just a little, he said, "Do you really care?"

In answer, she lifted her head far enough to kiss him. "But we should probably get dressed," she said. "It's getting colder out here."

"Mmm. I think I'll suggest that we glass this place in and install some kind of heater before winter."

"Then it wouldn't be a gazebo."

"Maybe not, but it would be more comfortable on chilly October nights." He kissed her and then eased away, reaching for their clothing.

Josie didn't say anything else until they were both dressed and ready to head back toward the house. Then, looking up at him, she said, "Thank you, Alex."

Surprised, he said, "For what?"

"For not making me—"

Alex touched her lips with a finger to stop the words. "You'll let him go when you're ready," he said. "I realize that now."

She wanted to say something else, to reassure him somehow, but he hadn't asked for reassurances. So she just nodded and walked beside him as they left the gazebo. And it wasn't until they were halfway out of the lighted maze that her hand crept into his.

"Alex, will you answer a question for me, honestly?"

"If I can."

"Are you and Daniel . . . up to something?"

He looked down at her, surprised again. "Up to something? That's an odd way of putting it. Makes us sound like two boys sneaking cigarettes out behind the barn."

She met his gaze, her own serious. "That wasn't an answer."

He looked away first, and they walked for several moments more in silence. Then, finally, he said, "Peter left a mess behind, sweet. We're just trying to clean it up."

"What kind of mess?"

Alex shook his head. "I think this is very much a case of what you don't know can't hurt you. You trust me, don't you?"

"Yes. But—"

"No buts." His fingers tightened around hers. "It turns out that my dearly departed *cousin* was a bigger son of a bitch than even I realized, and if we can't repair the damage he did . . . well, the family will suffer for it."

"But you won't tell me what it's all about?"

"I can't, Josie. Not yet."

They came out of the maze then and took the path that would lead them back to the house. There was enough light to see by, but when Josie looked up at Alex, she found his expression shadowed and unreadable.

Slowly she said, "You told me days ago that Amelia was up to something. And Daniel. You made it sound like a war, as if you believed they were somehow fighting each other. You even wondered how many of us would be left standing when it was all over."

"Did I say all that?" Alex shook his head. "Damned indiscreet of me."

Josie didn't let his light, offhand tone deter her. "Daniel and Amelia have always . . . grappled with each other. But since Peter died, it's worse. Much worse. It's almost as if they hate each other. Do they?"

"I don't know, sweet."

"Do you—do you know who killed Peter?"

"No."

Josie wanted to ask him if he had gone out that night after she had left him, but couldn't bring herself to. Instead she said, "All this is . . . connected, isn't it? Amelia and Daniel's fight, Peter's murder—and the mess he left behind. It's all tied together somehow."

"Leave it alone, Josie. You'll be better off if you'll just leave it alone."

His tone warned her, but she couldn't help saying, "Why do I feel as if, sooner or later, I'll have to choose sides?"

"I hope you won't," was all he said.

She let the subject drop then, unwilling to push him because he had been so willing to give her the time she needed. And when they went into the quiet house and upstairs, she answered his questioning look with a nod and went with him into his bedroom.

•　•　•

LAURA DID DECIDE to stay at the Kilbourne house over the weekend, and so arrived on Friday morning with a bag packed. She unpacked in the same suite in which she'd spent Wednesday night, and then went downstairs to find that Amelia was ready to sit for another sketch.

Laura had another idea. "Amelia, I know you have things to do; I heard what Josie told you about all the mail that's come in. And what I really need to do is get in some practice with my paints. I brought everything with me. Why don't I set up somewhere out of the way—the conservatory, probably, since there's plenty of light in there—and occupy myself for today."

Amelia hesitated, then nodded. "I think that's an excellent idea, child. I do have quite a few calls to return and notes to respond to, and I should go into the city this afternoon to see to several business matters. If you really don't mind being on your own today—"

"No, of course not, Amelia. I'll be fine."

The old lady nodded again. "Then I'll leave you to it."

So Laura got her paintcase and easel from her car and set up in the conservatory while Amelia and Josie settled down to work in the library. The house was very quiet, and as was so often the case, Laura had so far seen only those two. She had no idea where the others were.

She was restless, oddly on edge, and as the morning wore on, she was more and more conscious of a sense of waiting within her, a feeling of expectation she couldn't begin to explain.

Laura had positioned herself to take advantage of the view out into the gardens, deciding to practice by painting the section of the gardens that contained the arched footbridge. She tried to divorce her mind from her fingers, something that was fairly easy to do considering the thoughts and questions darting through her head. And it wasn't until Josie came to get her for lunch that she realized she had not been painting the footbridge at all.

"Hey, that's lovely," Josie said admiringly.

"Thank you." Laura dropped her brush into a can of turpentine and frowned at the canvas, baffled. The feathery strokes of color showed flowers and trees along the edge of a lake, with mountains beginning to rise in the background. It was a beautiful place—but Laura had no idea where it was or why she had painted it.

Josie didn't seem to notice anything wrong. "Ready for lunch?"

"Just let me clean this brush . . ."

Both Madeline and Kerry appeared for lunch, though there was no sign of Anne. Nobody explained where Daniel and Alex were, and Laura didn't have the nerve to ask. Afterward, forgoing her usual rest time, Amelia left for her afternoon engagements with Madeline, who had decided to ride along, since she had a doctor's appointment.

The family chauffeur, Laura was wryly amused to note, was a thin, upright gentleman with gray hair who was clearly on the shady side of sixty.

When the big Lincoln had gone, Kerry headed off to practice her music, and Josie, after checking to make certain Laura didn't want to join her, went for a walk in the gardens.

Laura returned to her painting, but the more she stared at it, the more restless and uneasy she felt. There was something wrong with it, although she didn't know what. Something missing. It bothered her. She caught herself pacing back and forth like a caged cat and abruptly decided that enough was enough. She needed to do something else for a while.

Remembering Amelia's advice to explore the house in order to better understand her, Laura thought about where she could go without invading anyone's privacy, and realized she hadn't yet seen the basement or attic. Since both had presumably been virtually cleared out for the estate sale, she doubted she would find anything interesting, but before she could think too much about it, she found herself moving back through the house.

AS SHE CLIMBED the stairs to the second floor, Laura wondered idly why it was the attic that drew her rather than the basement, and thought it might have something to do with the general atmosphere of the house. As dark and repressive as she found most of the house, the thought of descending into its bowels, so to speak, held no appeal for her at all.

She found the stairs to the attic easily enough, not far from her suite. The narrow stairs themselves were rather dark, but there was a switch at the top, and when she flipped it, several shaded bulbs that hung from the rafters glowed with life. They showed a vast space, roughly finished with unpainted, unpolished flooring and Sheetrock walls. There were no windows, and though the lights provided adequate illumination, there were shadowy places among the stacks of boxes and trunks, the old furniture, and the unidentifiable bundles of family possessions.

Laura was about to begin exploring when she caught a faint spark of light at the far side of the attic. She walked past two huge steamer trunks and several pieces of furniture that had for some reason escaped being sold, her attention focused on the far wall. There was something hanging on the wall, covered by an old blanket. A corner of the blanket had come loose, and she could see a bit of an elaborate frame and the glint of something shiny.

A mirror.

Even though the bottom of the frame seemed to be on a level with Laura's thighs, it was a huge mirror; she had to reach high to tug at the blanket that was tucked over the top of the frame. Wary of dislodging the mirror, she pulled carefully until the blanket began to slide down, then swept it off to the side and took a step back as the mirror was revealed.

She didn't know why it had escaped the sale, perhaps because it was a Kilbourne family heirloom or simply because there was little demand these days for so huge a mirror. But it was beautiful, the frame solid oak carved with an artist's skill and the glass polished to perfection.

But as always, Laura noted those things only in passing. She stared into the mirror itself, looking past her own reflection, over her right shoulder at the room behind her. The attic was so shadowy, so filled with odd shapes and silhouettes and patches of inky blackness, that it was like gazing on something mysterious and dreamlike.

And dreamlike, the reflection shimmered and changed.

There was a shifting of darkness, a faint movement, and her heart began to pound wildly against her ribs. She could have sworn she saw the room behind her transform, saw it become first a candlelit bedroom, then a parlor, a living room, another bedroom. And through those rooms, a man walked slowly toward her, changing as his surroundings changed, first dark and then blond and then dark again, his faces different, his clothing altering from one style to another.

Then the reflection shimmered faintly again, and Laura stared at Daniel as he came out of the shadows behind her. His eyes caught and held hers, and a certainty stronger than anything she had ever felt in her life swept over Laura with the force of a tidal wave.

It's you. It's you I've been looking for.

She couldn't move, couldn't even breathe. She watched him, felt him behind her. His hands touched hers, then glided up her arms slowly until they rested on her shoulders. His fingers curled under the collar of her silk blouse and pulled it aside, and he bent his head until his lips touched the skin he had exposed. She heard herself make a low sound, sensual beyond belief, and saw her head fall back to allow him more room to explore her neck. His other hand slid across her collarbone and surrounded her throat, tilting her head back a touch farther, his thumb and middle finger lying across her carotid arteries, and she felt her blood pulsing underneath them.

At some point, Laura closed her eyes, the reflection she had been watching less important to her, less real, than the sensations he was arousing in her body. Her blouse was unbuttoned and pushed off her shoulders, and her head rolled against his shoulder in a helpless response when his hands cupped her breasts through the bra. She heard another sound escape her, a sound of such immeasurable longing that the pain of it hurt her throat, and her hands went back, searching for and finding his hard thighs, gripping with all her strength.

"Laura . . ." His voice was low, rough. He turned her swiftly in his arms, and his mouth came down on hers, almost bruising in its hungry force.

She thought she was melting, merging into him somehow, her entire body burning. His mouth on hers seduced and compelled, drawing her to him as surely and completely as the moon drew the tides. She fumbled with the buttons of his shirt, blindly desperate, and felt him unfasten her slacks, felt the cool slide of the material down her legs, and she automatically stepped out of them and nudged off her loafers and socks.

His shirt finally gave way, and she pushed it off his shoulders. His chest was hard, and springy hair teased her fingertips as she stroked him, and the harsh sound that escaped him when he lifted his head to stare down at her trailed over her nerve endings like a caress.

He wasn't enigmatic now. His eyes burned and his rugged features were taut in a masklike expression of intense desire, and when he lifted his hands to frame her face, they were shaking. "God, Laura . . ."

Her mouth was wild under his and her hands fumbled

with his belt, somehow got the pants unfastened and pushed down over his narrow hips. Her bra was gone, and her breasts flattened against his chest when he held her fiercely against him. Laura felt the hard swell of his arousal and moaned when her body answered with a throb of need.

She wasn't conscious of moving or being moved, but suddenly she was lying on her back, completely naked now, the blanket that had covered the mirror a jumbled bed beneath her, and he was there with her. His big hands were on her breasts, stroking and shaping, his thumbs rubbing across her tight nipples in a touch like fire. One of his knees pushed between her thighs in a rough and primitive caress, and his mouth on hers devoured.

Laura had believed that she had experienced the full range of sexual pleasure before. But now she realized that what she had felt before this had been merely a healthy young body's response to simple physical stimulation. Like any sexual creature's, her body was designed to react positively to a male for whom she felt an attraction; when he kissed her, when he touched her, she experienced pleasure.

But when Daniel touched her, she felt something far beyond a simple physical response. It was as if every cell of her body lacked something only he could provide, as if she were designed to merge with him, created to dovetail perfectly with him because he was the other half of herself.

"Daniel . . ." His mouth was on her breasts now, and Laura didn't know how long she could endure the burning pleasure of it. Her fingers slid into his thick hair and she held his head against her, moaning. "Daniel, please . . ."

His lips slid up over the slope of her breast, up her throat, and slanted over her mouth. He kneed her thighs farther apart and then moved between them, and in a single powerful thrust was deep inside her.

For an instant they were both still, almost stunned,

their bodies as close as two people's could be. Then Daniel was moving, driving himself into her in a fierce, quickening rhythm, and Laura cried out because the pleasure exploded all through her body without warning, like nothing she had ever felt before. Dazed and trembling in the aftermath, she held him with what strength was left to her while he groaned and shuddered with his own shattering climax.

THE DRY, STALE air of the attic felt heavy, languid. Or, at least, that was what Laura blamed for her disinclination to move. Their bed was hard and unyielding, the thin blanket providing almost no cushioning between them and the unfinished wood flooring. With her head pillowed on his almost equally hard shoulder, she looked across his chest at the scattered jumble of their clothing, feeling her cheeks warm absurdly at the tangle of her panties and his shorts.

My God, what's happened to me?

What she had seen—what she had thought she had seen—in the mirror seemed very dreamlike in retrospect. Unreal. Of course unreal. But no amount of reason, no logical arguments, could change the certainty she felt down to her bones. In countless mirrors all through her life, she had looked for him, knowing that one day he would be there.

It was, like so much in her life, inexplicable. And Laura shied away from thinking about it right now, because she was half afraid of any answer she might have arrived at.

Realizing, suddenly, that there were other people in this house, that Josie might have returned from her walk or Amelia and Madeline from the city, Laura tried to force herself to move, to push back away from the hard heat of his body and the disturbing comfort of his embrace. But her muscles had barely tensed when his arms tightened around her.

"Not yet," he murmured.

She felt one of his hands moving slightly on her shoulder, his long fingers almost kneading, very gently, and wondered why that odd, probing touch made her feel as bonelessly contented as a cat in the sunlight. She kept her voice as low as his had been when she said, "The door isn't even closed, is it?"

"No one ever comes up here."

"You did."

"I was following you."

"I didn't even know you were in the house."

"I came back just after Amelia and Mother left." He was silent for a moment, then said, "When I came upstairs, I heard you going toward the attic. So I followed."

Laura didn't want to disturb this peaceful aftermath, especially since she was all too sure it would be brief, but she couldn't stop herself from raising her head from his shoulder and asking dryly, "Afraid I might find something up here?"

His harsh features were set once more in their unreadable mold, the pale eyes shuttered, and his voice was matter-of-fact when he said, "How could there be anything up here I would want to hide from you?"

Laura didn't know the answer to that, but it bothered her that he had replied to her question with one of his own. "I don't know," she said finally. "Why did you follow me?"

He answered that without hesitation. "Because I knew this would happen."

"How did you know?" *It was you in the mirror. All these years, it was you I looked for. Did you know that?*

He lifted a hand and touched her face, one finger tracing the line of her brow, the shape of her cheekbone. His thumb brushed across her bottom lip in a slow, gliding caress. "I wanted it to happen," he replied at last.

"And Daniel Kilbourne always gets what he wants?"

His mouth twisted slightly. "Don't. Don't turn this into a question of power. So much of my life is a question of power. But not this. You wanted it too, Laura. We both wanted it."

She couldn't deny it, didn't even try. And when his hand slipped to the nape of her neck and pressed gently, she didn't try to deny that want either. His lips played on hers, gentle at first and then hardening, demanding, and Laura didn't care why he had followed her up here. She didn't care about anything except feeling.

LAURA BUTTONED HER blouse slowly, trying to fix all her attention on the task even though she was intensely aware of him getting dressed just a couple of feet away. It vaguely surprised her that she was still so hypersensitive to his nearness, and it was more than a little disconcerting. A couple of hours of dynamic sex had only fed her appetite for him rather than satisfying it, and she didn't know if she'd be able to bear it if this was all he wanted from her.

"So, what now?" she heard herself ask, unnaturally calm.

He came to her immediately, completely dressed but with the tail of his shirt untucked, and framed her face with his hands to make her look at him. He was smiling slightly, but his voice was matter-of-fact. "Now we go on. I want more than an afternoon, Laura. Stay with me to-night."

She tried to think, tried not to let the determination she felt in him make the decision for her. "What about Amelia?" she murmured.

"What about her? This is just between you and me."

But it isn't. You know it isn't. His thumbs were rubbing back and forth across her cheekbones, and Laura wanted to tell him to stop because it wasn't helping her to think straight.

"Laura?"

She shook her head finally, hoping he'd just accept that. But when his eyes narrowed, she knew it wouldn't be so easy. Reluctant, she said, "I'm not trying to be coy or anything like that. It's just . . . I wouldn't feel comfortable spending the night with you here in this house."

"Because of Amelia?"

"Her—and the others. This is your family home." She shrugged, helpless to explain her feelings any clearer than that.

Daniel looked down at her for a moment, then nodded slowly. "All right. I'll respect your feelings—for now. But we both know that this between us can't be denied, don't we, Laura? We both know it's just beginning."

"Yes," she said, and wondered if he knew that she found the promise of that as terrifying as it was exhilarating.

Chapter 10

*A*melia didn't expect you to come back
to the house this afternoon, did she?"
Laura asked as they walked down the
main stairs to the ground floor. From the music room
came the quiet and soothing notes of some sonata she
recognized vaguely but couldn't name, and she thought
absently that Kerry did indeed spend a great deal of time at
her piano.

Daniel stopped at the bottom of the stairs, looking at
Laura as she paused on the first tread, and said, "No, probably not. I had a meeting canceled; otherwise I would have
been in the city until late. Why?" His eyes were unreadable.

"Just wondering." Her indifference wasn't convincing,
even to her.

But if Daniel wasn't convinced, he clearly wasn't curious enough to ask. Instead he took her hand and asked
casually, "What were you doing before you went upstairs
to explore? Painting?"

"Yes. In the conservatory."

"Amelia's portrait?"

"No. I thought I could use a little practice before I started on the portrait."

"You don't mind if I see it, do you?"

Since he was already heading for the hallway that led to the conservatory, and bringing her along with him, Laura's voice was a bit dry when she answered, "No, of course not."

He glanced at her as they walked down the hall, a genuine smile of amusement warming his face unexpectedly. "Am I being presumptuous? Taking too much for granted?"

Laura didn't quite know how to answer that. "I don't know. What are you taking for granted? That you can see my work? It isn't exactly secret, parked in the conservatory for anybody to see. Josie looked at the painting earlier. Besides, you've already seen some of my sketches."

"And that disturbed you," he said perceptively.

"Maybe." She shrugged. "I'm used to having my work seen and criticized; any artist is."

"Your commercial work, certainly. But you're very unsure of yourself with this kind of work, aren't you, Laura?"

"You know I am." He'd been standing right behind her when she had revealed as much the first day she'd come here. "But if I'm going to be successful outside the field of commercial art . . ."

He stopped in the doorway of the conservatory and looked down at her. "You'll have to get used to even more criticism?"

"And probably have to grow a thicker skin." She smiled. "Art critics aren't exactly known for their compassion."

"If a vote of confidence helps, you've got mine. I saw real talent in those sketches." Without giving her time to respond, he kissed her, briefly but not at all casually.

When he raised his head, he was smiling. "May I see your painting?"

Laura nodded, wondering if she'd ever be able to refuse him anything. It was a scary question, because she thought she knew the answer. She walked beside Daniel, her hand still in his, and stood beside him when they reached the painting of a place she couldn't name. The silence seemed to go on too long as he intently looked at it, his thoughts as usual unreadable, and Laura was just about to comment that she didn't know why she had painted this particular scene, when he spoke.

"Beautiful. You've captured the peace and grandeur. But you've forgotten the house."

She looked at him blankly. "The house?"

Daniel nodded and, with his free hand, indicated a lower corner of the painting, an area near the lake. "Here. The house was here."

"You . . . know this place? I mean, it's real?"

"Did you think it wasn't?" He smiled slightly as he gazed down at her.

"Well, since I thought I painted it from my imagination . . ." She looked at the painting, frowning.

"You probably saw a picture somewhere," Daniel said after a moment. "In a magazine, maybe. Things like that stick in our minds sometimes. Does it matter?"

Laura wasn't sure, but she thought it did. "This place—where is it?"

"Scotland."

That surprised her. "Have you been there?"

"Yes. As I said, you've captured it beautifully. One of my favorite places on earth." He turned and pulled her gently against him, releasing her hand so that he could put both arms around her. "Definite talent, just as I thought."

Easily distracted from the painting by the response of her body to his touch, Laura felt her arms slip around his waist and looked up at him a bit helplessly. "Daniel, we shouldn't—"

He kissed her, his mouth moving on hers with a lazy certainty that swiftly became something more urgent. As quickly as that, as easily as that, he ignited once more the overwhelming emotions and sensations she had felt in the attic. Her longing for him was intense and absolute, pushing everything else out of her consciousness, and if he had pulled her down to the tile floor there at the base of her puzzling painting amidst the flourishing greenery of the conservatory, she would not have uttered a word of protest.

But Daniel lifted his head finally, gazing down at her with eyes that were hot and a taut look in his face. "Christ," he muttered, and it sounded more like an invocation than a curse. His hands slid down over her bottom, and he held her harder against him.

Laura heard a sensual little sound escape her, but shook her head as she tried to fight the urgency of what she felt—and what she felt in him. "Daniel . . . we can't do this. Not here. Not now. Josie's probably back from her walk and somewhere in the house. Kerry's still in the music room. Amelia and your mother will be home anytime now. We can't . . ."

He didn't say anything for a moment, his hands still moving slowly on her, caressingly, in the intimate and unmistakable touch of a lover. Then he said, "Just how discreet do you think we can be?"

Laura thought of how rarely she was going to be without Amelia's company until the portrait was finished, and how even more rarely the house would be empty save her and Daniel, and realized only then how difficult it was going to be for them to spend any time alone together—especially given her reluctance to sleep in his bed. Before she could think of anything to say, Daniel went on in a deliberate tone.

"An occasional night at your apartment? Stolen minutes in the attic from time to time? Meeting out in the gardens somewhere, time and weather permitting? Do you really think that's going to be enough, Laura? For either of us?"

She drew a breath. "Correct me if I'm wrong, but if Amelia finds out about us, she won't like it. Will she?"

"Why wouldn't she?"

"She warned me against you, Daniel. Twice. It seems pretty clear to me that she wanted me to stay away from you, whatever her motives. And don't pretend you don't know that she never would have left me here in the house today if she had expected you to come home early."

"No, I suppose she wouldn't have."

"Well, then? It's obvious she won't be happy."

He was still gazing at her, but his eyes took on a distant look for an instant, and when he answered, his voice was thoughtful. "I don't know. Perhaps she will. The warning to you might have been intended to . . . draw out the chase, so to speak. To keep us apart as long as possible in order to drive the level of tension high. Higher. She might have thought I'd be more distracted if you were kept away from me, at least for a while."

Laura felt a little jolt. "Distracted from what?"

Daniel smiled slightly. "From the games we play. Don't tell me you haven't noticed."

"Are they games? Just games?"

"What else could they be?"

"A power struggle," Laura heard herself say. "A real one."

Daniel eased back away from her a bit, his hands moving to the less intimate area of her shoulders, as if he had been distracted from passion—or wanted to be. Laura dropped her own hands and linked her fingers together as she studied his face. There was something almost speculative in his expression for an instant, and then he was impassive.

"Is that so surprising? There's a great deal at stake in the finances of this family, including the future of everyone who lives here."

"And you feel Amelia would jeopardize that future?"

He seemed to hesitate, then said bluntly, "When I came of age eleven years ago, it was to find that Amelia had very nearly bankrupted the family. Oh, we looked good on paper, but in reality we were a few short years away from selling off property in order to keep up with loans and taxes. She had spent a fortune since my father died, and had little to show for it. Some incredibly expensive jewelry she keeps locked in her safe, mementos from a couple of world cruises she'd taken, ownership of several racehorses that had never won and never would. She'd neglected business or made bad decisions, invested in ridiculous schemes and absurd inventions, and spent money as if it meant nothing. I had no choice but to confront her with the facts."

Laura had no trouble imagining how tense that little showdown must have been, given Amelia's pride and obsessive need to control the people and events around her, and she couldn't help wincing inwardly. "I heard—that is, I read somewhere that Amelia technically controls the family business and finances as long as she lives. How could you get her to give up any control at all to you?"

"David's will was very specific; he established a kind of everlasting trust to be administered by various family members rather than an outright inheritance that would pass on to a descendant after his death—and out of his control. He wanted Amelia to run things while she lived, with control of the trust passing after her through the male line first: to my father, then myself or Peter, then my son if I should have one. So Amelia was left in control of everything—providing none of David's descendants could prove during her lifetime that she was a bad custodian, a condition that applies equally to anyone in charge.

"My father wasn't interested in the family business and didn't care how she ran things. Until about a month before he died, when something—I don't know what—made him uneasy enough to begin looking into the family finances. I imagine he found, or would have, the seeds of disaster I found ten years later. I'll never know. He was killed. Quite a coincidence, wouldn't you say?"

"Or just a tragic accident," Laura replied steadily.

Daniel nodded. "Or an accident. In any case, I confronted Amelia with plenty of proof she'd been a lousy custodian, and told her she had a choice. Either I took her to court to sue for control, or she'd give me control while remaining at least publicly and tacitly in charge of things."

"You had to know it'd be a fight from that day on," Laura said. "She wouldn't want the public humiliation of a competency hearing, but it must have been equally galling for her to know you were actually in control of the family business and finances."

"Which brings us back to the games Amelia and I play," he said. "She still has the legal authority to make decisions, since I haven't challenged that publicly, and for eleven years she's been testing the boundaries, pushing and pushing to see how far I'll let her go. Little things, mostly, small battles of authority. Relatively unimportant decisions overruled by her. Posturing at board meetings. Deliberately acting against my wishes in minor matters. And running things here in the house with an iron hand, of course, imposing her will and her tastes and preferences on the entire family."

"What about the rest of the family? Do they know how things really stand?"

"Alex does. Josie's probably guessed. As for the others, no. They assume I'm actively in charge because Amelia's getting older, but that I'm more or less following her wishes, not that I hold the actual power. It's a pretense Amelia very carefully keeps alive, though more outside this house than in. Mother and Kerry aren't interested, and Anne never sees beyond her own problems, so Amelia doesn't fight me much here. Or I don't fight her."

"Did Peter know?"

With detachment, Daniel said, "He found out when he tried to wheedle a European sports car out of Amelia when he turned twenty."

"Did he . . . try to get the car out of you after that?"

"No. He knew better. I expected him to live within his very generous allowance, something I made clear to him."

Trying to sort through all this, Laura said slowly, "Since you suspect Amelia had something to do with her husband's death, and your father's, aren't you concerned that she might try to get you out of the way?"

"I told you I didn't really believe she killed David," Daniel reminded her.

"Yes. And I didn't believe you."

Surprising her, he smiled.

"All right. Then let's just say that I believe in being cautious, at least up to a point. Amelia knows very well that I have a large envelope kept safely by the lawyers, to be opened in the event of my death—natural or otherwise. Nothing in David's trust says a descendant has to be alive when proving Amelia a bad custodian, and she knows it."

Laura felt a cold hand slide up her spine at even the possibility of Daniel's death, and the strength of the feeling shook her. Trying to push that aside, she asked distractedly, "What would happen in that case?"

"You mean, if I died childless, who would take over? Anne would be David's only living descendant. Control of the trust would change over to the female line. If Anne didn't want the job of managing things—and she wouldn't—then business decisions and family finances would be handled by a team of financial advisors and the family lawyers for the duration. That would continue unless and until Anne had a child to come of age and take over authority. If she dies childless, the trust is broken and Alex inherits everything outright."

"As the only blood Kilbourne left?"

"That's the way David wanted it." Daniel shrugged, adding, "And that brings us all the way back to where we started—with how Amelia would feel about us. Remember?"

"We didn't get that far off track," Laura murmured.

His hands tightened on her shoulders, but he didn't pull her closer. "Maybe not. It just took a while to explain why Amelia might be pleased by this. In any case, I think she just might be."

"But what if she isn't?" Laura looked up at him steadily. "And what about the others? I'm in an awkward position here, you know that. Even if the others believe I didn't kill Peter, I was still suspected of it—*and* of being his mistress. Then within a matter of days I—I end up in *your* bed? Jeez, it sounds awful even to me."

He did pull her close then. "Never mind how it sounds. How does it feel?"

She caught her breath, avoiding his intense gaze. "Daniel, don't."

"Why? Because you can't think clearly? Because you can't be sensible and rational? Neither can I." As he had in the attic, he framed her face with his hands to make her look at him. "I want you, Laura. I've wanted you since the first moment I laid eyes on you. And I don't really give a damn who knows that."

Without her conscious volition, Laura's hands lifted to rest on his chest. She could feel the intensity in him, the determination, and the force of it was almost overwhelming. Almost. "I just need a little time." Her voice was unsteady despite all her efforts, and she knew she sounded shaken. "Please, Daniel. Everything's happened so fast, I—"

He kissed her with a sudden, startling gentleness, and when he raised his head again, the intensity was gone—or hidden. He was smiling a bit ruefully. "I guess eleven years of battles with Amelia have taken their toll; I can't seem to stop trying to get my way. I'm sorry, Laura. Of course you need some time to get used to this, I know that. I think we can manage to be discreet, at least for a while."

She was a little surprised that he'd given in, but grateful too. "I just think . . . it might only take one more straw to break this family. I don't want to be it."

His thumbs brushed across her cheekbones caressingly, and then Daniel let her go. "We're not so fragile as you think, but never mind. It's probably a good idea to keep this to ourselves right now. Look, it's getting late, and I have some calls to make. Why don't I leave you to your painting?"

Laura nodded, conscious of feeling bereft when she forced her hands to drop from his chest. She didn't say anything until he turned away and went toward the doorway. "Daniel?"

He paused and half turned to look back at her, his brows lifting questioningly.

"You said Amelia might have warned me to . . . draw out the chase. To keep us apart as long as possible in order to distract you. How did she know? I mean, how could she be so sure you even wanted me?" *Since I sure as hell never guessed.*

Daniel smiled faintly. "Secrets don't live long in this house, Laura. It's something to keep in mind. I'll see you at dinner."

She stared after him for several minutes, frowning, grappling with the uneasy possibility that this afternoon Daniel had moved the most vital chess piece in the entire game. Was that why he had followed her up to the attic?

He wanted her, yes, Laura didn't doubt that—but he wouldn't be the first man to combine a pleasurable sexual conquest with some other deliberate purpose. And though his explanation of the power struggle between him and Amelia certainly rang true, there was more to it, Laura was sure. Something else was going on between those two, something far more dangerous than Daniel was willing to admit.

And Laura still felt herself very much a pawn.

It would be devastating, she knew, if she found out that the interlude in the attic and everything after it had only been a means to an end, a deliberate move by Daniel to accomplish God only knew what result in his struggle with Amelia. That was the kind of thing that could destroy a woman, especially if she felt too much for the man using her as a pawn. . . .

She pushed it all into the back of her mind and turned to her painting, desperate for something, anything, to keep her distracted, if only for a while. Her gaze fixed on that lower corner, where Daniel had indicated the forgotten house, and after a moment she found herself reaching for her paints and brush. When she tried to decide consciously what kind of house belonged there by the lake, her mind was maddeningly unhelpful. Finally she drew a deep breath and closed her eyes for a moment, then just dabbed her brush in some paint and began painting without thinking at all.

A small gray house took shape beneath her brush. A stone house. It had a thatched roof, and smoke curled from the stone chimney. There was a small garden plot, she realized, almost hidden from this angle by the little house; the edge of it could just be seen. And a woodpile off to the side. And there was a path down to the lake, where you went several times a day to draw water. And another path, much fainter, that led off through the woods to the nearest neighbors, miles away. And you couldn't see the barn, because the angle was wrong, but it was over there past that big rock. . . .

Laura shook her head, a little dazed, and stared at the painting. *I know this place. I've been here.* But how could she, if it was in Scotland?

"Hi, Laura. Hey—didn't mean to startle you."

She looked at Josie and managed a smile as her heartbeat returned to normal. *Jumpy. I'm getting so damned jumpy.* "Sometimes my imagination takes me . . . far away. Are you just now back from your walk? I thought you must have gone back into the house by now."

Josie smiled. "I needed to think about a few things, so I just sat in the gazebo. Didn't realize how long I'd been out there until I looked at my watch a few minutes ago. Is Amelia back yet?"

"I don't think so. I haven't seen her."

"Good, then I can be working busily when she gets home." Josie looked at Laura's painting, and if she thought the addition of the little stone house was a small amount of work to have completed in the hours since lunchtime, she didn't say so. Instead she said, "I like the house. Looks old, but sturdy."

"I . . . thought that corner needed something," was all Laura could manage.

"I think you're right. But it's perfect now." Josie smiled. "I'd say you're ready to start Amelia's portrait."

"I don't feel ready," Laura confessed.

Josie laughed. "Take it from me, when it comes to dealing with Amelia, you don't think about it—you just do it. You'll be fine, Laura. And the portrait will be fine."

"Thanks."

"Don't mention it. And now, if you'll excuse me, I'll get myself to the library, where I can be blamelessly working when Amelia gets home."

"I hear that." Laura wasn't going to ask, but heard

herself speak before Josie could do more than walk past her. "Josie? Has Daniel ever been out of the country?"

Josie paused, surprise crossing her expressive face. "He went to Hong Kong a few years ago on business. That's it, I think."

"He's never been to Scotland?"

Curiosity joined surprise on Josie's face. She shook her head. "No, not that I know of. Certainly not since I've been here. Why?"

"No reason. Just . . . something he said once. It's not important."

Josie didn't look particularly convinced of that latter statement, but accepted it. "Okay. See you at dinner."

"See you."

Laura turned her gaze back to her painting, faking absorption, but when she was alone once more in the conservatory, she stopped pretending. She was so confused she couldn't even think straight, and all her frustration and uneasiness found voice in a single murmured question.

"Damn you, Daniel, what are you trying to do to me?"

HE DIDN'T EXPECT Amelia to catch on to the change in his relationship with Laura right away. Laura, for all her expressiveness, could keep her secrets when she wanted to, he thought—and he knew damned well he could. So they had a bit of grace, a little time before the careful balance in this house would shift yet again.

Daniel stared down at a stack of financial reports on his desk, frowning, hardly conscious of Josie working quietly on the other side of the room. Had he revealed too much to Laura in telling her about his struggle with Amelia? It was difficult to know. He might have jumped the gun, but he had felt sure she was already on his side of the battle lines—and not just because they had become lovers.

Lovers. He felt his breathing deepen at the simple thought of that, his heart thud heavily in his chest, and closed his eyes, remembering her reflection in the mirror as she had watched him come toward her. There had been shock in her eyes, and recognition, and longing. And no hesitation. She had responded to him instantly, her sweet yearning tearing at his heart even as her sensuality stole his breath and clouded his mind.

He breathed in slowly, her haunting, arousing scent as real to him as though he were back in that attic, and felt the warm silk of her flesh beneath his lips and fingers. Gazed into green eyes alight with heated desire. Heard his name murmured in a voice husky with passion. Felt her arms around him, her body welcome him with its slick, searing heat and unbearable pleasure.

Dear God, it had been so long. . . .

"Daniel?"

He opened his eyes, focused on the papers lying before him. Breathed out slowly. When he looked up and across the room at Josie, he was in control. "Yes?" Only Laura could shatter his control. Only Laura.

"Are you all right? You looked a little . . . strange."

He felt a flicker of mild curiosity as to what she'd seen on his face, but dismissed it. He wasn't worried about what Josie knew, or guessed. She was discreet, and would no more tell his business to Amelia than she would Amelia's business to him. Besides which, she had her own concerns at the moment, her own secrets to keep. "I'm fine," he said.

She nodded a bit uncertainly, then pushed back her chair and rose. "Just thought I'd mention that it's nearly five. Since Amelia's upstairs resting, I told her I'd check on dinner before I go up and change."

Daniel nodded. "All right. I think I'll call it a day as well." Not that he'd gotten a damned thing done all the while he'd been sitting here, but there were a few advantages to being the boss, and one was not having people look over your shoulder to make sure you were being productive.

He waited a few minutes after Josie left, giving her time to check on the evening meal and head toward her own room, then locked the financial reports in the center drawer of his desk and left the library. He hadn't gone out to greet his mother and Amelia when they had returned an hour ago, though Josie had, and he had only spoken a brief greeting to Alex when he had arrived home not long ago. Since there was no music wafting out from the music room, he assumed Kerry was upstairs getting ready, as the others likely were.

He climbed the stairs, wondering if Anne would show her face tonight or continue to come and go like an unhappy wraith, avoiding all of them. Daniel felt a bit sorry for Anne, but at the same time knew that most of her troubles were all her own doing. She was too full of anger and resentment to be rational sometimes, and maybe it wasn't surprising that she snapped at every hand held out to her. Except for Peter's hand, which she had obviously accepted . . .

Reaching the second floor, Daniel paused and stared at Laura's door. Four guest suites in the main section of the house, and Amelia had put Laura in the one Daniel had to pass every time he went to his own bedroom. Coincidence? Hardly. That old woman would have made a fine inquisitor a few hundred years ago, he thought with grim amusement. She had a keen understanding of exactly how to torture her victims without shedding a single drop of blood.

He intended to walk past Laura's door and go on to his own room. He fully intended to do that. But he found himself instead going directly to her door and knocking softly.

She opened the door a moment later, a little flushed

and damp from her shower, her glorious hair loose around her shoulders and the silky green robe she wore clinging lovingly to her slender body. It took a space of several quickening heartbeats before Daniel could speak, and when he did he wasn't at all surprised that his voice rasped.

"Are you all right?"

Laura was surprised, by his presence and the question, and her eyes looked warily past him for an instant before she said, "Why wouldn't I be?"

Good question.

"May I come in for a moment?" And when she hesitated, he added quietly, "Nobody will know, Laura. Everyone's in their rooms getting dressed."

She stepped back, pulling the door open far enough for him to come into the sitting room, then closed it behind him. She didn't move away from the door but stood there, a bit stiffly. She was nervous, and Daniel didn't like it.

Crossing the space between them, he lifted a hand to cup her cheek and said, "Don't look at me like that. Why are you wary of me, Laura? What have I done?"

She hesitated, those green eyes uncertain as they searched his face, then shook her head a little. "Nothing. I guess I'm just jumpy with everybody back in the house." She eased away from him and moved restlessly across the room, stopping only when she stood before an elegant little side table with a gilded mirror hanging on the wall above it.

Their eyes met in the mirror, and Daniel moved toward her without consciously making the decision to do so. When he reached her, he put his hands on her waist and drew her slowly back against him. His hands moved over her flat middle slowly, the slide of silk over her skin warm and sensuous. He watched the reflection of her eyes darken, saw her lips part, and wondered if she could feel his heart pounding. He knew she could feel his desire for her.

He bent his head and pressed his lips to her shoulder, then nuzzled the side of her neck, breathing in her unique scent, and murmured, "Are you upset with me because we didn't use protection when we made love?" He saw surprise flicker in her darkened eyes when he raised his head, and thought she was startled because that fact was not something she had considered.

After a moment, she said a little huskily, "I'm on the pill."

"That didn't answer my question." He rubbed his jaw slowly against her soft hair, watching her face intently in the mirror.

"No, I'm not upset," she said finally. "I—I hadn't thought about it."

"And now that you have thought about it? We can use added protection if you want, Laura. But there's no reason for you to worry if we don't. I'm healthy and not infected with anything. Except you."

Her eyes flickered again, but her hands came up to cover his where they rested just beneath her breasts. "I'm healthy too. So I guess neither of us has to worry."

"Good." He didn't have to look at the clock on the nearby mantel to know that he was running out of time, but he hated to let go of her. "I don't suppose you'd be interested in being late for dinner?" he asked, hearing the wryness in his own voice.

She smiled. "Interested, yes. But I imagine Amelia would find it suspicious if both of us turned up late, don't you?"

"Yes. Dammit." He shifted his hold on her, turning her so that he could kiss her. It wasn't enough to satisfy his hunger for her; if anything, this taste of her just made the ache worse. But he had no idea when he would be able to

hold her or kiss her again, and couldn't ignore this opportunity.

When he finally raised his head, they were both
breathing raggedly, and the heated sheen of desire in her
eyes almost made him sweep her up and carry her off to
her bedroom—and to hell with Amelia. But the clock on
her mantel softly chimed the half hour just then, and the
sound of reality brought him back to his senses.

Reluctantly he eased back away from her. "I'd better
go. Come and check the hall for me—make sure it's
clear."

Laura nodded slowly and went with him back to the
door. She opened it cautiously and looked outside to make
sure no one would see him leave, then drew back and
nodded. "It's clear." Her voice was a little husky.

"Sneaking around at my age. If anyone else had asked
it of me . . ." He kissed her one last time, hating the
necessity of leaving her, then slipped out of her room and
headed for his own.

When he drew abreast of Alex's room, the door
opened, and the lawyer came out into the hall. He looked
at Daniel, mildy surprised, and said, "You're running late.
It's nearly six."

"I lost track of the time," Daniel said.

Alex glanced around them quickly and said in a lowered voice, "It's just as well I caught you. We need to
talk."

"You've found something?"

"Maybe. You'll have to judge for yourself."

"Is it urgent?" Daniel asked.

Alex pursed his lips thoughtfully. "Well, no more urgent than the situation. I should think it'd keep until tomorrow."

"All right. Can you get away in the morning?"

"Sure. Can you?"

Daniel chose to take that question as an inquiry into

the schedule of his usually busy Saturday mornings rather than something more personal—even though Alex's half smile told him that he apparently wasn't quite as good at hiding his feelings as he had thought. Or else Laura had somehow left her mark on him, visible for all the world to see.

He didn't ask, just said calmly, "I have some time around ten. Where can we meet?"

"Better make it my office. Something I want to show you."

Daniel felt his pulse quicken and looked at Alex with a narrowed gaze. "Something we can use?"

Alex was noncommittal. "Like I said, you'll have to judge for yourself."

Daniel knew the younger man too well to push, so he merely nodded and went on to his bedroom. He stripped rapidly and got into the shower, shivering under the near-icy water but making no effort to adjust the temperature. Cold showers at his age. And, adding insult to injury, it didn't help anyway.

It took him less than ten minutes to shower and dress, and he took the time to shave because he had a fairly heavy beard and he didn't want Amelia noticing that he had not, as was his custom, gotten rid of his five o'clock shadow. But he was still quick enough that when he went downstairs and strolled into the front parlor, the old grandfather clock out in the foyer was just striking the hour.

He was the last to enter the room aside from Anne, who in all likelihood wouldn't show up at all.

"Drink, Daniel?" Alex was playing bartender.

"Scotch." He took the glass and nodded his thanks, his gaze sweeping the room without—though it required a tremendous effort—lingering obviously on Laura. The glance was enough, at least, to tell him she was standing behind the couch nearest the window, facing the room warily as she had before. That she was wearing, improbably for a redhead but with stunning effect, a flame-red dress that was vaguely Oriental in design, a high-necked sheath that left her arms bare. It was made of silk, judging by the shimmer when she moved, and the way it clung to her body turned an exotic but otherwise sedate design into something starkly sensual. She wore her hair up, and pearl studs in her lobes were her only ornaments.

She didn't need anything else.

Daniel went to his usual place by the hearth, speaking casually to his mother and Amelia and greeting the rest generally, and thought how remarkable it was that he was able to string two words together that made sense, let alone behave normally enough that no one seemed to notice anything different about him.

"The others have been telling me about their day, Daniel," Amelia said. "How was yours?"

He had no idea whether she had found out that he'd returned to the house much earlier than expected, and merely said, "Busy, as usual. In fact, I have to go into the city tomorrow morning for a while."

"You work too hard, dear," Madeline said automatically.

"I'm fine, Mother." Daniel looked at her, wondering as he always did how she could be so conventional in some ways and so inexplicable in others. She played the mother very well, saying all the right things at the right moments, and grieving violently at the death of her son. Yet she hadn't grieved noticeably for her husband, and she would not, Daniel thought in detachment, grieve for him if he went before her. As far as he could tell, Madeline had never cared deeply for anyone in her life—except for Peter.

He had known that from childhood and might well have been scarred for life by the overt rejection, but Daniel had realized very young that it was not something lacking in him, but in Madeline. For whatever reason, there was room in her to love only one other besides herself, and for whatever reason, her youngest son had been the chosen one. Her husband and oldest son had heard all the right words and seen all the right smiles—and neither had made the mistake of taking them at face value.

"I'm sure you should at least take weekends off," she said now, looking up at him from the couch with an anxious smile and eyes that mirrored his own except for the slight vagueness of sedatives.

"I won't work after noon," he promised. That satisfied her, as he had known it would, and she lapsed back into silence and the numbing peace of drugs.

Daniel glanced toward the other sofa, where Kerry and Josie sat, and even the furtive glimpse of the still flame that was Laura was enough to make him feel a building heat of his own. Goddamn useless cold showers . . .

Laura spoke then, her voice huskier than usual—or maybe that was just his fevered imagination.

"Kerry, what was the music you were working on all afternoon? I recognized it, but couldn't remember the name of it."

"It was Beethoven," she replied. "The *Moonlight Sonata* mostly."

"It was beautiful," Laura told her. "The house was so quiet and the music seemed to fill it. Very peaceful."

"Did it help you with your painting?" Josie asked, looking back over her shoulder with a smile.

"I don't know if anything could do that," Laura replied with a faint laugh. "But it made my . . . frustration a bit less painful."

"Kerry, you can play for us after dinner," Amelia announced.

"Of course, Amelia." If Kerry disliked being chosen as the evening's entertainment, there was no sign of it in her sweetly inexpressive smile or her meek voice.

From his place as he leaned against the back of the

couch near Madeline, Alex asked, "Has anybody heard from Anne lately?"

Amelia's face seemed to set in stone, but she didn't reprove Alex.

"I saw her come in and then leave again this afternoon," Kerry ventured. "She's very unhappy, poor thing."

Amelia looked at her and said a bit dryly, "You're very generous, Kerry, I'll say that for you."

"Why? Because I don't blame Anne?" Kerry's smile remained unchanged, gentle and composed. "Whatever happened between Peter and Anne, it wasn't her fault."

Daniel looked at her in some surprise, since it was the first time in his memory that she had said anything against Peter. Criticism of Peter was seldom heard in the house, in fact, and Daniel fully expected Amelia to pounce on the remark. She did.

"Do you think Peter seduced her?" she snapped.

Kerry's voice remained perfectly gentle. "Of course he did, Amelia."

"And why do you think that?"

"Because he always did. He was a hunter, you know. He liked collecting trophies. He never used a gun, but I imagine he drew blood more than once. Anne was just another trophy to him. So was the woman who killed him." She paused, then added, "If it was a woman, of course."

There was hardly a thing anyone in the room could say after that softly devastating summation, and not even Amelia ventured to try. As for Madeline, she simply didn't hear it, whether because of the sedatives or merely because she chose not to listen.

Daniel wondered at Kerry's use of the word *trophy,* but didn't have time to reflect on it. They all heard a thud as the front door was slammed, hasty footsteps, and then Anne appeared in the doorway. She moved instantly into the room until she stood near Daniel, where she could see everyone and they could see her.

She looked around with a defiant lift to her chin and announced, "I just saw Brent Landry, and he says there's no evidence against me. Do all of you hear that? The cab driver *did* see Peter alive and well when I left, and Brent says I couldn't possibly have got back to the motel later in the right time frame. So I'm in the clear. I didn't kill Peter."

Daniel had never honestly thought Anne capable of killing—at least not the way Peter had been killed—and he was relieved to hear she had been eliminated as a suspect. But he was a logical man, and he couldn't help reflecting that with the cab driver's testimony, the window of opportunity for Peter's killer had now grown exceedingly small. So who had appeared after Anne had left the motel and stabbed a fully dressed Peter to death?

"So you can all stop talking about me behind my back," Anne told them fiercely.

Daniel waited to see if Amelia would point out that being innocent of murder eliminated only one of the sins of which Anne was presumed guilty, but it seemed that Amelia was in no mood for a scene tonight. When she spoke, it was mildly.

"We haven't been discussing you, Anne. But I am glad to know you're no longer under suspicion. Now perhaps you'll stop avoiding the rest of us. You do mean to sit down to dinner with us, I hope?"

"I'm not dressed," Anne said, uncomfortable now.

Daniel thought she looked as she always did, right down to her clunky boots, so he wasn't surprised when Amelia waved off the halfhearted protest.

"You look fine." She rose to her feet. "Shall we?"

As easily as that, Anne's return to the bosom of her family was accomplished. No one objected. No one even commented.

The others followed Amelia's lead in rising and leaving the room, including a subdued Anne, and since Laura walked out with Josie and Kerry, Daniel didn't get a chance to speak to her privately.

Not that he knew what he would have said. Something idiotic, no doubt, like asking her if she was all right when there was no reason she wouldn't be.

All through dinner he was overwhelmingly conscious of her sitting two chairs away. He hardly noticed Anne's hesitant attempts to talk to a smiling but distant Kerry. Barely heard Alex or Josie or Madeline when they spoke. But when Laura replied to some question Amelia had asked her, he heard every word, every inflection.

And when everyone afterward moved to the music room to hear Kerry play, he couldn't help finding a corner out of Amelia's sight and the attention of the others where he could look at Laura. He knew she felt his gaze, even though she didn't look at him once. While the slow throb of Beethoven's *Moonlight Sonata* filled the room, he stared at her and remembered once again the interlude in the attic.

She felt it, his gaze. Perhaps even his thoughts. Or maybe she was remembering too. He saw the silk over her breasts shimmer as her breathing quickened, saw color rise in her face. He watched her lips part and her fingers twine together in her lap. He was too far away to see it, but knew that a pulse beat quickly under the pale skin of her throat.

It had been nearly impossible for him to keep his hands off her before today; how, now, could he be expected to deny or ignore the hunger he felt for her? Today had given him a taste only, and there was no way on earth he could be satisfied with that.

Discreet? Christ, how long will I be able to hide it?

Not long.

He wondered if she had any idea at all how difficult it

had been for him not to reach out every time he saw her, not to touch her hand or her face or her bright hair. How difficult it was to be in one room when he knew she was in another somewhere in the house. He wanted her with him, wanted to look at her and touch her. Had to. It was why he had allowed Amelia to maneuver her into the house when every rational thought warned him of the price he might be called upon to pay for his reckless need to have her near.

He pulled his gaze from her with an effort and looked at Amelia, upright and composed as always, untouched by the riot of emotions he felt.

And what about you, Amelia? Are you just trying to distract me? To keep me from finding out the truth? Is that why you brought her here? Or are you up to something else? What do you really know about the mirror, Amelia? All of it—or only some? And if you know it all, how do you intend to use that knowledge against me?

How do you mean to destroy me without risking the power you love so much?

Daniel drew a silent breath and looked toward the piano without seeing it. He was doing all that he could, he reminded himself. Moving as quickly as he could. What other choice did he have?

He pushed the useless questions out of his mind and tried to concentrate on the music. But that was useless too. His gaze was drawn, again and again, to Laura, and by the end of Kerry's performance, Daniel was afraid that anyone looking at him would know, instantly and without question, just how out of control he felt.

No one seemed to, however, and as everyone moved—at Amelia's "suggestion"—across the hall to the den, where they would be expected to play cards or watch television or talk in order to while away her evening, he excused himself by saying that he had a few calls to make in the library.

Amelia nodded regally and began saying something to Kerry, who was walking beside her, while Anne moved ahead. Madeline was behind them, and Alex and Josie had lingered a moment in the music room, talking quietly. So when Laura passed him just outside the doorway, Daniel grabbed the opportunity. His hand caught hers for a fleeting instant, and he said, so low it would be inaudible to anyone else, "Come to me tonight. Please."

He saw the flash of green as she glanced up at him, but he didn't pause to try to read her expression. He turned away from her and went toward the library, knowing that if he was close to her a moment longer, no one in the family would be in any doubt of his feelings.

Chapter 11

*L*aura rubbed her left arm absently as she leaned against the window casing and looked out on the Kilbourne gardens. Not that she could see much. It was ten o'clock, and the scattered lights in the gardens were only faint pools of illumination dimmed and textured by the shadows of restless trees. The wind could be heard from time to time, moaning softly, and the coming storm had quite effectively blotted out the moonlight.

Not a pleasant night.

She had left the others downstairs a quarter of an hour before, telling Amelia that she wanted to come up here to her sitting room and "tinker" with some of her sketches before turning in for the night. And since Anne had, rather inexplicably, chosen to walk up with her on the way to her own room, Laura hadn't been given the chance to look for Daniel in the library even if she had wanted to.

She didn't want to think about how much she had wanted to.

Trying to distract herself and definitely not in the mood to tinker with her sketches, she found Dena's num-

ber in her purse and sat down on the comfortable sofa to
call the college student. She expected to get an answering
machine, assuming the younger woman was out on a Friday night, but Dena was in.

"Hi, Laura. I tried to call you earlier, but—"

"Yes, I'm away from home for the weekend. So I
thought I'd check in and see if you had more information
for me."

"You bet. Hold on a sec while I get my notes. . . ."
Dena was gone for a couple of minutes, then returned and
began speaking briskly. "Okay, we got lucky again—in
fact, I can't believe how lucky we've been. But I've told
you that, I guess."

"You've mentioned it. Go on."

"Umm . . . where is—oh, yeah, here it is. Well, as I
told you, Faith Kenley's sister, who was a prominent society widow and who inherited the mirror from Faith, died
in 1897 and her estate was sold at auction, in New York
City, in 1898. Attending that auction was a thirty-year-old
married woman by the name of Shelby Hadden, who,
you'll be interested to hear, collected mirrors."

"How do you know she collected them?" Laura asked.

"She's listed in the auctioneer's notes as a collector,
and it's mentioned in quite a few contemporary letters.
Seems she was pretty well known for it, at least during the
period of her life up to this point; no mention of it afterward. But she must have been fairly fanatical about it then,
because in one of his letters a year or so earlier, her husband seemed a little upset about what he obviously saw as
an unreasonable obsession."

Laura frowned as she gazed at nothing, then said, "You
got access to their letters?"

"Through a friend in New York who has access to the
relevant archives. Got a stack of faxes for you to see. Some
of Shelby's letters, her husband's—and letters from some-

body else I'm about to tell you about—plus a few newspaper stories. What happened was a big scandal, Laura."

"She met a man at the auction?" Laura ventured.

Dena was surprised. "How'd you guess that? As a matter of fact, she met a man a year or so older than her named Brett Galvin. Dunno how they managed to connect, since Shelby's husband was with her, but there's a letter from her to him dated a couple of days later, and it's obvious they've met on the sly since the auction."

"I see." Laura drew a breath. "Who bought the mirror? Shelby?"

"Yep. She mentions in that first letter to Brett something about how it must have been fate, both of them looking for a mirror that day, but she's the one who bought it. Anyway, they began an affair that, I gather from the few surviving letters from the period, was just about too hot to handle. None of Brett's letters from this period survived, probably because Shelby's husband destroyed them."

"He found out?"

"Oh, yeah. Not right away, though. In Shelby's letters to Brett, it's obvious that he's pushing her to divorce her husband and marry him, and she desperately wants to, no doubt about that. But she also has a little girl she obviously adored, and knew damned well she'd lose the kid if her husband had anything to say about it. She says she'd be willing to take the girl and run away with Brett without formally divorcing her husband, but she knows he'd hunt them down. And it's pretty obvious that although Brett's willing to raise Shelby's daughter, he most definitely wants Shelby to live with him as his wife, so that's what he's arguing for."

"Poor thing," Laura murmured. "It must have nearly torn her apart."

Dena sighed. "That comes across in her letters. If there had been no child, she wouldn't have hesitated, but she couldn't bear the thought of losing her daughter. In the end, of course, the choice was taken out of her hands. Her husband found out about the affair—nobody says how—and literally threw her out of his house with no more than her clothing and a few personal possessions— including the mirror, which, by the way, he shattered when he slammed it down on the sidewalk outside their house."

So that's how it was broken. "She went to Brett?"

"Nowhere else she could go. She had no family within hundreds of miles, and no friends that would have taken her in. This was before the turn of the century, remember; outsiders didn't interfere between a husband and wife. Brett tried to protect her as much as he was able, moving her into his house but bringing in a sister as chaperon. Nobody bought it, I'm afraid. If they weren't sharing a bed every night, they might as well have been as far as the gossip was concerned. According to public opinion, Shelby was definitely in the wrong—and they made her pay for her sins. So did her husband. He won custody of the child, smeared Shelby's reputation to hell and back, and as soon as the divorce was final, he left New York, refusing to tell her where he was taking her daughter. Shelby never saw the girl again."

"Jeez. Which one of us said this mirror seemed to be cursed?" Laura wondered, her gaze going to the mirror lying facedown on the coffee table beside her sketchpad.

"I don't remember, but it seems to have been prophetic. Want to hear the rest?"

"Just tell me there's a happy ending, dammit."

"Um . . . well, yes and no. Shelby and Brett moved to San Francisco, mostly to escape the scandal, and they were married there in 1900. For a few years, things were as good as they could have been; Shelby missed her daughter terribly, but she adored her husband, and soon they had two sons of their own."

"A few years?" Laura frowned, trying to grasp some elusive knowledge in her mind. "Wait a minute. Wasn't it about that time that the big earthquake nearly destroyed San Francisco?"

"Afraid so. 1906. Their home was destroyed—and their younger son was killed. Shelby was injured as well—something about her arm, but it's not clear exactly what happened to her. She complained in a letter or two later on that some nights she couldn't sleep for the ache, but there's no mention of her losing the arm or being disabled. Anyway, she and Brett managed to rebuild their lives and raise their remaining son. They had a lot of ups and downs, but their love never wavered. He had to travel some in business, so they wrote lots of letters to each other—I've got a few here for you to read—and they're so filled with devotion and passion that it's . . . almost embarrassing to read them. I felt like an intruder, you know? It's funny . . . I've never felt that way before in researching."

Laura was silent for a moment, then asked, "What about the end of their story?"

"Well, they lived together for nearly thirty years and died within days of each other in 1928 when a flu epidemic swept through the city. Brett was sixty-one; Shelby was sixty." Dena hesitated, then said, "You know, I have to say, I'd never really thought about romantic love very much. I mean, I've had my share of dates and crushes and lust—but never love. Maybe I never really believed in it. But these lives the mirror has passed through since it was made . . . it just seems to me that those couples loved each other in a way I can't even imagine."

"I know what you mean," Laura murmured, conscious of an ache deep inside her.

There was a little silence, and then Dena chuckled. "Hey, *you* didn't meet somebody special when you bought the mirror at that estate sale, did you? Hands

reaching for it on a shelf, eyes locking in fateful knowledge . . ."

Laura managed a laugh, glad that she hadn't filled Dena
in on any of the details of that day, including Peter Kilbourne's visit and subsequent murder—and very glad that
Dena was oblivious to current events and never looked at
newspapers less than forty or fifty years old. "Nobody was
anywhere near when I found that mirror," she said lightly.

"Too bad. I was hoping you could continue this love
thing the mirror seems to have going on."

*It was because of the mirror that I met Daniel. And the way I
felt when I first saw him . . .*

Laura pushed the turbulent questions in her mind aside
and managed to speak lightly yet again. "You don't know
if it *went* on beyond Shelby and Brett," she reminded the
young researcher. "Or do you?"

Back in her brisk mode, Dena replied, "No, not so far.
The Galvins' son, Andrew, inherited his parents' property
when they died. He continued to live in San Francisco and
never married. Died himself, an accidental drowning victim, at age fifty in 1952. So far, I've found out that his
estate was split up, much of it going to charity. It may take
me a while to track down where the mirror went, since it
wasn't mentioned specifically in his will or letter of instructions."

"Thanks, Dena. You've done a great job."

"Hold the applause until I track the mirror to the
Kilbournes' door. In the meantime, I'll leave these notes
and things in an envelope with the security guard at your
building, okay?"

"That'll be fine."

"And I'll call when I have more info. Good night,
Laura."

"Good night, Dena." Laura cradled the receiver and
sat for a time looking at nothing. Then her gaze shifted to
the mirror on the coffee table. Lovely, but such an ordi-

nary kind of thing, and so unobtrusive for something that had seemingly caused—or sparked—so much drama in so many lives. She didn't think Daniel had even noticed the mirror when he had been in here earlier; his gaze had never wavered from her. She leaned forward and picked up the mirror, turning it this way and that. She looked at her reflection, her gaze fixing as it always did on a point past her own shoulder at the room behind her.

Even though I know it's him I was looking for, I can't stop looking. Can't help expecting to see him there. As if he should be. As if the room is simply empty unless he's in it. And when I see him in a mirror, it's as if . . . as if I'm caught up in something beyond my control.

She put the mirror back on the coffee table, her fingers lingering to absently trace the intricate pattern stamped into the brass on the back. Then she leaned back with a sigh. *Think of logical things.* The history of the mirror, while fascinating and certainly moving, had so far revealed no connection whatsoever with the Kilbournes. In fact, as far as she could see, investigating the mirror had done little except to stimulate her already agitated imagination and fill her head with far too many irrelevant thoughts.

Irrelevant . . .

She got up and moved back to the window, too restless to sit any longer. Rubbed her arm absently. The storm was coming, she knew. It would be a bad one. Another hour, maybe two.

Come to me tonight. Please.

Had he lied to her about having been in Scotland? Why would he? Such an insignificant thing, after all. And that bothered her most of all, that he might lie about such a small and unimportant fact, because there were so many bigger and much more important things he could lie about, and Laura no longer trusted her ability to know when he was telling the truth. She hadn't doubted him when he'd said he had been to Scotland. . . .

God, so many questions. Had he told her the truth about the struggle between him and Amelia? Was he in the right, struggling to protect his family and preserve their way of life when Amelia would selfishly and recklessly squander their wealth? Was he being kinder than he had to be by allowing Amelia to present the appearance of authority even though that meant frustration and conflict for him? And was that all that was going on, this struggle for power? What, if anything, did it have to do with the murder of Peter Kilbourne?

And how was *she* tied in to all this? Was Daniel right in suggesting that Amelia had brought her into this house merely to be a distraction for him? If so, if that was all it was, then why was Laura so sure that he was somehow being very careful with her, holding something of himself back with utter deliberation and control? Because it wasn't real?

Come to me tonight. Please.

No, she didn't doubt his desire. His face had remained impassive as always, but she had felt his gaze tonight, his awareness, his . . . absorption in her. Once or twice she had even had the unsettling idea that she was reading his mind, seeing in hers images from their time in the attic and knowing he was thinking about that. It had required all the control she could muster to keep still and silent, to pretend indifference in the presence of his family.

But Laura had no idea if his desire was anything more than the physical, if his preoccupation with her was anything more than the sexual intensity common in a new love affair. Love . . . He had said they had made love. But she thought that would probably be his chosen phrase irrespective of any emotions involved; he would never be crass or vulgar given his upbringing and his reserved nature, and she doubted a more clinical description would appeal to him. So it meant nothing.

At some point, she thought, determinedly analytical,

he would no doubt refer to them as lovers, and that would mean nothing as well. Something she should keep in mind.

Come to me.

His voice was in her head, low and rough, taut with a soul-deep longing she felt herself. How could that not be real? How could he pretend so well if he felt nothing of this gnawing need that tormented her, this overwhelming yearning to be with him whatever the risk or the cost, to feel his powerful hands on her, his body close, so close to hers. . . .

Come to me.

Laura turned jerkily from the window and paced restlessly. A glance at the clock on the mantel told her it was nearly eleven. Still too early for bed. Desperate for something to occupy her attention, she took another shower, washing her hair this time, since she hadn't earlier. That took up ten minutes or so, with another twenty demanded to blow-dry the long, heavy mass of her hair and brush it until it gleamed.

She found herself smoothing on skin lotion in the scent she had used for years, and followed that by putting on her prettiest nightgown, long, emerald green, and silky, topped by a matching robe so sheer it was hardly worth the effort.

That was when she admitted consciously that she was going to go to him.

The admission made, there was nothing to do but wait. Laura sat on the couch in her sitting room and listened, hearing the wind from time to time as the storm neared. Hearing, faintly, footsteps outside her door at least twice as someone passed on the way to his or her room. It was a Friday night, when at least several of the family might be counted upon to be up—and probably out—late, but the worsening weather and lack of plans meant that everyone was home and likely to seek their own rooms by midnight.

Amelia, at least, always turned in by midnight, she had told Laura. Not that she slept much at her age, but there were always letters to be written or a good book to be read, and she enjoyed solitude. So she had said.

Laura listened to the little clock on the mantel chime midnight, just seconds before the full fury of the storm broke over the house. Thunder rolled and boomed and cracked, lightning flashed like strobes, and rain sheeted down, pelting the windows from time to time as the wind snatched at it.

She waited a few minutes longer, trying to hold on to patience by reminding herself of how embarrassing it would be to encounter someone outside her room dressed the way she was. But even that possibility couldn't do much to make her cautious. By quarter past midnight, with the storm still raging outside, she was slipping from her room and out into the quiet, deserted hallway.

There was a lamp near the top of the stairs to light this main section of the upper floor, and when Laura moved silently on thin-soled slippers into the west wing hallway, she found two more small lamps dimly illuminating that corridor. Almost holding her breath, she fixed her gaze on Daniel's door at the end of the hall and tried to move even more quietly as she passed other closed doors.

She was still several feet away when Daniel's door opened. Laura had no idea if he had heard or sensed her coming, or if he had merely assumed she would, but he was obviously unsurprised. His gaze traveled swiftly from her slippers to her face and then remained there, intent, his eyes a little narrowed. He stood back, holding the door wider so that she could come into his room, and when she had, he closed it softly behind her.

Laura barely noticed gleaming mahogany furniture or masculine decor, or even that the only light in the room came from a small lamp by the bed and the gas fire burning warmly in his fireplace. All she noticed was him. He had discarded his suit jacket and tie and had rolled up the sleeves of his white shirt loosely on his forearms. His gleaming black hair was a bit disheveled, as though he had been running his fingers through it, and there was tension in his face.

"I can't stay all night," she said huskily, determined to exert at least that much control over this.

He reached out and pulled her against him. "Then we'd better take advantage of the time we have," he murmured, his hands curving over her bottom to hold her even closer.

Laura caught her breath and slid her arms up around his neck. "You knew I'd come, didn't you?"

"How could I know? I hoped." His lips brushed her cheekbone, then covered her mouth hungrily.

Everything in Laura's mind, all the baffling questions and uneasy speculation, stilled in that moment. She didn't think, didn't want to or need to. She only felt. Her body molded itself to his, her mouth came alive to match his longing, and fire raced along every nerve in a shattering sensation that was almost but not quite pain.

She felt herself lifted and carried, felt the softness of his bed beneath her, but she didn't open her eyes. He was still kissing her, deep kisses that seemed like a drug she craved and could never get enough of. She was vaguely aware of shifting obediently to help him rid her of the nightgown and robe and her slippers, and knew her own fingers coped eagerly with the buttons of his shirt and then his belt and his pants. Still, she didn't open her eyes or say anything at all beyond murmuring his name when his mouth finally left hers to trace a searing path down her neck and over her breastbone.

Her nails dug into the hard, shifting muscles of his back when his lips closed over the tip of her breast, and Laura heard another of those unfamiliar sensual sounds escape her. The pleasure of his caress was sharp and potent, drawing her body taut instantly and creating deep inside her a hollow need for him that was so overwhelming it was almost frightening. Then his mouth left her flesh, and the ache of not having him there was unbearable.

"Look at me," he ordered, his voice low and rough.

Laura forced her eyes to open. The lamp by the bed lit half his face with a warm golden glow while leaving the other half in shadow, and she found the sight mesmerizing. Half known, half not, attracting her so irresistibly even as he made her wary, he was a mystery she desperately needed to understand. "Daniel," she murmured, as if answering a question he had asked or she had asked herself.

His hands slid underneath her, and instead of lowering his mouth to her, he lifted her to take his caress. Laura's back arched and she caught her breath at the strange sensuality of the movement, then moaned at the piercing satisfaction of having his mouth back on her aching flesh. He was holding her in place with one hand still beneath her back, while the other gently shaped and kneaded her breasts, and Laura didn't know how long she would be able to bear it.

He made her bear it. His mouth tugged at her nipples and his hand stroked her breasts and then slid lower, rubbing her belly, then lower still, and Laura cried out softly in wordless pleasure. Her thighs parted for him and her hips moved instinctively to his rhythmic touch, and Laura surrendered helplessly to the demands of her own desperate body. She couldn't see or hear or feel anything except the exquisite tension torturing her with its promise.

Daniel waited until she was shifting restlessly, until her fingers gripped his shoulders pleadingly and uncontrolled little sounds of frantic need came from her, and then he moved swiftly to settle between her thighs. Laura felt him push inside her, deep inside, filling the terrible aching emptiness, and she bit her lip to keep from crying out wildly, to scream because it felt so good.

His body lay heavily on hers and Daniel slid his fore-arms underneath her shoulders and held them with his hands as though he feared she might slip away from him. His face was taut, his voice a rasping whisper when he said, "Don't hold back, sweetheart. This is an old house; the walls are thick."

Laura barely noticed the endearment or his perception, because he was moving in a slow, lingering cadence that held her body rapt with a fierce tension that was, had to be, like the moment before life ended. She even thought, with some distant and detached part of her awareness, that nothing could feel so incredibly wondrous unless the price demanded for it was death.

She didn't care. The tension wound tighter and tighter, making her body jerk and undulate beneath his, drawing strange keening sounds from her throat, and al-lowing her to breathe only in sharp, shallow pants. And then, with shattering suddenness, the tension snapped, and waves and waves of throbbing pleasure washed over her.

She finally went limp, trembling, just as Daniel reached his climax, and her fingertips glided up his spine in an unthinking caress as he groaned and shuddered in her arms.

It was a long time before he stirred, and Laura luxuri-ated in the hardness of his body, the heavy weight bearing her down into the mattress. She was not the least bit un-comfortable, which surprised her given his size. A part of nature's design, she supposed, that men and women should fit so well together even with a disparity in size and build. In any case, she loved the way he felt, loved his warm breath against her neck and then his nuzzling lips, and when he lifted his head and raised himself just a bit on his elbows to look down at her, Laura was very much afraid that her blissful satisfaction showed.

He was smiling just a little, his face relaxed now, and those normally pale eyes were dark in the scant light of the room. "I don't want to leave you," he murmured, his forearms still under her shoulders and his hands tangled in her hair. "But if I'm too heavy—"

"No, you aren't." His fingers were moving lazily against her scalp, their bodies were still joined, and Laura felt such contentment she wanted to purr out loud. It was still storming, she realized vaguely, hearing a rumble of thunder. Or was this another storm altogether?

"Good." Daniel kissed her gently. "Maybe I should hold you here all night."

"You know I can't stay." The statement was neither as unequivocal nor as matter-of-fact as she meant it to be, since her fingers were stroking the nape of his neck at the time.

He kissed her again, this time with more hunger than tenderness, and she felt the faint stirrings inside her of his reawakening desire. "You can stay for hours yet," he told her huskily, his lips brushing across her cheekbones.

Laura wanted to remind him that he had business in the morning, that both of them would be expected to bear the appearance of people with a solid eight hours of sleep behind them, and that if they didn't, Amelia at least would certainly be suspicious. She wanted to say that. But his lips were moving over her face, teasingly avoiding her own hungry mouth, and by the time she finally managed to put a stop to his tormenting, there didn't seem to be much use in continuing the conversation.

THEY HAD SLEPT awhile, Laura realized when she woke around three-thirty as yet another storm vented its fury outside. When she eased up onto her elbow, a glance at his bedside clock told her the time, and she spent a good five minutes looking down at him as he slept. Utterly relaxed now, he looked younger, and the rugged planes of his face seemed softer, less harsh. He had unusually long eyelashes,

she realized, something that normally went unnoticed because they framed those strikingly pale and unreadable
eyes.

He lay on his back beside her while she lay in the circle
of his right arm, and on his flat, hard stomach his left hand
and her right were clasped, their fingers twining together.
Laura wondered which of them was so determined to hold
on to the other that the grasp hadn't loosened even in
sleep, and had the uneasy idea that it was her. Proof of that
was when she was able to slip her hand gently from his.

I'm clinging to him. Gotta stop that.

She wasn't yet ready to leave him and go back to her
own room, and she didn't want to wake him, since he
seemed to be sleeping deeply, but she was wide awake and
felt too restless to just lie there quietly. There was too
much to think about lying in his bed, she decided. Too
much to worry about. She'd be better off all around if she
found something to occupy her mind until he woke or it
got so late she'd have to go back to her own room.

She managed to slip from his loosened embrace without waking him, and knelt beside the bed among the jumble of their clothing on the floor. It amused her slightly
that their clothing had once more ended in a tangle. She
pushed his shoes and her slippers to one side, and laid his
pants and shorts over a chair near the bed. She fingered her
gown and robe for a moment before tossing them over the
arm of the chair, then shrugged into his white shirt.

Laura's art training had included studies of the nude,
and between that and an innate lack of undue modesty or
self-consciousness, she would have been perfectly comfortable roaming about Daniel's dim room naked. So she
was amused at herself for putting on his shirt.

Women always do this in books and movies. I wonder why.
Never having had a lover in the true sense of the word,
Laura had no experience with such things. But putting on
a lover's shirt instead of their own things seemed to be the

rule in books and movies, and created mild curiosity in Laura's mind. Then she turned her head to rub her chin absently against the collar of his shirt, and his scent caught her instant attention. *Ah. Now I understand.* She knelt there for several minutes just breathing in the slightly musky scent of Daniel, her eyes half closed, and might have remained there in a mindless heap for some time if a crash of thunder and the discomfort of the hardwood floor beneath her knees hadn't driven her to her feet.

She studied his bedroom as she hadn't before, noting the mostly heavy mahogany furniture and muted rugs scattered on the floor. There was an overstuffed burgundy armchair and ottoman near the fireplace, and a padded bench at the foot of the big bed. The draperies and bedspread were a dark green, the wallpaper in here a subdued stripe, and there wasn't a great deal to reveal Daniel's personality except for bookshelves on either side of the fireplace. She went to them and studied titles in the dim light, finding a number of old friends in fiction, numerous nonfiction volumes on finance and related subjects, and a couple of figurines that looked to her uncertain eye to have come from Hong Kong or some part of the Orient.

She wandered on, looking at quietly tasteful oils on his walls, none of which aroused more than mild interest until she saw the portrait hanging near the window. John Kilbourne, Daniel's father. It had to be, she thought, because this man was a slightly older edition of Daniel, with only a touch of gray at his temples and a more heavily lined face to indicate more years than his son had yet achieved.

Odd. Daniel's the living image of his father, and yet Madeline said that Peter was all she had left of John. Or did Daniel inherit the physical appearance while Peter got the personality of their father?

Laura made a mental note to ask someone about that and wandered on, ending up at the window that faced the rear of the house. Since Daniel's room was at the end of

the wing, his bedroom and bathroom between them
boasted windows on three sides of the house, but the best
view would be this window looking out over the gardens
just as Laura's window did.

She leaned against the casing and looked down on the
gardens, interested to see that the maze was visible from
this vantage point. The lights were still on out there, as
they no doubt were all night, and from here there were
fewer trees blocking her line of sight to the maze. It was a
weird, almost ghostly scene on this stormy night, the
shrubbery lights delineating the paths of the maze even as
the rain blurred and softened the lines and lightning
flashed sporadic harsh emphasis on the display.

It was the strobelike lightning that caught her attention, though she couldn't have said why. Because it was so
powerful, she thought, or because in the momentary bril-
liance of that light she glimpsed something that tugged at
her awareness. . . .

"Laura?"

She turned her head to look back toward the bed, and
caught her breath. Clearly, Daniel didn't have a problem
with nudity any more than she did. He was moving across
the room toward her, his grace catlike and his strength
stunningly explicit in rippling muscles and powerful limbs.
Big, rugged, starkly masculine, he was a blunt invitation
for any woman to learn just what her body was capable of
feeling.

That, Laura thought dazedly, was how a man should
always approach a woman—naked in the firelight. There
was something heart-catchingly primitive in the sight, and
long before he reached her, Laura felt the effect in her
thudding heart and sudden inability to breathe evenly. It
was like recognizing a primal force that would never,
could never, be contained or controlled except by its own
will.

Yes, you're that. You've always been that. And I've always been—

"I thought you'd gone," he said when he reached her, his low voice displacing the strange sensation his approach had created. He put his hands at her waist and drew her against him.

"I should go. It's almost four." She had the odd notion that she had been on the verge of . . . something. That some knowledge she needed had been right at the door of her awareness, almost within reach. But it was gone now.

He bent his head and kissed her, the initial gentleness deepening as always, and against her lips, he said huskily, "I should let you go. But I don't want to. Stay a little longer, sweetheart. Please."

Possible revelations slipped from her mind even as her arms slipped up around his neck, and all she could say in response was, "I want to."

After that, Laura wasn't at all surprised to find herself back in his bed, and when she next worked herself up on an elbow and looked at the clock, she also wasn't surprised to find that it was nearly five A.M. The storms had finally faded away, and it was very quiet in the bedroom.

"I know," Daniel said, one hand toying with her hair and a slight smile curving his lips.

"It's awfully late," she said anyway. "Or early. You have to go into the city in just a few hours, don't you?"

"Around ten."

Laura nodded, and hesitated before speaking again. She didn't want to disturb the peaceful contentment between them, but she also had no idea when—or even if—there would be another moment such as this, when the intimacy of the past hours might be expected to encourage truth, or at the very least diminish guardedness.

"What is it, Laura? What's wrong?"

"Wrong? Nothing. That is . . ." She shook her head

a little, then blurted, "Did you lie about having been in Scotland?"

"No," he replied calmly. "Who told you I hadn't been there?"

"I asked Josie," she confessed, uncomfortable now. "She said you hadn't."

"In the last five years, I haven't," Daniel said. "It was before Josie came to live here." His free hand moved to cup her cheek. "Why do you have to doubt me, Laura? I wish you could learn to trust me."

"I want to. But—but you haven't been completely truthful with me, have you?"

"About what?" His question seemed honestly puzzled, but his eyes were dark and abruptly shuttered.

It unnerved her. And it made her feel guarded herself, unwilling to show her own vulnerability when he had retreated from her this way. He was warding her off, protecting himself somehow, and she had to do the same thing. Frustrated and troubled, Laura fell back on the thing that had brought her to this family in the first place. "About the mirror, for instance."

He sighed. "Laura, listen to me. There is nothing I can tell you about that mirror. I don't believe it's connected in any way to Peter's murder, and as far as I know, it was just another piece of forgotten junk up in the attic. It brought you here, and for that I'm grateful, but beyond that I'm not interested in your mirror. And that is the truth."

She wanted to believe him, desperately wanted to. But she felt certain that among his seemingly honest and straightforward words lurked, somehow, somewhere, a deception. He knew more about the mirror than he claimed to. So why did he continue to lie about it?

Unwilling to call him a liar to his face, Laura said, "All right."

His hand slipped under her thick hair to the nape of her neck, and he pulled gently until she was closer. "No, it isn't all right." His voice roughened. "You've gone away from me."

Only after you went away from me. But she didn't say it out loud, unwilling to admit to him that his withdrawal had hurt. Instead, in a voice she tried hard to keep steady, she said, "I don't know what you want from me. What do you want, Daniel? If it's just this, sex now and then with no strings and no questions on either side, then tell me. I can't play your game until I know the rules."

His fingers tightened on her neck, and his face hardened. It was a brief reaction, lasting only an instant, but in that instant Laura felt an odd little shock that wasn't exactly fear but a tangle of respect and apprehension and a strange understanding. She couldn't explain how she knew, but she was certain that this man was capable of great violence, that it was an innate thing buried deeply in his nature and checked only by the rules and laws he chose to obey. And that it would never be directed against her.

"It's no game," he said very quietly, the momentary hint of intensity gone now. "Not this, not what's between us. You know that, Laura. You have to know it."

She did know that, or felt it at least. But she couldn't help saying, "I guess you have another name for it, then. Daniel . . . I don't expect or ask for bedroom promises. But I expect honesty. So if there's a question you don't want to answer, say so. Something you don't want to talk to me about, say so. Just don't lie to me."

He looked at her for a long moment, expression unreadable, his fingers moving gently against her neck. Then he sighed. "And if there are things I don't want to talk about to you at present? Areas of my life I'd rather not get into right now? Will knowing that make you hold yourself at a distance from me? Will it cause you to believe you can't trust me? Answer that with the truth, Laura."

She hesitated, then said, "I don't know. But I know I'd

rather hear the truth than a lie—even if that truth is only that there are things you don't want me to know."

It was his turn to hesitate, a moment longer than she had, and when he spoke, it was with deliberation. "Would it make any difference to you if that truth is that there are things I don't want you to know *at present*? When the tensions of today are past, when Peter's killer is found and my . . . current battle with Amelia is concluded, there'll be no more questions between us, no lies or evasions. Nothing left unanswered. I promise you that."

Laura found that response as tantalizing as anything yet said between them, and couldn't help thinking it might have been better for her to have gone on wondering if he was being truthful rather than to be bluntly told there were things he didn't want her to know. Because that knowledge was virtually guaranteed to madden her.

"Laura, I realize that isn't the answer you wanted. But it is the truth you wanted. And it's all I can offer you right now."

After a moment she pulled gently away from him and sat up, linking her arms around her upraised knees and gazing somewhat blindly across the room at the fire. "I wish I knew what that meant," she murmured. The bed moved under her as he sat up as well, and she felt his hand lightly stroking her bare back, his lips press briefly to her shoulder.

"It isn't a question of trust," he said.

"That's what it sounds like."

"No. I trust you. But I need . . . to be in control right now. And I can only do that in my own way. Something you have to trust in. I'm asking you to do that, Laura. To trust me. To be patient awhile longer."

"You ask a lot."

"I know. But do I ask too much?"

"That depends." She turned her head to look at him. "There's something I—I have to know. Something that's been bothering me since the first day I walked into this house. Are you . . . have you been using me somehow in this fight with Amelia?"

"No," he said instantly.

She searched his features uncertainly. "I felt—that day and since—that you were. That both of you were somehow using me like a pawn."

"Amelia was. Is. Maybe only trying to distract me—I'm not sure. But I never did, I swear. All I tried to do was . . . keep you here. I allowed Amelia to maneuver you when I might have been able to stop her, but it was only for that reason. Because I wanted you to be here."

"And when you followed me up to the attic? It wasn't part of a—a cold-blooded plan?"

Daniel released an odd little sound halfway between a laugh and a groan. "A plan? I wanted you so badly I couldn't think straight, much less plan anything. As for being cold-blooded, no. Never about you. Where you're concerned, my blood is a long way from cold, and any detachment far out of my reach. About you I can only feel."

Laura returned her gaze to the fire, trying not to let the seduction of his words sway her against her own reason, trying to think it through. He was asking her to trust him even while saying there were secrets he was keeping from her, and she just didn't know if she could do that. She *felt* that she could trust him, but her mind was filled with so many questions. . . .

"Laura?"

She felt herself nodding even before she was consciously aware of what her answer would be. "All right. Like you said, it's the truth I wanted. What I asked for. So I guess you aren't asking too much in return. I—have to get back to my room." Before he could move or say anything, she slipped quickly from the bed. She had to go around it to reach the chair where her things lay, but the steady gaze she could feel didn't make her self-conscious or disturb her at all. She got her nightgown and slipped into it and the sheer robe, then put one hand on the side of the bed as she bent to locate and put on her slippers.

As she straightened, Daniel leaned across the bed suddenly and caught her wrist. "Look at me," he ordered softly.

Laura knew that he would see she was still disturbed by all this, but there was nothing she could do about it. She looked at him.

His mouth looked a little hard and more than a little grim, but when he pulled her down far enough for him to kiss her, he didn't feel hard at all. His lips were soft and warm as they moved on hers, and seduced her so quickly that she felt her knees go weak and had to sit on the edge of the bed or she would have fallen. By the time he finally allowed her to draw away a bit, it required an effort for her to do so.

There was heat now in his gaze and his mouth had a softened, sensual curve. "Whatever else you doubt," he said in a rough voice, "never doubt that what we have is real and honest. And nothing's going to change that, Laura. Nothing."

Laura nodded slowly. "I know." *But just what is it we have, Daniel? What would you call it?*

He seemed about to say something else, but finally released her wrist and fell back on the bed, looking up at her with restless eyes. "Go on. If I don't let you go now, we'll still be here at noon."

She would have liked nothing better than to crawl back into bed with him, but Laura forced herself to get off the bed and go to the door. She hesitated there for an instant, looking back at him, then silently left his bedroom.

With no storm outside now, the house was deathly

quiet, and she found herself tiptoeing as she went swiftly down the long hallway. She had an eerie sense of being pursued, and so strong was it that when she finally reached her room and closed the door behind her, she could feel her heart thudding in a fast, frightened rhythm.

Do I have a guilty conscience, or what? It was a rueful question, and Laura didn't bother answering it. She knew the answer.

It seemed hardly worth the effort to go to bed now when she needed to be up in just a few short hours, but she was tired and knew those few hours of sleep would be better than none. She was halfway across the sitting room when something tugged abruptly at her attention, and she turned back to frowningly survey the room.

Lamplit, as she'd left it. Undisturbed. But as she started to turn away once more, she caught the flash of light, and this time she moved slowly to the coffee table. Her sketchpad was lying there, just as she'd left it. And the mirror.

Faceup.

Someone had been in this room.

Chapter 12

The law offices of Kennard, Montgomery, and Kilbourne occupied two floors of a downtown office building in Atlanta and were virtually silent on this Saturday morning. Daniel encountered no one as he made his way along thickly carpeted corridors to Alex's tenth-floor corner office, something that hardly surprised him. Though the firm was certainly busy enough during the week, the demands of their one client did not generally require working overtime, weekends, or holidays.

When he strolled into Alex's office, Daniel also wasn't surprised to find him dressed casually in jeans and a sport shirt; though he bowed cheerfully enough to custom and wore reasonably sober suits during the week, his tendency toward comical and sometimes downright garish ties spoke volumes for his less than staid personality. Even his office, certainly elegant enough at first glance, boasted a few odd items in ludicrous contrast, such as a full-color and possibly full-sized figurine of a Tasmanian devil wedged between law books on a shelf, and a gaudy silver trophy on his desk which proclaimed him the Best Kisser of the high school class of 1987.

He was working at a computer on his desk, fingers flying over the keys, and muttered, "Just a second," after glancing up to see his visitor.

"Not my business?" Daniel asked.

Alex grunted. "Yeah, but not what we need to talk about today. Just that nuisance suit. We go to court in a couple of weeks now, and I wanted to get this done. . . . Be with you in a minute."

Daniel accepted that and wandered over to a window that looked out on downtown Atlanta. Not that he cared for the scenery. In fact, he didn't even notice it. He just looked out, focused on nothing. He tended to be able to function on little sleep when necessary, but with an unusually active night behind him and growing anxiety over Laura, he was feeling more than a little edgy. Certainly too tense to sit calmly and wait for Alex, and too tense to be at all interested in scenery he knew well.

He shoved his hands into the pockets of his casual black leather jacket and settled his shoulders, wishing this whole damned thing was finished one way or the other. His patience was wearing thin. And he had the uneasy suspicion that time was getting short as well, though he couldn't pinpoint why. Perhaps because Peter's murderer was still at large, an unknown and possibly threatening factor, or perhaps it was simply that Amelia had been too quiet lately, too sedate. That was not like her, and it rang warning bells in his mind.

And right now she was back at the house, with Laura and saying God knew what to her. Dripping sweet poison, probably. Not something he liked to think about, especially given Laura's doubts about him.

"You know, there's a gym with a punching bag two floors up," Alex said. "In case you need one."

"What I need to punch is dead," Daniel said flatly,

turning to face the younger man but remaining by the window. "The worst thing I know of Peter is that he got himself murdered before I could beat the hell out of him."

"No, I don't think that's going to be the worst we know about him."

That dry statement did nothing to ease Daniel's mind. Nothing at all. "Oh, Christ. What have you found?"

Alex leaned back and opened the center drawer of his desk. "Well, I finally tracked down that lockbox of Peter's."

"What the hell took so long?"

"Hey, I think I did pretty damned good, considering the thing was in a bank outside Atlanta. In Macon, to be precise. I spent all of yesterday driving there and back. And I don't recommend the trip."

Daniel couldn't help smiling a little at Alex's indignation. "Sorry. My temper's a bit frayed these days."

"No, really?"

"Alex."

"Okay, okay. The bank VP wasn't thrilled about the situation and didn't want to let me at the box, but since I'd had the intelligent forethought to bring along letters of authorization from you and the firm as well as a copy of Peter's will naming me executor— By the way, how the hell did that happen? Been meaning to ask you."

"That Peter named you his executor? The first I knew of it was when Preston told us the will existed just before Peter's funeral. I imagine he chose you because he didn't want to choose me."

Alex grunted. "I think he did it just to piss me off. Must have known the last thing I'd want to spend my time doing would be wading through the garbage he left behind."

"Knowing Peter, I doubt very much that he expected to die at all—far less before he saw his thirtieth birthday.

Are you going to tell me what you found in the box, or what?"

Alex pulled a large, bulky manila envelope from his desk drawer and placed it on the blotter. "Take a look at this." He opened the envelope and upended it, spilling the contents onto his blotter.

Daniel stepped to the desk and looked down with a frown. In front of Alex were two bundles of cash, each bound with a rubber band, a tagged key that looked as though it would fit a safe deposit box, and a gun.

After a long moment, Daniel picked up the automatic, made sure the safety was on, and ejected the clip long enough to note that it was full. Then he replaced the clip and set the gun gently back on the blotter, and picked up a bundle of cash. "How much?"

"A hundred grand total," Alex reported. "Any idea how Peter could have laid his hands on that much cash when he always seemed to be the next best thing to broke?"

Daniel glanced at the gun once again as he put the bundle back on the desk. "No."

Expressionlessly, Alex said, "I would have said he was too nervous to steal. By using a gun, I mean."

"I would have said the same thing. Peter always looked for the easy score, the fastest way to get what he wanted with the least risk to himself. Convenience store holdups were hardly his style. Is the gun registered?"

"No. And since the serial number's been filed off, I can't trace it. God knows where he came by it."

Daniel nodded. "The key?"

"Another damned lockbox key," Alex said, morose. "The tag, you'll notice, has nothing but the number two on it. Why do I have the depressing feeling that I'm going to be chasing all over hell and half of Georgia tracking down Peter's stashes?"

Instead of replying to that bitter question, Daniel asked, "When was this box opened?"

"Six months ago. And according to the bank records, Peter never came back after he opened it."

"Any way to track the money, find out where it came from?"

Alex shook his head. "Old bills, well used, nonconsecutive numbers. I even had a friend of mine with the police check out a few bills just to make sure I wasn't missing something, that they weren't marked or whatever. He told me there was no way of knowing where this stuff came from."

"A friend you can trust?"

"Yeah, he owes me a few favors. I didn't tell him it was connected with Peter, and he didn't ask. Don't worry— he's in a completely different department from Brent Landry."

Daniel nodded and moved back around the desk to sit down in Alex's visitor's chair. "Well, what do you think?"

"I think Peter was up to no damned good," Alex replied flatly, leaning forward to prop his elbows on the desk. "But as to how he got this money . . . Look. We know he gambled, something the police haven't discovered yet but very likely will. Possible enemies there, but why would any of them kill the golden goose? If he was dead, he couldn't pay for his losses, and the people who held his markers damned sure wouldn't be applying to his estate for payment."

"Agreed," Daniel said, frowning. "And since we haven't yet been able to determine how much he owed and to whom . . ."

"A dead end—if you'll pardon the pun." Alex wasn't smiling. "We're also reasonably sure that Peter was less than honest in his other dealings."

"Yes," Daniel said. "But being less than honest is one thing, treason is another."

"Have the schematics shown up in some nice convenient place where we hadn't yet looked?"

"No. But we can't be sure they've been sold."

"So you haven't reported them missing?"

"How can I? One hint of this gets public and Kilbourne Data is finished—to say nothing of the family reputation *and* my own. With no proof, we'd only be ruined by rumor, innuendo, and lack of trust. If, on the other hand, the design shows up somewhere in the Middle East, then it's treason."

"And you're the one left holding the bag. Especially now that Peter's gone."

Daniel shifted restlessly in his chair. "As bad as Peter was, I still can't bring myself to believe he'd commit treason."

Alex shrugged. "Maybe it wasn't so bad, to Peter. Maybe he wouldn't have called it treason. Daniel, he didn't like answering to you. He didn't like being on an allowance that didn't stretch to cover things like high-stakes poker and trips to Vegas and foreign sports cars. It was galling to him that everyone knew he had no power in the family business. So maybe he decided to take a big risk for the first time in his life. Roll the dice, everything at stake. If he won, he could live more than comfortably on some beach somewhere for the rest of his life. If he lost . . . well, look at this stash. To me it says one of two things. Either Peter needed to hide the money and gun for whatever reason, or else he had it laid by in case he needed to make a quick exit."

"And you favor the latter explanation."

"It makes the most sense to me, given Peter's nature. If there was going to be trouble, he'd run like a rabbit."

That was true enough, and Daniel knew it. "And the second lockbox key? Another stash?"

"Maybe. Even bad gamblers get lucky from time to time; if he'd had a run of good luck in the last couple of years, Peter could have socked away a few hundred thousand by now. Or . . ."

"Or?"

Alex sighed and began putting the money and gun back into the envelope. "Oh, hell, Daniel, you know what I'm thinking. That microcassette tape I found in Peter's room. There's only one reason a man like Peter would have taped the sex and pillow talk between him and the wife of one of the most prominent men in Georgia politics, and it wasn't for posterity."

"We don't know that," Daniel argued.

"No, we don't know for sure. Whitney Fremont has been in Washington with her husband for the past couple of months, and neither of us is willing to fly up there and ask her if Peter was blackmailing her. Since she was attending a diplomatic reception in our nation's capital the night Peter was murdered, we can be fairly sure she didn't use the knife, but how do we know this cash didn't make its way from her bank account into Peter's hands as hush money?"

"He still had the tape," Daniel said, continuing to play devil's advocate.

"Yeah, he did. A copy, maybe. Or he intended to bleed her more than once before handing it over. Maybe she wasn't smart enough to demand the tape, or maybe he lied about having destroyed it. But any way you look at it, Peter had something that lady would have paid plenty to keep secret. And to Peter, it probably looked very much like easy money. Money he could hide away in case he needed it later." Alex paused, then added, "And I think we both know that if Peter did find blackmailing easy money, then Mrs. Fremont wasn't likely to be his only victim. Hell, we have no idea how long this might have been going on. It was never difficult for him to get a woman into his bed, and Peter would have been amused by the idea of combining business and pleasure. So there may well be more of his victims out there, and one of them might have got fed up with paying hush money."

Alex was saying nothing Daniel hadn't already said to himself, but hearing it spoken aloud made it worse somehow. "The pride of the Kilbournes," he said now rather grimly. "Lecher, gambler, thief, blackmailer—and possible traitor. It's a wonder he lived as long as he did."

"The question is, how much of this will the police uncover before they find his killer? And the big question is, which of Peter's bad habits got him murdered?"

"And the biggest question of all," Daniel said, "is how much of this is Amelia involved in?"

"ARE YOU GOING to allow me to see this one, child?" Amelia asked.

Laura looked beyond the canvas to where the old lady sat in the fan-back wicker chair, and said lightly, "Can I wait awhile to answer that? As I said, this is sort of a trial run—that's why we're doing it here in the conservatory. I just want to work with the oils with you as subject and find out if I know what I'm doing."

"And as I said, Laura, I understand the difference between preliminary and final work. I promise not to judge you too harshly."

There was little Laura could say to that except, "Very well, Amelia. I'd rather you waited at least until the end of this session, though. Give me a chance to get as much done as possible."

Amelia smiled. "Of course."

Laura turned her gaze back to the canvas, where the shape of Amelia was pale flesh and hair and stark black clothing, with no texture yet, no shadows or highlights. Not even a face, really, just the shape of one, featureless. For some reason, that last made Laura feel uneasy, and she immediately began working on Amelia's dark eyes.

"You seem distracted today, child. And you look tired."

Laura had expected Amelia to comment sooner or later on what she knew was obvious, so she was ready with a casual answer. "I'm like a cat when it storms, restless and uneasy. I didn't get much sleep last night. But I'll be fine, Amelia."

"I see we share some of the same traits. Storms make me fidgety. This time of the year, with so many of them, I usually end up walking the halls of the house all night. As I did last night."

Laura looked at her. *How the hell do I paint those guileless eyes? Was it you in my room, Amelia? And if it was, why don't you say so? Why play with me like a cat with a mouse? Is that just something you like to do—play with people?* But all Laura said, calmly, was, "You should have knocked on my door. We could have played cards or worked on the sketches."

She half expected Amelia to call her bluff, but all the old lady said was, "Now that I know storms make you restless too, I'll remember that. Next time."

Going back to her painting, Laura could only hope that her own expression was as blandly innocent as Amelia's. But she doubted it. She *was* tired, and in the bright light of today, last night's events—all of them—seemed dreamlike. Now, thinking about them, letting the memories filter through her mind, they seemed even more unreal. She could hardly believe she had gone to Daniel's room, that they had spent hours together and made love with such intensity that even now there was a lingering soreness in her muscles and an unfamiliar and unnervingly sensual feeling of languor throughout her entire body.

She could hardly believe she had as good as told him he could—with her blessing, yet!—keep the truth from her. What *was* the hold the man had over her that he could persuade her to accept things against all rational thought?

She hadn't seen him at all this morning; he'd already

left the house when she came down to breakfast around eight-thirty. And she doubted he'd be home before afternoon. Was his appointment this morning ordinary business, or would he have declined to talk about it if she had asked?

"Laura?"

She frowned at painted dark eyes that still weren't right, then lifted her gaze to meet the real ones. "Hmm?"

"I need to go check on lunch, child. Can you do without me for a little while?"

Laura was a little startled to realize so much time had passed, and even more surprised when she saw how much work she had done on Amelia's face in the painting. Her fingers quite definitely had ideas of their own and seemed to work better when guided by—she assumed—her subconscious attention. God knew her thoughts had been elsewhere. "Yes, of course," she murmured, studying the shading and highlighting that had caught those distinct cheekbones and the gracious but somewhat enigmatic smile and the elegant nose. But those eyes still weren't right. . . .

Amelia let out a little laugh, but said nothing else, just rose and went into the house. Laura, knowing that she'd have to stop work soon for lunch, stood back studying the painting as she absently cleaned her brushes.

"Hey, that's pretty good."

She wasn't startled this time, but only because she'd heard Anne's clunky boots on the tile. "Thanks," she said, looking at the older woman. "Still a lot of work to do, though."

In the restless way of someone who didn't know what to do with her hands, Anne shoved them into the pockets of her long skirt, and fixed her gaze on the painting. But Laura doubted she was really looking at it, because when she spoke it was about something else entirely.

"I guess you think I'm pretty awful."

So, it's my turn to accept the olive branch, huh? Anne had been determinedly and methodically making peace since last night, singling out the members of her family one by one, and though Laura didn't think the attempts were mere lip service, she did think it said a lot about Anne's self-centered nature that she wanted her transgressions forgiven. By everyone, even a visitor in the house.

Mildly, Laura said, "I think Peter was very charming and very hard to resist."

Color burned across Anne's excellent cheekbones, and she shot Laura a swift, almost resentful glance. But then she seemed to remember that she was here to redeem herself, and drew a breath. "Yeah. Yeah, he was. He knew just what to say to you to make you forget . . . things."

Laura didn't ask what things, preferring to steer the conversation away from the bedroom. "Anne, you said once that Peter was killed because of the way this family does business. What did you mean by that?"

Anne frowned, her gaze still fixed on the painting. "They're ruthless, both of them. Daniel and Amelia. Winning is all that counts. It's the way Kilbournes have always done business."

"So Peter had to win?"

"He was being closed out, pushed out by Daniel. Treated like an idiot, like what he thought didn't count for anything. And Amelia used him to run her errands, for God's sake, as though he were a servant. He couldn't take that, could he? Not a Kilbourne."

Laura could almost hear Peter's smooth and charming voice, see his incredibly handsome face, as he told all his troubles to his cousin, winning her sympathy and her loyalty. Eventually getting her into his bed, surely a triumph since their blood relation would have made the brief affair even more titillating to a man like Peter. She wondered if it had occurred to Anne at all that a man of nearly thirty who complained of being treated badly by his family even as he seduced his own cousin was not a man who could be counted on for truth.

"What did he do?" Laura asked softly. "You said he had plans."

Anne had her hands out of her pockets now and was rubbing her thin upper arms absently as though she were cold. "He did. Big plans. He told me. As soon as the money came in, he was going to show everybody."

"What money?"

"The money he was expecting. He said a friend was . . . investing in his future. Something like that. First he had to do another one of Amelia's stupid errands, take care of the pitiful bones she threw his way. And then he was going to get his money."

"What was he going to do with the money?"

"He was going to start his own business." Anne's chin lifted defiantly as she looked at Laura. "One to compete with the family. He already had people lined up, managers and designers and computer experts, and he was sure he could take some of those government contracts away from the family. He could have bid lower, you see, outbid the family, and once he got his toe in the door, everybody'd come to him with other contracts. He had it all planned."

Laura didn't know much about business, but it seemed to her that Peter's "plans" had been vague at best. Of course, it was possible that Anne herself was simply vague, that Peter had drawn up more detailed plans, but it still sounded to Laura like the impractical, grandiloquent daydreams of an embittered man who badly wanted to show up his more successful brother.

"When did he tell you about it?" she asked casually. "Not that last night?"

"No, a couple of days before that."

"But you believe he was killed because he had to win? Because he had to best the family? Best Daniel?"

Anne nodded decidedly. "I think so. I'll bet it wasn't a

friend he got the money from at all, but one of those shady types he knew. He thought I didn't know about them, but I did. I saw some of them with him a few times when he didn't know I was around. I'll bet anything that he borrowed lots of money from them or talked them into investing in his business, and later, for some reason, they turned against him and killed him."

With a more logical mind than Anne's, Laura spotted the fallacy in that argument immediately. With money invested or loaned to Peter, and presumably already spent, why would his "partners" then kill him and so destroy any chance they might have had of getting their money back? It made no sense. But the knowledge that Peter *had,* apparently, consorted with criminal types made Laura wonder if the field of possible murderers was not wider than any of them had suspected.

"You might be right," she said.

"I know I am. It's silly to think some woman killed Peter. He was very strong, you know, and perfectly able to defend himself."

Laura didn't bother to tell Anne that, according to the newspapers, Peter had been sitting on the bed when the first blow was struck, and that since the knife had punctured his heart, he had most probably died before he would have even thought about defending himself—hence the acceptable idea that a woman could have done the deed.

"Laura— Oh, Anne, you're here. Good. Lunch is ready." Amelia had, as usual, approached quietly, and appeared in the doorway of the conservatory with a suddenness that startled both younger women.

Recovering quickly, Laura laid her brushes aside, and she and Anne accompanied Amelia back inside the house to the dining room. They found Madeline, Kerry, and Josie there waiting for them, and it took Laura the several moments while they all gathered round the table and sat down to figure out what was different.

For the first time she could remember, Josie was not wearing dark colors. She had on a lovely pale green sweater and white slacks and looked both a little vulnerable and radiant.

"Josie, dear, white slacks in October?" Amelia was surprised, just faintly disapproving.

"It's after Labor Day," Madeline agreed, but clearly more by rote than out of any real interest.

Laura saw Josie flinch almost imperceptibly, and said, "I think you look terrific, Josie. Pale colors suit you beautifully." She was perfectly aware of having thwarted Amelia's attempt to dominate Josie, and she didn't care. If Amelia was trying to mold the younger widow into a replica of herself—something Laura had suspected since her second visit to the house—then somebody definitely needed to prevent her from succeeding.

Josie sent her a grateful glance and said casually to Amelia, "I think I'll start wearing brighter colors, Amelia."

Kerry spoke up then, placid and gentle as usual. "Laura's right, they suit you."

Tartly, Amelia said, "Spoken by a woman wearing the most dreadful sweater I've ever seen in my life."

Laura was a little surprised, since Amelia was usually honey-sweet to Kerry even while criticizing her, but Kerry merely smiled at Amelia and unfolded her napkin.

She has her own armor. Laura caught Josie's glance and knew they shared that thought. Then the uniformed maid came in to serve lunch, and conversation around the table became general.

Laura paid only cursory attention to what was being said. Her mind was occupied by the information Anne had shared about Peter. If anything, she thought, these new facts only clouded an already murky situation. Maybe Peter *had* been killed by some mysterious underworld figures, but Laura had the notion that if that had been the case, he would most probably have been shot and his body might never have been found. Still, Peter had obviously expected and probably received money from someone in the days before his death, and that might have had some connection to his murder.

People were being killed for money all the time, that was certain. So Peter might have been. If he'd had a large sum of money with him, for instance, he could have been robbed and murdered. What had looked rather like a crime of passion might instead have been one of frantic haste. Or he could have been robbed and killed by a junkie so out of his mind that the repeated stabbing might have seemed reasonable.

Laura shivered a little as her vivid imagination instantly conjured a sickening image, and looked around the table to distract herself. She found that Anne had unfortunately reverted to her previous behavior and was making sulky comments about the food being bland and wondering why it was that her wishes couldn't be followed occasionally.

"If you want something with more spice," Amelia told her impatiently, "then order a pizza to be delivered. Cook follows *my* wishes, Anne, and will continue to do so."

Anne laughed, an ugly sound. "You mean she will until Daniel decides to take over, don't you, Amelia? Peter told me all his secrets and all the family secrets. Like that lovely old rumor that you killed your own husband, hit him over the head and pushed him into the swimming pool. Did you, Amelia? Does Daniel have proof? Is that what he's holding over your head? We both know he's been the one in charge for years. The one who really runs things. He just lets you pretend, lets you act like you're the one with the power. He *lets* you, Amelia."

"Anne," Josie warned softly.

"You keep out of it," Anne snapped. "I'm sick and

tired of you always butting in, pouring oil when nobody asked you to, kissing up to Amelia and Daniel—and now Alex, literally. Is he good in bed, Josie? Would Jeremy approve of you screwing his cousin?"

That knife must have been a sharp one, because Josie went white and dropped her gaze to her plate, and didn't say a word in reply.

Laura had no idea where this sudden venom had come from, and she couldn't begin to guess what Anne hoped to gain by it—except perhaps some kind of payback for the humiliation she had suffered. Whatever had triggered the change, Anne's eyes were hard and bright, her mouth was a thin slash in her pale face, and her voice was so brittle a touch would have shattered it.

Laura wished now she had been paying attention to the conversation.

Amelia sat ramrod straight in her chair, two spots of color burning high on her cheekbones and her eyes so dark they were like holes in the world. Kerry continued placidly to eat, while Josie pushed the food around on her plate without looking up. Only Madeline and Laura were looking at Anne, and Madeline wore a slight frown rather than her usual vacant expression.

"Stop saying those things, Anne," she said. "You know none of it is true."

Anne lifted her glass in a mocking little toast. "Here's to Madeline, who wouldn't admit to trouble in the family if it was her ticket into heaven. Let's see . . . it's called *omertà* in your family, isn't it, Kerry? The famous vow of silence?"

"Not since we left Italy three generations ago," Kerry replied somewhat dryly, barely looking up from her plate.

"Well, still, I'm sure you know all about it. Sweet, silent Kerry, with never a harsh word for anybody. A widow without ever being a wife. That's true, isn't it,

Kerry? Want me to tell them another of Peter's little secrets?"

Kerry looked at her, and the scarred side of her face darkened, betraying some emotion the rest of her face never showed. Evenly she said, "You're obviously going to say whatever you want, Anne."

Before she could, Amelia spoke, sounding more upset than Laura had ever heard her sound. "Anne, if you can't behave in a civilized manner, leave the table."

"Leave *Daniel's* table, Amelia? Why on earth would I want to leave *Daniel's* table? I haven't heard the master's voice requesting it—"

"You're hearing it now." His voice was very quiet, but it ended Anne's tirade so abruptly and effectively that it might as well have been a roar. Daniel stepped into the room, his pale gaze fixed on Anne, and granite would have been softer to the touch than his face appeared. "I don't know what's wrong with you, Anne, but this stops now. Don't make me do something we'll both regret."

Whatever scorn she felt for the others, it was obvious Anne respected or feared Daniel too much to fight with him. With those angry spots of color burning in her otherwise pale cheeks, she shoved her chair back, threw her napkin on the table, and rushed past him without a word.

In the thick silence left behind her, Daniel glanced around at each of them, said, "I'll see to it that doesn't happen again," and left the dining room.

Kerry folded her napkin neatly and in a colorless voice said, "Amelia, I believe I'll go and practice my music. Excuse me, please."

Amelia didn't object. In fact, though her own meal was unfinished, she barely waited for Kerry to leave the room before saying, "And I believe I'll go upstairs for my rest now. Laura, child, do forgive me, but I don't think I'll be able to sit for you again today."

Since she sounded actually frail and looked it, Laura

hurried to say, "Don't worry about it, Amelia, please. I can occupy myself for the day."

"Thank you, child. Madeline, if you'll give me your arm . . ."

"Of course, Amelia." The two women had lived together in this house for more than thirty years, and whether or not there was affection between them, there was certainly knowledge and a degree of understanding. Madeline rose and offered her arm gravely, and the two women went slowly from the room.

Laura drew a breath and let it out slowly. To Josie, she said, "What got into Anne? I mean, my mind wandered for a minute and I never heard—what set her off?"

"I don't think there was anything," Josie replied, obviously baffled. "All I heard Amelia say to her was something about how there was no good reason to change the wallpaper in Anne's room. Such a trivial thing. But it seemed to be the last straw as far as Anne was concerned, because things went from bad to worse in a hurry."

"All that . . . spite . . . over wallpaper?"

Josie shrugged. "I guess. Or maybe she was still smarting over our having learned *her* little secret last Saturday and felt like evening the score."

Laura absently folded her napkin beside her plate. "Daniel said he'd make sure it didn't happen again."

Answering the unspoken question, Josie said, "He signs the checks. If anybody can make Anne toe the line, it's Daniel. He's always been pretty easygoing with her, I think because he felt sorry for her after she lost her mother the way she did. But today she went way too far."

"I would say so," Laura murmured, wondering which of Anne's venomous barbs had been on target.

Faint color rose in Josie's cheeks, but her voice was steady enough when she said, "She's always had it in for me, of course. Amelia says she's jealous of me, but I think it's something else. When Alex first came here, she . . ."

"Was interested?" Laura finished delicately.

"Yeah. I don't know if he even realized it, but I did. Later, when he and I . . ."

Laura nodded. "She is the type to take competition badly, and rejection even worse. Um . . . it's none of my business, but I think Alex definitely ended up with the right lady."

Josie smiled at her. "Thanks. You know, he told me everyone in the house knew about us, but I didn't want to believe it."

"Secrets don't live long in this house," Laura heard herself say.

"Isn't that the truth. Especially, according to Anne, any secrets Peter knew." Josie shook her head and pushed back her chair, rising. "Well, I think I'll go and find something to do at my desk. Unless you'd like some company?"

"No, thanks anyway." Laura rose as well. "I think I'll go walk in the gardens before this weird weather turns nasty again."

"Shall I give you a hint about the maze?" Josie asked with a smile.

Laura hesitated, then nodded. "Yes, please. Dammit."

"When there are three choices, always pick the middle path."

Doubtful, Laura said, "That's a hint?"

Josie laughed. "A good one if you have a decent sense of direction. How long should I give you before sending out a search party?"

"Oh, couple of hours, at least."

"Done. Enjoy yourself, Laura."

"I'll do my best."

But it wasn't out of any playful sense of fun that Laura sought out the intricate puzzle of the maze. She had to get out of the house for a while, for one thing, feeling uneasy and anxious as the atmosphere of the place got to her. She needed to be alone, needed to think about a few things.

And with the lure of Daniel in the house, so close and so tempting, she needed distance to keep her head clear.

At least, she hoped that would do it.

The storms of the previous night had left the garden glistening in the cool October sunlight, and the air smelled clean. Laura walked briskly along the path to the maze, comfortable in her long sweater and skirt. She met no one along the way, though she did spot a gardener working industriously in a bed of evergreen azaleas about twenty yards from the entrance to the maze. He didn't look up, and Laura didn't call attention to herself as she passed through the leafy doorway.

On this bright afternoon, the maze didn't seem nearly as claustrophobic as it had seemed the first time she'd been here, and she found it wasn't at all necessary to look up and reassure herself that there was sky above her head. This time, trusting the subconscious that seemed to guide her painting hand so well, she merely walked without worrying over decisions. She found herself choosing the middle path whenever there were three options, but the other choices were made on some level of her mind that seemed to find the maze familiar.

It wasn't until she reached the center without making a single wrong turn that Laura realized what she had done. In her idle mind, a finger had traced an intricate pattern stamped into brass, following a continuous line that led to the center and the heart holding two initials. The mirror.

She made her way slowly to the gazebo, not noticing the beauty of her surroundings today. Went inside and sat on the foot of the chaise, seeing nothing except the image of the mirror as clear as a photo in her mind.

It had always reminded her of a maze, that pattern, but she simply hadn't made the connection until now. "Idiot," she told herself without heat. It had been right in front of her—literally. Seen last night from Daniel's window, she had finally recognized it subconsciously, because that was the only vantage point she had yet found that showed the entire maze clearly.

But what did it mean? A mirror that was a key to a maze . . . or a maze fashioned after a one-of-a-kind design on the back of a mirror? The mirror had come first, since it had been commissioned—far away from here in Philadelphia—in 1800. The maze, according to Josie, had been planted here in the 1950s by David Kilbourne. Was that when the Kilbournes had come into possession of the mirror? Had David bought it somewhere for his wife, and later had the maze follow the mirror's design?

Would Amelia have tossed unwanted into the attic a gift from her beloved David?

She would have if she really did drown him in their own swimming pool.

Laura leaned forward and put her elbows on her knees and her chin in her hands, frowning. If Amelia had killed her husband, Laura had a strong hunch she wouldn't be confessing to it, not now after forty years. But would she confess to knowing more about the mirror that had brought Laura here than she had yet admitted? Probably not. It *had* been more than forty years, after all.

And even if she did say that, yes, it had been a gift from David long ago—so what? She wasn't likely to remember any more than that; considering the wealth of this family, Amelia had probably gotten a great many gifts in forty years, and one brass mirror would hardly stand out in her mind.

Laura had the depressed feeling that Dena's final report on the history of the mirror would end with David Kilbourne buying it at a flea market or antique shop somewhere and that would be it. End of story. Nothing to explain why Peter had tried to buy it back from her decades later. No hint that it had had anything to do with his murder. Nothing to explain the evasiveness she felt in Daniel about the mirror.

And certainly nothing to explain why Laura herself had searched all her life for the tarnished brass mirror she had found in the Kilbourne garage one Saturday morning.

Dead end.

"No. It means something. It has to."

"What means something?"

He had approached without her awareness, which said a lot for the mirror's power to grip her thoughts and emotions. Now she sat up straight and looked at Daniel, and instantly she had trouble thinking about anything but him.

"What means something?" he repeated, stepping into the gazebo and towering over her. His voice was husky, and when Laura met his gaze she was immediately aware of all the long hours since she had left his bedroom. Too many long hours. Languid heat spread slowly through her, warming and softening the muscles that had been sore earlier, and her heart began to thud hard against her ribs.

Hardly aware of speaking, she said, "The maze. Where did David get the design for the maze?"

"From a stranger in a bar," Daniel said absently. "It's an interesting story. Remind me to tell it to you one day." Then he went down on his knees.

Laura caught her breath when his big, warm hands touched her ankles and began sliding up, pushing the hem of her long skirt higher. She wanted to remind him that it was the middle of the day, that anyone might be strolling through the maze and happen upon them here, but somehow the words wouldn't emerge. She could barely breathe, and she couldn't look away from the hot glitter in his eyes.

"I've been thinking about this all day," he said, his hands on her thighs now. "About you. Remembering last night." His fingers slid up the outer curves of her hips and hooked into the waistband of her panties.

Laura felt herself lifting up a bit to help him as he pulled the scrap of cotton and lace down her legs. Letting the panties fall where they would, he put his hands back on her, this time easing her legs apart as he pushed the skirt high on her thighs. She caught her breath when he gently stroked her inner thigh, and then her mouth was opening eagerly under the hungry pressure of his, and her hips were pushing toward him, her arms going around his neck.

It was like a tide washing over her, a living thing too powerful to resist. She wanted Daniel, right now this minute, and nothing else in the world mattered except that. She was hardly aware of the sounds coming from her throat, little purrs and whimpers of pleasure. She could only feel. His shaking hands on her breasts, wildly exciting even through her bra and sweater. His mouth feeding on hers as though he needed the taste of her to live. The softness of his hair beneath her fingers and the strength of his arms and the hard delight of his body.

And then he was inside her, stretching and filling her, and Laura cried out, her legs closing around him as her body arched to push herself even closer, to take more of him, all of him.

The pleasure washed over her in waves of heat and throbbing delight, building and building until it reached a crest of ecstasy so overwhelming that she lost herself in it.

There were tears on her face when Laura finally came back to her senses, and in that naked moment she accepted a truth that would no longer be denied. She was in love with Daniel Kilbourne.

Chapter 13

$\mathcal{J}$ osie fixed her gaze on the doorway of the library when she heard the front door open and close. A moment later, Alex appeared.

"What the hell are you doing working on Saturday?" he demanded, far more abrupt than usual.

His tone might have made her bristle, but Josie could see that he had something on his mind, something that was worrying him. So she merely said, mildly, "I'm not working, actually. I was just writing checks, paying a few personal bills."

His frown lingered for a moment, but then he laughed shortly and came into the room. "Sorry, sweet. My day has not been a lot of fun so far. How about yours?"

"Oh, it's been okay, if you overlook Anne having some kind of breakdown over lunch and asking, among other things, if Jeremy would approve of me—um—having sex with his cousin."

Alex sat down on the corner of her desk and stared at her, brows lifting. "I gather she used a less polite term?"

"You could say that. You could also say that in a few

short minutes, Anne managed to insult, expose, and alien-
ate everyone at the table—with the possible exception of
Laura, who was merely stunned."

Reflectively, Alex said, "I've got to start coming home
for lunch."

Josie couldn't help laughing, but she also shook her
head. "It was horrible. She even attacked Kerry, saying she
was a widow without ever having been a wife—and I've
never seen Amelia so frozen after Anne got through nee-
dling her about her not really being the one in charge. If
Daniel hadn't come in and shut Anne up, I don't know
what would have happened."

Alex took her hands and drew her to her feet. "You
shouldn't let her get to you, Josie. She's a resentful and
unhappy woman and gets pleasure out of causing as much
trouble as she can. Just ignore her."

"It's a little hard to do that when she's announcing at
the top of her voice that we're sleeping together."

He looked at her steadily. "So she announced it. So
what? Did the sky fall? Did Amelia fire you on the spot
and order you from the house? Did everyone look at you
in horror?" *Did the ghost of Jeremy rise up in wrathful condem-
nation?*

He didn't ask that last, but Josie heard it anyway. "No.
But I felt so . . . defenseless somehow. And it hurt to
have my private business laid out in front of everyone
without so much as a by-your-leave."

"But you didn't feel guilty?" he probed. "Or
ashamed?"

"No," she replied slowly, a little surprised.

Alex smiled. "Then we're definitely making progress,
sweet." He kissed her, lazily but with a difference Josie
could feel and yet couldn't define. "Maybe Anne's little
scene had some redeeming value, after all."

"I don't think Daniel thought so," Josie said a bit absently. "I've never seen him look like that before."

"How did he look?"

"Hard as nails and about that unbending. After Anne ran from the room, he told us it would never happen again, and then I assume he went after her. I haven't seen either of them since, but I'm willing to bet he told Anne she'd better behave herself from now on, or else."

Alex grimaced. "Not what he needed at the moment. I'll tell you something, sweet—it's not a barrel of fun being responsible for this family."

She looked at him searchingly. "Are you and Daniel still . . . cleaning up after Peter?"

"Something like that. Also not much fun."

"And you still won't tell me about it?"

"Josie, there's nothing you could do to help, and no reason for you to be worrying along with Daniel and me. We'll get to the bottom of it sooner or later, and then I'll tell you everything. All right?"

She eyed him. "You Kilbourne men are secretive as hell. Except for Peter, of course, who appears to have told Anne every blessed secret he knew."

"Did he, now? That's interesting." Alex's greenish eyes took on a faraway expression briefly, then cleared. He smiled at her. "Well, never mind. Why don't we get out of this depressing house for a few hours? I'm sure we can find something to do."

"I should check and see if Amelia wants me—"

"It's Saturday. Whatever Amelia might want can wait." He got off the desk, still holding her hands, and said casually, "By the way, though I didn't get a chance to mention it this morning, you look great today."

Josie felt herself color, and thought it was ridiculous for her to be blushing like a schoolgirl. "Thanks."

He smiled at her and, gently, said, "I don't think Jeremy would mind. As I recall, black was never his favorite color."

A sudden lump in her throat made it impossible for

Josie to speak, so she merely nodded and went with him from the library, wondering if he had any idea at all that she had stopped apologizing to her dead husband for what another man had taught her to feel.

AS THEY WALKED slowly back through the maze toward the exit, Laura looked down at their clasped hands and wondered if it mattered to him that she loved him. He had to know. She doubted she was capable of hiding her feelings where he was concerned, not now, and besides that, from the day they had met he had seemed attuned to her moods and emotions. Surely he knew. He had brushed the wetness from her face with gentle fingers but hadn't questioned or commented, and he'd been virtually silent since. Did he know? Did it matter to him at all?

"You're very quiet," he said finally.

Laura gathered all the casual calm at her command and said, "I've just been ravished in a gazebo. I'm entitled."

He stopped and looked down at her, smiling slightly. "And I didn't even say hello first, did I?"

"No. You said something . . ." Laura felt a slight sense of panic when she realized she couldn't remember whatever it was he had said. *Oh God, will I ever be the same after this?*

With his free hand, Daniel tipped her chin up and kissed her. "Hello."

"Hello. Somebody could turn that corner up ahead and see us, you know. In fact, somebody could have gotten an eyeful just a few minutes ago."

Dryly he said, "After Anne's little display in the dining room, you surely can't doubt what I said about secrets not lasting long around here."

"No," she agreed with a sigh. "In fact, since she seemed determined to expose everybody's secrets, I half expected her to blurt out that I was in your room last night."

"How would she know that?"

Laura hesitated, then said, "She could have been in the hallway and seen me."

"Her bedroom's in the east wing, on the other side of the house; what would she have been doing near your room or mine?" Daniel frowned slightly as he looked down at her.

She knew the perception of that searching gaze and tried to avoid it. "Oh, you're right. It's just that I was the only one in the dining room she hadn't attacked, and I figured I was next. Did you hear much of what she said?"

"Most of it. Laura, has something else happened? Something worrying you?"

She hesitated again, uncertain, then said, "While I was in your room last night, someone was in mine."

He frowned again. "How can you be sure of that?"

Laura hadn't planned to tell him she had the mirror with her, though she *had* considered just suddenly showing it to him in order to study his reaction. But she heard herself say, "When I decided to stay here over the weekend, I brought the mirror with me. When I left my room last night, it was lying facedown on the coffee table. When I came back, it was faceup."

After a moment, his face showing no reaction to the information, Daniel said, "Amelia often walks the halls at night."

"So she told me."

"Did she admit to being in your room?"

"No. But . . . I got the distinct feeling she was toying with me. Do you think it was her rather than Anne?"

"I think it's more likely."

"Then she *was* toying with me."

Daniel touched her face gently, his fingers lying against her neck and his thumb brushing her cheek. "Maybe. Or maybe she just didn't want to admit to invading your privacy."

A little puzzled, trying to understand, Laura said, "It seems to me, given the history between you two, that you'd always think her motives negative ones. But you don't, do you? Daniel, why do you let it go on? The way Amelia's . . . testing the boundaries with you, struggling to get her own way, has got to be stressful, maybe even dangerous. Yet you've let it continue, all these years. Why? To spare Amelia embarrassment?"

With a slightly wry smile, Daniel said, "Call it quid pro quo, as Alex would say. You'd never know it now, but Amelia was very kind to me when I was a boy. My father spent time with me, but Mother was . . . distant. Completely wrapped up in Peter. Amelia paid attention, talked to me, took an interest. For a while we were very close. It made a difference, Laura. In my life. I can't forget that."

Laura didn't say anything for a minute, just searched his hard face intently. Then, finally, she said, "But it's all coming to a head now, isn't it? The struggle, the tension between you two. It's almost visible in the air sometimes. You'll have to stop it."

"I'll have to stop it," he agreed quietly. "Soon."

"She'll hit back. You know she will."

He nodded. "I know she'll try. But there's nothing I can do about that right now. I have other things that concern me more at the moment."

"Such as . . . what Peter was up to before he was killed?"

Daniel's hand fell away from her face. "Guessing?"

"Putting the pieces together. He *was* up to something, wasn't he? Trying somehow to raise money to finance his ambition? Is that what got him killed? Did he try to get that money from the wrong place, the wrong people?"

"I don't know." Daniel turned and continued down the path through the maze, still holding her hand.

"And you don't want to talk about it." Laura wasn't surprised, but tried to hide the pang of hurt she felt.

His fingers tightened around hers. "No, not now. You said you could accept that, Laura."

"I need to have my head examined," she muttered.

They reached the exit of the maze just then, and as they walked out onto the path that would take them back through the garden, Daniel said, "Why? Because you're willing to give me the time I need?"

"I just wish I understood," she replied with a sigh. "I still don't know what you want from me, Daniel."

He stopped, looking down at her. "Don't you?"

Laura had no trouble at all in interpreting the shimmer of heat in his eyes and had to clear her throat before she could say, "Besides that."

Daniel smiled. "I want to know all about Laura Sutherland."

She blinked. "You do?"

"Yes. Where you were born and grew up, about the family you aren't close to and the other people you have been. Likes and dislikes. Politics and philosophies. Which side of the bed you prefer. Things like that."

"That's . . . a tall order."

"We have time. Hours yet until we have to dress for dinner, and I doubt anyone will disturb us out here. Walk with me, Laura. Talk to me."

She glanced down at their clasped hands and said slowly, "If we spend the entire afternoon out here together . . ."

"Everyone will know we're lovers?" His voice was calm. "Someone knows you weren't in your room last night, Amelia probably. I doubt the others will be much interested. I know I promised to give you time, and I'll try not to . . . overwhelm you. But I find I'm liking secrets less and less these days. I'm not ashamed of being your lover, Laura, and I don't really give a damn who knows."

"I didn't say I was ashamed. But we've known each other barely more than a week—"

"And so we might offend someone's delicate sensibilities? If it doesn't trouble us, then why should we care what other people think? Laura, if it *really* bothers you that everyone will know we're lovers, then I'll go back to the house and leave you out here. No one's seen us yet; the maze is only clearly visible from my window. We'll pretend we barely know each other when there are other people around, that we're indifferent. We'll keep the truth a secret as long as we can, if that's what you want. Maybe you can slip into my room tonight after everyone's asleep, or I can come to you. For a few hours. And then tomorrow we go back to pretending once again. Is that what you really want?"

Laura gave in, to him and to her own yearnings. "No. It isn't what I want. But, Amelia—"

"I doubt Amelia will say much. But if she does, I'll handle her." He lifted her hand and kissed it, an oddly graceful and intimate gesture for a man with such a powerful, rugged appearance. "Now, walk with me, please. And tell me all about Laura Sutherland."

She decided later that it was the kiss that did it, snapping the last wispy threads of her resistance and making her throw caution to the winds. In any case, she walked with him, and they talked.

The gardens were very quiet and peaceful, and they weren't interrupted as they strolled the paths, pausing from time to time to sit on the scattered benches, and pausing more than once to take advantage of a particularly secluded spot.

Daniel asked questions and Laura answered them, telling him more about herself than she had ever told anyone. He talked as well, filling in some of the details of his life when she asked, being more open than she had expected.

Laura thought she was probably behaving too much

like a woman in love, but there was nothing she could do about it. Just as he seduced her so easily with his touch, he now seduced her with his attention, his absorption in all the details of her life. He made her forget everything but him, made her world tunnel until it contained only the two of them and these lovely gardens.

It wasn't until they went back to the house to dress for dinner hours later that she remembered what he'd said about David getting the idea for the maze from a stranger in a bar, and by then the opportunity to ask him about it was lost, at least for the moment.

WHEN LAURA ENTERED the front parlor just before six that evening, she hardly knew what to expect. Not from the others—and not from Daniel. Since she and Daniel had encountered no one during the afternoon, even while coming back through the house to go to their rooms, there was no way of knowing if they had been seen, their intimacy noted. So Laura was braced for any reaction from the others. As for Daniel, what she was uncertain of was how he would behave toward her in the presence of his family.

It was one thing to protest a secret relationship, but quite another to romance a lover before the curious eyes of others, she thought. And he was, besides, a reserved man, controlled and not given to emotional displays. At least, so she would have said before he had walked through the gardens holding her hand, pulling her behind practically every tree in order to kiss her until her knees buckled.

They were still a bit shaky, dammit, and it appeared to be obvious to anyone who cared to study her.

"You," Alex said lightly as soon as she walked into the parlor, "look like a woman in need of a drink. What can I get you, Laura?"

"I don't drink," she said. "Usually. Sherry?"

From his habitual place behind the wet bar, Alex smiled at her and fixed the drink she had requested. He and Josie were the only ones in the parlor, and when Laura took her drink and retreated to her usual place behind the sofa nearest the window, the other woman offered her a smile of sympathetic understanding.

"Ignore him. You look fine. Gorgeous, in fact."

Laura looked at Josie's long dress, which was a stunning silvery sheath, then glanced down at her own elegant black dress and couldn't help but laugh at the color reversal. "Thanks, so do you."

"Transformations," Alex noted lazily as he leaned on the bar, "are fascinating, don't you think?"

"Not if you're the one transforming," Laura told him ruefully.

"Amen," Josie said.

"Uncomfortable," Laura said with a nod.

Josie sighed. "To say the least. And unnerving to not know yourself anymore."

"To not be able to control yourself," Laura murmured, she thought under her breath, and sipped her drink.

Alex began to laugh.

"Bastard," Josie said affably.

"Sorry, sweet, but if you two could see your faces!"

Josie glanced up at Laura from her position on the couch. "His biggest character defect is misplaced levity. You may have noticed." She didn't react at all to the endearment, other than with a slight rise in color.

"The ties gave him away," Laura said.

Alex looked down at the one he was wearing currently, a violent multicolored vision of characters from a popular comic strip which clashed beautifully with his sober dark suit, and said, "I resent that."

"Resent what?" Daniel asked as he came into the room.

"They're casting aspersions," Alex told him, automatically fixing a Scotch and handing it over as Daniel passed. "Attacking my tie."

"I wouldn't worry. That tie can probably defend itself."

Josie and Laura both burst out laughing, and since Laura was still laughing when Daniel came around the sofa to her side, she didn't have time to stiffen up when he put an arm around her waist and kissed her.

"You look beautiful tonight," he said huskily.

Laura looked somewhat dazedly up at a usually hard face altered amazingly by tenderness, and decided that she'd let the rest of this family or anybody else think anything they liked about her if her reward was having him look at her like this. "Thank you," she murmured.

Without an ounce of self-consciousness, Daniel kept his arm around her, his fingers moving slightly at her side as though he couldn't touch her without also caressing her. As for Laura, she discovered without much surprise that her body had a mind of its own, leaning against his with a sensual familiarity about as subtle as neon. She only just managed to stop herself from opening up his suit jacket and burrowing in to get even closer to him.

Either he saw or sensed her feelings, because there was a pleased glint in his eyes. But Daniel didn't say anything about that. Instead he looked across the room at Alex and asked, "Have you seen Anne?"

"Nope." Alex apparently felt no need to comment further on transformations, though he was smiling faintly. "But given what Josie told me about what happened at lunch today, I wouldn't expect her to show her face for a while. Did you read her the riot act?"

"More or less. Then she stormed out of here, and I haven't seen her since."

Josie sighed. "You know her, Daniel. She'll come home when she's thought of some way of blaming her tantrum on someone else."

"It was worse than a tantrum this time," Daniel said somewhat grimly.

Whatever else he might have added to that was lost as Kerry came into the room, drawing their attention with her innate grace—and the fact that tonight she was wearing a dress even Amelia wouldn't be able to find fault with. It was a long, high-necked dress that left her arms and shoulders bare, and the simple style made her look fragile rather than thin. It was a shade of deep burgundy, and the color lent warmth to her pale skin and glints of light to her hair.

As she normally did around the family, she wore only minimal makeup rather than the heavy stuff designed to hide her scars, yet even so they seemed less obvious than usual. Her expression was as serene as it always was, but there was a spark of something in her eyes, life that hadn't been there—or had been hidden—before.

She's stopped playing Amelia's game, Laura realized, wondering if the scene at lunch today had produced a different result than the one Anne had intended.

"The usual, Kerry?" Receiving a smiling nod, Alex fixed her drink and handed it over, and she went to join Josie on the sofa near the window. She smiled at the others, accepting Daniel and Laura's closeness without a blink.

"You look great," Josie told her. "Why haven't I seen you wear that color before?"

"Probably for the same reason I haven't seen you wear *that* color," Kerry replied, her soft voice faintly amused. "I think we've both been . . . taking the path of least resistance."

Curious, Josie said, "I know what knocked *me* off the path; how about you?"

"A realization," Kerry answered without answering. "Slow in coming, but here at last." She lifted her glass in a little toast, sipped, then said with a tiny smile, "Amelia won't be happy tonight."

Laura had just been thinking the same thing. To all appearances, today Amelia had lost at least some of her domination over Josie and Kerry, to say nothing of Anne's attack at lunch. And there was still no way of knowing what her reaction would be to Laura's very public defection into Daniel's arms.

Before anyone could comment aloud, Madeline came in, dressed and made up flawlessly as usual—and vague as usual. If she even noticed a couple of the more obvious changes in the group she joined, it wasn't apparent. She accepted her usual drink from Alex and went to her usual place on the other sofa, murmuring greetings to the room at large.

Laura glanced up at Daniel, remembering his comment about his mother's distant attitude toward him. He was looking at her, detached as always, but Laura had some idea now of the hurt he must have felt as a boy, and what it had probably cost him to earn that priceless detachment. For the first time, she felt angry at Madeline. Two sons, and it had been the worthless one with the shallow charm and easy smiles she had preferred rather than the more complex and definitely superior Daniel.

How could any mother choose like that?

Then Laura met Madeline's gaze fleetingly across the room, and the pale eyes so superficially like Daniel's were utterly vacant. They didn't really see Laura. They didn't see her son, or her son's arm around Laura. They didn't see anything. They didn't care about anything.

Laura put her hand over Daniel's at her waist and smiled at him when he turned his head to look down at her in an instant response. His face softened, his eyes flickered with sudden heat, and he pulled her a bit closer.

That was what Amelia saw when she came into the room. The two of them looking at each other as if no one else existed. And she saw Josie wearing a pale dress and looking nothing like a widow, saw Kerry wearing a dress that suited her beautifully. Perhaps she saw her grip on her family loosening.

Laura tore her gaze from Daniel's with an effort when she heard Amelia's cane tapping, and she saw the old lady as she paused in the doorway. She thought she saw that face of aged beauty quiver a bit, but if she did it was a fleeting reaction. Dark eyes unreadable, Amelia came into the room and took her accustomed chair and her accustomed drink from Alex.

"You all look very nice tonight," she said, and there was in her voice the faintest suggestion of effort, as if the accustomed words no longer fit.

I can almost feel sorry for her, Laura thought. And then, in surprise, *I can paint her now. I know I can.*

"Someone should have built a fire," Amelia said, gazing toward the unlit gas logs in the fireplace. "It's chilly tonight."

"Allow me," Alex said, and crossed the room to light the fire, a quick and simple procedure.

"Thank you," Amelia murmured.

Looking at her, Laura thought there was something rather forlorn, even bewildered, about Amelia tonight. Though she was as upright as always, she seemed smaller and somehow less substantial, the iron gone from her backbone. And she looked older, that haughty face less taut, the lines around her eyes and mouth more apparent.

No one seemed willing to break the silence, and Laura wondered if everyone else was as relieved as she was when they heard the front doorbell ring. Even more, she wondered if Amelia was as conscious as Laura was of the fact that this time Alex didn't ask for permission before responding to that summons.

Alex came back into the silent room a few moments

later, his expression somewhat guarded. "Again, it isn't a social visit," he said.

Brent Landry was behind him. The police lieutenant was, as before, soberly but elegantly dressed and looked quite at home in the parlor. Also as before, he went to the fireplace, where he could see everyone in the room, and murmured a greeting to the group. One of his black brows may have lifted a fraction of an inch when he saw Laura and Daniel standing as they were, but that was his only reaction.

"We were about to sit down to dinner," Amelia told him, frosty but not nearly so incensed as she had been the last time.

"I'm sorry, Miss Amelia. But there's a matter I need to clear up in my investigation, and it won't wait."

"Have you found out who—?" Madeline was looking at him, her eyes intense now.

As before, his voice gentled. "No, not yet. We're still eliminating suspects."

"How many enemies could one young man have?" Amelia demanded, grim.

"Enough to keep us busy," Landry replied very politely.

Her lips tightened. "Very well, get on with it."

His penetrating gray eyes swept the room slowly, settling at last on Kerry. "I have a few questions for you, Mrs. Kilbourne."

She looked up at him, expressionless.

"Kerry was in California when Peter was killed," Josie said. "What could she know about it?"

"Perhaps more than you might think," Landry replied, his gaze still fixed on Kerry's face. "Mrs. Kilbourne, were you aware that your husband had gambling debts?"

"Yes," she replied matter-of-factly.

"Before you married him?"

She hesitated almost imperceptibly. "No."

"Were you aware that, two months ago, your husband participated in a high-stakes poker game in the private back room of an Atlanta club, losing over three hundred thousand dollars in a single night?"

It was Alex who first broke the silence with a muttered, "Jesus."

Kerry said, "He didn't have that kind of cash."

"No," Landry said. "He didn't. But he knew the manager of the club rather well, and the manager accepted his markers. Do you have any idea of whom I'm speaking, Mrs. Kilbourne?"

A very faint smile curved Kerry's lips. "I would imagine you mean my brother."

He nodded. "Lorenzo DeMitri. Did you know that your husband owed that kind of money to your brother?"

"Yes."

"It didn't surprise you?"

"Nothing Peter did surprised me."

Amelia spoke up then, directing harsh questions to the detective. "Are you saying that this gambling debt is why Peter was murdered? That Kerry's brother had something to do with it?"

Landry's gaze shifted to Amelia, but only fleetingly. "I'm saying that this is . . . another avenue to explore, Miss Amelia. Mrs. Kilbourne, were you aware that your brother had your husband physically thrown out of his club just two days before he was murdered?"

"I was in California then."

"But were you aware that the incident took place?"

"At the time, no."

"When did you learn of it?"

"While I was in California."

"How did you learn of it?"

Kerry drew a little breath. Her hazel eyes were clear and calm. "When my brother called my father."

"To report the incident?"

"No. To explain why the club was in possession of worthless markers totaling over three hundred thousand dollars. The club, as you well know, belongs to my father."

Landry's eyes narrowed. "Then your brother had no intention of trying to redeem those markers?"

"He knew they were worthless. So did my father."

"Then why were they accepted in the first place?"

Kerry smiled. "Peter was family."

Skeptically, Landry said, "Do you expect me to believe that your brother, a hard-nosed businessman, coolly and calmly accepted hundreds of thousands of dollars of worthless markers simply because they were from his brother-in-law?"

"It's the truth," she said.

"And your father accepted this as well? He gave no order that your brother should attempt to redeem the markers?"

"No."

"He wasn't furious at your husband?"

"Angry, perhaps. But he knew Peter too well to do more than shrug it off and tell Lorenzo that Peter wasn't to play at the club again."

Landry stared at her for a moment, then said, "Would it surprise you to know that your brother was seen that night less than two blocks from the motel where Peter Kilbourne was killed?"

Kerry shrugged. "Not especially. Lorenzo has many interests. They keep him busy."

Alex spoke, his lazy voice belying his very sharp eyes. "Come on, Brent. Surely you don't believe DeMitri killed his brother-in-law over gambling markers—however staggering the total. What would he have to gain? A dead man can't redeem markers; at least with Peter alive there was a chance to collect."

"Maybe the chances were better with him dead," Landry said. "Mrs. Kilbourne, were you aware that your father had insured your husband's life to the tune of one million dollars? And named you as beneficiary?"

Kerry looked faintly surprised, then considering. "No. But it sounds like something he would do. He knew how Peter was with money, and probably wanted to make sure I'd have some kind of independence if I were left alone." She smiled. "And I can assure you, Lieutenant, that neither my father nor my brother would ask me to use insurance money to pay Peter's debts—even those he owed to them."

"I think this avenue has a dead end, Brent," Daniel said quietly. "Unless, of course, you have some kind of evidence that Kerry's brother—or someone in his employ —actually met with Peter the night he was killed."

Landry glanced at him, then returned his gaze to Kerry. "One final thing, Mrs. Kilbourne. If your father wasn't angry at your husband, then why did he place a call to Peter Kilbourne's private number here at the house on the afternoon he was killed?"

"He didn't," Kerry replied. "I did."

"Do you mind telling me why?"

In a very gentle tone, Kerry said, "Yes, I do mind."

"That's enough, Brent," Alex said. "Kerry was three thousand miles away, and nothing she and Peter discussed could be pertinent to your investigation."

For a moment it seemed that the detective would insist, but then he nodded. "I agree. Unless new evidence comes to light which would alter that."

There was a little silence, and then Amelia said, "If you're finished, Brent, we would like to have our dinner now."

Not visibly discomfited by her asperity, Landry merely inclined his head politely and said, "Of course, Miss Amelia. Please do forgive me for delaying you. Never mind, Alex—I'll see myself out."

Nobody moved or spoke until they heard the front door close quietly behind Landry, and then it was Amelia who rose to her feet and said as though nothing out of the ordinary had occurred, "It's apparent Anne isn't going to join us, so we won't wait any longer."

Laura obeyed the slight pressure of Daniel's fingers, and they lagged behind as the others got up and obediently followed Amelia from the room. When they were alone, she said, "That was unexpected—to me, at least. Did he strongly imply that Kerry's family was in organized crime, or have I been watching too many gangster movies?"

Daniel began guiding her toward the bar, where they could leave their virtually untouched drinks, and said, "Too many movies. However, rumor has it that both her brother and father are ruthless when it comes to business, and not too picky about which side of the law they stand on. That private back room at their club is evidence of that."

"Then why forgive Peter's debts? Just because he was family?"

"Maybe. Or maybe there's more to the story than Kerry's willing to tell."

Laura thought there was probably a lot more, but she and Daniel had to join the others then and there was no time to discuss possibilities. Especially as the rest of the family followed Amelia's lead and at least outwardly acted as though nothing unusual had happened. In fact, Amelia behaved as though the entire day had been normal, allowing no mention of Anne's outburst or Landry's visit to pass her lips, and simply ignoring the minor rebellion when Daniel seated Laura in the chair beside his own rather than in her accustomed place at Amelia's right hand.

Instead she directed the conversation as if nothing had changed, inquiring after everyone's day and suggesting that a game or two of bridge would fill the evening nicely.

Alex and Josie were both good players, Kerry passable, and as for Laura—

"Count us out," Daniel said, pleasantly but firmly. "We have plans for the evening."

Laura thought that was a little high-handed, to say nothing of disconcerting, but since his hand touched her thigh beneath the table just then, stroking lightly in a caress she felt easily through the thin material of her dress, she couldn't seem to find the words or the will to protest. She glanced down the table to see Amelia's lips tighten slightly, but the old lady merely nodded in regal acquiescence and went on arranging everyone else's evening.

With the meal over, the family made their way back toward the den, with the exception of Daniel and Laura, who stopped at the foot of the stairs.

"Plans?" she said.

"Plans." He put his hands on her waist and pulled her against him, smiling. "Spending the next few hours in my bed while I try to persuade you to spend the rest of the night there."

"Daniel . . ."

"Laura, what does it matter if we sleep together all night in that room? Who does it concern except us?"

She told herself that she gave in simply because she was still weary from the night before and lacked the energy to fight him. But the truth was that she knew she wouldn't be able to leave him that way again, slipping from his arms and his bed in the darkness before dawn as if what they had done there were wrong.

And it turned out she wasn't nearly as weary as she had thought. . . .

IT WAS A little after midnight when Laura woke to the peaceful quiet of Daniel's firelit bedroom. He was still sleeping deeply, on his stomach beside her with an arm flung across her middle and his face nuzzled in her hair. Laura couldn't figure out why she was awake. Considering the past few hours, she was surprised she wasn't blissfully unconscious.

She stretched a bit, cautious, and felt her muscles quiver a protest at being asked to do anything but just *be*. They certainly wanted her to snuggle closer to Daniel and go back to sleep. Her mind, however, was wide awake and busy sifting through the events of the day.

Sighing at her own perversity, Laura slid out from under Daniel's arm, careful not to wake him, and slipped from the bed. She found his shirt and put it on, then wandered across the room to the window that looked out on the gardens and the maze.

It was calm out there, the scattered lights showing hardwood trees beginning to go bare-limbed after the recent storms had snatched at their fading leaves, and still shrubbery, and empty benches. The maze was alight, but softly tonight without a storm's harsh attention. It was probably chilly but not cold, a moonless night that was motionless and calm.

So why did Laura feel so uneasy? Because there were things Daniel refused to talk to her about? Because Anne had too suddenly laid bare too many of the family secrets? Because it was becoming more and more apparent that Peter had been worse than the family black sheep, and because his young widow was a smiling enigma? Because Amelia had been different tonight, changed in some way Laura sensed and saw yet could not define?

Because she was helplessly in love with Daniel Kilbourne and knew with stark certainty that she would never survive it if he didn't love her too . . . ?

In the stillness below, a hint of movement caught Laura's eye, and she turned her head a little to watch a cloaked figure leave the conservatory and slip out into the gardens. Even farther away now than she had been when she had seen the same thing from her own window, Laura frowned and tried to decide who was going out for a postmidnight walk. In the enveloping cloak, it could have been anyone.

"Laura? Sweetheart, come back to bed."

She started to tell him about it, but decided that enough secrets had been exposed for one day; let whoever it was enjoy their nighttime ramble in peace. Turning away from the window, Laura returned to Daniel's bed.

KERRY REACHED THE center of the maze quickly tonight. It was a brisk walk of considerable distance, but she wasn't the least bit out of breath when she reached the gazebo. She went inside and for a moment stood looking around at the inviting interior that she had created so painstakingly here. It was her haven. The simple furniture with its soft cushions, the filmy curtains ready to veil the world outside, fresh flowers in delicate vases. Simplicity.

Everything here was simple. Uncomplicated. Just as it appeared to be. Her escape into clarity.

She absently plumped up a pillow or two, then sat down abruptly on the foot of the chaise, her cloak swirling around her, and stared at nothing.

It was barely ten minutes later when a footstep drew her attention, and she looked up as Brent Landry came through the doorway of the gazebo. He stood there, the gray eyes fixed on her face holding an expression of entreaty, his own handsome face a little pale. There was a long silence, and when he finally spoke, his voice was husky.

"I'm sorry," he said.

Kerry didn't reply, just sat there looking at him for another long moment of silence. Then, in one movement, she rose and went into his arms.

Chapter 14

*I*f you had called me Mrs. Kilbourne one more time," she murmured, "I think I would have screamed."

They were lying close together on the chaise, their clothing scattered and only her cloak protecting them from the chill of the night. But it was enough.

Brent tightened his arms around her. "I didn't want to do that. You understand, don't you? Why I had to?"

She was silent a moment, her breath warm against his neck, then said, "I understand that your job is to find out who killed Peter. And I understand that you had questions you needed to ask me. And I think . . . I even understand why you faced me with those questions the way you did. Because you knew I'd have to answer in that house, with all of them watching and waiting. You knew I couldn't get away."

He sighed roughly. "We've been lovers for nearly a year, Kerry. And in all that time, how much have you told me of your marriage? How much have you told me of anything that mattered in your life, anything that mattered to you? Nothing. You slip into my arms like a ghost, something I can hold more in my imagination than in reality. An hour maybe, and then you're gone again, and all I have is the memory."

"I don't want to talk when I'm with you," she said a little wistfully. "I just want to feel. Is that so wrong?"

"What's wrong is that you won't let me in, won't let me get close to you. Won't let me love you."

Brent was still amazed by this, by the power of it and by the way it had all begun so suddenly. Seeing her at Amelia Kilbourne's annual New Year's bash, a huge and glittering affair to which only friends and VIPs were invited, he had been surprised more by her fawnlike shyness than by the scars almost hidden by excellent makeup. She had been Peter's wife for more than two years then, but never accompanied him in public, and since Brent had missed the last few of Amelia's New Year's parties, it was the first time he had met her.

Even now he couldn't explain what had happened. All he knew was that he had discovered her later, virtually hiding in the conservatory far from the rest of the party, almost numb with unhappiness. He had touched her face quite without meaning to, the scarred left side because it was his right hand that had reached out to her and because all her pain had been there and he had wanted to ease that. She had looked at him with huge eyes, her bottom lip quivering, and then she had come silently into his arms.

It had been a strange, frantic coupling, accomplished standing in a dark corner behind a bristly green plant thrusting its leaves in their way. Her skirt hiked up, his pants unzipped, both of them panting and straining and left so weak afterward that they clung together for a good ten minutes before they could let go of each other. And still no words, no plans, no promises. Her clothing put right, Kerry had slipped back into the house silently, and he had let her go because he'd had no idea how to stop her.

She had called him a week later, saying that she was going to be in the city that day, and asked hesitantly to see him. He had suggested his apartment. And it was like the first time, hurried and desperate and starving. She had been astonishingly awkward and inexperienced, especially for a woman married two years to Peter Kilbourne, but so sexually open and giving, so eager, that she almost broke his heart.

As she was dressing to leave that day, she had asked him if they could go on meeting. Tentative and vulnerable, she touched something in Brent that had never been touched before. Though his nature was to question and probe, he asked Kerry nothing at all. He just said yes.

They met weekly at his apartment for a while, but it was an ordeal for her to come into the city, and so when it was warm enough, she suggested they meet at the center of the Kilbourne maze. It was easy enough for her to get a copy of the gardener's key so that Brent could let himself in the back gate, and she obviously felt that the security codes were safe with a police officer. As for secrecy, the maze could hardly be seen at all from the house except from a window or two; only the roof of the gazebo could be seen. And there was virtually no chance of discovery, since they always met late at night.

As the months passed, Brent had learned some things about Kerry even without asking questions. That she was innately sensual, her skin so sensitive that the lightest touch aroused her. That she was very intelligent as well as observant, with a fine appreciation of irony. That while she was shy, she was also self-possessed, and articulate on those rare occasions he'd been able to persuade her to talk. That she was starved for affection. That she believed she was ugly.

He had, late one night after losing himself in her and realizing starkly that he never wanted to be found again, asked her to leave Peter and marry him. She had been surprised, then oddly, sadly, amused.

"Oh, Brent, I could never saddle you with an ugly woman."

"What?"

In that same gentle tone, she said, "I know what I am. Too thin and too pale and too plain, and scarred into the bargain. One morning you'd wake up to me beside you, and you'd realize what a mistake you had made."

"You're wrong," was all he could think of to say in his shock, wondering if Peter had carved those cruel words into her soul, if his rejection was the cause of Kerry's pain.

"No, I don't think so. I look into mirrors. I see what's there."

And no matter what he had said after that, no matter how honestly he had told her she was beautiful and sexy, Kerry would only smile and shake her head. She accepted that he desired her, unsurprised by his hunger because she shared it and no doubt thought it was an appetite that could be satisfied by even plain, imperfect food. But she would not believe she was anything but ugly.

Now his arms tightened around her again, and Brent said, "I've never asked because you made it plain you didn't want to talk about him, but . . . is it because of Peter that you won't let me love you? Did he hurt you?"

She pushed herself up on an elbow to look at him, her face still, then said, "If we have to talk about him, I want to get dressed first."

Brent didn't ask why, he just said, "Promise you won't bolt back to the house as soon as you get your shoes back on."

Kerry smiled slightly. "I promise."

He wasn't sure he believed her, but released her anyway, and they both dressed quickly in the chill of the night air. Kerry didn't sit down on the chair or chaise, but wandered around the interior of the gazebo, touching this and that, avoiding his gaze as she told him, finally, about her marriage to Peter.

"I was nineteen when I first saw him. Still living at home with my father, here in Atlanta. Dad had just met the woman he'd marry a few months later, but he was single then and liked having people around him. Especially young people. Peter had met my brother—through the poker games, though I didn't know that then—and Lorenzo had invited him to a pool party at our house. After that, he came over often to use the pool, like all Lorenzo's friends did. Unlike the others, he spent time with me."

She stopped wandering and looked out into the clearing around the gazebo, her expression reflective. "I suppose Peter didn't know how *not* to charm a woman. Or a girl. It came as naturally to him as breathing does to other men. I had been . . . sheltered I guess is the word. Most of my time was spent with books and my music. I didn't have any friends. He was the first man to pay attention to me. To flatter me. And he was so beautiful. . . ."

Brent waited, forcing himself to remain silent.

Kerry's shoulders lifted in a faint shrug. "Of course, you can guess what happened. I fell in love with him. I wasn't very good at hiding it. Everyone could see how I felt, especially Peter. And he was . . . kind. Still flattering me and paying attention, letting me dream. But nobody was more surprised than I was when he asked me to marry him a few weeks later."

She turned and faced Brent, leaning back against the gazebo's half wall. There was a little smile on her face. "He said all the right things. And did all the right things. Want to hear how he took my virginity the night before our wedding?"

"Not particularly," Brent said.

Kerry nodded, unsurprised. "But you want to hear the rest. Okay. He married me. And brought me here to introduce me to his family."

Surprised, Brent said, "You hadn't met them?"

"No. It was a whirlwind courtship, remember. And we were married in the office of a justice of the peace just two days after he proposed. There wasn't time." She shrugged again. "I'll say this for the Kilbournes—they tend to be courteous in the face of disaster. They all must have been appalled when Peter brought me home, yet they never showed me anything but kindness.

"I knew that Peter and I were to live here in the house. I didn't know we'd have separate bedrooms, but in those first few weeks, it didn't matter. Peter usually slept in my bed. Then, gradually, he slept there less and less. He didn't offer explanations or excuses, he just went to his own room. By the time we'd been married six months, I—I had to practically beg him to come to my bed."

Brent gritted his teeth and said nothing.

Kerry's eyes were distant, focused on the past. "He was always . . . polite. When I went to him, when I begged him, he always made love to me. Then one morning, after one of those nights when I had begged him to touch me and he had slept in my bed, I woke up and saw him looking at me. He smiled quickly, but . . . I had seen. What was in his eyes, his face. After that, I never asked him to make love to me again. And he never did."

"Why the hell didn't you leave the bastard?" Brent demanded harshly.

She blinked at him, and her hand lifted to rub her left cheek in a brief, telling gesture. "Dad had married and moved to California; I knew my stepmother wouldn't welcome me back home. My sister was married with a family, and Lorenzo had his life. I was nineteen, untrained for anything. Ugly. All I wanted was a place to hide." She shrugged jerkily. "This place was as good as any other, and better than most. No one demanded I do anything, go anywhere. I was left in peace with my books and my music. Peter was always polite, even kind once he realized that

I didn't expect him back in my bed and wasn't going to object to his other women. In time I think he was even grateful to me, because whenever one of his conquests got too demanding, he could always flash his wedding ring and talk about the wife who wouldn't divorce him."

"Kerry . . ."

"My life could have been a lot worse," she said steadily. "My marriage could have been a lot worse."

Brent shook his head helplessly. "But, Christ . . . is that why Peter married you? Because he wanted a wife who'd be willing to stay at home and not give him any trouble?"

She looked at him, and that odd little smile appeared again. "Oh, Brent. Haven't you realized yet?"

"Realized what?"

"Why Peter married me." There was a glimmer in her eyes, but the tears didn't fall. "My father bought him for me."

After the first moment of shock, Brent began to understand, the pieces falling into place even as Kerry went on steadily.

"Lorenzo had allowed him to run up staggering debts at the club because he was a Kilbourne. He and my father had no idea that Peter couldn't get his hands on the family money, and Peter kept them in the dark about that as long as possible, charming them and making promises. Like all gamblers, he was convinced his luck would turn. So he kept on playing, and kept on losing.

"By the time my father finally realized there was no way Peter could pay off the debts, I was very obviously in love with him. Dad was involved with his new young girlfriend, and he saw a way to get me off his hands—and get something in return for writing off Peter's losses. So he told Peter he had a choice. Dad would take the markers to Daniel and Amelia, exposing Peter's gambling and his debts, or he'd tear up all the markers if Peter would marry me and be kind to me." Her smile wavered a bit. "Probably the only bargain in his life that Peter kept."

Brent drew a breath and released it slowly. "When did you find out about all this?"

"While I was in California. Peter had gone to Lorenzo with some tale of how he had a windfall coming, and Lorenzo let him play at the club, promising to stand good for the money. Until then, the rules had been spelled out clearly; Peter could play only with cash on the table, and when that ran out, he was out of the game. But he somehow managed to charm Lorenzo into letting him play on credit that night. Then the game got out of hand, and Peter ended up losing more than three hundred thousand dollars, just as you discovered. Lorenzo threw him out of the club and told him not to come back until he had the money. But he never expected to see it, so he called Dad to report what had taken place. Dad was so furious that he blurted out to me what had really happened almost four years ago."

"Which is why you called Peter."

She nodded jerkily. "I guess I hoped he'd deny it. That he'd say he had married me because he wanted to—even if he had changed his mind later. But he didn't. He just laughed and said I should be flattered . . . because my dowry had been markers worth more than half a million dollars."

"Son of a bitch," Brent muttered.

After a moment, Kerry said, "I hung up on him. It was the last time we spoke. I don't know who killed him, Brent, but I know who didn't. Dad didn't have anything to do with it, and neither did Lorenzo. As far as they were concerned, the losses were chalked up to bitter experience. Fool me once, shame on you; fool me twice, shame on me. Peter fooled them twice. But they wouldn't have made me a widow because of it."

Brent nodded and, absently, said, "I never liked Lorenzo for a knife anyway. A gun's more his style."

Kerry smiled slightly. "You had no idea of my background when we got involved, did you?"

"No, I didn't." He looked at her, abstraction fading.

"I was never mixed up in any of the illegal things my father and brother did."

"You don't have to tell me that." He crossed to her and put his hands on her shoulders. "Kerry, do you think I don't know you by now? Do you honestly believe that all these months I met you here just because I had an itch that needed scratching?"

She was silent, just looking at him, then swallowed and said softly, "When you found me in the conservatory that night, I was hiding because I'd seen Peter slipping off to his bedroom with a beautiful model. Even then, even after all that time when I'd known he had other women, seeing him do that hurt so much I was sick with it. And then you were there, looking at me as if it mattered to you that I was hurting. And when you touched my scars, so gentle and caring . . ." She drew a little breath. "Brent, you've made me happy. Made me feel things I never thought I could feel. I want you to know that I'll always be grateful—"

His hands lifted to surround her face, and Brent cut her off with a rough curse. "Stop it. I don't want your gratitude."

Her eyes remained fixed on him, almost painfully intent. "Don't you? But how can I not be grateful? You make me feel like a woman, Brent."

"You are a woman. A beautiful, sexy, exciting woman I love with everything inside me."

Her bottom lip quivered and tears shimmered in her eyes. "How lovely that sounds," she said wistfully.

Brent groaned and rested his forehead against hers for a moment. Then he kissed her without an ounce of gentleness tempering his naked desire, and when he tore his lips from hers they were both shaken. "Listen to me," he said hoarsely. "I'm twelve years older than you are, Kerry. I've had other women, other relationships. I know what I want and I know what I feel. I love you. Believe that. Get used to it. Because I'm going to convince you. And I'm going to marry you."

"But—"

He kissed her again to cut off the protest. "No. No buts. If you want to be conventional, we'll wait until spring or summer, but you will marry me." After that, he didn't wait for another protest or anything else; he just kissed her one last time and then left her there in the gazebo, dazed and wondering.

It was nearly three in the morning when Kerry finally made her way slowly back to the house, following the path through the gardens with blind familiarity, and she was so preoccupied that she probably wouldn't have noticed anything strange under the little arched footbridge even if the lights had been bright enough to show her what lay half in and half out of the water.

LAURA WOKE RATHER abruptly from uneasy dreams and opened her eyes, and for a moment she didn't know where she was. But only for a moment. Raised on an elbow beside her, Daniel leaned down to kiss her with heart-stopping tenderness.

"Good morning," he murmured.

She smiled slowly, the nameless anxiety of her dreams fading. "Good morning."

"I think I could get used to this," he said, surveying the curtain of her bright hair spread out on his pillows, and her pale shoulders rising from deep green sheets. "Jesus, you're even beautiful first thing in the morning."

Laura blinked, then laughed. "Thank you. How long are you going to keep on surprising me?"

"Am I? How was that surprising?"

"Well . . . I don't know. It just seems out of character for you to say things like that. I didn't expect you to."

He kissed her again, smiling just a little. "You didn't expect me to tell you that you're beautiful? That I can't keep my hands off you?" His hand found her stomach under the covers and slid upward until his long fingers closed around her breast. "That I want you all the time, even when we've just made love and I'm so drained I can barely breathe?"

He pushed the sheet and blanket down to her waist and watched his hand caress her, watched her flesh respond instantly to his touch. "You didn't expect me to say that sometimes I have trouble believing you're real, that I'm half afraid someone's going to wake me up and I'll find it was all a dream?"

He leaned down to her, his mouth toying with one hard nipple while his thumb brushed the other rhythmically. Then he raised his head and smiled at her as his hand slid down over her stomach and under the covers. "You didn't expect me to say that I love the way you respond to me, especially when I do this?"

Laura made a little sound and reached for him.

"WHY NOT GO ahead and move your things into my room?" Daniel asked as he accompanied her to her room so that she could dress for breakfast. Since they had shared a shower in his room, she was wearing his robe and carrying the clothing she had worn the night before.

Laura sent him a faintly harassed look as they came into her sitting room. "I'm not even supposed to be staying in the house, let alone your room. I meant to go back to my apartment every evening. That was the plan."

"Make new plans," he suggested.

Since Laura wasn't quite ready to burn her bridges to the extent of moving in with him, she merely said, "I'll just be a minute," and escaped into her bedroom.

She half expected him to follow her, but he didn't, and she quickly began getting dressed, choosing casual jeans and an oversized sweater, since church wasn't on the agenda. Daniel didn't go to church, he had told her without emphasis or further comment, and the rest of the family wasn't particularly religious. Since Laura had a somewhat intense aversion to organized religion herself, that suited her.

She was sitting on the bed putting on socks when she glanced up and realized that she could see Daniel's reflection in the mirror above her dresser. He was standing at the coffee table, gazing down at either her sketchpad or the brass mirror, an odd expression she'd never seen before on his face. It was as though he saw something he both loved and loathed, something that could influence him more than he liked or wanted to admit.

While she watched, he bent and picked up the mirror. Straightening, he held it in both hands, turning it slowly. He seemed lost in thought, and those thoughts were clearly troubled ones. And then he shook his head a little and leaned down to put the mirror back where he'd found it.

Laura waited until he stepped away from the coffee table, then called out lightly, "Nearly ready."

"Good, I'm starved," he called back.

She finished putting on her shoes, then went into the sitting room as she was tying a scarf at the nape of her neck to hold back her hair. Mildly she said, "You told Peter to buy the mirror back from me, didn't you, Daniel?"

Standing by her fireplace, he looked at her with a faint smile. "Yes."

Laura hadn't really expected him to admit it, so he had surprised her again. "Why?"

"Let me ask you something." His voice was casual and yet—not. "You said you were going to have a researcher look into the history of the mirror. Have you done that?"

She nodded slowly. "We've gotten as far as the late 1920s. Dena—my researcher—should be reporting again in a few days."

It was Daniel's turn to nod. "When you have the complete history of the mirror, then we'll talk about it. All right?"

"Why wait until then?"

He came to her and put his hands on her shoulders. "Because I'm asking you to."

Laura let her head fall forward briefly to rest against his chest, then looked up at him with a halfhearted glare. "You're doing this deliberately, aren't you? Torturing me. Daniel—"

He put a finger against her lips briefly, his expression intent now, serious. "Please, Laura. It's . . . important to me."

Swayed in spite of herself by his gravity, she finally nodded. But she couldn't resist saying, "At least you aren't lying to me and saying it's just a piece of junk from the attic."

"I'm sorry about that," he said, taking her hand as they left the sitting room. "At the time, it seemed the best thing to do."

She sent him a baffled look. "And I thought I was curious about it before."

"Not too much longer now, and all your questions will be answered." He smiled at her. "I promise."

Laura hesitated, then said, "At least tell me this. Did the mirror have anything—anything at all—to do with Peter's murder?"

"I don't see how it could have."

"Does it have anything to do with—"

"Laura. I'm not going to play twenty questions."

She sighed. "It was worth a shot."

He chuckled, but when they reached the first floor, asked seriously, "Did you have nightmares last night?"

"I don't know. Why?"

"You were restless. I nearly woke you once because you seemed so distressed. But then you calmed again."

Laura thought about it, then shrugged. "I have a vague memory of being upset, but I don't remember why. Sorry if I disturbed you."

"You didn't disturb me. I was watching you sleep."

Laura was rather grateful that they reached the dining room then, because she didn't quite know what to say to that. She was also grateful, though surprised, to find only Alex and Josie at the table.

"Where is everybody?" she asked as she and Daniel began to help themselves from the buffet on the sideboard.

It was Josie who answered. "Kerry's sleeping in; she usually does on Sundays. Amelia was awake with the birds as usual and is now up in her room writing letters. Anne's still among the missing—in fact, I don't think she came home last night. And I believe Madeline finished breakfast early and went for a walk in the gardens."

"That's what I dreamed about last night," Laura realized. "The gardens."

"Was it an entertaining dream?" Alex asked politely.

She couldn't help laughing as she brought her plate to the table and sat down. "Sorry. We were sort of discussing dreams before we came in here, and I couldn't remember mine. When Josie mentioned the gardens, a bell went off."

"So what did you dream?" Josie asked, sipping her coffee.

Laura thought about it, and the longer she did, the more uneasy she felt. "It was one of those strange dreams where everything seems distorted. Peculiar shapes, odd angles, off colors. I was lost out in the gardens, because I kept taking dead-end paths. No matter which way I went, I ended up at a wall or a thicket of bushes or some other dead end. And the paths were getting narrower and narrower, and I knew if I didn't find my way out quickly, they'd disappear altogether."

"So what happened?" Daniel asked as he joined her at the table.

Laura felt her face warm as she remembered. "Well . . . somebody called to me, told me which was the right path. And I got out."

Daniel didn't say anything, but she thought he knew that it had been his voice she had heard. She also thought that Josie and Alex could guess, judging by their quick exchange of glances and faint smiles, but neither probed.

"I dreamed about mermaids," Alex said thoughtfully. "I wonder why."

Laura and Josie looked at each other with identical expressions of rueful understanding, and Alex exclaimed, "It wasn't *that* kind of dream!"

"When men dream about mermaids," Josie told him severely, "it's *always* that kind of dream."

They were still discussing the subject sometime later when Daniel and Laura finished breakfast and left the dining room. By tacit consent, they went back through the house to the conservatory, headed for the gardens.

As they passed the barely begun portrait of Amelia waiting patiently on its easel for Laura's return, she said, "I've got to work on that."

"Amelia won't expect you to work on Sunday," Daniel said.

Laura started to say that it was her own mind rather than Amelia's wishes that urged her to work on the painting, but in the end said nothing else about it. She didn't want to have to explain to Daniel how odd she was feeling right now, because she couldn't explain why, even to herself. All she knew was that she felt more anxious than she had her first day here, oddly conscious of time passing and inexplicably convinced that there would not be enough of it.

I have to hurry. I have to get the portrait done.

"You're very quiet," Daniel observed as they walked across the open yard and took the path that would lead eventually to the maze. He put his arm around her shoulders so that they walked more closely together.

"Am I?" Laura was gazing ahead of them, her eyes tracing the path uneasily.

"Too quiet. What's wrong, Laura?"

"I don't know. I just feel—" She stopped suddenly as the little arched bridge came into sight.

"Laura?"

She actually took a step back, then forced herself to stop. Looking up at Daniel helplessly, she said, "I can't. There's something wrong with that bridge . . . and I can't cross it."

Rather to her surprise, Daniel didn't even make an attempt to reassure her that there was nothing wrong. Instead his arm tightened briefly around her and then let go, and he said, "Wait here."

Laura wanted to run, to turn and bolt for the house, but she made herself stand there and watch as he continued along the path to the footbridge. The closer he got, the more anxious she became, and she almost called out to him not to cross the bridge.

But he didn't cross it. He put one foot on the bridge and held the handrail as he leaned over it a bit to see the concrete supports below. Then he went very still. There was a good thirty feet separating them, but Laura saw his face whiten in shock. He didn't move for a long moment, then turned away and came back to Laura.

"What?" Her voice was thin, frightened.

Daniel put his hands on her shoulders. His voice stony, he said, "It's Anne. She's dead."

After a long moment, Laura said unsteadily, "I dreamed about dead ends."

Daniel pulled her into his arms and held her tightly.

"IT WAS AN accident, wasn't it?" Josie asked Brent Landry. "She just fell. Slipped somehow and—and fell." Alex, sitting on the arm of her chair, put a hand on her shoulder and squeezed it gently.

Brent shook his head slightly. "The handrail of the bridge is too high for her to have fallen over it if she just slipped. She had to have been pushed—with considerable force—to land the way we found her."

"It still might have been an accident," Daniel argued. "A quarrel that ended with a shove, not meant to injure. Dew on the bridge, her foot slips . . ."

"It's possible," Brent said. "But I don't see anyone rushing forward to claim an accident, do you?"

"You aren't saying it was one of us?" Alex demanded.

They were in the front parlor, everyone except Amelia and Madeline, both of whom had remained in their rooms after Daniel had told them about Anne. Daniel and Laura were sitting on the sofa nearest the window, Kerry was on the other one, and Josie and Alex occupied the chair in which Amelia usually sat. Brent Landry stood by the cold hearth.

It was early afternoon, and Anne's body had been taken away only minutes before. With it had gone the police officers and technicians who had worked to gather evidence, leaving only Brent behind.

In answer to Alex's question, Brent said evenly, "We'll know more after the postmortem, but right now it looks like Anne died yesterday evening sometime between six and midnight. The gardeners had gone for the day, and the only staff inside the house were the cook and one maid. The front gate was closed with a guard on duty. The rear gate was locked, with no sign of forced entry. None of the motion detectors around the fences were disturbed. So you tell me, Alex. Who else could it have been?"

"None of us would have killed Anne," Kerry said quietly.

Brent glanced at her, then allowed his gaze to sweep the others. "As Daniel said, a quarrel might have gotten out of hand. If the evidence points that way, and whoever was involved comes forward, the DA would most likely consider it an accidental death. Involuntary manslaughter, perhaps."

He paused, then said, "It's no secret that Anne's temper was . . . explosive. She might even have instigated the argument. Was she upset about anything yesterday? Angry at anyone?"

Josie and Laura exchanged glances, but it was Daniel who answered dryly, "Everyone, I believe, with the exception of Laura. There had been a scene at lunch."

"What kind of scene?" Brent asked.

"The unpleasant kind." Daniel shrugged.

Brent looked at him, waiting, but when it became obvious that was all Daniel chose to say, he looked at Josie. "Why was Anne angry?"

Josie lifted her hands in a helpless gesture. "I don't know. She'd been simmering since last week when you exposed her affair with Peter. But she'd also gone out of her way Friday evening and yesterday morning to—oh, make peace with everyone or try to. Then, at lunch . . . she just exploded."

"What happened?"

Josie glanced at Daniel questioningly, and it was he who said, "She did her best to insult everyone, that's all. Par for the course where Anne was concerned."

Brent drew a breath and let it out slowly. "Daniel, I

know you'll go a long way to protect your family; I respect that. I know that as far as you're concerned, what happened yesterday at lunch is not my business. But it is. I have to find out how and why Anne Ralston died, something I would think you would also want to know. No matter what the answer is. Because, unlike Peter, Anne didn't die in an anonymous motel room across town. She died here. Literally in your own backyard. And no one in this house is above suspicion, because someone in this house knows how and why Anne died."

There was a long silence, and then Daniel looked at Josie and nodded. Quietly, without emphasis, Josie repeated the gist of Anne's tirade. Then she added, "But none of it was worth fighting about. We all knew Anne, knew how she was. And . . . once she said what she did, there was no taking it back. Why would any of us have confronted her about it later?"

"Besides which," Alex said, "we were all fairly occupied during the evening. Drinks in here at six, then your little production, you may remember. Then dinner. Afterward most of us went back to the den, and we played bridge."

"Most of you?"

"Josie and me, Kerry, and Amelia. Madeline was watching an old movie on TV, I think."

"How long were you together?"

Alex shrugged. "I think the party broke up sometime after ten."

"And you went your separate ways?"

"More or less. Amelia said she had letters to write. Madeline said something about a book. Kerry went to the music room; we could hear her playing, because Josie and I stayed in the den for a while. Then we went upstairs." He paused, then added, "To my room."

Without comment, Brent made a note in the little

black notebook he carried, and then looked at Daniel. "What about you?"

"Laura and I were upstairs," Daniel said. "In my room. Together."

"All evening?" Brent asked.

"And all night," Daniel replied calmly.

Brent nodded, again without comment, and made more notes. When he spoke again, it was briskly. "Did any of you see or hear anything out of the ordinary?"

Laura spoke for the first time, hesitant. "I saw something. But it was after midnight, so it wouldn't matter—would it?"

"What did you see?"

"I looked out the window and saw someone leave the conservatory. Whoever it was wore a cloak or something, and I couldn't tell—"

"That was me," Kerry said. "I often walk in the gardens at night." She looked up at Brent, and a faint quiver disturbed the serenity of her expression. "I walked over the footbridge twice. But I didn't notice anything."

Brent nodded and made another note. Then he looked at Daniel. "I doubt Amelia would have had the strength to shove Anne, but I'll need to talk to her. And your mother."

Daniel frowned and shook his head. "Not today. They were both upset when I told them about Anne, naturally. And Mother's sedated."

"Tomorrow, then." Brent looked at him steadily. "They may have heard something, seen something. I have to talk to them, Daniel."

"Don't expect me to like it."

"No, I never expect miracles." Brent smiled slightly, then sighed and closed his notebook, sliding it into the inner pocket of his suit jacket. "We've roped off the area around the footbridge, and I'd appreciate it if that could be left undisturbed for a day or two. I'll send one of my people out to take down the tape as soon as possible."

"All right," Daniel said. "I suppose there's nothing new on Peter's murder?"

"No." Brent hesitated, then added, "My superiors would probably have my badge for saying this, but we may never know who killed Peter, Daniel. So far every lead has faded away to smoke. The investigation will continue, of course—but I have to be honest. As things stand now, there's no good suspect, and no evidence pointing to one."

Josie said, "It's only been two weeks."

He nodded. "I know that. As I said, the investigation will continue; there's no statute of limitations on murder. But if murders aren't solved quickly, they tend not to be solved at all. I just wanted you all to be prepared."

"Great," Alex muttered.

Brent looked at Daniel. "I'll be back tomorrow, probably in the afternoon, to talk to Amelia and Madeline." And when Daniel nodded reluctantly, added, "In the meantime, if any of you remember anything or think of something that might be helpful, let me know."

There was a little silence after he left, and then Kerry got to her feet. "I never liked Anne, but I never wished her harm. Do you suppose her death had anything to do with Peter's?"

Alex frowned at her. "How could it have?"

"I don't know." Her expression was tranquil. "But two violent deaths in the same family within two weeks seems a bit much—even for the Kilbournes." Without waiting for anyone to respond to that, she strolled from the room.

"You know, she's right," Alex said a bit ruefully to Daniel.

He grimaced. "It had occurred to me. But I'm

damned if I can see any connection—other than their affair."

Sighing, Josie rose and said, "All I know is that there are arrangements to make, and I might as well get started. I'll have to try and contact Philip Ralston in Europe. He has to be told."

"Nice call to get on a Sunday night," Alex murmured as he too got to his feet. "Assuming we can track him down. I'll help, sweet."

Josie didn't thank him verbally, but her hand slipped into his as they left the room.

"Glad those two are finally going public," Daniel said absently. "It's about time."

Laura leaned her head against his shoulder. "Mmm. Daniel, do you think Anne died somehow because Peter did?"

"I wish I knew."

She was silent for a moment, then said, "I should leave, go back to my apartment. Amelia won't be thinking about the portrait, and—"

Daniel shifted so that he could put his hands on her shoulders. His gaze was very intent, and there was a look of strain around his mouth. "Laura . . . I have no right to ask you to stay here, especially after today. I couldn't blame you if you decided to get as far away from this family as possible. But—I'm asking you to stay. I need you with me."

There were many questions Laura could have asked him, but none of them seemed important in that moment. So she merely nodded and went into his arms.

IT WAS FAIRLY late that night when Alex and Josie went up the stairs together. Dinner had been virtually silent, with no one bothering to "dress" for the meal, and not even Amelia had been able to pretend that nothing out of the ordinary had happened. She had retreated to her room soon after, as had Madeline, while Kerry had ordered the car and gone out without explanation. Daniel and Laura had remained downstairs for a while, but had gone up sometime before.

"What a day," Alex murmured as they reached the second floor and walked down the hallway.

"Tomorrow won't be much better," Josie reminded him. "More questions, more arrangements—and don't forget the press."

Alex groaned. "Lovely. And I have to go chasing after box number two."

"Box number two?"

He slipped an arm around her waist. "Just Peter bent on pissing me off from the grave."

"Is that supposed to make sense?"

"Probably not. Ignore me, sweet. Let's just say I'm not looking forward to the next few days."

"No. Neither am I." They had reached her bedroom, which was first in the hallway, and she looked at Alex hesitantly. "Would you . . . stay with me tonight?"

He glanced at the closed door, which had not yet admitted him, and then looked at Josie steadily. "Because it's been a lousy day?"

She shook her head. "Because I want you with me."

Alex waited.

Josie knew what he needed to hear. "I can promise we'll be alone in there. The picture that used to be on my dresser isn't there anymore. I put it away in a photo album where it belongs. It's there with pictures of my parents, and pictures of me on a pony, and high school graduation. Memories. Just pleasant memories tucked away where they belong."

Slowly, Alex began to smile. "Well, it's about damn time. Which side of the bed do you prefer, sweet?"

ello, stranger." Cassidy came into Laura's apartment on Monday afternoon, and as her friend closed the door behind her, she added, "Are you home to stay, or—"

"No, just picking up a few things." Laura avoided her friend's searching look, going behind the breakfast bar to pour her a cup of coffee. "I was surprised to find you home this early. Shouldn't you be at work?"

"They're painting my office, so I got the afternoon off."

Laura nodded and set the coffee cup on the bar. "Here, this is fresh."

"Never mind the coffee," Cassidy said, sitting down at the bar and reaching for the cup despite her statement. "I've been reading the papers today. Is it true? Was she murdered?"

Laura picked up her own cup and sipped, then shrugged. "We don't know yet. The lieutenant who's investigating is supposed to come to the house in about an hour to talk to Daniel."

"How's the family taking it?"

"According to their various personalities." Laura smiled. "Amelia has rallied after a bad weekend. Anne obviously slipped, she says, and though it's a terrible tragedy, we have to get on with our lives. Pretty much the same way she was when Peter was killed, smiling and aloof. She decided it would be a good idea for us to work on the portrait this morning. Daniel was inclined to suggest—forcefully—that she wait at least until after the funeral, but I reminded him it would keep Amelia occupied while he and Josie dealt with all the calls and the police. And I wanted to keep busy myself."

"So you spent the morning painting Amelia?"

Laura nodded. "Kerry spent the morning with her music. Josie, as I said, helped Daniel, and Alex went into the city. Madeline ordered the car early and left; she said she had a friend she'd promised to visit, but it looked more to me like she was escaping. Not even the sedatives could shield her from that place in the garden roped off with bright yellow tape."

Cassidy looked at her steadily. "And how is Laura holding up? You're looking a bit taut, friend, and sounding ragged."

"I'm feeling that way too." Without much expression in her voice, Laura filled her friend in on most of the details of the weekend, sketching the events and characters. She also admitted her changed relationship with Daniel matter-of-factly, though she didn't go into detail about it.

"You're in love with him," Cassidy said.

Laura lifted her cup in a small salute of acknowledgment. "Surely that doesn't surprise you?"

"No, not especially. But that you're virtually moving in with him so quickly like this—that surprises me. Laura . . . are you sure you can trust him? I mean, trust him not to hurt you?"

"Hurt me? You mean—"

"Well, Anne might have been pushed, right?"

"Daniel wouldn't hurt me." Laura didn't realize it until she said it aloud, but she was as sure of that as she had ever been of anything in her life. Surer. "And he didn't hurt Anne. I know it."

"Okay, if you say so. But there are other kinds of hurt. You're in love, but is he in love with you?"

Laura hesitated. "I don't know. Sometimes, when he looks at me, I think he is. I know he . . . he feels something for me. Oh, hell, Cass, so much has happened since we met, I just don't know. I've barely been able to think. But he said he needed me with him, and that's why I'm going back there."

Cassidy looked at her searchingly, with almost detached curiosity. "I always wondered what you'd be like in love. It's body and soul for you, isn't it? Absolutely all of you."

Laura laughed shakily. "Unlike you, yes! I think I always knew it would be this way, and that's why I was so cautious for so long. Until I met Daniel. With him . . . I'm happy, Cass. I mean, when it's just the two of us, nothing else matters. It's like I've . . . come home."

After a moment, Cassidy said, "Then I envy you that. But as for the rest, it sounds like a real mess. It's obviously getting to you. Like I said, you're looking awfully tense. And what's that stuff about you dreaming and then not being able to get near the footbridge? You've never been psychic, have you?"

"Not to my knowledge. Daniel accepted it so matter-of-factly that we haven't even talked about it, but *I* don't know where it came from. And I don't know why it is that I feel this urgency to finish Amelia's portrait. I worked like a demon on that thing this morning—it's nearly finished, I think. Even Amelia was pleased. Of course, she thinks it's just a practice portrait."

"But it isn't?"

Laura stared at her and felt an odd chill. "No. It isn't. It's the only portrait I'll ever do of Amelia."

Cass shivered suddenly. "You're scaring me, friend."

"I'm scaring myself." Laura turned away briefly to pour fresh coffee, then said in a steadier voice, "Maybe it's just that house having its effect on me, or more of my odd whims and notions—but I know what I know, Cass. There won't be another painting of Amelia."

"Are you . . . afraid something might happen to you? The way it did to Anne?"

Shaking her head, Laura said, "That I don't know. I don't feel *afraid*, really, just uneasy. But more than before. I keep wanting to look back over my shoulder, and I think you'd have to peel me off the ceiling if somebody yelled 'Boo' real loud." She let out a little sound that wasn't really amused. "It's probably just the house. I mean, God, look at everything that's happened there, in that family. Is it any wonder you could cut the tension with a knife? Is it any wonder I'm having unsettled dreams and looking over my shoulder?"

"Don't go back there," Cassidy said definitely.

"I have to."

"Why? Because Daniel's there?"

"Yes. Because he's there. Because it isn't finished."

"What isn't finished? The portrait? The story of the mirror? Your love affair?"

Laura managed a smile. "All of the above. And who killed Peter. We still don't know that."

With an impatient gesture, Cassidy said, "I give up. You're hell-bent to get *yourself* killed. I can see it now. Amelia's finally going to crack and push you down the stairs, in the best tradition of Gothic heroines. Or Madeline will slip some of her sedatives into your drink one night and shove you out a window because you smiled at her the wrong way at dinner. Or Daniel—"

"Daniel won't hurt me," Laura interrupted.

"Now I know what they mean by crazy in love. You certainly are."

Laura set her cup on the counter and said lightly, "Maybe so. And if I crash and burn, you can say you told me so. In the meantime, though, would you keep watering my plants for me? And keep an eye on the place?"

"Oh, sure." Cassidy got off the bar stool, shaking her head. "Nuts. She's nuts."

"Thanks."

"Just send me a postcard from the asylum, huh?"

Later, as Laura drove herself back to the Kilbourne house, she thought about the conversation with Cassidy and wondered once more at her own inexplicable feelings. The only portrait she'd ever do of Amelia? Where had that certainty come from?

It was a question she couldn't answer, just as she couldn't answer the question of why it had upset her so much to read the material Dena had left for her at her apartment building, the copies of letters written just after the turn of the century. She had done that first upon returning to her apartment, and the letters that Shelby Hadden had written to her lover and then husband, Brett, had left her almost in tears. Dena hadn't been kidding when she had referred to the intense passion between those two, but it was the utter devotion they shared that had gotten to Laura. They had been through hell in order to be together, but both clearly felt the prize worth the price they had paid for it.

I just envy them, that's all.

Shaking off the wistful thought as she reached the Kilbourne house, she parked her car near the garages and then went into the house through a side door off the kitchen, taking the back stairs up to the second floor. She had brought only a small bag with her, and unpacked her things in the guest suite rather than Daniel's room. She didn't know why she was still so reluctant to move her things there, especially since no one in the house could be in any doubt as to their relationship, but her inner voice was still resisting and so she listened to it.

She went downstairs, and found Daniel working at his desk in the library. She knocked softly on the doorjamb. "If I'm interrupting—"

"I'll thank you for it," he said, pushing his chair back and holding out his hand to her with a smile.

Laura came to him, finding herself pulled smoothly onto his lap.

"I missed you," he said, kissing her.

When she could, Laura said, "I was only gone a couple of hours. But I missed you too." She linked her fingers together behind his neck, trying to keep it light, casual. "You must have been busy, though. Has the phone finally stopped ringing?"

Daniel shook his head. "As of this afternoon, we have a service, and it's taking all calls."

"Probably a good idea. Where is everyone?"

"Josie's upstairs getting the latest batch of letters from Amelia. Kerry went for a walk in the gardens, I assume taking the path that doesn't go near the footbridge. Alex should be back anytime now." He frowned. "So should Mother."

"Isn't Lieutenant Landry due here soon?"

"He called to say he'd been delayed a few minutes."

"Did he say—?"

"No. Just that something interesting had turned up. He can be a cryptic bastard when he wants to be."

"Speaking of cryptic"—Laura nodded at the papers spread out on his desk—"what is all this?"

Daniel looked at her a moment as if debating, then said, "Preliminary designs for an aircraft tracking system. And various work logs and sign-in sheets for the research and development lab."

A little surprised, Laura said, "Is this the kind of work you do? I thought your end was finance."

"That is my end." He grimaced slightly. "As far as the science of this stuff goes, I'm out of my league."

"Then what are you doing?"

"Looking for fingerprints." Daniel shook his head. "And finding only the ones that aren't the least bit helpful."

"I see Landry isn't the only one who can be cryptic when he wants to. Daniel, if this is one of those things we aren't talking about yet—"

"It was," he admitted frankly. "But it looks like the whole damn thing's going to be public sooner rather than later, and I want you to be prepared."

"That sounds ominous."

He looked grim now. "It won't be pleasant."

Before he could say anything more, Alex walked into the room. The young lawyer was dressed casually in jeans and a Georgia Tech sweatshirt, but carried a businesslike satchel briefcase. And he said a single, succinct word to Daniel.

"Bingo."

Laura felt Daniel tense, and quickly got off his lap. "I'll leave you two."

Daniel held her wrist to keep her near. "No, Laura, you might as well hear this now."

Alex asked instantly, "Has something happened?"

"I got a call," Daniel told him. "They've moved up the meeting. If I can't produce the schematics by the end of the week, my name is mud."

Baffled, Laura looked from one to the other. "Daniel?"

"It's a long story," he told her, "but the short version is that we believe Peter stole a set of plans from the lab before he was killed. Very important plans, designed for the military. Plans that certain other powers would pay a great deal to get their hands on. And our government is not going to be happy with me when they turn up missing."

"But if Peter took them—"

Daniel shook his head and released her wrist. "All the evidence points to my having taken them. Peter must have lifted my keycard at some point and used it; all the logs agree that I was the last one in the vault before the plans disappeared."

"But anyone would know you couldn't have done it," Laura said.

Daniel sent her a quick look, a glint of something in his eyes flashing too quickly to be read, but all he said was, "My good character won't count for much with all the evidence against me. Alex, you found the second lockbox?"

"Yep. I played a hunch and tried Macon again. Sure enough, he had a box at another bank."

To Laura, Daniel said, "Among other things, we found a key to a safe-deposit box in Peter's room after he was killed. Needless to say, we were hoping to find the plans. But no luck so far." He explained about the first box and its contents, then looked at Alex questioningly. "And this one?"

Alex set his briefcase on the desk and opened it. "No plans, I'm afraid. Definitely another stash, though. But not money this time." He dropped a handful of audio cassette tapes on the top of the papers Daniel had been working on, then stacked four videotapes there as well. "I stopped by the office to check these out. And I'm real glad I closed and locked my door first. Want to take a guess?"

Daniel picked up a couple of the audiotapes. One was labeled *Andrea,* while the other bore, also in Peter's handwriting, the name *Melissa.* The videotape on the top of the stack was labeled *Gretchen.* Each label also had a date, several going back at least three years. "Christ," Daniel muttered.

"If he wasn't already blackmailing them, he undoubtedly planned to," Alex said. "I just checked quickly, but what's on these tapes—audio and video—would destroy a couple of marriages for sure, and at least one political future. I didn't recognize three of the women, but I think we can safely assume they would also have had a lot to lose if Peter had played these tapes for their nearest and dearest."

Daniel's face was impassive, but instinct made Laura put her hand on his shoulder. He didn't react visibly, just looked at Alex and said, "Now it's becoming clear where he found his gambling money the last few years."

"Yeah." Alex began putting the tapes back into his briefcase. "I'll destroy these."

"No," Laura said. When both men looked at her questioningly, she said, "You have to let those women know that it's over. Hand them the tapes and tell them. Otherwise they'll never be sure that Peter's blackmail stopped with his death."

Daniel looked back at Alex. "She's right."

"Okay." Alex grimaced. "It's not a chore I'm looking forward to, but I'll take care of it as discreetly as possible. Identifying those three I didn't recognize might be a problem, though."

"Do your best."

It was Laura who said slowly, "All those women had a strong motive to kill Peter."

Alex looked at Daniel, his brows raised, and it was obvious to Laura that the two men had discussed the subject.

Daniel reached up to take Laura's hand from his shoulder and hold it in his. He leaned back in his chair and gazed up at her steadily. "I don't approve of people taking the law into their own hands, but in this particular case, all my sympathies lie with the women Peter blackmailed. If one of them found a desperate way out of an impossible situation, then maybe she was justified. He sure as hell wasn't."

"In other words," Alex said, snapping shut his brief-case, "we aren't passing this information on to the police."

"You don't condone that decision?" she asked him.

"As a matter of fact, I do. I've always said it would be poetic justice if one of Peter's women finally got the upper hand with him. But it's a dubious opinion for someone in my line of work, so don't spread the word around." He smiled at her, then looked at Daniel. "This stuff should be safe enough here at the house for tonight. I'll lock it in my safe at the office tomorrow and start tracking these ladies down."

"Thank you, Alex."

"Don't mention it." The lawyer took his briefcase and left the library.

"I can see now why you didn't want to tell me," Laura murmured. "It must be awful for you, knowing your own brother could do these things."

"The worst of it," Daniel said, "is that I never really doubted he could. Except for the plans—that surprised me."

"Why? You didn't think him capable of it?"

Daniel sighed. "I didn't think he'd sell his country's secrets, no. Even more, I didn't think he'd frame me in the process."

"Why would he? Did he hate you that much?"

"I never thought so." Daniel frowned suddenly, his gaze moving to the papers spread out on his desk. "But—"

Josie knocked on the doorjamb. "Brent's here. He wants to see all of us in the front parlor." She grimaced slightly. "Again."

Daniel looked across the room at her a moment, then nodded. "All right." He released Laura's hand and began gathering up the papers to put them into his desk drawer.

To her, he said, "Why do I have the feeling that Brent is going to tell us Anne was definitely pushed?"

"We knew it was likely," Laura reminded him.

He slid his chair back and stood up. "It must have been an accident."

"Of course it was." Laura's fingers twined with his as he took her hand, and they moved toward the door. She had some idea of what he was feeling right now. As Brent had said, this death had occurred in the Kilbournes' own backyard and it seemed a virtual certainty that someone in the family was involved.

It was a very short list of suspects.

"I WAS IN my room all evening," Amelia told Brent coldly. "Writing letters."

"Did you go to your window? See or hear anything?"

"No." Amelia sat upright as usual in her chair, and the dark gaze fixed on Brent was distinctly unfriendly. "What do you mean, she was pushed?"

"I mean just what I said, Miss Amelia. The medical examiner found marks on Anne's shoulders, just where someone's hands would have been if they were trying to shove her backward. And over the handrail of the bridge."

"Surely you don't even imagine that I could have pushed her," Amelia snapped.

"I doubt you would have had the strength," Brent agreed, unmoved. "On the other hand, Anne was thin and light, and it wouldn't have taken much to push her backward, especially if she was off balance at the time."

"I never left my room," Amelia said, spacing every word for emphasis.

Alex said, "We all had alibis for Saturday night, Brent." Sitting between Josie and Kerry on the sofa nearest the door, he appeared relaxed, but his greenish eyes were sharp.

Brent looked at him. "There was plenty of opportunity for any one of you to slip out at various times during the evening, and you know it. You weren't all together after dinner. And even when several of you were together, there could have been an opportunity to slip outside."

"None of us did," Alex said flatly.

"The medical examiner puts the time of death between eight P.M. and one A.M.," Brent said. "You said yourself that the group down here broke up around ten and scattered."

"Well, some of us paired up," Alex reminded him, glancing at Josie and then looking across the coffee table at the other sofa, where Daniel and Laura sat. Madeline had not yet returned from visiting her friend.

Brent shook his head slightly. "As I'm sure they taught you in law school, when lovers alibi each other, there's always room for doubt."

"Maybe," Alex returned in an even tone. "But in the absence of evidence to the contrary, they are alibis you have to accept."

"For the moment." Brent turned his gaze to Kerry and, for the first time, appeared visibly affected by the interview. His face tightened, and when he spoke, his voice was less impersonal than it had been. "Since the ME has widened the window for the time of death, I have to ask you if you saw or spoke to Anne in the gardens on Saturday night when you went out."

"No." Kerry looked up at him, her expression serene as usual. Gently she added, "I would have remembered. Anne hated the gardens. I would have been surprised to see her out there."

Whatever Brent might have replied to that was lost as the front door slammed and Madeline hurried into the room. She didn't appear as flawless as usual; her sweater was slipping off one shoulder and her hair was a bit mussed. Her pale eyes were bright and clear, and she was carrying an armful that included a long, fat plastic tube closed off at both ends, two videotapes, a small black note-book, and a large manila envelope.

Dropping everything onto the big, square coffee table in front of Daniel, she said breathlessly, "There. I told you I knew all of Peter's secrets."

In the startled silence of the room, Daniel leaned forward and picked up the plastic tube. He unscrewed the cap on one end and reached in with his fingers, drawing out a rolled-up bundle of blueprints.

They might as well have been in an alien language to Laura, so technically complex that no layman would have had a clue, but she heard a little sigh escape Daniel as he looked at them, and she felt his relief when he began rolling them back up to restore them to the protective tube.

From the other sofa, Alex asked quietly, "Is it—?"

Daniel nodded, then looked at Madeline. "Mother, where did you get all this?"

She smiled at him. "Why, from one of Peter's secret places, of course. I know about all of them."

Daniel gestured slightly with the tube still in his hand. "Do you know about this? Do you know what this is?"

Nodding, she said matter-of-factly, "Those are the plans Amelia got him to steal for her."

The silence in the room was complete. Conscious of her own numb shock, Laura glanced from face to face, seeing that her incredulity was shared. Even Brent Landry, who had been very much in command of the room before Madeline's entrance, stared at her now with a frown and perplexed eyes. But he didn't say anything. No one said anything, not for a long moment.

Then Amelia stirred and let out a short laugh. "Don't be absurd, Madeline. Why would I have done such a thing?"

Her daughter-in-law looked at her with a pleasant half

smile, obviously still pleased to be able to prove that she alone had been privy to all her beloved Peter's secrets. "Why, because you wanted to ruin Daniel, of course."

Laura thought she heard Landry murmur, "Jesus," but he was the only one to voice the sick dismay visible on several faces.

Not Amelia's face, of course. She merely looked at Madeline with scorn. "We'll have to get your doctor back over here, Madeline. Clearly he needs to monitor your medications more closely. Or commit you."

Madeline looked around the room at the others, then said defiantly, "I know what I'm saying. And it's the truth. Peter was supposed to sell the plans to a broker representing one of those countries in the Middle East—I forget which one. Amelia set it all up. She'd done it before, you know, years ago, and still had contacts."

"Years ago?" Daniel's voice was wiped of all emotion, like his face.

Eagerly Madeline nodded again. "In the forties, during and just after the war. Because of the money she could make. She was always expensive, you see, and she liked the money. She had access to the company's military designs, to all the plans. So she sold some things. Until David found out, that's what Peter thought. Because he must have found out what she was doing; what other reason could she have had to kill David?"

"She's out of her mind," Amelia said very quietly. "Can't you all see that? For God's sake. Daniel? Can't you see she's sick?"

Daniel didn't even look at her, just kept his gaze fixed on Madeline. "She sold some of this country's military secrets to the enemies?"

"Yes, she did. David had done so well with the business, and there were lots of government contracts. Since she helped keep the books then, it was easy for her to take things. Well, not take. Copy. Peter said she told him how she'd done it, and then she gave him her list of contacts. But most of them were dead; you see, she hadn't had anything to sell them since just after the war and so had lost track of most of them. But one found a broker for her, so she and Peter could sell the plans."

Daniel drew a short breath. "Why hadn't Peter sold the plans as they'd intended? Why were they still in . . . his secret place?"

For the first time, Madeline's bright satisfaction in herself faltered. "He—he was supposed to meet them that night. The night he was—was killed. He wasn't sure he was going to the meeting, that's what he told me that afternoon. He didn't trust the broker. And the more he thought about it, the less he liked the idea of having everyone think you had done it. But when he—he was killed, I thought it was probably because of that. Because the broker was bad. And I thought the broker must have taken the plans, so I never thought to go to Peter's secret place and look."

Laura felt utterly numb and couldn't even begin to imagine what Daniel must be feeling. His face remained completely impassive, and his tone measured.

"Mother, if you thought you knew who might have killed Peter, why the hell didn't you say something about it?"

She looked surprised. "Because they were secrets, dear. I couldn't betray Peter's secrets, could I? And I was so upset besides, all I really wanted to do was sleep and forget."

"I told you she was out of her mind." Amelia's voice was stronger now, clearer. And self-righteous. "Don't you see, Daniel? Don't you understand what Peter was trying to do? With you in jail, control of the company would have passed to him."

"No, Amelia," Daniel said slowly. "Legally, you're still in charge. So Peter would have had to take you on before he could claim control, and he didn't know enough about the business to successfully do that."

Her lips tightened, and those dark, dark eyes flashed. "He hated having to come to you for everything, hated having to beg. *He* wanted to ruin you, Daniel. *He* wanted to see all your pride in the dust, all your arrogance shattered."

"I think it was you who wanted that." Daniel's voice was so low it was almost, but not quite, inaudible. He set the plastic tube on the coffee table and picked up the little black notebook. Slowly, seemingly unconscious of every eye in the room on him, he leafed through the pages. "Names, dates, routes of contact. I doubt Peter would have known weapons brokers born forty years before he was."

"Don't be a fool!" Amelia said harshly.

Daniel studied the notebook a minute longer, then looked at Amelia. "Damned by Peter's own words, Amelia. He wrote it all down. All of it, including your instructions on how to use the keycards and get into the vault. Did you forget he always did that because his memory was so bad? Or did you simply hope it would all be over so quickly that it wouldn't matter? That I'd come home from my business trip to find myself suspected of treason? Was that it? Or were you just so desperate to destroy me that you were willing to take any chance to do it?"

She stared at him, that aged face stripped bare of its haughty elegance and showing the bare bones of hatred beneath. Her thin mouth writhed in a snarl. "Did you think I'd spend the rest of my life kowtowing to you, Daniel? Watching you run things when it was supposed to be me?"

"You were *running things* into the ground, Amelia." His voice was flat, his gaze locked with hers. "Was I supposed to stand by and let you bankrupt this family?"

For the first time, their power struggle was out in the open, the raw emotions and potent intelligence of both obvious to those around them. Nobody else said a word, nobody else dared to step in the middle of an old, deadly quiet conflict.

"That wouldn't have happened," Amelia snapped.

"Oh, no? It was going to happen, Amelia. One more diamond necklace, one more losing racehorse eating his head off in Kentucky, and this family would never have been able to recover from the loss. I had to step in, to stop you from throwing money away."

"It was *my* money." Her voice was fierce. "David left me in charge, left me to make decisions on how things were to be run—"

"Did he? I wonder, Amelia. I did some checking, you see. And David had been scheduled to see Preston Montgomery about his will—the very day he was killed. Interesting coincidence, wouldn't you say?"

Amelia's mouth tightened and her eyes flashed, but she remained silent.

"Maybe Peter was right to think David must have found out what you had done. Is that what happened? Did David confront you with it? Maybe outside, near the pool, so the servants wouldn't hear? Did he tell you that he was going to change his will and the trust, to take everything away from you? Is that when you picked up something heavy and killed him, Amelia?"

"You're as crazy as Madeline," Amelia said coldly.

"No. But that old crime doesn't matter much except to us, does it, Amelia? If there was no evidence against you then, there certainly won't be now. You got away with it." Daniel drew a breath, then said, "But I couldn't let you get away with ruining the family. I had to do whatever was necessary to stop you."

"Did that have to include humiliating me? Constantly challenging my authority even in this house? Oh, no,

Daniel, I think not. I think you enjoyed it, just the way you've enjoyed fabricating this entire—"

"I have proof." His voice dropped, the words falling like stones. "You know that. And perhaps it's time the others knew it too. I have proof, plenty of it, that you were criminally irresponsible at best and wantonly destructive at worst. Any judge would have been satisfied, Amelia, with what I had to show. You would have been stripped of all power, all authority, and left with no more than a small allowance and the right to live in this house until you died. Publicly humiliated. But I didn't do that, did I? I didn't drag you into court for all the world to see."

Quite suddenly, in a chilling turnaround, Amelia was calm. Even smiling. And her voice was contemplative when she said, "That was where you made your mistake, Daniel. Your only one, really."

"Oh? And what was that?" As thoughtful and conversational as she was, Daniel, with the ease of an old habit, slipped back into their polite game.

"You didn't use your weapon, your evidence, when you should have. It gave me time, you see. And just how long did you think I would go on waiting for you to stop playing your little game and take me to court so you could do it all legally? No longer than I had to, certainly. But I couldn't just . . . get rid of you. There was that little matter of the letter you'd left to be opened in case something happened to you, and your evidence against me. So there was only one thing to do. Ruin you."

Amelia rose to her feet, erect as always, not leaning on her silver-headed cane. "I had hoped that Peter did meet with the broker that night. I assumed he was killed so as to avoid payment." She might have been talking about the weather for all the emotion she showed. "I also knew that you had discovered the missing plans. But I was certain that, given enough time, the plans would surface—with your fingerprints all over the transaction. All I had to do in the meantime was to keep you . . . reasonably distracted, so that the search for the plans wouldn't have your full attention. So that you wouldn't realize what I had tried to do, and take me to court before I could see you finished. Luckily, a distraction presented itself." Her gaze flickered to Laura, and she smiled. "That was easy enough."

"You failed, Amelia," Daniel said quietly.

"I didn't fail. Peter failed." She let out a soft laugh that was like dry leaves rustling in a cold wind. "Men have always failed me."

"Beginning with David?"

"No. Beginning with my father. But that's a long story, and I'm feeling very tired right now." She smiled. "I'll tell it to you tomorrow, perhaps."

"I'll look forward to it." Daniel's voice was still low, still courteous.

And Amelia was still smiling as she went slowly, erectly, from the room.

There was a long, long silence, and then Brent Landry stirred and addressed Daniel for the first time since Madeline's entrance. "You could press charges."

Daniel was staring down at the notebook in his hands. "No, I couldn't. The plans weren't sold. My reputation will be unharmed. And there's no evidence to connect her to the theft of the plans. She committed no crime."

"If she killed her husband—"

Looking up at the detective then, Daniel said, "If you want to investigate a forty-year-old *accident,* good luck. If there was no evidence then, do you expect there to be any now?"

"She might have killed Anne—" Landry began.

"Oh, no, she didn't do that," Madeline said brightly.

Daniel looked at his mother for a long moment, then slowly rose to his feet. "Mother . . ."

Madeline must have seen something in her son's face, because she took a step back and laughed nervously.

"Don't look at me like that, Daniel. I didn't mean to kill her, of course. It wasn't *intentional*. But she kept going on and on about knowing all Peter's secrets. And she kept *telling* people what he'd told her in confidence. Betraying that confidence. And then, out in the garden, she . . . taunted me. She said I hadn't known all of Peter's secrets, that he'd kept things from me. So I told her to shut up and—and I pushed her. And she fell."

Shaking her head with a little grimace of dissatisfaction, she added, "I would never have betrayed Peter to the rest of you, of course, but I had to prove it. That Anne didn't know his secrets like she said. I did. I knew all his secrets, all his secret places . . ." Her voice trailed off, and she smiled.

Alex seemed to shake himself out of the limbo of fascinated horror that had gripped most of the people in the room, and said, "None of this is admissible, Brent. She wasn't advised of her rights."

"She wasn't being questioned," Brent murmured.

Madeline looked at them, frowning as though they were speaking a foreign language. She pulled at the sweater slipping off her shoulder, seemed to realize that she looked less than her usual flawless self, and shook her head with a little "tisk" sound. "It's almost time for dinner, isn't it? I should go and get ready . . ."

As she went vaguely from the room, Laura rose, said, "She shouldn't be alone," and started after Madeline.

"I'll come with you," Josie said, and did.

Daniel looked down at the notebook he was still holding, his mouth a grim slash. "She isn't responsible, Brent. And it was an accident."

"That's clear enough," Alex agreed.

Brent hesitated. "I'll speak to the DA. Given the circumstances, Madeline still under sedation because of Peter's murder . . . he may decide that prosecution would benefit no one."

Daniel nodded. "Thank you."

Brent nodded toward the notebook. "I'll need to take a look at that, Daniel. Peter might have been killed by someone he was supposed to meet that night. If there are names . . ."

After a moment, Daniel tossed him the notebook. "Discreetly? There's no point in making any of this public if we don't have to."

"I'll do my best." Brent frowned at him. "Do you mean to say that you intend to take no action against Amelia? After everything she did to try and destroy you?"

Daniel sat back down on the sofa and reached for the manila envelope on the coffee table. His expression still unemotional, he said, "No, it has to stop. If Amelia had not been involved with the business, she would never have known about the plans for the new design. I can never allow her that kind of access again, and until she has no legal authority . . ."

"A court battle?" Alex asked.

"I no longer have a choice."

Brent looked from one to the other. "That's it? Her punishment is to be publicly tossed out of the business?"

It was Kerry who murmured, "Weren't you listening? That may well be the worst punishment she could face."

"But she probably killed her husband," Brent said. "And possibly created a situation whereby Peter was killed. And it sounded to me as if she would have attempted to have you killed, Daniel, if there had been any chance she could have gotten away with it. Surely that deserves more than public humiliation?"

Daniel looked up at him, and Brent thought there was something both inflexible and certain in his expression. "Justice is always meted out. Eventually. Amelia will have to face a higher court."

There was another little silence, and then Kerry rose and told Brent, "I'll show you out."

Brent went with her, but paused at the door to look back at Daniel. "You'll—get help for her?"

"For which one?" Alex murmured.

But Daniel was nodding to Brent. "I'll get help for her."

A moment or so later, they heard the front door open and close. Kerry did not return to the parlor.

Daniel opened the manila envelope and pulled out the contents. His mouth twisted. "Stills—presumably from one of these tapes or the others we found." He started to return the black-and-white photographs of various naked women doing various things with Peter Kilbourne to the envelope, then paused and looked at Alex. "*One* of Peter's secret places, she said. This stuff was in *one* of his secret places."

Alex stared at him, then groaned. "Oh, shit."

Daniel nodded. "We'll have to talk to Mother. Later. When she's . . . able. Find out what else Peter might have hidden away." He sighed tiredly and returned the photos to the envelope.

"Great." Alex climbed to his feet, his face showing a mixture of disgust and awe. "What a day. Look, I'm going to go call Madeline's doctor—if Josie hasn't already. How much should I tell him?"

"As much as you have to." Daniel shrugged. "As much as he needs to know to help her."

Alex nodded, hesitated a moment, then said, "Do you know what I find incredible about all this?"

"What?"

"That we still don't know who killed Peter. It's as if some ghost walked in off the street, killed him, and then vanished into thin air. All the secrets laid bare in the last couple of weeks, and we still have no idea who killed Peter. I wonder if we'll ever know."

Daniel wondered the same thing.

• • •

IT WAS NEARLY seven that evening when Laura knocked tentatively at Daniel's door. She heard his voice and went in, finding him sitting in the armchair by his cold hearth.

"The doctor's with Madeline," she said quietly, coming to sit on the hassock at his feet. "Josie had a tray sent to Amelia's room and told the cook to just set out food on the sideboard and anybody who wants can serve themselves."

He nodded slowly, his eyes fixed on her face. "You should eat something."

"I thought I'd wait for you."

"I'm not hungry."

Laura hesitated, then leaned forward and put her hand over the one resting so still on his thigh. "I'll go away if you'd rather be alone."

His hand turned under hers and grasped it strongly, just this side of pain. "No." A faint tremor disturbed the granite stillness of his face. "I need you with me, sweetheart."

"Then I'll stay." Without thought, she lifted his hand and cradled it against her cheek.

Daniel seemed to catch his breath, and the granite cracked a bit more. His eyes were like silver. Unsteadily he asked, "You do love me, don't you, Laura?"

Perhaps oddly, it didn't surprise her that he would ask. Nor was she surprised to hear herself reply, "I've always loved you. Even before I knew you. Didn't you know that?"

Daniel closed his eyes briefly. "I only know how long I've loved you. God . . . so long . . ." He reached for her and pulled her onto his lap, holding her tightly.

Laura burrowed even closer, absorbing his warmth and his hardness, trying to give him whatever he needed of her. Body and soul.

"Stay with me," he murmured, granite crumbling finally into shards of pain and the emotional weariness of battles long fought and bitterly won. "Just let me hold you for a while."

To Laura, there was no place on earth she would rather have been. Murmuring her love, she turned her face up for his kiss, and as always the first gentleness became something searingly urgent and unstoppable. It burned away pain and healed bitterness, and when at last they found their way blindly to the bed, it forged yet another thread of belonging between them.

LAURA MOVED HER things into Daniel's bedroom that night.

AND SOMETHING ELSE happened that night. Ending a generations-long tradition of violent death, Amelia died quietly. In her sleep.

Chapter 16

*J*ust over a week later, on a cool Wednesday morning in mid–October, Laura stepped back from the easel and nodded absently to herself, and dropped her brush into a can of turpentine on the small table that held her paints and other brushes.

"Finished?" Daniel asked.

She looked up, smiling, to see him coming from the house out into the conservatory, where she'd been working. "Finished."

He joined her, slipping an arm around her waist, and they both studied the portrait of Amelia begun before she died. It showed an elegant old lady, her high-necked, turn-of-the-century black gown starkly formal against the background of the casual fan-backed wicker chair and lush green plants. Her dark, dark eyes were secretive, her small smile enigmatic, and something in the tilt of her chin spoke of ruthless self-interest.

"You've captured her," Daniel said. "Congratulations, love. You're an artist."

Laura smiled at him, and as they walked back into the

house together, said, "I have to say, I feel pretty confident. If I can put Amelia Kilbourne on canvas, I can put anyone there."

"We'll hang it in her parlor, I think. Perfect place for her."

"Even Amelia would probably say so," Laura agreed.

Amelia might also have been pleased to know that her death had created a sensation. Coming so soon after Anne's death and Peter's murder, there had of course been speculation of suicide at best—and murder at worst. But an autopsy had shown clear evidence that Amelia had died of a stroke. Not even the tabloids had been able to do much with that fact, though they had naturally tried.

Still, the past week had been difficult for everyone. After some thought and a doctor's evaluation, the DA had chosen not to prosecute Madeline, so Anne's death had been officially noted as accidental. More tabloid fodder, of course. And though Anne's estate had been minimal, Amelia was found to have a considerable personal fortune in addition to all the legal ties that had bound her to Kilbourne Data and other family businesses; Daniel and Alex had spent long hours in the past week wading through all the complex legalities.

In fact, this was the first day that Laura and Daniel could look forward to spending any time together, since Daniel had gone into the city with Alex for what both had hoped would be only a couple of hours earlier in the day.

"Did you get finished up?" Laura asked now.

"We did all we could for the day, at the office, anyway. It'll take months to get probate on Amelia's will, but the legal transition of power in the business has been smooth enough, thanks to David's foresight." Daniel shrugged. "As for the rest of it, we can do that as well here. Alex is still trying to track down all the women Peter was probably blackmailing and return the tapes to them, and he wants to talk to Mother now that we can. We have to make sure we've recovered everything Peter had hidden away."

Laura knew he wasn't looking forward to that, but also knew it was necessary. They probably would have asked Madeline before now about Peter's other "secret places" and what they might contain, but she had been under the care of a new doctor, and he had okayed the questions only in the last day or so.

"Is that where Alex is now? With Madeline?"

Daniel nodded. "I think he just wants to get Peter's business behind him. The rest of this is draining enough without also worrying if there are more women out there terrified of their secrets being exposed."

As they turned by mutual consent toward the library, Laura slid an arm around his waist and said, "At least they won't have to be terrified much longer. Josie went up to sit with Madeline after you two left this morning; Madeline seems to find it easiest to talk to her, so I'm sure she and Alex between them can find out what else might be hidden."

There was a fire burning in the library, and the drapes were open to let in the weak October sunshine, so the room looked much more cheerful than it had once upon a time. They sat down on one of the long leather sofas, and Daniel pulled her across his lap, smiling at her.

"Have I thanked you for being so caring and thoughtful with Mother these last days? Believe me, I'm grateful."

Laura shook her head a little. "It hasn't been just me. Josie, Kerry, and I didn't really talk about it, but between us we can keep Madeline company and make sure she's all right. That new medication the doctor put her on seems to be helping; she's calm, but not drugged the way she was. I think she'll be all right, Daniel. I really do."

He half nodded, but said, "We've still got some hard ground to cover, with Mother as well as everything else. You know that, don't you?"

"I know that. But we will get through it."

Daniel touched her face with gentle fingers and looked at her with restless eyes. "I don't think I could have borne any of this without you, love. These last days, especially. Just knowing you'd be waiting for me when I came home, that you'd be sleeping with me in our bed, made all the difference. I love you. So much."

Laura rubbed her cheek against his hand and smiled at him. "I love you too."

He hesitated, then said, "I know you've barely had a chance to think, and I know I should give you time. But I also know without a shadow of a doubt that I want to spend the rest of my life with you. Say you'll marry me, Laura. Please."

She looked at him for a long moment, her eyes searching his face. "You're so sure," she murmured.

Daniel nodded, a muscle tightening in his jaw. "I'm sure. I knew we belonged together that first day, when I walked in and saw you here. Didn't you know it too? Didn't you feel it?"

Slowly she nodded, still just a bit wary, maybe even frightened of something so powerful that had taken over her life so suddenly and unexpectedly. "I felt it. I didn't understand what it was, but . . . I know I love you, Daniel. I know I loved you then."

He surrounded her face with hands that weren't quite steady. "I won't rush you to the altar, love, but I need to know that's where we'll end up. Say you'll marry me."

On some level of her mind, Laura was aware that they had things to talk about still, and that they did need more time to be together. But she also knew, as certainly as he seemed to, that this was right.

"Yes." Her arms slid around his neck as he drew her closer and kissed her, and she felt more than heard herself murmur the acceptance again against his lips, as though it had to be repeated.

They were still in that general position, Laura lying half across his lap and cradled against his chest, their faces close together, when Alex walked into the library a few minutes later.

"Sorry, folks," he said, more casual than apologetic, and not at all embarrassed; with his romance as well as theirs out in the open, scenes such as the one he was interrupting had been fairly common in the last week.

Laura forced herself to sit up beside Daniel, and stared at the large cardboard box Alex was placing on the coffee table before them. "What is this?"

Alex sat down on the other sofa. "Well, according to Madeline, Peter asked her to keep this for him. It was in her closet. She says he put things in it from time to time, but that she never looked. Because it was one of his secret places." He grimaced slightly and looked at Daniel. "Anyway, I thought you should take a look and see if it's what I think it is."

With a slight frown, Daniel leaned forward and opened the flaps of the box. Inside was a veritable tangle of objects and garments. There were very simple things: a needlepoint bookmark, a tiny porcelain clock, a scented candle. But along with those things were several pieces of jewelry such as a gold bangle bracelet and a lady's wristwatch. There was a little fold-out fan, a tiny bud vase, a small and nearly empty bottle of expensive perfume, a silk scarf, one suede glove—and a pair of bright pink lady's underwear.

"It was the panties that gave me a clue," Alex said.

"Christ, I thought he gave this up in college," Daniel muttered.

"Gave up what?" Laura asked.

He sighed. "They're trophies, love. When he was in high school, Peter began . . . collecting some personal possession from every girl he had sex with. Stole them, actually. He said the girls never knew, that that was part of the fun. When I found out, I told him it was an insulting and distasteful thing to do, and he said he'd stop. I thought he had."

"This could be old stuff," Alex pointed out. "But Madeline did say he put something new in from time to time. If she's right . . ."

Laura looked into the box, both queasy and curious. For a moment all she saw was a jumble of objects and colors, bright and shiny things such as a child might have collected. When she first noticed the scarf, it was more with puzzlement than anything else, a vague sense of where-have-I-seen-you-before in her mind. She reached in and drew it from the box, her fingers examining the texture of the silk, her eyes studying the colors. Then the pad of one finger brushed the threads of embroidery, and she stared down at a neat monogram.

Realization dawned slowly, one fact after another listing itself in her mind with cold clarity. Possibilities and probabilities falling neatly into line. Two people who had acted in ways entirely characteristic of them.

It had been right in front of her the whole time.

"Oh my God," she whispered.

Daniel put his hand on her thigh. "Laura? What is it? What's wrong?"

She turned her head to look at him, cold and miserable, hoping she was wrong but very afraid she was right. "I think I know who killed Peter."

LAURA STARTED TO open the thick manila envelope that had been waiting for her with the security guard at her apartment building, recognizing Dena's handwriting on the label, but decided that could wait. The last installment of the mirror's history, no doubt; so much had happened in the last week that she had all but forgotten her young researcher was still working on tracing the mirror to the Kilbournes' door. The envelope was bulky, and Laura thought there was a small book of some kind in it, but she still resisted the urge to look and see. Instead she left it on one end of her breakfast bar.

She went to her door when the bell rang, and Cassidy came in with a somewhat dry, "Now it really is 'Hello, stranger.' Do you realize it's been more than a week since I saw or spoke to you?"

"Sorry, Cass. A lot's happened."

Cassidy grunted. "No kidding. I've been reading the papers. Are you just passing through again?"

"More or less." Laura poured her friend a cup of coffee and slid it across the bar when Cassidy sat down. Then, casually, she reached into the pocket of her jeans and pulled out a folded square of colorful silk. "I wanted to get this back to you, for one thing."

"Hey, where'd you find that? Jeez, I was so afraid I'd lost your birthday present to me! Where was it?"

Laura drew a breath, feeling cold and miserable because until that moment she had hoped against hope that she had been wrong. "In a box of Peter Kilbourne's sexual trophies."

Cassidy was looking down at the scarf in her fingers, and though she went white, for a moment she didn't move or speak. Finally, softly, she said, "I might have known he'd cut notches in his bedpost, the bastard."

"You met him at the bank, didn't you? The bank where the family did business." *Right in front of me the whole time . . . a connection I missed.*

Cassidy nodded slowly, still looking at the scarf. "He came in sometimes, mostly taking care of business for his grandmother. He just flirted at first. Then, about six months ago he asked me out."

"And you . . . fell for him?"

"Like a ton of bricks." Cassidy smiled without humor and looked up at her friend. "For the first time with me, it was . . . body and soul. I'd never felt like that before. So . . . consumed by another person."

Laura shook her head, bewildered. "Cass, you never said a word to me. Never even let on that there was someone new in your life, someone important to you. Why?"

"Because I knew you'd disapprove. He was married, after all. And because . . . it was so exciting, to have a secret lover."

"Is that why I never saw him around this building? Because it had to be a secret?"

Cassidy shook her head. "Oh, Peter would have preferred the comfort of my bed to a motel's. He liked his comfort. But I said no. I guess . . . I thought if I didn't sleep with him in my own bed, I could pretend the worst of it wasn't real, wasn't happening. That I wasn't sleeping with a married man . . . who had no intention whatsoever of divorcing his wife." The ghost of a wry grin flitted across her face. "Isn't it wonderful how we can talk ourselves into things we *know* are bad for us?"

"What happened?"

"What do you think?" Cassidy's laugh was brittle. "He got tired of me, of course. The same way he got tired of every other woman who crossed his path. There I was mooning over him and clinging to him and making all these rosy plans for a future that was never going to happen, and he was already lining up his next hot piece. His cousin. His own cousin. Knowing him, I'm sure he thought forbidden fruit would taste sweeter. And it was something he hadn't done before. That would have been a novelty."

Laura forced herself to go on calmly despite the ache she felt. "How did you find out about Anne?"

"It was the day of the estate sale. I hadn't seen him in more than a week, and I was getting desperate. That's why I talked you into going over there. I think I knew he was trying to brush me off, but I wouldn't let myself believe it.

I couldn't let myself. I loved him so much it just didn't seem possible that he wouldn't love me back."

That pensive statement brought a lump to her throat, but Laura still somehow managed to keep her voice even, her questions detached. "You saw him at the sale? When we split up?"

"Yes. I got past the guards and slipped around to the back, thinking that maybe I could find a way inside the house. Or see him through a window, maybe." She smiled so briefly it was only a memory of self-mocking humor. "I was that far gone. Anyway, I did see him. He was in the conservatory—with Anne. They were . . . he had his hands on her."

"That's why you were so angry later. Not because you'd lost that table you wanted. Because of what you'd seen."

"I'm surprised you noticed. That mirror was all you had on your mind." Cassidy shrugged.

"Would you have told me the truth if I had asked?"

"No, probably not."

There was a little silence, and then Laura said, "What happened that night, Cass?"

The beautiful blonde seemed miles away—or weeks in the past. When she answered, her voice was almost absent-minded. "I'd heard her say something about meeting him that night at the motel, and I realized how far they'd gone. That they were lovers. He had slept with me just a week before, but that night he was going to sleep with his cousin, and it wouldn't be the first time."

"What did you do?"

Cassidy stirred and looked at Laura. "I went there, of course. I was supposed to be at a party with that guy I'd seen a few times—my window dressing. But it was easy enough to slip away without anyone noticing; most every-body was drunk by then anyway."

"Were you?"

"No. I'd told my date I'd be the designated driver, so he could drink all he wanted. I had the keys, so I took his car. The motel was across town; it was after eleven when I got there."

Laura closed her eyes for a moment, then asked quietly, "Were you planning to kill him?"

Cassidy's blue eyes were very clear, and she was smiling a little. "I know you'd like me to say no, but the truth is I'd been thinking about it. Very calmly, in fact. I had even stolen a butcher knife from my hosts that night and hid it in my purse. Just in case. But it didn't have to happen. If Peter had only . . ." She shook her head. "But he didn't."

Laura tried to brace herself inwardly, forcing her mind not to shy away from considering a scene her imagination had conjured so vividly so many times. "What happened, Cass?"

"Anne was just leaving," Cassidy said slowly, frowning as if remembering was difficult. "I was parked down the street a bit, and I could see the door of their room clearly. He went to the door to say good-bye to her, and he wasn't dressed. I knew he would be taking a shower. I knew him. I sat in the car for a while, until I saw his shadow move across the blinds while he got dressed. Then I went to the door and knocked, and he let me in."

"He wasn't surprised?"

"Yes, he was. But Peter always thought he could charm his way out of any situation. I guess he never realized how angry I was."

Laura swallowed. "I guess not."

Cassidy looked at her friend, and her frown deepened. "I don't remember doing it. I remember that we talked first, but I'm not sure what was said. Except one thing. I told him I loved him, that I'd forgive him for Anne, all I wanted was for him to love me. I would have gotten down on my knees, I think. Begged him. But . . . he laughed so hard he had to sit down on the bed. And I guess that's when I did it. When he laughed at me, at my love. Because the next thing I knew, I was looking down at him. And he was dead."

It took all the command over herself she could muster for Laura to say, "You must have been covered in blood."

Shaking her head, Cassidy said, "No, not really. There was some, but not a lot. And I was wearing black pants, you know, and a black silk blouse. I got a towel from the bathroom to wrap the knife in, and a wet washcloth to take with me. I got most of the blood off my hands and—and face in the car. Then I stopped by a convenience store and washed again in the rest room."

"What did you do with the knife?"

"Well, that night, I came by the parking lot here and locked it in the trunk of my car. So my date wouldn't see it, you know. Later, I got rid of it. In a dumpster on the other side of town." Cassidy shrugged. "Anyway, I went back to the party. They hadn't even missed me."

Sounding as helpless as she felt, Laura said, "My God, Cass. It—it never showed. You never seemed different, not to me."

"You always said I was good at compartmentalizing myself. I guess I am." Cassidy straightened and flexed her shoulders absently. "Well, that's my sordid little tale. Did you tape it, Laura? My confession?"

"No," a new voice said quietly. "But I did."

Cassidy turned on the bar stool and looked toward the hallway that led to Laura's bedroom. Two men were coming out. Both were tall; the one in front was a bit shorter and more slender, with dark, hawklike good looks. Cassidy had seen him on the TV news.

"You're Landry," she said. Then she looked at the powerful, rugged man behind him, and said, "And you're Daniel. I suppose you and Laura are going to get married?"

Daniel nodded, more compassion than anything else in his eyes when he looked at her. "Yes. We are."

"And they lived happily ever after." Cassidy slid off the bar stool. She was smiling. "That was the ending I wanted, you know. The one I thought I deserved. The one they promised us as kids. But I guess they'd never heard of Peter Kilbourne."

"I'm sorry," Daniel said.

She looked at him, a little surprised, then nodded. "I see you are. So am I, as a matter of fact. But none of us can change the past, can we?"

"No. None of us can do that."

Her gaze moved to Landry, and she said, "Well?"

He nodded very slightly. "Cassidy Burke, you're under arrest for the murder of Peter Kilbourne. You have the right to remain silent . . ."

Laura didn't listen to any more, and she didn't watch Cassidy being led away. She just walked around the bar and went into Daniel's comforting, loving arms. And cried.

IT WAS ON the following Friday afternoon that Laura remembered the manila envelope. She had brought it back to the Kilbourne house with her more or less automatically, dropping it into a drawer in Daniel's room on top of a stack of her own underthings. And hadn't given it another thought, until today.

She was alone in the big house except for the cook and two maids busy cleaning the ground floor. Daniel was at his office, Alex at his; Josie had taken Madeline in for a doctor's appointment; and Kerry had taken a book and gone out to the maze to enjoy one of the last warm days they would have for a while.

Laura expected to be on her own for at least a couple of hours, and it seemed like a good time to read the rest of

Dena's research and learn the rest of the mirror's history. It was the only thing still a question mark in her mind, the only mystery left unsolved, and she thought it might be why she still felt just a tiny bit wary. It was time to deal with that.

She took a cup of hot tea upstairs with her and went into his—their—bedroom. The big armchair made a very comfortable place for her to curl up and read, and the room was peaceful. She opened the envelope and dumped its contents onto the hassock. There were several typed sheets of paper clipped together, and a fairly small leatherbound book with a rubber band holding it closed and a note in Dena's scriptlike handwriting.

Read the report first, Laura.

Intrigued, Laura left the small book on the hassock and leaned back to read the typed report. It opened with a brief note from Dena, just a reminder of where they had left off, with the deaths of Brett and Shelby Galvin. And then the report continued briskly.

In 1952 a man named Mark Coleman, 23, bought an old silver mirror at a secondhand store near San Francisco. The clerk told him that if he was interested in mirrors, he might want to attend a church auction being held nearby the following Saturday. The church was selling items donated to them by the estate of Andrew Galvin (Brett and Shelby Galvin's surviving son, who had done very well in shipping and died, unmarried, at 50 by drowning). Mark went to the church auction, where he bought the brass mirror.

And where he found Catherine Archard.

She was 18 when they met, and deeply religious. She was also, from all reports, somewhat fragile, both emotionally and physically. Apparently, Mark's courtship of her was slow and gentle;

letters from Catherine to friends are filled with her happiness. Next to her God, she loved Mark.

A year and a half after meeting, they were engaged. Then, on Christmas Eve, 1954, just weeks before their wedding, Catherine and Mark apparently had some sort of disagreement, the nature of which he never confided to anyone else. She got in her car and drove off into a heavy rain. He followed in his own car. Catherine, known to be an uncertain driver, lost control and went over an embankment. Before Mark could get to it, the car burst into flames.

That's all I could find about the accident.

Mark Coleman was apparently devastated by his loss. Some friends even say he was still grieving ten years later, when he was killed in a plane crash.

He willed all his possessions to charity, including, specifically, the mirror. An antiques dealer from San Francisco bought the mirror, along with various other items. He reportedly placed the mirror in his shop—and there is no record of it being sold. The dealer went out of business in the early 1970s; his stock was liquidated. But there is no further mention of the mirror.

Here the trail stops, somewhere between 1964 and 1974.

Postscript: Laura, I can't really explain the enclosed journal. Maybe you can. When I contacted a friend at a California archive for news clippings and so on relating to Catherine Archard and Mark Coleman, she found a few of Catherine's letters for me (copies appended). And then, the very next day, she was browsing at a junk shop and found the journal. She called it an incredible coincidence, and FedExed it to me immediately. After reading the journal, I'm not sure I'd agree that coincidence had anything to do with it. But you'll have to let me know what you think. Read the whole thing, when you have time. But it's the final entry I especially want you to read. I'm almost afraid to draw my own conclusions . . . but if you think about it, the journal entry offers an explanation of sorts for the mirror's history.

Let's talk about this.

Laura shook her head, baffled and curiously uneasy. She read the copies of Catherine's letters first, studying the childish, loopy handwriting and the sweet sentiments—mostly about Mark, although there was a good bit about her church and her God as well.

Laying the sheets on the hassock, Laura picked up the journal and removed the rubber bands holding it closed. She flipped through the pages quickly, not reading but noting the strong, clear handwriting so neat it was almost print. She found the last entry, dated October 23, 1952, and beginning abruptly.

When the clerk told me that the estate of Andrew Galvin had donated items to be auctioned for charity, I could hardly believe it. It's always been difficult for me in concept—the death of a child of a previous life—but this is the first time I've been faced with the cold fact of it. My God, I could have gone to San Francisco and met Andrew, this son of my last life! I could have known him as an adult, a man older than I am myself. Strange. And unsettling. As I have so often before, I feel a guiding hand, destiny's touch, perhaps, for Andrew's death has enabled me to find the mirror once again. And to find her. Her name this time is Catherine.

She's very young, just eighteen. Very gentle and serious. Very devout. I will have to be patient.

Laura sat for a long time, not moving, gazing at nothing. Thoughts tumbled through her mind so rapidly she could barely grasp them. All the inexplicable events and feelings of her life began to come into focus, to finally make sense to her—if, that is, she accepted one very simple impossibility as truth.

And, dear God, how could she do that?

IT WAS JUST before five when Daniel came into the bedroom, and as soon as he saw the papers spread out on the hassock, the journal, he went cold to his bones. He looked around quickly, saw her standing at the window, and the relief was so great he nearly groaned aloud. Instead he went as far as the chair and put his hand on the back of it, looking across the few feet that separated them with so much hope and fear, he felt raw.

"Laura?"

She didn't turn, and when she spoke her voice sounded almost absentminded. "You said that David got the idea for the maze from a stranger in a bar. Tell me about that."

There could be no more prevarication, Daniel knew. No more lies, no more evasions. Between them now there could only be stark truth.

He drew a deep breath and held his voice steady. "In 1955, David was in San Francisco on business. In a hotel bar, he met a grieving young man who had buried his fiancée the year before. The young man had a mirror made of brass lying in front of him. A mirror with an elaborate, mazelike pattern stamped into the metal. The young man had had too much to drink, and he talked. He told David that the pattern stamped on the mirror was called Eternity, that the mirror had been specially commissioned to celebrate . . . an eternal love. And while David traced the pattern over and over with a finger, the young man told him a fantastic story about reincarnated lovers. They talked until dawn, and then the young man took his mirror and left. The story haunted David. When he came back home, he had the maze put in. And as you can see, he remembered the pattern very well."

"You can only see it clearly from this window," Laura murmured. "This was David's room, wasn't it?"

"Yes."

She turned, finally, leaning back against the window casing. Her face was pale but calm, and he couldn't read her eyes.

"Laura—"

"It was you, wasn't it? That grieving young man in the bar. It was you. Ten years before Daniel Kilbourne was born."

Daniel nodded slowly. "It was me. Another face, another time. But me."

"And you were grieving . . . me."

He nodded again. "I made a mistake. I told you about us too soon. Your faith was too absolute to allow for such a possibility, even coming as it did from the man you loved. You were . . . distraught. Frightened. You ran from me. And you died that night." He tried to steady his voice. "And I lived on, ten eternal years without you. I swore I wouldn't make the same mistake again, Laura. I wouldn't tell you the truth until I was certain you were ready to hear it."

"That's why you didn't want to talk about the mirror."

"Yes."

She was silent for a moment, then murmured, "I've always hated Christmas. And never knew why."

Daniel took a step toward her, but stopped when she

held up a hand warningly. She wanted the distance to remain between them. At least for now. *Please God, let it only be for now* . . .

"I don't remember," she said. "I . . . feel things. But I don't remember."

"I know. You never do. It's one of the crosses I've had to bear, that you don't consciously remember me. Or us."

"But you remember? What do you remember, Daniel?"

"At first, in childhood, there are only flashes, dreams. As I get older, the memories slowly come into focus. By the time I reach adulthood, I know the truth. And I begin searching for you."

"But what do you *remember?*" she asked, suddenly intense.

He drew a deep breath. "I remember the first time I ever saw you, a long, long time ago. I remember every face you've ever worn, even more clearly than I remember my own. I remember the times we were able to grow old together, and the times when our lives were short. I remember our tragedies, and our triumphs. I remember every place we've ever lived together, every home we've had."

"Scotland," she realized suddenly. "My painting."

Daniel nodded. "We were happy there."

She looked at him searchingly. "We weren't always happy?"

He hesitated. "It hasn't always been easy for us, Laura. Sometimes I found you after you'd already been promised to another man. Sometimes our lives were torn by violence. But we always knew we belonged together."

Still her eyes searched his face, and Daniel couldn't tell if she looked at him in wonder or in doubt. "Why can't I cut my hair?" she asked abruptly.

"Because of something that happened long ago," he answered readily. "You lived in a small village, and when I found you that time, you were already married. An arranged marriage your father had forced you into—had virtually sold you into. And it was a very unhappy marriage, even before I showed up. There was no way out for you, not then, but we had to be together. We took . . . insane risks." He paused, then went on with more difficulty. "When your husband found out, he beat you terribly and cut off all your hair. He meant it to be a badge of shame, a kind of scarlet letter proclaiming you an adulteress. You weren't ashamed of loving me, but in cutting off your hair, he hurt you far worse than he did with his fists and words. You swore no one would ever again cut your hair against your will. In every life since, you've worn it long."

"What happened?" Laura asked. "In that life, what happened to us?"

In a matter-of-fact tone that came from lifetimes of reflection, Daniel said, "I killed your husband and we ran away together. It was a hard life, but we had each other. That always got us through."

Laura shook her head a little. "This is so hard to believe."

"I know, love," he said gently. "But it's the truth, I swear to you."

"The mirror. It's been . . . guiding us? To each other?"

He nodded. "I don't know how. I've learned to accept that there are patterns in fate, threads of destiny we always seem to follow. Like the mirror. Ever since I had it made for you, it's been somehow involved in our meeting each other in a new life. This time . . . I have no idea how it ended up here, in this house. With this family. If I had to guess, I'd say that Dad probably found it in a shop somewhere and brought it home for Mother. He was always doing that when they were first married, buying her things she never had much interest in. But all I know for certain is that when I saw the description of the mirror on the inventory, I thought there was a chance it was ours. And sent Peter to you to buy it back."

"If you thought it might be our mirror," she said slowly, "then why did you send Peter? Why not come yourself?"

"I was afraid," he answered simply. "Afraid it wouldn't be our mirror. That it wouldn't be you. Afraid to hope, after so many years without you. Then Peter came back, and when he told me about your collection of mirrors, I knew it was you. It had to be. Mirrors fascinate both of us, they always have. In fact, Peter needled me a bit that afternoon, saying that you were probably my soul mate because of the obsession with mirrors."

Daniel frowned suddenly. "That must have been what Amelia overheard. She made a comment later—the first time you came here—about the mirror. All I could think was that David must have told her something when he had the maze put in. And maybe he had. Or maybe she simply overheard my conversation with Peter. In any case, she knew enough to suspect that you would be the perfect distraction for me. And so she brought you into the house."

After a long moment, Laura drew a breath and let it out slowly. "There's one more thing I need to know."

He took a step toward her, his heart thudding, once again afraid to hope. "What, love?"

"Is this . . . our last life? Or only our next one?"

Daniel smiled. "I can't see the future, Laura. Only the past. But I can tell you this much. We always live as if this is the last life we'll be given. Because it may well be."

Laura moved away from the window and crossed the space between them. Looking up at him gravely, she said, "Then we'd better get started on it, don't you think?"

"Laura . . ."

"I love you, Daniel." Her arms went around his neck

and her body pressed close to his, and her smile was so tender it almost stopped his heart. "And I want this life to be the best we've ever had."

As his head bent and his lips touched hers, Daniel had no doubts at all.

ABOUT THE AUTHOR

KAY HOOPER, who has more than four million copies of her books in print worldwide, has won numerous awards and high praise for her novels. Kay lives in North Carolina, where she is currently working on her next novel.

Look for Kay Hooper's next novel

Haunting
Rachel

available Fall 1998 in hardcover
from Bantam Books

Here's a sneak peek.

"It won't take long," Thomas said reassuringly. "A week, maybe a bit more. Then I'll be back."

"But where are you going? And why does it have to be now?" Rachel's demand held all the impatience and indignation of a nineteen-year-old about to be deprived of the company of her fiancé at a somewhat inconvenient time. "Tom, you know Mercy's giving that shower for me on Thursday, and—"

"Honey, men are never welcome at those things. I'd just be in the way." He was still soothing but also a little amused, and smiled at her with the complete understanding of a man who had known her since her auburn hair had been worn in pigtails and at least two of her front teeth had been missing. He was ten years her senior, and at that moment every year showed.

Rachel didn't exactly pout, but when she sat down in a chair by the window, it was with a definite flounce. "You promised. You said there wouldn't be any more of these mysterious trips of yours—"

"There's nothing mysterious about them, Rachel. I'm a pilot, and I deliver cargo. You know that. All right, I know I said there wouldn't be any more trips out of the country, but Jake asked me to do him a favor, and he *is* my boss. So, just a quick run down to South America."

"You promised," Rachel repeated, not much interested in reasons. Her one uneasiness about marrying Tom was due to the fact that he sometimes made promises blithely only to find later that they were difficult, if not impossible, to keep. She was somewhat doubtful that would prove a good quality in a husband.

Thomas put his hands on the arms of her chair and bent down, focusing on her all the charm in his definitely charming nature. "Would it make you happier if I said that Jake's giving me an extra week off if I take this run? That's another week in Hawaii, honey. Think about it. Lazing around in the sun on Waikiki, breakfast on a balcony with a magnificent view—and shopping. Lots more time for shopping."

She couldn't help but smile. "You know that isn't my thing."

He chuckled. "Yeah, but you're no slouch at it. Come on now, and give me a smile. Say you're not mad anymore. I'll have a miserable few days if I fly off knowing you're mad at me."

It was virtually impossible for Rachel to resist his blandishments, a fact both were well aware of, and her sigh held resignation as well as a touch of resentment. "Oh, all right. But you'd better not hang around down in South America. Just remember what'll be waiting for you back home." She wreathed her arms around his neck and kissed him.

The passion between them had been nearly impossible for them to handle since the night of her sixteenth birthday and their first real kiss; familiarity had not bred anything except a better understanding of just how powerful desire could be, especially when it went unsatisfied. Though Rachel's willpower was shaky where he was concerned, Thomas, very conscious of the years between them and of her youth, had decided for both of them that sex would wait until marriage.

It wasn't a decision Rachel was happy with, and this wasn't the first time she had made an attempt to force his hand.

His voice was a little ragged when he pulled back slightly and muttered, "Stop that. I've got to go."

Rachel didn't want to let go of him. "You'll miss me. Say you'll miss me."

"Of course I'll miss you. I love you." He gave her a brief kiss and then unlocked her arms from his neck and straightened. "Make my excuses to your parents about tonight, all right, honey?"

She sighed again. "Right. And I get to spend a boring Saturday night all by myself. Again."

"Just three more weeks, and that will no longer be a

problem," Thomas reminded her. "I promise, honey, no more lonely nights for either one of us."

"I'll hold you to that."

Rachel walked with him to the front door of her parents' house, received another quick kiss, and stood there watching him stride down the walkway to his fast little car. He loved speed, Thomas Sheridan did, whether on the ground or in the air, and often teased her that she was the only love in his life that characteristically moved at a lazy pace.

He turned and waved before opening his car door, and Rachel admired the way the sunlight glinted off his pale silvery hair. He was a rare blond Sheridan on a mostly dark family tree, so different from his raven-haired sister Mercy that both had frequently maddened their mother by speculating humorously about blond-haired strangers in her past, despite Thomas's undeniable resemblance to his dark father.

"See you in a week or so, honey," Thomas called out.

He slammed the car door before Rachel could respond in kind, so she merely waved. She watched the car until it vanished from her sight, then went back into the house to tell her parents that her fiancé would not be joining them for dinner that night.

Rachel woke with a start and sat up in her bed before she even knew what had awakened her. The room was filled with the somber light of dawn, and she was astonished to see him standing near the foot of the bed.

"Thomas? What're you doing back so soon? I—" Her voice broke off as though it had been cut by something sharp. It wasn't right, she realized. *He* wasn't right. She could almost see the curtains through him. A coldness seeped into her body, into her very bones, and she heard herself make an anguished little sound when Thomas seemed to reach out toward her, his handsome face tormented.

Rachel stretched her own hand out toward him, but even as she did so, he was gone. And she was alone in the stark dawn.

Thomas Sheridan's plane never reached its destination, and no trace of it was ever found.

It was no more than a glimpse of movement on a street corner that caught Rachel's attention. She turned her head more or less automatically, drawn as always by the glint of sunlight off silvery blond hair. She expected to see, as she always had, a stranger. Just one more blond man who would, of course, not be who she wanted him to be.

Except that it was Thomas.

She stood frozen, with four lanes of cars filling the space between her corner and his, and when their eyes met, she almost cried out. Then the light changed, traffic began moving briskly, and a noisy semi blocked her view of the corner. When the truck had passed, Thomas was gone.

Rachel stood there until the light changed again, but when she rushed across the street, there was no sign of him.

No. No, of course, there wasn't.

Because it hadn't been him.

Realizing that her legs were actually shaking, she found a table at a nearby sidewalk cafe where she could keep an eye on that corner, and ordered a cup of hot tea.

It hadn't been him, of course.

It was never him.

"Are you all right, miss?" the waitress asked when she returned with the steaming cup. "You look sort of upset."

"I'm fine." Rachel managed a smile she doubted was very reassuring, but it was enough to satisfy the young waitress. Left alone again, she dumped sugar into the tea and fixed her gaze once more on that corner.

Of course it hadn't been Thomas. Her mind knew that. It had only been a stranger with a chance resemblance that had seemed stronger because distance had helped it seem that way. And perhaps a trick of the light had helped, as well as her own wishful thinking. But it couldn't have been Thomas. Thomas had been dead nearly ten years. No, they had never found a body, or even the wreckage of the plane, but Thomas's life had certainly ended somewhere in the impenetrable depths of a South American jungle.

Even though he had promised to come back to her.

One more promise Thomas had not been able to keep.

Her knees were steady once more when Rachel finally got up nearly an hour later and left the cafe. And she didn't let herself stop or even pause when she passed the corner where a memory had so fleetingly stood. Knowing that she was late helped her walk briskly, and common sense pushed the memory back into its quiet room in her heart.

It was after three o'clock on this warm and sunny Tuesday when she went into a building in downtown Richmond. She went up to the fourth floor, and entered the law offices of Meredith and Becket, and was immediately shown in to see Graham Becket.

"Sorry I'm late," she said at once.

"Rachel, you didn't have to come down here at all," Graham reminded her as he moved around the desk to take her hand. "I told you I'd come to the house."

"I needed to get out." She shrugged, then gently reclaimed her hand and sat down in the visitor's chair.

He stood looking down at her for a moment, a somewhat rueful expression on his face, then went back around the desk to his own chair. A tall, dark, good-looking man of thirty-eight, and a highly successful attorney, he was accustomed to female interest.

Except from Rachel. He'd been her father's attorney for nearly ten years and one of the executors of his estate since Duncan Grant and his wife had been killed when their small private plane crashed shortly after takeoff eight months ago. He knew Rachel fairly well, but knowledge didn't stop Graham from hoping that one day she would notice he was a man who was closer to being one of her contemporaries than her father's.

And a man, moreover, who had been half in love with her for years.

She had never noticed.

"More papers to sign?" she aked, her slight smile transforming her merely pretty face into something inexplicably haunting.

Graham had tried to figure out what it was about that

smile that made Rachel instantly unforgettable, but to date had been unable to. Her features, taken one by one, were agreeable but not spectacular, very even and regular. Her pale gray eyes were certainly lovely, but the dark lashes surrounding them were more adequate than dramatic, and her nose might even have been a trifle large for her heart-shaped face.

If a man was being critical about it.

Her gleaming auburn hair framed that face nicely, but it was unlikely that fashion mavens would copy the simple, shoulder-length style. Her mouth was well-shaped and her teeth straight and white, but there was nothing especially memorable about either.

Despite all that, Rachel had only to smile that slow smile of hers to become a stunningly beautiful woman. And it wasn't only Graham who saw the transformation; he had heard more than one man and a number of women comment on it over the years.

Solemn, Rachel was pretty; smiling, she was extraordinarily lovely.

"Graham?"

He recalled his wandering thoughts and opened a file folder on his desk. "Yes, more papers to sign. Sorry, Rachel. But I did warn you that Duncan's estate was complex."

"It's all right. I'm just wondering when it'll all be over."

He looked at her across the desk. "If you intend to keep a hand in the business, it'll never be over. But if you mean to accept Nicholas Ross's offer to buy you out . . ."

"I'm still thinking about that. Do you think Dad would have wanted me to sell out, Graham?"

"I think he expected you to. The past few years, your life hasn't been in Richmond except for holiday and vacation visits home, and those were brief. Ever since you moved to New York, I think he realized it wasn't likely you'd come back here to live."

"Yes—but I don't have to live here to keep the business. I could hire a manager to run my half, you know that. Between you, Nicholas, and a manager taking care of things day to day, I'd have to show up only periodically for board meetings."

He nodded. "True enough."

"I don't know beans about investment banking, so I could hardly be a hands-on boss anyway. And all those investments Dad had personally, they're so diverse there's no way I could keep track of them on my own." She seemed to be arguing with herself, frowning a little. "At the same time, several of the companies Dad invested in aren't in a position to buy out his interest right now, so I'd have to find other investors if I wanted out. That, or take a loss. Either way, it means time and trouble."

Graham looked at her searchingly. "In a hurry to get back to New York? I thought you said you'd taken a leave of absence and didn't mean to go back until summer."

"That's what I said, and what I meant. But . . . I don't know, I'm getting restless, I guess." She shrugged. "I'm not used to being idle, Graham."

After a moment, he said, "But it's more than that, isn't it? It's memories. The house is getting to you."

Rachel got up and went to stand before a window that offered a view of the busy street below. Graham remained in his chair, but turned it to keep watching her, and when she remained silent, he went on quietly.

"After Thomas was killed, you couldn't wait to get out of that house. Went back to college first and then to New York. And your visits home even then were always brief, because you were always busy."

"Trying to make me feel guilty for neglecting my parents?" Her voice was a little tight.

"No. They didn't feel neglected, if that's been worrying you. They understood, Rachel."

"Understood what?"

"How much of your past was bound up in Thomas. How old were you when you first knew you loved him? Twelve? Thirteen?"

Rachel drew a breath. "Ten, actually. He came to pick

up Mercy from my birthday party, and he kissed me on the cheek. I knew then."

It required an effort, but Graham kept his voice dispassionate. "And since his sister was your best friend, you saw a lot of him. I imagine he was at the house quite often even before you two began dating. You were sixteen then, weren't you?"

She didn't seem surprised by his knowledge, probably attributing it to her father and casual conversation rather than any extraordinary interest in her. "Yes."

"So Thomas spent a lot of time at the house. Years, really. All the time you were growing up. Eating meals in the dining room, sitting with you in the den, listening to music in your bedroom, walking by the river. That place is filled with him, isn't it?"

After a moment, she turned and leaned back against the window casing. She was smiling just a little, wistful, and it made her beautiful again. "Yes, the house is filled with him. And even now, after all these years, it hurts to remember him."

"Of course it does. You never really let him go, Rachel. You couldn't. There was no funeral where you could say goodbye, just a memorial service when his parents had finally given up hope. And, by then, you'd bolted off to college where there weren't any memories of Thomas. For you, there was never any . . . closure."

She looked at him almost curiously. "You knew him, went to school with him. Was it so easy for you to accept his death?"

"Easier than for you, because I was never close to him. I wasn't . . . emotionally involved. His death was a tragedy and I was sorry, but no memories haunted me."

She hesitated, then let out an unsteady laugh. "Haunted. That's a good word. I thought I saw him today."

"What?"

"On a street corner while I was waiting for the light to change. I looked across—and there he was. I could have sworn it was Thomas."

"What happened?"

"A truck went past, and when I could see the corner again, he was gone. I ran across and looked, but . . . My imagination, I guess."

"You guess?"

"Well. My imagination, of course."

"Or just a man with blond hair," Graham said steadily.

"Yes. I know."

"But this isn't the first time you thought you saw him."

Lightly, she said, "I'm going nuts, is that what you're saying?"

"What I'm saying is, don't let memories and wishful thinking become an obsession, Rachel. Thomas is dead. Don't you believe that if he were alive, he would have somehow got word to you, that he would have managed to come back to you?"

"Yes. Yes, I do believe that." *Because he came back to me once, came back from death to say goodbye to me.*

She had never told anyone about that, not even on that horrible dawn when she had awakened both her parents and insisted her father get in touch with Thomas's boss because she was certain something terrible had happened.

"Then you know that what you saw was simply someone who looked a bit like Thomas." Graham's voice was still matter-of-fact.

Rachel felt a faint flicker of amusement as she returned to her chair. "I think you really are worried about my sanity, Graham. Well, don't be. I was shaken at first, but my common sense asserted itself pretty quickly. I know I didn't really see Thomas on a street corner."

Except for that first instant, when she had been sure . . .

"I'm glad. But, Rachel . . . if you need someone to talk to—"

"Thanks. But I think it's just as you said. I never got the chance to say goodbye to Thomas, and I've never faced up to all the memories at home. It's just something I'll have to work my way through." She smiled at him. "Now, didn't you say something about papers to sign?"

• • •

The house where Rachel had grown up was an elegant Georgian mansion built on extensive acreage on the James River. The house was more than two hundred and fifty years old, and had been in the Grant family for much of that time. Remodeled from time to time by various Grants, it now contained such luxuries and conveniences as carpets, closets, and bathrooms, as well as modern wiring, central heat and air conditioning. Yet it had maintained its graceful air despite those changes, and was considered one of the most beautiful houses in Richmond.

Rachel got out of her mother's sedan at the front drive and stood for a moment studying the house. Not for the first time, she wondered if she was being hasty in even considering selling the place. Yes, the house was far too large for one young woman who didn't care for entertaining and didn't have to in her work—the only real excuse for a single person to own such a place. And, yes, there were too many memories here, many of them painful. And her uncle Cameron wanted it, would enjoy it, and would keep it in the family at least a while longer.

But it was her home. She had actually been born in this house, with a doctor in attendance, since her parents had been determined to uphold that tradition. Until she had gone away to college and then moved to New York, Rachel had always lived here, just as her father and grandfather before her. Her roots were here.

Did she really want to give it up? And if she did, were her reasons the right ones? Or was she just being cowardly in wanting to run away once more without facing the pain of loss?

Not questions that were easily or simply answered, she knew. Shrugging them off for the moment, Rachel went into the house. She was greeted just inside the door by the housekeeper, Fiona, who was dour as usual. A part of the family for more than twenty years, Fiona, now in her late middle age, moved more slowly these days, and her superstitious nature could be a trial at times, but she loved this house and took excellent care of it.

Which was why she resented any intrusion into her routine.

"That Darby Lloyd has been sending things down from the attic all day. How'm I supposed to do my work with those men of hers tramping up and down the stairs, Miss Rachel?"

Rachel had known Fiona too long to be disturbed by the forbidding stare or acid complaint. Laying her purse on a side table in the large entrance hall, she merely shrugged and said, "You know it has to be done, Fiona. We have to have a complete inventory and appraisal of everything in the house—and that includes the attic."

"But she has the second floor hallway filled wall to wall, and I can't even vacuum—"

"Fiona, just be a little patient, all right? I'll go speak to her about blocking the hallway."

"If you can get through," Fiona said with a sniff.

Rachel was able to get through the upstairs hallway with a bit of maneuvering. A family could fill a large attic with an astonishing variety of furniture, especially over generations and many shifts in style and taste; items partially blocking the hallway ranged from Revolutionary chests and Regency tables to—of all things—a sixties style beanbag.

"My God," Rachel said when she finally managed to make her way up the fairly narrow staircase to the attic. "Has this family kept every blessed stick of furniture ever to cross the threshold?"

"That would be my guess." Somewhat harassed, strands of her coppery hair escaping from the casual ponytail she wore and a smudge of what looked like soot on her otherwise creamy nose, Darby Lloyd came around a huge wardrobe with a clipboard in her hand. "Sorry for the stuff in the hall, but there was no other way to sort through everything."

Rachel waved a dismissive hand. "Don't worry about it."

"Well, I know Fiona's upset." Darby grimaced. "One

of my guys swore she put a hex on him when he asked if he could leave a Chippendale desk at the top of the stairs."

"She doesn't really hex people," Rachel said.

"Never underestimate the power of suggestion. Ten minutes later, Steve developed a migraine. Sam had to take him home. Which is why I'm up here alone and at my wit's end. Do you know, I think there's a Queen Anne desk in that far corner, and I can't get to it. That's very frustrating, Rachel."

Rachel had to smile at Darby's intensity. A friend since elementary school, Darby had remained in Richmond after college, starting her own interior design company with a generous investment from Duncan Grant's firm. She was also an antiques dealer, which was why she was nearly drooling at what she was finding here in the attic of this old house.

"You'll get to it eventually," Rachel reminded her soothingly. "Have you started the list of things you want to buy for your business and things you think you can sell for me?"

Darby rolled her eyes. "Have I ever. In case you don't know, there's a fortune in this attic alone. Aside from all this glorious furniture—most of which is in fabulous condition, by the way—I've found three trunks so far, all filled to the brim with the kind of stuff to make an interior designer's mouth water. Vases, candle holders, figurines, picture frames. Jeez, Rachel, it's going to cost me a fortune to buy what I want just from in here."

"I told you we'd work something out. I'm in no hurry for the money, you know that."

"Thanks, Rachel. I'll check with you first, of course, before taking anything away. There might be a few things you want to keep for yourself, maybe transport to your apartment in New York."

Like most of the people around her, Darby assumed Rachel would be selling out and leaving Richmond, an assumption encouraged by Rachel's attitude and decisions so far. It wasn't something Rachel disputed, even though she was still wavering and uncertain about what she meant to do.

So she merely nodded in response and said, "Sounds good."

Rachel went to her second-floor bedroom and stood at the doorway looking down the hall toward her parents' bedroom. Though she had gone through her father's desk here at the house as a business necessity, she hadn't yet been able to sort through his and her mother's personal belongings. It was something she knew she had to do, not a chore she could put off on anyone else. It would take time and require decisions, and so far Rachel had simply not been up to the task.

And still was not.

She went into her bedroom, a room she had been allowed to decorate for herself when she was sixteen. Since Rachel had inherited her mother's elegant taste in antiques, even as a teenager she had not been fond of the fads and often peculiar color combinations in vogue with her friends; her room was decorated in quiet tones of blue and gold, the furniture virtually all Louis XV pieces, delicate and lovely.

Rachel was comfortable in the room, and after so many years more or less took the stunning antiques for granted. She went into the adjoining bathroom and turned on the faucets to fill the big oval tub, deciding that a hot bath might ease her tension and soothe the restlessness she couldn't seem to get rid of. It only half worked, but half was an improvement, and by the time she climbed from the tub half an hour later Rachel definitely felt better.

She wandered back out into her bedroom wearing a silk robe, and went to stand at a window that looked out over the front drive and lawns. Plans for the evening were simple; dinner, probably with her uncle Cameron who was currently staying in the house, and then television or a book. It had become her routine.

"Jetsetting heiress, that's me," she murmured to herself wryly.

The irony, of course, was that she could have jetted off

to wherever she wanted—and simply had no interest in doing so. Money was not one of the things Rachel had ever had to strive for, and so it was not something that represented success or achievement to her.

Achievement, to Rachel, was bound up in the designs she created as an apprentice to one of the best New York fashion designers. After years of hard work, she had the satisfaction of knowing that in the fall her designs would be shown under her own name.

But that was months and months away, and in the meantime she had to decide just how much of her past she wanted to abandon.

Rachel sighed and began to turn away from the window when a flicker of movement down by the front gate caught her attention. There was considerable distance between the house and the gate, but what Rachel saw was clear enough.

And definitely real.

A man with silvery blond hair was standing at the gate looking up toward the house. He was very still for a moment, and then he made an oddly hunching movement of his broad shoulders that might have been a shrug or some gesture of indecision. He turned and walked away, and was hidden immediately by the high brick wall and numerous tall trees.

Rachel lifted a hand as though to stop him, but her flesh touched nothing except the cold glass of her window.